The General's Gift

By Omayra Vélez

Copyright

The General's Gift

Library of Congress Cataloging-in-Publication Data

Names: Vélez, Omayra, author.

The General's Gift/Omayra Vélez

Description: Florida: [2023]

Identifiers: ISBN 978-1-959443-14-8 (paperback)

ISBN 978-1-959443-13-1 (hardcover)

ISBN 978-1-959443-12-4 (eBooks)

Subjects: Behui, Yakuta, Palermo Kingdoms (Imaginary Places)–Fiction. | Fantasy

Fiction. | Romance fiction. | BISAC: FICTION / Fantasy / Romance | FICTION / Action & Adventure. | FICTION / Fantasy / Romance / Action / Adventure.

Classification: LCC

Omayra Vélez Publisher

eBook ISBN 978-1-959443-12-4

www.omayra-velez.com

Dedication

For Aunt Elba, we share more than a diagnosis. We share the love for Christ.

Table of Contents

CHAPTER 1

A Ransack

Boom! The bed shook, startling Olympia awake. She woke naked, between two bodies, her heart racing, and tried to find something familiar. It all seemed like a nightmare. The last time she roused at the sound of a blast was when she was a child. Her grandfather had died in a raid on their home, but that happened over twenty-six years ago. The memory from her childhood merged with the present when the loud sound of a cannon was accompanied by the pandemonium of men running back and forth outside the door.

"What is going on?" asked Sir Edgard.

"It sounds like a mixture of fire magic and black powder. We are being attacked. Let's go," said Prince Wallen. The two men shot out of bed.

"You—woman—get up, and dressed, but stay in my room until I send someone for you."

The men searched for their pants, shirts, and boots. They dressed in a rush, leaving the room in a hurry, taking their overcoats with them. Olympia pushed the covers aside; with trepidation, she got out of bed. She needed to see the commotion happening outside. Running to the window her foot snagged on the prince's belt making her stumble and fall against the window sill, leaving a mark on her arm. When all the courtesans arrived the previous night, torches lit up the courtyard of the castle, but now the blasts filled the sky with light. It reminded her of the fireworks shows that colored the skies in her home city of Nolia to celebrate New Year's Eve, in the glorious Kingdom of Palermo. *"Oh no, they have lightning mages."*

Being this close to war made Olympia's nerves shatter. A week ago, when she left the Il Palazzo di Roberti brothel, her master promised she wouldn't be in harm's way. Hah, who would have known the war was going to reach her?

Chicho, the brothel's owner, seldom let her entertain too far away from the capital, but Prince Wallen had paid a handsome sum of gold for her.

The cold air made her shiver, turning her entire body cold, while her heart beat faster than a fox's when chased in a hunt. Guards, mages, and archers stood on the battlements, firing. Her tired body tensed at the sight of unbridled magic coming from over the battlement and there was still an hour before dawn.

Stepping away from the window, she closed it with trembling hands. Her memories from her childhood came back to her. Her father held her in his arms as he ran down the stairs of the family manor. Fire consumed the matronly house from top to bottom, but fear was all she remembered as her father carried her over his shoulders. At such a high vantage point, she could see her mother with terror as she ran, holding her older brother by his hand. Olympia shook her head, trying to whoosh the memories away.

She hastily retreated from the window and tried to distract herself by going to look at herself in the opulent mirror that stood in between two mahogany dressers. Her black hair which had been made up in long braids, now hung in wavy strands having come loose during the night. Olympia touched her golden collar. The cold metal was a constant reminder of her reality.

The hated device always caught her hair when she worked with uncaring men. She worked at untangling her from around the collar as she tried to fix her braids, fixing them back up and out of the way. Her arms and body hurt after a night of Exotic service to the men in the room.

Olympia hated having to service more than one person at the same time, but in the end, it didn't matter what she liked or disliked—Chicho's word was final. Her smeared makeup made her eyes seem even more swollen and tired than she expected. She went to the bathroom, took a washcloth, dipped it in water, and tried to cleanse her face as best she could.

"Olympia, hurry! You must move fast." Talking to herself only happened when nervous.

"Where is my clothing?" The previous night she had entered wearing little clothing, and the animals had torn her lingerie off in minutes. Her bustier lay in shreds on the floor. Moving fast, and trying to open one of the prince's wardrobes, she almost cut her arm with the lock before giving up the attempt.

She then went to the second wardrobe and opened it easily. In it, she rummaged and found several pieces of clothing; taking out a pair of black pants, a white shirt, and a belt. Olympia hoped the prince would never miss the items of clothing. In haste, she put on the pants. Not surprisingly, they were big on her. Without doubt, she needed the belt or the pants would fall from her hips. The shirt was also too large, but she put it on buttoning it all the way to her neck. To finish the outfit, she found a long black scarf from the floor of the wardrobe.

BOOM! Olympia moved away from the wardrobe, running back to the window; she searched for the maker of the noise. A portion of one of the battlements had collapsed. Blast after blast came from the ramparts of the castle. With each booming sound, she jumped a little. A draft from the window made her shiver, bringing her back into focus. Fear all the way to her soul encouraged her to back away from the window.

Olympia needed her shoes. She looked everywhere in search of her sandals. In every corner, under the bed, even shaking out the covers on the bed, but she could not find them from the previous night. Instead, she chose to search in the wardrobe once more for a pair of the prince's shoes.

After searching for a few moments, she found a pair of boots. She needed socks but could not find any. The boots were too big, but by this point she no longer cared. She had worn men's clothing before; this was not the first time. By the time Olympia started looking for a coat, a young man unceremoniously opened the door. He entered the room with the gumption to get things done. The young man stared at Olympia and gave her a sad smile. The teen could not have been more than fourteen, but he already had a rifle, ready to join the battle.

"M'lady, come with me; Prince Wallen wants you and the other women to be together. Please, follow me," said the young servant. Olympia placed the scarf around the collar and snatched a short blue coat from the wardrobe as she left the prince's room. Following the servant, they ran down the hallway, where he knocked on every door along the way. The young man ushered forward the women who exited the rooms to join Olympia.

"M'lady, I thought we were far from the borders between Behui and Alhambra," said Lyla, the youngest.

"We will talk later. Let's go, run." Olympia took Lyla by the hand, hastening her pace behind the servant.

"The boss will not like this. Chicho will require compensation if anything happens to any of you," said Tapa, the women's bodyguard that Chicho had sent to guard his workers. They ran through the hallways until their flight was arrested in front of a set of tall double doors at the far end of the second floor. The young man pushed open the doors to an enormous room.

When the women entered, they could see books lining the walls from floor to ceiling. Olympia's only thought was that she loved books. All the women looked scared as they entered.

"Oh," she sighed in wonder, "this must be the prince's library?" Olympia had never seen such a wonderous thing.

"Not his main library. This room used to be a bedroom, but Prince Wallen loves books and once he'd filled the walls with books he moved to another room," said the servant as he turned away and left.

Tapa, their bodyguard, barked out an order to the women. "Wait inside the room; I will stay outside the door." Baam! The door slammed shut without another word.

Olympia turned to look at the solid mahogany door that now imprisoned them. Through the central window, she could see fire and lightning raining over the battlements. The night turned into morning, as Olympia's fears ran wild, but she kept her counsel. Some women wept, others whispered among themselves, while others managed to sleep, but Olympia sat vigil, silently.

Many hours later, the grandfather clock chimed again as it had throughout the night, this time to indicate the half hour. It was 8:30 in the morning. As the morning progressed, the sounds of battle continued. The women sat on sofas around the room, trying to relax by playing word games, but every time a cannon fired, they all jumped. Olympia needed to calm her nerves, so she walked over to the prince's desk on the far side of the room. She sat in the chair, removed her scarf, and unapologetically, started to rummage around.

On top, she found a fountain pen, ink, and some paper. One of the pages had a red dot on its corner, which gave her enough inspiration to write a short story, so she took it. Writing always calmed her a little; this time, it was the only thing Olympia could do. While trying to keep distracted writing her story, one of the girls came to stand next to her.

"M'lady, you smell like alcohol but don't look hungover. How do you do it?" asked Lyla, the youngest one of the women.

"No, I didn't drink a drop; I never do. That bastard, Prince Wallen, poured an entire bottle of cognac over my body last night." Olympia took a sniff at her arms. "Yuck, I reek." Leaving the desk behind, she walked to a cushioned chair, sat and closed her eyes. A headache slowly formed at the back of her head.

BOOM! A cannon blasted, and Olympia closed her eyes tight.

"When do you think we can leave this place? The servants haven't brought us any food and I am hungry," said Meleni.

"M'Lady, I am thirsty," said Catalina.

"I have no idea when they will bring us food or water. Tapa didn't say anything about food and I know you are tired, but all we can do is wait. The servants will be here soon," said Olympia.

"Is there a lavatory in this room? I need to relieve myself," said Lyla.

"Can you wait?" Meleni asked, eyeing Lyla.

"No!" Lyla crossed her legs in her chair. After Lyla's comment, Olympia remembered when she was young. Now, at thirty-one years old, youth seemed like a lifetime ago. Something had to be done, so she went to the door and knocked.

"Hello Tapa, we can't be in this room all day. We are hungry, thirsty too. Some of us need to use the lavatory," said Olympia. Tapa opened the door.

"A servant told me this room has a lavatory closet at the far end to the left. Wait patiently, and be quiet. I'll try to get you some food and water."

"Can I go with you?"

"No! None of you can leave this room," said Tapa. He locked the door behind him, upsetting Olympia.

"Tapa said we can find a lavatory at the end of the room to the left."

The women walked to the far end of the room, where they found a hidden door behind the bookshelf. The women used the lavatory. They even washed their arms and necks, trying to take the unpleasant pong from their skin. Relieved, the women sat back down on the sofas. All except Olympia and Lyla who went to the windows to watch as the men ran back and forth across the castle ramparts, carrying weapons and injured soldiers. The hours passed as the women continued to wait for Tapa and their food.

A blast, louder than previous ones shook the foundations of the castle, and some dust fell over the women's heads.

"Oh no, I think the enemy have breached the inner walls of the castle!" said Lyla, still looking out the window.

"Walk away from the window." Olympia pulled Lyla away from the window.

“Aren’t any of you afraid? Because I am terrified,” said Meleni, and she huddled into the sofa’s corner, in front of the fireplace.

“We will be fine. Tapa is outside. He will not let anyone enter the room,” said Lyla, giving her teacher a half smile. Olympia felt sorry for Lyla. Tapa was a buff man; but what could one man do against an army?

“It would be awful if they got us, but it will be worse for you, M’Lady,” said Catalina, playing with a strand of her blond hair.

“Why?”

“Yes, M’lady, you as an Exotic, with your beautiful face and body, those men will hurt you if they catch you,” said Lyla.

“You all forget, you are as beautiful as me, if not more. We must stay together, do you all hear me?” asked Olympia. The women nodded.

BOOM! Another loud blast came, but this time it seemed closer. Olympia, the only Exotic, covered her face with her hands, rubbing her temples cringing at the thought of war. BAM! This time, blasts and screams came from within the castle walls. The sounds of rifles, of blasts, of lightning causing destruction everywhere, all made her want to leap up and run away. The five women now huddled together on the sofa. Battle sounds being overshadowed by Olympia’s own pounding heartbeat. Her ears were ringing, causing her breathing to become more rapid. She felt faint. The woman next to Olympia cried.

BOOM! BAAM! BANG! Shots, blasts, women’s screams; the sound of people running outside the door. AH! More screams, now those of men … then—silence. Olympia grabbed the scarf from where she had left it on the desk and wrapped it around her neck; she needed to cover her golden collar. All the other girls had bronze or silver collars. They would stay together.

Lyla cried in her teacher’s arms. Olympia knew she had to calm Lyla down, but couldn’t think of anything. She wasn’t good at consoling people. At the moment, she wanted to take a brief glance through the window, but Meleni and Lyla would not let go of her.

A few minutes later, the door snapped open. The women jumped as a dirty-as-sin soldier entered the room. Olympia's fears sprung to life. An Alhambra soldier entered with a rifle, pointing it straight at them.

Olympia participated on hunts many times. She had hunted animals with others of the aristocracy. It was expected of an Exotic. Now she knew what prey must feel when cornered. A cold sweat streamed down her back; feeling the coldness she trembled. All the blood drained from her face and her hands shook. "Will this be my end?" she wondered to herself.

They had no part in the fight. They were from a neutral kingdom. Palermo had not entered the war between Alhambra and Behui. Olympia could not talk or move. She stared at the end of the rifle.

"We are not citizens of Behui, Alhambra, or Yakuta; surely, they must let us go," whispered Catalina, the smallest of the women.

They were not the prince's property. As hired personnel, they must have had some rights. Olympia had expected to be in the castle for just one night and be returned to her master the next day. They were supposed to have been on a train back to Palermo following the noon meal.

Things sucked, but she suspected it would get a lot worse, really fast. Olympia wanted to crawl into a dark, cold cave. With every movement of her body, Olympia's head pounded. Her headache had moved from the back of her head to between her eyes. Light felt like daggers entering her eyes.

"Aren't we lucky? What do we 'ave 'ere? Are ye servants 'iding in one of the master's rooms?" asked a blond soldier covered in mud.

"These are whores. Can ye no smell sex on them?" asked a second bearded soldier who came inside the room after the blond soldier. Of all things, Olympia was offended by his comment.

"We are not servants or common prostitutes. We are courtesans," said Paulina.

"Oh, excuse me; let me inspect yer arm. Curtis, do ye think we could have a turn with any of them?" suggested the hairy man. Paulina stepped forward, showed her right wrist to the man, but a tall, equally dirty man entered the room, pushing her aside.

"All you women come with me," said the tall man. He manhandled the women, forcing them to stand in a straight line.

"Now lookie here, are these beautiful spoils of war?" asked a fourth bearded soldier who entered the room.

"These are courtesans, they—" the blond man was interrupted before he could finish talking.

"One moment, we don't belong to Prince Wallen. We are rented personnel. We are from Palermo," said Paulina.

"Woman, we don't care where ye come from or who's yer master; now move next to yer friends," said Curtis.

"Wait, you need to check all of our trade tattoos; there are differences between us." Olympia felt a little braver after Paulina's show of courage.

"I know the difference between a prostitute and a street walker. Now be quiet, ye lot. Stay in yer line," said the tall soldier as he inspected the right wrist of one women after the other, but as the soldier was about to check Olympia's tattoo, a man in a knight's uniform came to the door and called him.

"No, you are making a mistake; you need to look. There is rank between—"

"Shut up whore; I tried to be nice to ye. All yer yapping, don't let me think," said Curtis.

"Please, you need to check—"

Curtis slapped Olympia and said "Quiet!"

"What are they?" asked the knight, entering the room in a hurry.

“They are definitely high-quality courtesans,” said Curtis, pushing Olympia to the side.

“Take them to the General’s tent; these are expensive loot. Can they understand our language?” asked the knight.

“Two of them can, but the pretty one with the black hair can’t keep her trap shut,” said Curtis.

“Gag her if she can’t keep quiet; I hate women who can’t keep quiet when you ask them to,” said the knight and left. The soldier tied each of the women’s hands, and then linked them all to a long rope to keep them together.

“All of you women follow me. Y’all gave me a headache, so I don’t want to hear another word,” said Curtis, pointing his index finger from Paulina to Olympia’s face. Olympia walked in front of the other girls, trying to shield them. Darkness filled the hallway, so when they stepped out the door, Olympia almost fell over the body of a man with a bullet wound to his back.

“Oh no! This can’t be,” said Olympia. Tapa lay face down in a pool of his blood. Each woman made a gasping sound as they stepped out of the room. Olympia’s hands shook when she could not control her anxiety.

“Move, hurry; I don’t have all day,” said Curtis. As the women walked down a darkened set of stairs and along a long hallway, they could see blood-covered walls, with dismembered men lying here and there, and Olympia heard screams coming from the rooms she passed.

“Can you hear those cries?” asked Lyla.

“These brutes are hurting someone inside these rooms,” said Meleni.

“This is scary,” whispered Lyla.

“Don’t worry; all will be fine if we keep our wits.” Olympia said with trembling words and more courage than before. They walked slowly, making sure not to step onto any of the dead bodies. The soldiers escorted them out of the castle, pushing them forward, but Olympia stumbled as they walked out. The screams, dismembered bodies, guts of men splattered on the floor and the semi-darkness inside the castle made it all seem like a nightmarish hell that she just wanted to escape from and get outside. But when they finally did step outside, the light of day blinded her, and reality sank in making her want to cry, but she didn't. Olympia raised her hands to cover her eyes.

Her ears rung again; her stomach pinched with pain like no other, which made her gag. A few seconds later, she turned her face, trying to let go of what little she had in her stomach. The aftertaste of putrid vile left her wanting to shout, but once Olympia had vomited, her head felt a little better. The other women were trying to help Olympia, but the man holding the rope pulled it, making the other women stumble and fall as they tried to avoid Olympia's vomit.

Once outside, the reek of gunpowder, blood, and feces assailed their senses. Dead bodies littered the castle grounds, but in front of the fountain in the middle of the courtyard, the soldiers piled the dead along with those still living, but maimed and in the throes of death. Men of varied ages lay in every direction; one had his eyes open, staring. Olympia turned her face, not wanting to see the glaze of death that covered the dead man's eyes. Olympia tried to take the shallowest of breaths, but still she could not avoid the gagging sensation, as she hunched over. The next minute, she had vomit on her pants and shoes.

"Yuck!" Olympia said straightening her back, wanting to die, but she cleaned her mouth with the sleeve of her shirt. Her own smell made her gag again, but this time she took control of herself.

"Young man, I need you to listen to me. We are from Palermo. We are rented personnel. We don't belong to the Lord of the castle. The law says we must return to our land. You are making a mistake," said Olympia.

"I don't know nothing about no law," said Curtis.

"At least look at each of our trade tattoos. We are highly educated. I am an Exo—" she tried to say. The soldier slapped her; he took a dirty rag from his back pocket, and placed it in Olympia's mouth. "I tried to be nice and told ye to shut yer trap." Curtis pulled her by her arm.

"Olympia, please, when they take your gag off, don't talk. Heaven knows what these animals will do to you. Look at how they are treating us as we are now. They didn't care to check your trade tattoos." Meleni glared at the men surrounding them.

"They are filthy animals, all of them," whispered Lyla.

"Stop talking," shouted the old bearded man.

The soldiers made the women stand in a line in front of the castle wall while men were catcalling and whistling. Olympia frowned at the surrounding men wanting to slap all of them. It was infuriating having to stand outside under the scorching sun. None of them were street walkers.

However, she didn't look like an Exotic. Olympia had covered her Exotic-tattoo and her golden collar, with her shirt and scarf. The sleeves of her coat covered the multiple tattoos of her skills on her right wrist. Her braids were loose, she smelled like sex, alcohol and vomit. Her dry mouth made her want to jump into the nearest water well. Her eyes stung with the sweat that poured from her brow. The heat was making Olympia dizzy, but she stood tall. The other girls' faces were turning red from the sun. Olympia turned around, giving her back to the sun, and the other women did the same.

"I hope they take us away from here soon. This heat is making me so thirsty," said Meleni.

CHAPTER 2

The New Acquisition

Four hours later, once the men finished plundering the castle, the soldiers marched the five women several miles to where the invading force had made camp. Olympia and her friends did their best not to flag or fall down as they were prodded and pulled toward their unknown destination or future.

Upon reaching the camp, they walked through a maze of soldiers, tents, and carts. There were animals in pens, carts full of goods, and weapons everywhere they looked, but Olympia became more nervous when she saw some common street walkers strolling about the camp. She hoped they would not end as sex slaves. Once they reached the largest tent in the camp, Curtis removed Olympia's gag, giving her time to take a few deep breaths before he escorted her and the other four women inside.

Olympia's eyes adjusted to the darker interior where she saw four tall men talking among themselves. One had a scar on his face which scared her. He stood tall, wearing expensive-looking armor. She took him for the highest commander, so was unsurprised when Curtis made them line up beside each other in front of him.

"My Lord, please undo my bindings and look at my—" Curtis slapped Olympia once more, prohibiting her from finishing her sentence.

"I should have kept your mouth covered."

"Quiet, I want this one gagged. I hate it when women speak without being addressed," the oldest man in the tent said. A soldier stepped forward with a gag. He muzzled Olympia, but left it loose enough for her to breathe.

"Yer Grace, we found these five high-class courtesans hidden in the castle," Curtis said.

“They are all beautiful; by our laws, they are all spoils of war,” one of the four commanders in the group said. The man with the expensive armor addressed the women. Paulina translated for her friends in hushed words.

“One of them speaks our language. I am General Joshua Caleo, the Duke of Coldwell from Alhambra, and you five are mine now.”

“Your Grace, we have several things to discuss, including what you wish to do with the women?” the youngest of the four men said.

“What do you think I should do with them?” asked General Caleo.

“I don’t know, Your Grace. Prince Wallen didn’t have many women in his hold. They may not belong to the prince, but we can’t stop our march to deal with women,” said Commander Linder.

“It doesn’t matter. If they were inside the castle, then they are part of the loot,” the oldest of the men said.

“Fine, I have five company commanders and five women. They will be gifts. Call the resident Trade Official and my company commanders. All my knights did an outstanding job,” General Caleo said.

The five young women stood next to each other. As the General kept giving orders, they waited. The Trade Official entered the tent with his books and ink bottles. A few minutes passed when four filthy men wearing dirty armor entered.

“Where is Lord Wolfson?” asked the General.

“Lord Wolfson said he had to attend to something first. He said he would be here as soon as he was done,” said the messenger.

“Lord Wolfson has no sense of urgency. When I give an order, I expect it to be obeyed. What does he think? Does the man have lieutenants? These Yakutan men have no respect for authority. So be it; Matteo will have to take the leftovers.” General Caleo, Duke of Coldwell said.

“Gentlemen, these five are courtesan prostitutes found in the castle. I am gifting one to each of you. Take your pick, you will choose in order; the highest ranking in the peerage chooses first. Earl of Leon, you go first, select one from all five. However, you must mark the one you pick as yours to keep. I want these women cared for and protected. They are too beautiful, so I don't want any of you tossing my gift aside," the General said.

"How about this? I'll mark mine with my house crest, making her my mistress. My mark will protect her." The Earl of Leon said.

"Great idea, I'll do the same," said another man. All the others agree to mark the women with their house crests.

"Fine with me, we will have the Trade Official do all the required documents. So, which one will you pick, Lord Leon?" asked General Caleo. Olympia opened her eyes wide. She came to Behui with four of her friends from the brothel, women she had personally trained.

"Oh, I want the youngest," said the red-bearded man, Earl of Leon.

Oh no, Lyla, she just got her certificate as a dancer and is barely a courtesan, with only a few months of owning her full license. The man appeared twenty years older than her, thought Olympia.

"Nice choice, my friend; now mark your new mistress." The Earl of Leon took a pincer from the corner, took a log from the fire outside the tent, and placed it on the side. He heated his signet ring until it became as red as a chilly pepper. The Earl of Leon took his ring with a smaller hand pincer, burning his seal on Lyla's left wrist.

"Aaaahhhh!" Lyla screamed in pain.

"Thank you for my gift," said the Earl. After, he signed the trade's official registry. The Earl of Leon took his woman, leaving the tent with a smile.

"Barron Toleo, it's your turn to choose," said the General.

"Too easy, I take the little blond one with the brown eyes," said the tall man.

“A tall man and a little thing; I hope you don’t break her in one lay,” said one of the General’s aids, while all the other men laughed. Barron Toleo did the same as Lord Leon. He branded his little blonde woman, making sure to not cause her further pain.

“Thank you, General, you all have fun,” said Barron Toleo after he had signed the trade registry; he left the tent with Catalina.

“That one is beautiful. She has the looks of the people from Albria. Why is she gagged?” one of the commanders asked.

“The gagged one can’t stay quiet. Do you want her, Sir Yaibar? The Albrian looking may be the teacher of the others. What say you? It’s your turn next.”

“Oh no, I have enough with a nagging wife, I don’t need a yappy mistress. The brunet with the big bust, I take her,” Sir Yaibar said.

Sir Yaibar branded her, signed the Trade Official registry, got his papers, took Meleni by the arm, and Sir Yaibar also left with a smile on his face leaving the tent door opened. As the day waned, the soldiers moved barrels, goods, and lit torches around the camp. All around the camp the soldiers had made campfires, providing lots of light. Olympia wanted to run, when an attractive man with dark brown hair, wearing black armor entered the tent, surprising Olympia with his demeanor. Many different types of men have come and gone through her life as an Exotic, but this one attracted her attention.

Olympia liked his ice-blue eyes, but she didn’t like the blood caked on his arms. His eyes seemed full of something Olympia had not seen since she was a child, some type of rare quality, maybe kindness. He had his sleeves rolled up to his elbows, while a bloodied cloth was wrapped around his big left hand.

“Lord Wolfson, you have finally arrived. What happened to your hand?” asked the General Caleo, Duke of Coldwell.

“Ah, it’s nothing; one of the prince’s knights didn’t want to die,” Lord Wolfson said.

“Ha, ha, ha, I had one of those myself; he left a nasty cut on me leg,” said the last commander, waiting to choose.

“General, I am sorry it took me so long to be here, but my stallion needed tending. I don’t like others touching my horse.

“I understand now. Your Takapian horses are the finest in all Yakuta. You were called here to gift you for bravery in battle. Fine, Sir Wheelan, it’s your turn to choose.” General Caleo said. The General took off his chest plate, sat on a chair, when a page came from the side of the tent. The young man took the armor pieces, leaving as he came—in silence.

“I want the curvy one with the big hips. I like my women with meat on her bones,” said the young knight. He branded the woman, did the paperwork, and left, holding Paulina’s hand.

“I don’t understand what is happening here,” Lord Wolfson said.

“I had five courtesan prostitutes looted from the castle. I choose to give each away as sex slaves to my top commanders. The others already chose theirs, based on noble hierarchy. You were not here to choose first, so they all chose ahead of you, leaving you … the leftover. The last one is beautiful. Enjoy your new sex slave. They were courtesan prostitutes, by what I was told. So, they are trained to please,” General Caleo said. A page entered just then, bringing the General a tray with a tankard and food. The General drank but pushed the food aside.

Olympia stared from one man to another. They would not reduce her to being a personal sex slave. She was the best Exotic in Nolia. Olympia was present as a favor from her master to Prince Wallen. This had to be a nightmare, but she was wide awake.

“I thank you for my gift, but Yakuta abolished slavery many years ago. Also, I don’t need a woman in my ranks,” said Lord Wolfson with his brow furrowed.

“Do not deny me. You are insulting my honor by refusing my gift,” said the General, as he stood up. Lord Wolfson stood tall, his lips drew thin, almost disappearing under his mustache and beard, and his hands balled into fists.

“Please accept my apologies; I don’t want to cause any insult. I understand people in Alhambra do things differently than us. I will take my gift and give you a gift in return as a show of respect. I offer you a colt born from Pearl, my prized mare. The colt was born last summer. I will send it to you upon my return to my father’s castle.”

“My son and I always wanted one of your Takapian horses. So, I accept your gift,” the General said. Lord Wolfson bowed his head. He was about to take Olympia’s hand when the General spoke.

“Wait, I made all the other knights register the courtesan with each commander’s house seal. The others marked their women with their house crest on their left arm. Since you are highest in the peerage, you should not do any less. Since you are from Yakuta, we should use a Yakutan Trade Official to generate the certification, but there isn’t one here. So the one from Alhambra will have to do it instead,” said the General.

“Slavery was abolished in Yakuta several years ago, so I can’t own slaves in my land. Certification will be invalid.”

“We can erase the slave-tattoo of her old master for you,” said the Trades Officer.

“Yes, erase the tattoo. Mark her with my house crest, just like all the other lords did. Also, add my name to her left wrist,” Lord Wolfson said.

“My Lord, when you return to Yakuta, you must erase the trademark-tattoo and register her as a mistress under your house,” said the Trades Officer. Lord Wolfson nodded.

“What is your name?” asked the Trade Official.

“My name is Matteo Hanno Arnold Sean Wolfson.”

The official untied Olympia's hands letting a young Arcane mage who had come with the trade's official, take her hand to perform an incantation on Olympia's wrist. The Arcane Mage said words in a language Olympia didn't know making the slave-tattoo disappear.

Once he was done, the Trade Official came and added the tattoo of a mistress in its place. Taking his ring off, Lord Wolfson heated it. Lord Wolfson didn't look at Olympia; he just branded her on her left wrist. Olympia screamed as the ring touched her skin, but her gag muffled the sound. The intense pain weakened her knees, but Lord Wolfson held her in place.

She would take a thousand tattoos, but not one brand. After the Trade Official tattooed the name Matteo Hanno Arnold Sean Wolfson on Olympia's left wrist, all was done. The Trade Official filled out some papers for Lord Wolfson to sign, and so did General Caleo, Duke of Coldwell and his aids.

"Thank you for my gift, General," he said.

Lord Wolfson took Olympia by her upper arm, said good night and left in a hurry. It was night by the time they left; walking in silence, Olympia in pain with her gag and Lord Wolfson with his apparent anger. They walked to a far corner of the encampment, to where all the tents were green. He entered the largest green tent on his side of the camp, to which Olympia followed behind him. Once inside the tent, he took the gag from her. She moved her mouth to relive the pain from the gag.

"Listen, Miss, I don't know if you can understand me. Can you speak Yakutan? What's your name?" asked Lord Wolfson.

"My name is Olympia Corona Takatsu. I can speak Palermian from the southern cities, Behuian, Yakutan, Catalagac, modern Albrian, and Parshtishi."

"Wait, what kind of prostitute are you? How come you know all those languages?"

Lord Wolfson's surprise made Olympia chuckle. Olympia took off her scarf, unbuttoned her shirt, moving her head so she could show her golden collar, left breast, and the mark of the Exotic.

"I am a slave Exotic Courtesan Prostitute," Olympia said, her deep amber eyes directed at him, unmoving.

"That twisted man, Duke of Coldwell. So now I have an Exotic! I don't need a prostitute, let alone an Exotic. I don't want a woman, and most certainly not a mistress. This shit is not happening to me. Were all the other women Exotics also?"

This man must prefer the company of men.

"No, I was the only one."

"Lord of the heavens above, why do I have to be the lucky one? I don't allow prostitutes to visit my company as they just distract my military mages, and now I have a high-ranking courtesan in my camp. You, simply being in my campsite, will bring problems. How did no one notice you were an Exotic? Since you are an Exotic, you should belong to the General."

"The soldier checked the other women's tattoos, but when it was my turn, someone called the soldier, skipping me. Later, he never reached me. A young soldier tied my hands together, gagged me, rendering me incapable of disclosing my status or my specialty. Since I was in the company of the other women, they mistakenly assumed I was the same as them."

"You smell like stale, unadulterated liquor. I don't allow my men to get drunk in this camp. Do you need to have a drink every day? If you require a daily drink, you will have a big problem here."

"I don't drink. A decanter of cognac was poured over me last night." Olympia didn't want to give any further details.

"Fine, now I'm stuck with you. Let me see your right arm. I need to know all your skills." He looked at her wrist. Olympia did what he asked of her, while taking the opportunity to glance around the tent. She had to make some changes, if this place was where she had the misfortune to live.

"We will continue marching with General Caleo to our next target. I don't use prostitutes or Exotics. As I've already said, I consider your trade a distraction among my men—one that I don't need in war. The only women I allow in my camp are three powerful master battlemages, who can kill any man that is stupid enough to try to hurt them." Lord Wolfson sat on the only chair, forcing Olympia to continue standing.

"Since I am your slave mistress, how should I address you, my Lord?"

"You are not my slave. King George abolished slavery over eight years ago. I can't have slaves, so I've gifted you your freedom. As for what you can call me, I am Lord Wolfson to all my men, but since you are my mistress, call me Matteo." He rubbed the back of his neck and closed his eyes.

"Would you answer me another question?"

Lord Wolfson nodded.

"Why don't you like me?" Olympia asked with her arms crossed. Lord Wolfson opened his eyes. He regarded Olympia with tired eyes.

"Miss, I don't dislike you. I just don't know you. I don't give my trust to just anyone. My trust is earned. In your case, you are a total stranger. Also, I reserve my counsel when it comes to people of your trade."

"Why?"

"I don't partake in the dubious delights of prostitution." Lord Wolfson said, wincing as he touched his injured hand.

"All the nobles I have met make use of Exotics. Why do you deny yourself?" Olympia asked, surprised.

"The god I serve doesn't like us to partake of prostitutes."

"I have entertained Sheshlia, Liaba and Parla priests and bishops. In which faith do you believe? The men of the cloth from those religions don't follow your rules." Olympia's astonishment surpassed her curiosity.

“I am a Benanti,” said Lord Wolfson. As they spoke, he busied himself by unwrapping his injured hand and pouring some water over it, cringing a little when cleaning the wound. He then re-tied a new piece of clean cloth around his hand.

“You follow the Morai faith? Wait! You don’t look, Morai,” Olympia said.

“I am not Morai, but my family and I follow their faith.”

“Why follow that restrictive faith? It makes little sense to me.” Olympia considered him a puzzle.

“It’s a long story, and I don’t have the time or the energy to tell it. Suffice to say, we follow all the tenants and in my family we all worship together.” Lord Wolfson stood up, took off his pauldrons, placing them beside his weapons. Lord Wolfson took a deep breath.

“Most men don’t care about faith,” Olympia said, rubbing her aching head.

“As you get to know me, you will discover I don’t care what other men do. I care what my sons, family and my people do. My conviction is to my g-d, my king, my family, and my men.”

“I haven’t met any man that has kept his hands away from me. My experience with men has been one of pleasure or pain.”

“Miss, you are a beautiful woman. I am sure you were successful in your trade. A woman with all your skills could have accomplished a high level of renown. However, I warn you. Here, you will not work in your trade. If you value your life, you will abstain from enticing my men.”

“I can’t help men looking at me. Will you punish me for what others do?” Olympia could not believe the man would blame her for other people’s actions.

“Listen to me; as long as you keep your Exotic ways to yourself, you will live a peaceful life. My men will keep to themselves or if they don’t, I will kill them myself. In my camp, you are not a prostitute. I will treat you as one of us, as long as you act like a lady.”

Lord Wolfson removed his chest plate and leather bindings from around his waist. He placed them next to his other armor pieces while he continued looking at Olympia. He had a sweat-covered inner shirt, which he quickly took off staying shirtless. The man had hair on his chest. She liked a hairy chest. She wanted to touch him, but she kept her arms crossed and her eyes on his face.

The Lord reached into his trunk, took out a pocket watch, and looked at the time. He closed the lid of the trunk and placed the watch on top, when a little light from a torch outside made the watch shine. Olympia marveled at the beauty of the timepiece.

The old piece seemed worn, but still held a shine. Olympia wandered over to the trunk, admiring the watch face and noticing it was pristine, with no trace of dirt. Her Grandfather had a pocket watch like this one. She loved pocket watches. In her opinion, they were one of those attractive things every gentleman needed to carry. Trying not to breathe, she wanted to listen to the magical tick-tick-tick marking each second. They reminded her of how life would pass, regardless of her decisions.

Is it bronze or gold?

For the moment she forgot where she was and what had happened. She gingerly picked up the watch to look closer. It was encased in metal with a glass face. There was an intricate vine carved on the metal, over and around the glass. As she admired the design, much to her surprise, the metal covering opened. The piece had the most exquisite hands moving so delicately against a black-on-white watch face.

Tiny numbers adorned the outer edges of the watch face, and on every quarter hour line there was a mystical symbol. Each time the second hand passed over the mystical marking, it shined red. With gentle hands, she touched a dial on the side, noticing it also had another button below it. Olympia closed the metal covering.

Carefully, she turned the watch over and found a 'W' engraved centrally on the back. The W was adorned by a wolf with tiny rubies for eyes, standing on his hind legs, with his front paws on top of the W. Olympia had only seen one similar watch in her life. It was her mother's father's pocket watch, but his watch had an S for Skylar on it, with a stag carved around the S. Olympia smiled at the lovely memory of her beloved grandfather.

The old man had given her and her younger cousin, Ultima, a new doll every year for their birthdays. They shared a birthday date. Many years back, when the revolution happened in Albria, her family had to run for their lives, but she never found out what had happened to little Ultima or her parents. Olympia was deep in her musings when Lord Wolfson spoke again.

"You appear to like my watch," Lord Wolfson said, a small query in his voice. Olympia jumped, placing the watch back where she found it.

"Yes, my grandfather had one similar to yours."

"My watch has been in my family for generations. It was my many-greats grandfather's. He gave it to his son, and so it has gone down the line of generations until my grandfather owned it. He gave it to my father when he married my mother. My father gifted it to me when I married my wife, Leonora. One day, I will pass it on to my eldest son, Ivan, on his wedding day. It's a family tradition." He took the watch, placing it back in his trunk.

"It only has one wolf on the back of it. Why is that, and who made it?"

"Only one Wolfson goes to war when we are called. A friend of the family made it for the first Lord Wolfson."

"One is such a lonely number." Olympia gave him a sad smile.

"I must think what to do with you. Having you in my company of men is a nightmare I don't want."

"Well, I have many skills. Some might be beneficial to you, but my specialties are languages and mathematics. I am an intellectual." Olympia said walking to the tent's entrance and looking around outside.

Lord Wolfson quickly pulled her back inside the tent, closing the tent's entrance. "Please, you must stay inside the tent," said Lord Wolfson. He sat in his chair and took off his boots, then leaned forward, elbows on knees and pressed his eyes with the ball of the palm of his hand. Olympia thought she saw a smirk developing under his mustache and beard, but when he looked up, she only saw a frown.

He raised his arms, stretching his back, then sat back. He relaxed his arms on his lap, and closed his eyes. His tired body resembled a knackered working horse.

Olympia could hear him mumbling something.

Is he praying? Oh, I am with a prude!

She could not believe her ears. It was fine by her, if he didn't want an Exotic. In the end, she was going to find a way to escape. She starting moving toward the tent entrance again. She needed to return to Palermo. The lifestyle of living in tents was not for her. The best Exotic in the entire city of Nolia had a standard of living and this was not it.

"Please," she heard him say, "stay inside the tent." She wondered how he even knew she had moved since his eyes were closed.

She turned her back to the tent flaps and looked back at him. Galivanting through the wilderness with a prude, Lord of nothing, would not become Olympia's new lifestyle. She was an intelligent woman, returning home should be an easy task.

CHAPTER 3

Life Changing Occurrence

With her back to the entrance, Olympia stood watching Lord Wolfson as he finished his prayer. Taking a deep breath, he leaned down and removed his socks. Once barefoot, he walked past her to the entrance, stuck his head out, and shouted. "Olsen, come in here."

A few minutes later, a blond man walked into the tent. "Yes, my Lord," said the man.

"This here is my new mistress, Miss Olympia Tasatsu." Lord Wolfson pointed at Olympia.

"No, it's Olympia Takatsu!"

"Take Miss Olympia to Cook for some supper. She must be hungry. Take her to Tony, the healer. Have him give her something for her burned wrist and those rope marks on her arms; make sure Tony helps her with all her injuries. Provide her with water to wash, and give her a new pair of pants, a shirt, anything she needs to travel with us," said Lord Wolfson.

"The Miss will need a better pair of traveling boots. Those look too big for her," said Olsen.

"Yes, get her a new pair of boots and a warm coat. Make sure she has the clothing she needs before bringing her back. If you encounter any problems, come directly to me. Keep the men away from her. Do you understand?" asked Lord Wolfson.

"Yes, my Lord," said the tall man.

"Go with Olsen, but do not talk to anyone in my camp," he said, looking directly at Olympia. "Olsen, have Tony come over. I need him to heal my hand."

Olympia left with Olsen. He had long, dark blond hair, caught up in a ponytail. He wore his gray shirt with the sleeves rolled up to his elbows, showing his tattoos that revealed he was a two-handed-sword warrior and a battlemage from Alhambra. That alone, was a curiosity for Olympia since in Alhambra mages were few. Add to that, battlemages never worked as personal assistants to a Lord.

How could an Alhambra mage be working for a Yakutan Lord? Curious!

Olsen's dark green eyes followed her every move. His body appeared odd to her, because his back, arms, and neck seemed bulky for his trim waist. He led her to a big cart full of things hidden under a tarp, but although there was space to enter the tent-like structure, there was room for only one person to walk around. A man rummaged inside it whistling.

"Hey Tony, step out here," said Olsen.

"What ya doing?" said Tony from inside the tented cart.

"I'm fine, but do you have any salves or ointment for burns?"

"What? Ya got burned in the raid?" asked Tony in his Yakutan-Parshtishi accent.

"Nah, I only got some scrapes, nothing major. It's the Boss's new mistress. She just got branded, and she's got rope burns on her arms too."

"What? The Boss got a mistress! Since when does our commander let women into his camp?" asked Tony, poking his bald head out of the tented cart.

"I don't know, and I don't care. It's not my business. Lord Wolfson saved my life twice, so I will serve him until the day I die without question," said Olsen.

"Woe—Woe, I'm just asking. I'll get the salve." Tony shook his head while going inside the tarped cart. He searched around, and stepped out with a small bottle in his hands.

"Olsen, could he give me something for a headache? My head feels like it is splitting in two," said Olympia. Tony gave her a curious look that made Olympia think of a scolding teacher. Tony went back to hunt some more.

"Hurry, Tony, it's late, and she still needs to eat," said Olsen.

“Alright, alright, give a man a chance,” shouted Tony from inside the tarp. After a minute, he stepped out.

“Here ya go. This salve is for the burns. This powder is for the headache.” Tony gave a little green bottle and a small pouch of powder to Olsen.

“What does she need to do with this?”

“She needs to add the powder to her warm tea, stir it well, then drink it all. Have her add some honey to her tea. The powder is quite bitter. The powder will help with the headache. For her wrist and arms, she must wash the burned area with clean wuata and soap. Once the area is cleansed, using clean hands, she can apply a little of the salve on the burns. She needs to keep the area clean. Use it until the area is healed. Ya hear me?” asked Tony.

“Thank you, Tony. Also, the boss needs you to go to his tent. His hand needs healing. Please don't tarry. Lord Wolfson's hand looks infected,” said Olsen.

“I'll go to him in a minute,” said Tony. He went to fumble again inside the crowded cart. Olsen handed the green bottle and pouch to Olympia.

“You heard what Tony said. You must follow his instructions.”

“Olsen, what is wuata'?” asked Olympia and Olsen chuckled.

“It's water. Tony has a peculiar way of talking. He is a good man, though.”

Olympia took what Olsen gave her; and placed them inside her pants pocket.

After they left the area of the healer's cart, they walked to the communal eating area. The aroma of roasted chicken made her mouth water. Olsen made her a plate of chicken breast, bread, and roasted corn. He poured a large cup of tea and added a generous portion of honey, and then led Olympia to an area away from the men to eat. He stood by her side. Olympia sat by herself and ate all her food—the first meal Olympia had all day.

She added the powder from the pouch to her tea and stirred it well so the honey would hide the flavor, exactly as

Tony had instructed. Olympia drank it all and hoped the powder would help with her headache. Once she finished eating, Olsen took her plate and gave it to Cook's assistant. They walked to the other side of the camp, where they found water barrels. He took three huge leather skins and filled them with water.

"Here, Miss, these three water skins should be enough for you to wash." Olympia took one skin of water, and Olsen carried the other two. As she walked through the camp, the men were eyeing her, and some even gave her lascivious looks, but they carried on walking until they reached another man who appeared to be buried under a cartload of items.

"Hey Timo, where are you, man?" called Olsen.

A huge man, as tall as a mountain, was organizing things inside several enormous trunks, but with only his right arm and hand, as his left were missing.

"What ya need, Mage?" asked Timo with his head in a trunk.

"Will it kill you to call me by my name?"

"Yar is a mage; besides, I can't remember names. So, what ya want?" asked Timo.

"Would you find me the smallest pair of pants you have, a new small shirt, small undergarments, a pair of the smallest boots, and a small wool coat?"

"What ya dressing, a child?" Timo finally lifted his head out of the large trunk to take a look.

"What in all the red fires of hell is a wench doing in camp? Get her out of here. Don't let the Boss see her. Lord Wolfson will have yer hide, if he finds ya with her. Ya know wenches are not allowed in camp!" said Timo.

"Miss Olympia is the Boss's new mistress. And don't you start. I am sure Lord Wolfson will explain her presence to us later."

"Oh hell, this will be a pain in the arse. These men haven't had a woman in over a year. The Boss better hide her good. Although Lorna, Beni, and Willow are female, they are master battlemages. They can light up to hell the arse of any man, big or small. The three of them have served with the Boss since his years at the Academy, but her! She looks like a helpless kitten." He took a breath and almost as an afterthought, asked "But why are ye with her?"

"The Boss order me to care for her needs," said Olsen.

"Best of luck to ye," said Timo.

"Just give me what I need; I don't have all day," said Olsen. Timo passed all the things to Olsen.

"Here, Miss, a change of clothing; let's take you back to Lord Wolfson's tent. I think it's best for you to wash in his tent. Here, you carry your clothing and I'll carry the water." Olsen led Olympia back to the tent. Olsen called out to his commander before entering the tent. They found Lord Wolfson reading a book, sitting on his chair in nothing more than his pants. Admiring his hairy chest, sizable muscles, and several scars, Olympia found him sexy.

"You are back fast. Did you do all I asked?" Lord Wolfson looked at Olsen expectantly, who simply nodded affirmative.

"Olsen said it was best for me to wash in your tent, and I agree."

"Yes, agreed. The other lords let street walkers tag along in their camps. Not me; I don't want any distractions. My men are mages and warriors, here to do a job, not lie with women of the night. Olsen, tell Tonka, Logan, and Warren to bring my tub in here," said Lord Wolfson.

Olsen left the tent, to return a few minutes later with three other men carrying a metal tub. The men entered the tent, placed the tub in the middle, and left. Olympia stood behind with the three skins of water, no soap, and with no towel for her to dry herself.

"My Lord, I need a few things to wash," said Olympia.

"What do you need?" he asked.

“Do you have a bar of soap and a towel?” Her unpleasant odor made her irritable, but she tried to be pleasant. Lord Wolfson went to search in his trunk. He took out a towel, a piece of soap, and gave it to her. He donned a shirt, and left the tent without another word.

Taking a deep breath, Olympia closed her eyes and began to relax.

Finally, a much-needed bath!

She poured two of the three skins of water into the tub, undressed, took the bar of soap and stepped in. Olympia shivered in the cold, but then breathed in the scent of the soap as she tried to lather. As expected, it was a low-quality soap which neither lathered well, nor had much of a scent at all. She shivered again as she poured some of the remaining skin of water over her body.

Olympia was accustomed to scented soaps and lotions. The whole thing was well beneath her usual level of care, but it was a bath. She had decided to keep quiet, and at the first opportunity, she would escape back to Palermo. Olympia rinsed the remaining soap off her body, took the towel, dried well, and dressed. Her burned arm hurt. So, she applied the salve to her burns. Her skin felt instantly better. A few minutes later, Lord Wolfson returned to the tent.

She eyed Lord Wolfson’s dark brown hair and it seemed that he kept it free from lice, so she decided to risk it. “My Lord, do you have a comb?”

He went back to his trunk again, and this time he took out a comb and passed it to her. Olympia combed her long black hair, braiding it afterward.

“Olsen, come back,” shouted the Lord from the tent’s entrance. Olsen was back within minutes.

“Take her dirty clothing and burn it. Also, take Miss Olympia far from camp to answer the call of nature. I don’t want the men near her.”

Olsen nodded. Olympia left with Olsen. He tossed her dirty clothing on the central pyre and took a torch. They walked far away from the camp, where Olsen found a secluded area in the forest for her.

"Hurry, do your thing," said Olsen, stepping away. Olympia had never urinated outside, so it took her a few minutes to make her body respond. After she was done, she stepped back from behind the bush. She found Olsen playing with blue lighting in one hand.

"Does it hurt? I mean the lightning in your hand." Olsen smiled.

"No, it feels good. Let's go."

"Lord Wolfson has the water-mage marking on his body. So, he is a mage, but is he a also warrior? Is everyone in this camp a mage?"

"Our commander is both a warrior and a mage. He commands the mages' company in this battalion. Most of us here are mages, but he also has archers and a few regular soldiers," said Olsen, as they walked back to camp. Olsen stopped near a group of men to give them some orders. Once Olsen finished talking, they walked back to Lord Wolfson's tent. The men ogled her as she walked through the camp. She had never been surrounded by so many men.

When she entered the tent, she a saw the tub was full of bloodied water, and Lord Wolfson's hair was wet. He combed his damp hair, and then stuck his head outside the tent to call out to his men.

"Tonka, Logan, Sheldon, come in here. Remove the tub from my tent," shouted Lord Wolfson. Within seconds, the three men came in, and as the men took the tub out, they glared at Olympia. She felt like a ham on display.

"Where am I going to sleep?" asked Olympia. Her exhausted body ached, but her headache was going away. She had slept little the previous night.

"You will sleep here with me." She was about to protest just as Olsen entered with a bag full of furs and another man joined him with a bag of linen. After the men left, Lord Wolfson made a pallet in the corner of his tent.

“I hope you paid close attention to what I just did. You need to learn how to make your own pallet.” Mollified, Olympia went to her pallet.

“Wait, before you go to sleep, I must do something.” Lord Wolfson came over to her carrying a large set of pliers which he used to cut the golden collar from Olympia’s neck. When the collar came off her neck, heat drained from her body. Her eyes watered. She had worn a collar for twelve years, but now it lay in pieces on her lap.

“I will give the pieces of the collar to Olsen,” said Matteo. Olympia could not take her eyes off the wretched broken loop.

“Now that this piece of shit is off you,” Matteo picked the collar and tossed it to the side, “I have a few things I must tell you.” She looked up at him expectantly.

“First, I don’t want to hear you are messing with my men. I gave orders to my men to stay clear away from you. And now I am giving you the same order. You must stay away from my men. I have three women in my camp. They may talk to you if they wish, but the female mages will be busy with their tasks, so I don’t want you bothering them when they are working.”

“Second, if you cause any of my men step out of line and I find them alone with you, I will kill the man, *and* I will kill you. Do you understand?” His emotionless face made Olympia nervous.

“Third, whatever task I give you to do, do not question it. Just, do it. Afterward, you report to me. I demand loyalty from my people. I protect my people when they are loyal, but I kill traitors. Do you understand?”

“Yes!” Olympia furrowed her brow.

“Good, now go to sleep,” said Matteo.

Olympia wanted to run away, punch the man, slice his neck, and hide, all at the same time. Her situation was vile. She turned to remove her clothing off.

“What are you doing? Get dressed, woman.”

“I can’t sleep with clothing on; it’s a hot summer’s night. It is uncomfortable for me to sleep with clothes on in the summer. Plus, I want the linens to stay clean,” said Olympia.

“Then you must get used to the idea of sleeping with your shirt and pants on every night. This is a camp full of men. Anyone can come into my tent and find you naked,” said Matteo.

“What about if I sleep in one of your long shirts? I can’t fall asleep, if I’m hot. I have been like this since I was a child. Please, I am tired and need to sleep tonight,” Olympia pleaded. Matteo went to search in his trunk, took out one of his nightshirts, and tossed it to her.

“Use this, but I don’t want to see you outside of the tent in your nightshirt. You must be clothed when outside at all times. Do you understand?”

“Yes, I promise.” After, he stepped out of the tent, she took the shirt to her face and sniff it. It smelled clean. She put on her nightshirt and went to sleep. Needing to relax, she repeated in her mind the names of the twenty-two sons and daughters of her master, Chicho, who often worked in the brothel. After that, she recited the names of the thirty-three grandchildren of her master. The repetition lulled her mind, and despite her tired body hurting, she fell asleep some way through the recitation.

CHAPTER 4

At Lord Wolfson's Camp

When Olympia awoke, she felt like she had serviced four men in one night. She didn't want to think of what had happened the day before, but those memories invaded her mind. Upon waking, the first thing she perceived was Matteo asleep on his pallet. Dawn was still an hour away, but she could hear the birds chirping and a little light from the fire shined through the entrance of the tent. Thoughts continued to flutter through her mind.

Oh, how I hate to be out in the open. I miss my room, my bed, and baths with oils; my goodness, how I miss my lotions. All this noise in the morning is going to be a problem. I'm expected to live in a tent from now on with a man who doesn't like me and may kill me. I don't have the safety of the brothel. This can't get any worse.

Olympia remained on her pallet, but she needed to relieve herself. She was hurting, so she got up, got dressed, and peering left and right first, she stepped out of the tent. All was quiet at that early time in the morning. Most of the men had not awoken yet, so creeped out quietly. Out of nowhere, one of the guards came out. He grabbed her arm, startling Olympia.

"Where are you going? The Boss said to guard you," said the young guard.

"I need to relieve myself," said Olympia.

"Follow me." The young man took her to a far distance from the camp and pointed at some shrubbery of prickly bushes.

"Do your business. Hurry, I don't have all day," said the young man.

Olympia stepped behind the bushes. Again, the same as the night before, she had difficulty relieving herself. "This is so undignified," whispered Olympia to herself.

The young man watched her the entire time and it bothered her. She went over to the guard. "What is your name?" asked Olympia.

"My name is Palov."

"Thank you, Palov; take me back, please," said Olympia. Palov gawked at her from head to toe. He smirked, but he walked her back to her tent in silence. Lord Wolfson was already getting dressed when she entered the tent.

"Where were you?"

"I needed to relieve myself; or do I need your permission to do my natural business?" asked Olympia, eyeing Matteo.

"I don't want you walking about my camp. You are to do your business and return to the tent as fast as you can."

Matteo placed his hands together up, against his forehead and said a silent prayer. A few seconds passed. He raised his head as though looking at the sky, but his eyes remained closed.

"Olsen will be back, and he will take you to get your morning meal. Olsen is the only man in this camp you may ask for anything aside from me," said Matteo. Without looking at her, he left.

Olympia wanted to throw a shoe at him, but her Exotic training took hold of her. She knew she had to keep calm. In the end, she was an Exotic; keeping calm was part of her trade. So, Olympia got undressed and laid back down to sleep.

Olympia woke some hours after Lord Wolfson had left the tent. She dressed quickly, and was trying to figure out how she could escape this rigid man with his absurd rules. They were not too far away from the town of Gael, the one where she had first arrived three days ago. In Gael, there was a train station, but how was she going to escape? Nothing came to mind. So, she left the tent to wait for Olsen outside, to start her day. She waited for almost an hour, but boredom overtook her, so she went to walk around and stretch her legs. After she passed the carts with the clothing, she found the water barrels. A man as tall as Olsen was there serving water.

"Hello, I am thirsty. Would you give me some water, please?" asked Olympia.

"Here you go," said the man, giving her a wooden cup of water. His trade tattoo was visible when he served her the water. The man in charge of distributing water had a fire mage's and hunter's tattoos.

"You are Logan. The one that took the tub away. Does it take long to learn how to be a hunter?" asked Olympia.

"Miss, the Boss said never to talk to you. Please drink your water and return to his tent. Olsen should be there waiting for you." Logan took the cup back and pointed to Lord Wolfson's tent.

She left, looking back at the man.

"This lot really obey their master's orders," she whispered to herself. After walking around the camp for a few more minutes, drawing the attention of all the men. She got tired and returned to the tent. Olsen was waiting for her when she returned.

"Where were you? I've been here waiting for you. Master Wolfson will get angry with me if I don't keep you company."

"I was thirsty, and you were not here, so I went to get some water," said Olympia.

"Next time, wait for me. I'll take you to the water barrels. Now let's take you to break your fast." They walked through the camp. They arrived at the stock fire on the other side of the camp, where she met Cook.

"Hello, Cook, this is the Boss's new mistress. She is to be with us from here on until we return home," said Olsen.

"I saw her arrive here yesterday. Welcome to the company, young Lady," said Cook.

"Thank you," said Olympia.

"If you find her walking around, send her back to the commander's tent," said Olsen.

While they were talking, Timo, appeared, staring at Olympia from head to toe.

"She is a little thing. How is the commander going to keep this one safe?" asked Timo.

"Everyone is a little thing compared to you, Timo," said Cook.

"And you must not engage her in conversation," said Olsen.

"Yeah, the Boss explained her presence yesterday. I don't know about you, but I think it's a bad idea having her around," said Timo.

"Mind your own business. The little thing was a gift from General Coldwell. You know how the Alhambra people are. They have fragile egos. Company excluded, huh Olsen," said a woman with long red hair. She had braids with colorful strings attached to her hair. The woman had a fine scar which crossed from her left ear down her neck.

"Hello, I am Willow. I am one of the three female Master battlemages. I'll give you fair warning to stay far away from the youngest of the men. The Boss will kill you if he finds you fraternizing with," she paused, "well, all the men really."

"Hello, Miss Willow; it is lovely to meet you. Yes, I understand; he has already warned me. What type of mage are you?" asked Olympia.

"Just call me Willow and I am a lightning mage."

Willow, seemed like she could kill three men with her bare hands. She was enormous.

"Well, we are here for her meal," said Olsen.

Cook served her some porridge, gave her a cup of tea, and they left to sit by the corner of the stock fire.

"You'd best eat quickly. The Boss doesn't want you hanging around camp longer than necessary," said Olsen.

Olympia had no reply. She ate her meal as fast as possible. Once finished, Olsen returned her to Lord

Wolfson's tent, where he left her alone. Olympia didn't want to think about what life would be like in this camp.

Most of the men in the camp looked like boulders; if any of them wanted to assault her, there was nothing she could do. The thought made her nervous, but Matteo said she was safe. So, she undressed again and returned to her pallet, to sleep once more.

Sometime later, Matteo entered the tent.

"Woman, what are you doing sleeping? It is midmorning, not time for you to sleep." Olympia sat up, startled. She woke from a dream of a castle with numerous trees and horses.

"I am an Exotic. We work during the night, and we sleep in the mornings. My body is used to sleeping until the midday meal. I can't help it."

"You need to get used to sleeping at night. Anyway, I have news. We are going to break camp today. We will be leaving early tomorrow."

"Where are we going?" Olympia sat upright on her pallet.

"We are moving forward. The battalion is taking more ground in the Behui lands."

"I have a request. I think it is best for me to learn how to defend myself. I don't like how your men look at me," said Olympia.

"My men will not get near you. I gave them an order, and my orders are always followed. Moreover, you will never be near the battlefield, so you don't need to learn how to fight," said Matteo.

"But why?

"Because I have no women warriors in my camp aside from three female master battlemages. You will not be near the battleground. The General's camp stays behind, and so will you. The fighters go forward to fight, and the camp stays well back. You will be safe. My men are more than capable of fighting any mercenaries." Matteo took his sword and was about to leave his tent when Olympia held his arm.

"Would you reconsider? I feel helpless. This situation is frightening to me. Besides, I need something to do."

"Woman, listen to me. You have nothing to fear. My men and I will protect you. We are a company with a considerable number of mages, and I don't foresee any problems along our way. A little later Olsen will give you something to do." He tossed the maps he carried in his hands over his pallet to search in his trunk for something. Olympia took the time to read the map.

"Matteo, listen, please; I have another proposition. The town of Gael is where we traveled to when we arrived here in Behui. I read your map. We are not too far away from the town. Since you never wanted a prostitute, and now I am an imposition, would you consider returning me to my people?

"All you need to do is contact my owner once we're in Gael. I know he will pay you for all my expenses. I can make it to Palermo on my own. I am sure my master will remunerate you handsomely for my return. I am very valuable for my master. My clients must arrange my time months in advance" Olympia said holding on to Matteo's arm.

"Now you listen to me; the Trade Official erased the slave-tattoo placed by your previous owner. I took your collar away. You have my name and my crest on your left wrist. This mark is not a tattoo an Arcane Mage will take away. This brand was made by fire. You are not a slave anymore."

"Are you sure?" asked Olympia.

"I am a mage, not a man of the law, but if a mark is not on you then it means you are free. You should be happy. I will treat you like family as long as you are with me. So, get used to the idea. You have a family, and you are not a slave anymore."

"I have an Exotic-tattoo. That is my trade. My taxes are—" Olympia wanted to shout, but he interrupted her.

"Woman, enough! You are mine now, and as long as you are with me, I forbid you from practicing your Exotic trade. In this place, you are not a prostitute." He eased her hand away from his arm. "And get dressed! What is it with you and being in a nightshift almost naked?" said Matteo, as he left the tent.

Olympia stood back, exasperated. This man didn't understand how her trade worked. An Exotic had expensive taxes to pay. Her taxes were going to accumulate and he didn't care. The worst part was all the free time she had, and nothing for her to do. She sat and stewed in her thoughts, paced the interior of the tent, and thought some more. A mage came later with her midday meal.

"Hello Miss Olympia. Olsen is busy so he sent me with your meal. Eat while it's hot. I'll come back later for the plate." Logan was as brawny as Olsen.

Olympia ate her food. Thus far, she hated her new life. This was going to be one dull afternoon.

Olympia listened to the men breaking camp. She sat on the chair for a little while, but curiosity took the better of her. So, she went to comb through Matteo's things and his trunk. He left it unlocked, so she opened it. In it she found the religious book Matteo was reading the day before and a second book of prayers.

They were the religious books of the Morai. Why would he be reading a religious book when he should be thinking of war strategy? Olympia could not understand him. So, she placed the book back where she found it. She had no interest in the religious practices of the Morai.

Olympia continued looking through Matteo's belongings, where she found several shirts, pants, socks, and other items of clothing. The pocket watch wasn't in the trunk. He must have taken it with him. Olympia searched for other books, but found no others. However, tucked in a corner of the trunk, she found a bag of gold coins.

This is my opportunity. I should take the coins, and at the first opportunity, run away. I can reach a town with a train station on my own and buy a ticket to Palermo.

But she heard a sound outside the tent. Someone was coming, so she closed the trunk and stepped away. She had to plan things out. After a few minutes went by and no one entered the tent, boredom took hold again. Olympia needed something to do, so she stepped outside and searched for Olsen. Men were everywhere, all working on dismantling the camp. She called to one man.

"Oh, excuse me, young man, I need help. Where can I find Olsen?" asked Olympia, but the man ignored her. She then spotted Logan.

"Wait, Logan, I need to talk to Olsen."

"I'll get him." He nodded and ran away. A few minutes later Olympia felt a tap on her shoulder.

"Logan said you were looking for me. What do you need?"

"Do you have any books I could read or something I could do? I have worked all my adult life and I'm accustomed to being fully occupied, but with not a thing to do inside this tent, I am bored senseless."

"I have a book you may read; I'll bring it later. In the meantime, the Boss has several shirts that need mending. You can do that," said Olsen.

"There's one problem—I don't know how to sew. Sewing is not one of my trades." Olympia was insulted.

"Everyone knows how to sew. What are you talking about? Sewing, at least for mending things, is not a trade. It's a life skill."

"Well, I have never had to do it," said Olympia.

"Follow me," said Olsen, in an irritated voice.

Olsen entered Lord Wolfson's tent, opened his trunk, took out a shirt, and tossed it to Olympia. He then reached back into the trunk and found a box, and from that box he found some thread and a needle. "Come, I'll show you how it is done. Afterward, you can do it yourself," Olsen said exasperated.

Olympia said nothing. She just looked at Olsen incredulously. Olympia had never done anything so beneath her station in life. Olsen sewed a patch on one shirt; then he gave a pair of socks to Olympia along with other items of clothing.

"You were an Exotic. So, I guess you learn fast. I have already shown you how to thread the needle and make stitches. In an hour of two, I'll come back to check on you," said Olsen, as he left the tent. Olympia wanted to scream. She didn't want to sew. Sewing a man's shirt was humiliating for her as an Exotic.

Olympia took a deep breath; she counted to ten in three different languages, then she walked back and forth in the tent for a little while. After some time, she calmed herself down and sat looking at the clothing. Taking a deep breath, she took the thread and needle and tried to sew the shirts. Olympia knew she wasn't doing such a good job, but it was her first time with a thread and needle.

Time passed, when Olsen entered the tent, he had brought her some tea. He checked the work Olympia had done and said "Not bad. I'll be back later for the cup." He left her alone again.

Olympia had never had to repair anyone's clothing. So, this gave her a renewed conviction to find a way back to Palermo.

ଔଔଔ

Lord Wolfson didn't return to his tent the entire day. The men worked diligently all day long. Day turned to night, and he appeared in the tent as dirty as a Nolia street urchin in the late afternoon.

"I need you to step outside and not re-enter until I call for you," said Lord Wolfson. Olympia didn't say a word. She stepped out of the tent, sat on a log, and waited. A few minutes later, three men brought the metal bathtub into the tent. This was followed by the same three men entering with buckets of water. Olympia could not believe what she was seeing. He was bathing and not asking her for help.

Once he bathed and the men returned to remove the bathtub, Lord Wolfson called Olympia back in. She entered and found the man dressed and reading his religious book.

This man is definitely a prude!

"Why didn't you ask me to help you bathe?"

"I didn't need your help," said Matteo.

"I don't understand. I am your sex slave, here for your service."

"Didn't you hear me the first time? You are part of my family. I do not own slaves. Woman, you don't have the slave-tattoo. Why do you think I would ask you to help me?"

"I am an exquisitely trained Exotic. Aren't you even a little intrigued about what I could do for you?" Olympia smiled at him.

"All my life, I have kept my promises. Those include the ones to my g-d. I already told you; I don't use the services of Exotics or prostitutes. The moment you stop thinking of yourself as a prostitute, then I will consider seeing you as a possible mate." He looked tired.

"Matteo, you make no sense to me."

"I have said this to you before. You *will not* work as an Exotic. The General gave you to me. I branded you with my house crest, so I will treat you as I treat all the female members of my household—with respect and decorum." Lord Wolfson went to his trunk and looked around in it.

"Here, if you want to know why I do the things I do, read this book. It will help you understand. Keep it safe. It belongs to my father. Now, go to sleep. We will have a long day tomorrow." He handed the religious book to Olympia, removed his pants, and lay on his pallet.

Olympia did not believe him. She knew it was a matter of time before he would make use of her Exotic ways. All she had to do was wait.

Early the next day, Olympia was startled awake by a shake of her arm.

"Olympia, wake up," said Lord Wolfson, leaving the tent door ajar. She got up, dressed, and stepped outside. Olsen was already waiting for her. He took her to relieve herself and, afterward, to break her fast as the men dismantled their commander's tent. They finished breaking up the camp. When it was time to ride, Olympia followed Olsen. He fetched his horse and kept her company until Lord Wolfson approached leading his own horse.

Lord Wolfson mounted his horse and reached down to her. "Give me your hand," said Matteo.

"What?"

"You will ride with me. We don't have a horse for you. So, give me your hand and place your foot in the stirrup. Your wrist says you can ride horses." Matteo continued to extend his hand to Olympia as he spoke, so she took his hand and did what Matteo asked. He pulled her up onto his horse.

She had ridden horses many times on hunts, and when young. Olympia loved horses, and Lord Wolfson's stallion was majestic. Olsen had previously told her the horse was one of the Lord's prized Takapian horses. They rode all morning, but Olympia started fidgeting and kept shifting her weight in the saddle. Her legs were cramping with the unaccustomed position.

"Woman, please stop moving. It is exceedingly uncomfortable to ride with another person in my saddle. You are crushing my balls," said Matteo.

"I am sorry, my Lord. It is hot, and my legs are cramping, plus my back hurts. I'm just trying to get some relief for my achy legs."

"I suppose you need to walk, if your legs ache," he said, a slight note of exasperation in his voice. Matteo halted and dismounted before lowering Olympia from the horse. Afterward, he remounted, and called to the company to move on. He made her walk along with the others. Olympia's legs felt like jelly after hanging for so many hours, but now she had to walk in the mud. But once she dismounted, she felt a little cooler. Not having a hot body behind her felt better.

Olympia stretched her legs and tried to keep up with the group, but her boots didn't help. It rained the night before. The humidity made her perspire; sweat dripped into her eyes. The boots Olsen gave her got heavier with each step as they were sucked into the mud, making her feet hurt. Olympia followed the group, but she lagged.

A fine drizzle began to fall as she walked. It refreshed her from the heat, but also made it difficult for her to see. Carts kept passing her by, splashing mud as they passed. One moment Olympia was looking to the side, but the next thing she knew, she was on the ground on all fours. Muddy water splattered over her face and hair. Wincing when she tried to stand up, one man came running and picked her up as if she was a small child.

"Thank you," said Olympia.

With rough hands, the older man held her tight and placed her on her feet. He made sure she stood up straight before speaking. "You're welcome," said the burly man.

"What's your name?" asked Olympia.

"Oh, my name's Flint. Are you hurt?"

"Yes, I hurt my ankle."

"That's no good," said Flint.

"What is your job here? Have you served Lord Wolfson for long?" asked Olympia.

"I'm many things, but now I'm the smithy of the company. I have served the Wolfson family since the Boss was a cub."

Olsen galloped past where Olympia stood toward his commander.

"My Lord, Miss Olympia fell and hurt herself," shouted Olsen.

Lord Wolfson rode back to Olympia. When he arrived at Olympia's side, he dismounted his horse and grabbed a skin of water from a side bag.

"Olsen, stop the men; let them take a break. What happened?" Lord Wolfson shouted as he went to stand next to Olympia.

"The little lassy fell hard. I think she needs the healer," said Flint.

"Thank you for your help, old friend," said Lord Wolfson. Flint nodded, stepping away.

"Here, drink, you look flushed. Also, take some water and splash your face. It will refresh you." Matteo passed the skin of water to Olympia.

"Thank you."

"Where does it hurt?" asked Matteo.

"My ankle," Olympia said rubbing it.

"Olsen, call Tony and ask him to give her care," said Lord Wolfson. He helped Olympia hop away from the road to sit on a log on the side of the path. Tony arrived soon after and went directly to help Olympia. He removed both her boots and checked her ankle and feet.

"Yo, Olsen! This little lady needs socks; these boots are far too big for her," said Tony. Olsen nodded. Tony rubbed his hands until they shined green. He placed his hands over Olympia's ankle and held them there for a short while. Afterward, he wrapped her ankle with a long piece of gauze. Tony gave her a section of clean cloth and a small skin full of water.

"Here, Miss, finish cleaning your face and hands," said Tony. Once he was done, he packed his things in his bags.

"Thank you," she said, Olympia.

Tony nodded, giving her a smile. "You're welcome. Now make sure you wear socks with these boots. Put these leaves in your tea. It will help with any swelling that may come later," said Tony. He picked up his things, leaving a pouch of leaves for Olympia's tea.

“Wait here. I’ll get you socks from Timo,” said Olsen. Olympia cleaned her face and her hands the best she could. Olympia’s tired body needed rest after having walked and fallen.

Lord Wolfson listened to everything Tony had said. After Tony was gone, he knelt in front of Olympia.

“How are you feeling after Tony’s ministrations?”

“I feel much better.”

“Tony is an excellent healer. Listen, Olympia. I am sorry I made you walk. You are going to ride with me again. I’ll make a harness for my horse for you to rest your legs. Us Wolfson’s can be a little harsh at times, I’ll be better. I promise. Wait for Olsen to return, then come find me. I’ll help you mount the horse when you come back to me. We are leaving in thirty minutes.”

After he finished speaking, he stood up and left, not giving her a chance to respond. *Did Lord Wolfson just apologize to her?* Olympia could not believe it. No man had ever apologized to her. She was deep in thought when Olsen returned with a pair of socks.

“Here, Miss, these are new. I am sorry I didn’t think to get you socks before.”

“It’s fine. These look like they will keep my feet dry and warm. Thank you,” said Olympia. And here was Olsen apologizing also. These men were weird.

“You are welcome,” he replied.

Olympia put on her socks and boots moving her foot a little at a time not wanting to hurt the foot and ankle again or more than it already had been. Matteo helped her mount the horse when it was time to leave. He was as good as his word. He’d made a harness for her to rest her feet.

She had never been with a man like him. What made him different? Nobles, for the most part, loved her talents in bed. They praised her skills, but that was the extent of the interaction. Lord Matteo Wolfson appeared to care about her. He seemed to care about everyone in his command. Olympia sat up straight in the saddle.

She held on to the horse's mane, and thought about how her life had changed so drastically in just a few days. She still wanted to go home, but these men were unlike anyone else she had been around before.

CHAPTER 5

On the Way to War

They rode for five days. Olympia had seen little of Willow, and the other two female mages had not yet introduced themselves to her. She and the men were not allowed to talk with each other, and although she met Willow on the first day, she had not had the opportunity to speak with her again. During the next five days, Olympia rode with Matteo, but he talked little to her.

Olympia could hear the cling-clang of the pots and pans hanging off the rucksacks of the soldiers as the company moved along the path. After five days of rain, mud covered everything, including between Olympia's breasts. She could not understand how dirt got in to every crevice, even there. Lord Wolfson's soldiers traveled together, as all the companies in General Caleo's Army went up a mountain.

Apparently, Commander Lord Wolfson's company was the only one composed almost entirely of mages from Yakuta. The other companies in the battalion were soldiers and archers from Alhambra. Every night, they stopped and made as small a camp as possible. The men would erect a medium tent that would fit her and Lord Wolfson, but most nights, his trunk stayed in the cart which carried all his personal things.

She hated every minute she spent with the dirty men. Olympia only had one bath on the first night she had come to be with the Mage's company. By the fifth night, she decided she was going to take a bath whether he liked it or not. She stank, and so did he. Olympia could not tolerate her awful stench anymore.

She didn't *want* to complain; it wasn't like anyone would listen to her. Her hair was a mess, and her clothing needed tending. The wilderness was no place for an expensive Exotic. After they made camp, same as always,

Olsen came to take her to Cook for supper. Olympia made her request known.

"Olsen, I need to take a bath. Women can't go for so many days without washing."

"It's only been five days. Can't you wait?"

"It's four days too many. And no, I can't wait. I need to wash. Please, I only need some water—just a little bit of water, for a quick wash … and some privacy. I will not ask for anything else for an entire day. I promise—not a thing for a whole day," pleaded Olympia, with her hands together as though in prayer.

"Fine, after you eat your supper, I'll take you beyond the camp perimeters so you can wash," said Olsen, and Olympia smiled.

"Thank you."

"You have a way with words. Are you a mage?" asked Olsen.

"No, I'm not a mage," said Olympia. Olsen chuckled as they walked to where Cook had sectioned off a small area for him to work. The mage was true to his word. They went to the quartermaster's cart to ask for a clean pair of pants, a shirt, a towel, and soap. Timo even gave her a clean pair of undergarments. Olsen took three skins of water; and walked with Olympia to where Willow and two other women were waiting together.

"Olsen, you are late," said Willow.

"We don't have much time," said a brunette woman.

"I am sorry, but we had to stop over at Timo's to pick up a few things. Miss Olympia, you have already met Willow. These two are Master Mage Lorna and Senior Master Mage Beni. They are the other two women in our camp. The women were going to take a bath, so I asked them if you could tag along with them. I will go with you. The Boss wants me to stay nearby you at all times. I will not be far away, though obviously out of sight. All you need to do is shout, and I'll be with you in seconds," said Olsen. Olympia nodded. The three women looked and stank like they had played all day in a pigsty.

"Come follow us," said the redheaded Willow. Olympia followed the women. They didn't walk far from the edge of the camp. Olympia carried her things and a torch. Olsen carried the water. Once they reached a far enough place, Olympia passed Olsen the torch. Olsen walked to a safe place away from trees and bushes. He stuck the wooden part of the torch into the ground.

"Ladies, go ahead and wash. I'll be a few steps away. Call me when you are done," said Olsen.

"Just go; she will be fine with us," said Lorna, her purple eyes twinkling.

"I already told you. I can't go too far. The Boss assigned me the role of guardian," said Olsen.

"Fine, just go so we can wash," said Beni.

It was a dark summer night, but the forest's gloominess made Olympia shudder as she undressed.

"Oh, my word, look, Beni, she has the tattoo of an Exotic," said Lorna.

"The Boss told us you are his mistress, and some of the men say you were a prostitute because of your tattoo on your wrist, but no one said you were an Exotic," said Willow.

"How did an Exotic come to be a sex slave for the General?" asked Lorna.

"It's a long story, but in summary, when the soldiers took me as a spoil of war in the last raid, no one bothered to check my specialty."

"I have never met an Exotic," said Beni.

"Is it true the Trades Office gives you a unique tattoo that says the level of pain you can endure?" asked Willow.

"Yes!" Olympia showed them her tattoo on the side of her groin.

"Incredible! Is your tattoo imposed, or do you ask for it?" asked Beni.

"The pain marking is something the Trades Office allows us choose to have. Even slaves have a few rights in Palermo." Olympia said taking the first water skin and letting it wet her body. She hurried to wash, but as she lathered her body, Olympia saw a man watching from a distance. Not able to make up who he was, she turned her back to him and continued washing as fast as she could.

"I think a man is watching us bathe," Olympia said to Beni. Beni lifted her hands. Blue light came from her hands, making the bushes move left and right.

"I will kill you, if any of you men are out in the woods watching us bathe," said Beni.

"What? We had peeping eyes?" asked Willow.

"Yeah, Olympia thought someone was peeping while we bathed," said Beni.

"Forget them, but let's hurry," said Lorna. The women washed quickly, dressing as fast as they could. Olympia, dressed in her new clothing, took the dirty clothing, and shouted.

"Olsen, we are done!" A few seconds later, from the bushes, Olsen appeared.

"Let's go," said the mage.

"Ah, I think I saw a man watching us bathe," said Olympia.

"Did you notice who he was?" asked Olsen.

"He was too far away. He stood in the dark," said Olympia.

"I tried to pull him into the light with my magic, but whoever was there must have run away fast," said Beni.

"I'll let the Boss know. Let's go," said Olsen. The women gathered their things, leaving fast. Once they were back at camp, the women waved goodbye to Olympia, and Olsen took her to Lord Wolfson's tent.

"Later, I'll take you to a creek when we find one so you can wash your dirty clothing," said Olsen. Olympia could not believe what she had just heard.

"I have never washed clothing in my life."

"There is nothing to it. Like all of us, you will learn quickly. Don't worry," said Olsen, and he left her by the tent. Matteo was reading his religious book when Olympia arrived at the tent.

"Go to sleep, woman."

Olympia spent the day thinking of Meleni, Lyla, and the others. She wanted to see the other girls. The women were her students. They had come to the prince's castle with her, and she felt responsible for them. Olympia wanted to make sure they were being treated well by the other knights.

"I have a request," said Olympia. Matteo stopped reading.

"What do you want?"

"Will it be possible for me to visit the other women that were found with me in the castle? I was their teacher. They were under my care," said Olympia.

"Why do you want to visit them?"

"I want to make sure they are well," said Olympia.

"There is nothing you can do if they are not well. So, no, you can't visit them. It is best for you not to know what happened to them. Now go to sleep."

Olympia wanted to shout, but she just turned and removed her shirt. Lord Wolfson left the tent when she took off her pants. Olympia smiled. He was an enigma to her. She folded her clothing, as she undressed. Lord Wolfson entered the tent and found her naked. He turned, leaving the tent again to re-enter a few minutes later.

"Get on your pallet and go to sleep, woman," said the Lord.

"I have a name," said Olympia.

He took a deep breath. "Go to sleep, Olympia." He removed his shirt and pants, lay on his pallet, and turned his back to her.

ଓଓଓ

The next day, they reached a clearing where they made camp. She heard they were going to fight a Behui battalion.

The men set up camp in less than a day. They had all prepared their war gear and were prepared to be in the area for several days.

Olympia waited until Olsen took her out for her morning meal, and as usual he abandoned her once he had returned her to the tent. She took Matteo's under-armor and put it on, including his helmet. Olympia left the tent and walked over to the Alhambra side of the camp. She looked like a child dressed in a grown man's armor, but no one said anything. Olympia found herself in Sir Yaibar's encampment, where she walked around, being careful not to disturb any of the soldiers.

Olympia searched for the leader's tent. When she found the tent, she surveyed the area to ensure no one was looking before she entered. Inside, she found Meleni naked from the waist up, sleeping. Olympia took off her helmet.

"Meleni, it's me, Olympia." Meleni woke, startled. A surprised smile appeared when she saw Olympia.

"What are you doing here? It's so good to see you. I wondered what happened to you," said Meleni.

"I am fine. I just wanted to know if you are well. I have been worried about all of you."

"For the most part, I am fine. Come sit down. I am so happy to talk to someone. I've been lonely," said Meleni. Olympia sat next to Meleni.

"Are you being fed? Is he giving you what you need?" asked Olympia.

"Sir Yaibar gives me all I need except the freedom to walk around camp. I even have to do my natural needs in the tent," said Meleni.

"That is awful," said Olympia.

"Sir Yaibar always wants me naked from the waist up. He comes in and out of the tent during the day and likes to touch me. I am only fully dressed when we are traveling. How about you? Has your master made use of your Exotic talents?"

"No, Lord Wolfson hasn't even touched me," said Olympia.

"What? Does he prefer the company of men?" asked Meleni.

"He said his religion prohibits him from enjoying the use of prostitutes."

"What kind of crazy is your man? I have never heard of such a religion for humans."

"It is the Benanti," said Olympia.

"You mean the Morai religion? Your new master is a Morai?" asked Meleni.

"No, he is not, but he follows their religion," said Olympia.

"Do you know why?" asked Meleni.

"No, I don't, but I must go. I still want to find out how the other girls are doing."

"I hope they are fine," said Meleni. Olympia stood up from the bed when Sir Yaibar entered the tent.

"What are you doing here?" asked the Lord.

"Please don't be angry. She was my teacher. Please don't be angry, she only came to visit for a few minutes just to talk. We are lonely. We need the company of other women so we can talk," said Meleni.

"Woman, who is your master?" asked Sir Yaibar.

"Lord Wolfson," said Olympia.

"You," Sir Yaibar pointed at Olympia, "wait here. I am calling your Master to come get you." He left the tent in a hurry.

"Oh no, I must leave. I want to go visit the other girls," said Olympia.

"No, you can't leave. My master called your man. You will be in trouble," said Meleni. Olympia peeked outside the tent flap, and saw a man standing guard by the tent's entrance. She had to go back inside. A few minutes later, Sir Yaibar arrived. He entered the tent with an angry demeanor.

"Leave the tent, woman. Your master is here for you," said Sir Yaibar. Olympia exited the tent. Lord Wolfson and Olsen stood outside waiting for her.

"My Lord, you should not let your woman walk about alone in other commanders' camps. Your woman could get hurt. It was a miracle I found her," said Sir Yaibar.

"Olympia will not bother you again," said Lord Wolfson. He grabbed Olympia's arm and pulled her out of Sir Yaibar's camp, almost dragging her back to his tent.

"Get in!" he shouted.

Olympia walked inside, expecting a beating.

"What were you thinking? You know you can't be wandering about without Olsen? And to go to another commander's camp, alone! You're insane."

"I'm sorry. I just wanted to visit Meleni and the other girls. It is so lonely for me. Women have always surrounded me, but here I have hardly anyone to talk to. It's just, I need …"

"Enough! I told you it was best for you not to approach the other women, and now you made me look as though I am weak; that I can't control my woman. What will my men do? I don't want you walking about alone. You are only to be out with Olsen or if needs must, with anyone he leaves you with for a short time. Now stay in the tent." He stomped out, leaving Olympia seething with anger. She did nothing wrong. She only wanted to check on her friends. That wasn't a crime. Irritated, she did the only thing she could do—take a nap.

ଔଔଔ

Olympia planned to talk to Olsen. She needed something to do aside from mending clothing or she would go crazy. When Olsen came to get her for the midday meal, she asked.

"I need something to do. I have mended all of Lord Wolfson's things. Please talk to Lord Wolfson. I need a job."

“Calm down, I have talked to the Boss about this, and I have an idea. Let me get your meal, and later I’ll show you what I have in mind,” said Olsen. He took her to Cook. Olympia had her midday meal, and after she ate, he took her to a far corner of the camp where the smithy had his shop.

“Hey, Flint, how are you doing?” saluted Olsen.

“Oh, hey Olsen, what can an old man do for ya son?” Flint had a massive fire going in a makeshift oven.

“You already met Miss Olympia.”

“I do, the little lassy. What? She needs something?” asked Flint.

“Yes, she needs a job, something easy to do. I figure you could train her to sharpen some of the short swords,” said Olsen.

“For sure, I need help. The Boss took Ridley away from me and sent him to fight. I need help here,” said Flint, smiling and revealing his gappy front teeth under a bushy mustache.

“Olsen, wait, I’ve never worked with metal.” Olympia said, holding Olsen’s arm before he left.

“It is easy work. I’ll come get you later,” said Olsen, and he left.

“Mr. Flint, I am not good at working with my hands. I haven’t even cooked a meal in my life,” said Olympia.

“Come, little lassy, sharpening swords is not hard. I’ll show ya. All you need to do is follow my instructions,” said Flint.

Later, the company was supposed to go out on a campaign against a group of Behui soldiers. They took a day to train and another day to organize all their men. In the afternoon, Lord Wolfson walked briskly, approaching from the direction of the General’s camp, with two soldiers holding a third man in chains. When they reached the center of camp, his rage was evident in the way he held his sword.

“OLSEN, CALL ALL THE MEN,” shouted Lord Wolfson. Olympia was with Flint, sharpening a sword on a whetstone. Flint got up and she went with him. They walked to the center of camp as all the men gathered around their leader. Lord Wolfson stood on the healer’s cart with his sword in hand. Willow walked to stand close to Olympia.

“What is going on?” asked Olympia.

“I’ve seen the Boss angry before, but now he is furious. I am sorry to say this, but Sal is fucked,” said Willow. Olympia walked in between the men, and she stood on a stump. She wanted to see what was going to happen.

“Now, all of you, listen to me. You all know I protect those loyal to me, but I hate treason and thievery. This man was caught trying to steal from the quartermaster of one of the knights from Alhambra. Everyone is aware of my rules. Stealing is a crime at my camp. You two, push him to his knees.” The soldiers did so.

“They are lying. Those Alhambran dogs lie all the time,” said the young man.

“Lord Wolfson, this man was caught trying to rob rum from Lord Leon’s camp,” said the soldier holding him.

“They are lying,” said the captive.

“We both caught you doing it,” said the second of the soldiers holding him.

Matteo jumped down from the healer’s cart, rushed over to where the young man was on his knees, and cut off his head with a clean two-handed sword stroke. Blood gushed from the decapitated man’s body. It splattered on Lord Wolfson’s face and his chest. The head rolled to where Olympia was standing. She jumped back. She could not believe what she had just witnessed. When Lord Wolfson gave such quick judgment, all the hair on her body stood on end.

“To any of you even considering taking what is not yours, remember what judgement he received from me. I kill thieves and traitors,” said Lord Wolfson, pointing his sword at the man’s head. His taut stature relaxed and he walked away. Olympia could not believe his conviction and sense of justice. She slowly followed Flint and Willow back to the smithy, listening to the two of them discussing how the decapitated man was a drunk, and how they had told him repeatedly to stay away from liquor.

If Matteo killed one of his men for attempting to steal a bottle of rum, she didn't want to know what he would do to her if he thought of her doing something he thought was wrong. Olympia had to be more careful if she wanted to live.

CHAPTER 6

We Are Going Home

Lord Wolfson spent his days training his men for the upcoming battle. Scouts reported that in the Behui battalion there were many mages, Krapens, and soldiers posted throughout the Lagan mountains. The Alhambran forces wanted to push the Behuian battalion far back into Behuian territory, as deep as possible. General Caleo's intention was to gain some of the Alhambran Morai lands that the Behuians had stolen in a previous war.

Lord Wolfson divided his men into three groups. He didn't have many foot soldiers, so after the cannons fired the first round, he would need to bring the mages into the fight. To this end, he separated the water mages from the lightning mages to prevent them from clashing their magics. Lord Wolfson also organized the few archers he had, placing them behind the mages. He gave his mages time and space to work their strategy, knowing it was best to leave them choice in how to use their magic.

All morning, the knights planned and discussed the different war strategies they could use to fight the battalion of Behui. Then, from a distance, Lord Wolfson saw a sizable group of men approaching. The company bore Yakutan colors. As it turned out, they were a company of mages from the province of Gare. It was a larger company than his. General Caleo sent a messenger to Lord Wolfson. Matteo dropped what he was doing and went directly to General Caleo's tent.

"Lord Wolfson, we received a message from the approaching company. It is from Yakuta. Do you know Prince Peletano Hightower?" asked the General.

"Yes, I do. The prince is the nephew of King George. The son of his sister, the Princess Royal Nívea, and her husband, Lord Gareth Hightower, the Duke of Vurthas," said Lord Wolfson.

"The King's messenger is coming to greet us. I want you to be here with us when I deal with him," said the General. An hour later, a knight in black armor rode toward General Caleo's tent, escorted by four soldiers. The knight in the black armor dismounted his horse and approached. The man's grass-green eyes and light-brown hair reminded Matteo of his friend Lord Caleb Hightower.

"General," the knight inclined his head toward General Caleo, "I am Prince Peletano Hightower. I see I have made good time. I am here at the behest of my uncle, King George of Yakuta."

"Welcome. I am General Joshua Caleo, the Duke of Coldwell, Commander of this battalion from Alhambra. You have made good time, indeed, but why has the King of Yakuta sent a second company of mages?"

"King George has sent me to join your forces and replace Lord Wolfson," said Prince Peletano.

"Hello, Your Highness; I am Lord Matteo Wolfson, here as the Mage Commander on behalf of King George. What do you mean replace me? Why is that necessary?" asked Lord Wolfson.

"Your uncle, the Duke of Trenton, has died without an heir, and our King has proclaimed you the heir to the Trenton Dukedom, but to claim your inheritance, you must return to Yakuta and go to the city of Highcove. There you are to register your claim and pay the Dukedom's taxes. Furthermore, your father has fallen gravely ill, so you may have two titles to claim upon your return," said Prince Peletano.

"Your Grace, I am at your service. I can only leave if you release me," said Lord Wolfson.

"Lord Wolfson, you must return at your king's behest. After all, Kind George has sent a company of mages to replace your company," said General Caleo, Duke of Coldwell.

"Thank you, Your Grace. I'll start dismantling my camp immediately, which should take two days in all. If you'll excuse me, I'll take my leave now."

"Go, I bid you good travels," said the General.

An hour later, Lord Wolfson found the prince setting up his own company's camp.

"Lord Hightower, your brother Caleb and I graduated from Warwick Academy the same year. We were good friends while we were at the Academy and after. How is he doing?" asked Lord Wolfson.

"My brother Caleb died in Tsestelago. One thing consoles us is that he died a warrior," said Prince Pelatano.

"I am so sorry. You brother was a good man and an even better mage." The men talked a little about the war. Lord Wolfson said goodbye to the Prince and all the other knights, and then left in haste.

Olsen, who was in Lord Wolfson's attendance throughout, had heard the men speaking both in General Caleo's tent and later in the Prince's camp. He stopped his master as they were walking back toward their own camp.

"My Lord, it will take you several months to return to Yakuta. I am one of the few Master Lightning mages the Kingdom of Alhambra has. I am also a horse trainer. I owe you my life. I am both bound and honored to serve you. I wish to defect to Yakuta. Will you accept my duty and my service?" asked Olsen.

"You are coming with me. You are my first lieutenant and right-hand man. I don't care what anyone says. Mages in Alhambra may only serve the king, but not in Yakuta. I accept your defection, and conscript you to the service of King George of Yakuta. I hereby bring you into the house of Wolfson. In my camp, you are free. Let's go. We have to register you, and we have a lot to plan," said Lord Wolfson.

"Thank you, my Lord. May I be so bold as to ask if Logan can come as well? He also wishes to defect. We both want to serve Yakuta."

"He only needs to talk to Willow. She is his platoon leader. We will make sure both of you stay with us," said Matteo.

"My Lord, what are you going to do about Miss Olympia? It will be hard to travel with a woman so fragile," said Olsen.

"She will be coming home with me. I will not leave her behind to fend for herself in any town or city along the way."

"Miss Olympia keeps saying she wants to return to Palermo," said Olsen.

"I will not send her back to be a prostitute. My faith compels me to help her. I don't care what she says—she is mine."

ଓଓଓ

The day the company from Yakuta arrived, the soldiers in Lord Wolfson's company were all happy to hear news from home, some even received boxes. Even Olsen was smiling when he came to take Olympia for supper, which she found was odd. Olsen never smiled. But later, when Olympia was getting ready to sleep, Matteo entered the tent looking distressed.

"We are leaving the General's battalion. We will be returning to Wolfson Castle, my father's lands in Yakuta. We'll be leaving in two days, as soon as the camp is packed. So, early tomorrow morning, we must start packing all our things," said Matteo.

"I don't understand. Why are you leaving the fight? We just got here. You've spent days training your men and preparing for this battle."

"I must return. My uncle died, and he left me his inheritance, and my father is also severely ill, so my king has called me back to my land. I may have two accept titles and the responsibilities therein. I must take possession of the land soon," said Matteo.

"How do you know all that?"

"The company that just arrived came from Yakuta. King George sent it to replace me and my men. They brought the news."

“How long before we reach your land?” asked Olympia.

“It will take a little over three months for us to reach the city of Highcove and the mountains surrounding my uncle’s land. After that, we’ll have another two to three weeks before we reach Wolfson Castle.”

“Four months! I can’t last that long outside, in the open. I have never lived outside the protection of a home or a brothel,” Olympia said, looking scared.

“You will be fine. My men and I will not let you come to any harm.” He took his pocket watch, looked at the time, and put it away.

“What time is it?”

“It’s ten to nine. I have a few things I must do. Go to sleep. We have a busy day tomorrow,” said Matteo, and he left Olympia alone.

They left the battalion two days later, traveling as fast as they could. Three days went by, stopping late in the afternoon and spending each night in temporary light camps. Every night, the men made a small tent for Lord Wolfson that fit two people. Olympia was glad Matteo ensured she had enough space for her things. He would be busy all day, come to the tent late, and fall asleep soon after. During the day, they rode, interminably, making only a few stops along the way.

While traveling, Olympia had nothing to do and no one to talk with. She passed her time watching the men on their horses, on foot, and driving carts. Beni rode not too far from her, and Willow rode next to Olsen. They seemed to be having a lively conversation. Olympia envied the women. She wanted to be part of the conversation. Riding with Matteo was quite dull. He said little. Olympia mostly recited poems in her mind or would mumble songs to keep from falling from the horse, but this day was different.

She kept herself busy by watching the others while they worked, and she noticed young Sheldon, Lord Wolfson’s cart driver, had hurt both his arms. The poor young man could barely keep the horses in line when they were packing to go. Olympia looked around, and no one seemed to care about Sheldon. She could not stop wondering how he got injured.

Sheldon had no help when they stopped for the night. He had to manage all Lord Wolfson's belongings by himself, even the heavy stuff. A trunk almost fell on top of him as he was unloading the cart. Olympia wanted to run and help him, but Lord Wolfson had said never to approach the men, so she stayed by her tent.

She had to talk to Matteo. According to his map, which he let her read, they were going to pass by a town with a train station. So, she intended to ask him to take her to the town and let him know about Sheldon. After supper, Lord Wolfson entered the small tent, and was removing his leather armor, when Olympia approached him. She thought this was as good a time as any.

"My Lord, I read your map and found that the town of Kelsing is nearby. It has a train station."

"And? What are you saying?" asked Matteo.

"Please, if you go to the town of Kelsing and contact Chicho di Roberti, the owner of the brothel Il Palazzo di Roberti in the East district of Nolia, he will negotiate my return."

"No, I must return to my castle post haste. I don't have time to deviate from my path. I have plenty of problems to deal with right now."

"But it will only be a few days, three days tops," said Olympia.

"No, I will not go out of my way." Matteo looked directly at her, as though trying to imprint his decision.

"Please, I, my boss promised me a deal."

"But, Olympia, you don't have your old slave-tattoo. You are a mistress now."

"Matteo, I have a trade I don't li—" Olympia started to plead.

"You will not be a prostitute," said Matteo.

"How do you know? I have the tattoo, so I must pay taxes."

"How many times am I going to tell you? You have nothing to fear, if you are with me, you–are–not–a–prostitute." He said each word distinctly, trying to make her understand.

"Fine! I don't want to argue. I have something else I need to bring to your attention. It will be quick," said Olympia.

"What is it?"

"When we were riding here, and then setting camp, didn't you notice that young Sheldon has injured both of his arms? He needed help to load and unload your cart, but no one came to his aid. Could you have someone assist him? He can't be older than fifteen, and many of those things are very heavy, and now with injured arms, he could carry those injuries for life."

"No one told me Sheldon was hurt. I'll tell Olsen to have Tony check on him and assign a man to help the lad." Matteo searched in his trunk. He took out his prayer book.

"Another thing," said Olympia.

"What now?" Matteo glared at her.

"I don't want to pester you, but could you consider teaching me how to shoot a bow?" She quickly continued when he looked at her, incredulous. "Please listen. I am bored. I can help around here. I could gain a new skill, maybe help by going hunting."

"Are you kidding me? No, I don't want you out with the men alone, hunting or anything else. Why don't you ask Olsen to teach you how to work with the horses if you are bored. I promise that when we reach my lands in Yakuta, I'll figure out a way to deal with the issue of your taxes. At the moment, we are in enemy territory. I have the safety of my entire company to worry about. Please, woman, no more talk of you going out hunting," said Matteo, slamming the book shut and leaving the tent.

Olympia lay on her pallet waiting for Matteo until late that night, but it was near midnight, and he was still out. So, she settled down and fell asleep.

Two days later, as the daylight was waning, they stopped and made camp for the night. Olympia waited until the men erected the tent for them, but on this night the men didn't put up the small tent as on previous nights—they set an even smaller tent that barely accommodated one person. She made herself useful by making herself an unobtrusive pallet outside the tent, where she could sleep out of the way, and tried to make Lord Wolfson's pallet in the very limited space inside the tent.

It was going to be a long night if she had to sleep outside the smaller tent, but the tent belonged to Lord Wolfson and she was just his mistress. He was already in a bad mood. They had snags along the way, and were forced to make many stops—including a stop to mend a tire on one of the carts, which took several hours. He had called his lieutenants and gave orders to be ready to travel early the following day.

The men collected a sizable quantity of firewood for cooking. Cook said they were going to have a stew for supper. Olympia had a headache, augmented by all the different odors around her. She hated the smell of manure, dirty men, and the journey's grime. It made her want to regurgitate; at the moment she wanted to die. She could feel a bout of anxiety beginning to overtake. So, she tried to take deep, calming breaths, but the foul odors made her gag every time she did. Olympia figured distance would help, so she walked to the edge of camp where she overheard a group of men talking.

"That whore is a beaut'," said one of the men.

"I wish I could have a tumble with her," said a man with a long beard.

"Ye better shut up. The woman is the Boss's mistress. Ye're dead, if the Boss hears you talking like that," said the man who appeared to be the oldest.

"Ha, I watched her bathe. The wench is ripe for the taking. I'll catch her alone, and she's mine," said one redheaded man.

"And I'll tell ye, ye be dead if ye do that," said the oldest man.

Olympia stepped away. She ran back to camp to where her tent was. It was scary to know the men were talking about catching her alone. She had to say something to Matteo, but he would ask her what she was doing away from the tent area. It was a conversation she didn't want to have. Her headache worsened, so she waited for Olsen, trying to relax her breathing and calm her nerves. He arrived a few minutes later.

"Miss, are you ready for supper?" asked Olsen.

"Yes, uh, where has Lord Wolfson been all evening? I haven't seen him," said Olympia.

"The Boss has been tending his horse with Flint all this time. Runner threw a shoe. He needed a new one, and we don't have a replacement. Flint doesn't have the right type of oven to make him new shoes. So, the Boss is trying to get something done in a makeshift oven," said Olsen.

"I think Lord Wolfson loves that horse more than anyone else in this camp."

"Miss Olympia, we are at war. Here our horses pull our carts and carry us around. We value our animals, but I will tell you something about my master. Our boss would give his life for any one of us. I've seen him in battle, and until you fight in a war with a man like him, you will not understand." Olsen didn't say anything else.

Olympia listened and decided to pay more attention to Lord Wolfson or the Boss as his men called him, and his people. As had become the routine, she went with Olsen to share her supper with the others. Cook made a stew as promised, which they ate with enthusiasm, sopping up the gravy with bread. Where did Cook manage to make bread? Olympia didn't know, but she was happy to have it.

She sat and waited for Matteo by the outside entrance of the tent. It was already late into the night; a hot, airless night, but the sounds of the night made her shiver. She felt like something or someone was watching her. It was an eerie feeling—one she had never experienced before.

Lord Wolfson appeared a little while later. He looked tired when he placed his sword and rifle at the tent's entrance. He removed his leather armor and put it with his boots beside his weapons. Lord Wolfson sat, said his prayer.

"It is too hot and uncomfortable for both of us to sleep inside. You stay here, and I'll sleep out there." Matteo spoke with gentle words. He moved his pallet just outside the tent entrance. Olympia was shocked. Never in her life, had a man shown her any respect or made concessions for her wellbeing.

This man behaved so differently from all the other men in her life, but still she knew it was only a matter of time before he would make use of her Exotic ways. In her experience, all men were ultimately the same; they only wanted one thing from her.

He laid on his pallet outside, while Olympia snuggled inside the tent and tried to sleep despite her headache. Listening to the sounds of the night lulled her to sleep.

CHAPTER 7

We Found Trouble

The next day, Olympia woke an hour before dawn. She still had a headache, making her cringe at all the loud sounds, especially the ones the men were making around the camp. She always hated early morning noise, but it bothered her more than usual that morning. Exotics worked nights and woke late in the morning. She had traveled with Lord Wolfson for a little over ten days already, and she still didn't enjoy waking up early.

The men broke camp in less than half an hour. They collected all their things in a rush and packed the horses. Olympia stood next to Matteo's stallion, Runner. The horse kept nudging Olympia's back and she kept flapping her arms, trying to stop the horse from bothering her. But Runner kept playing with her hair using his snout.

"Stop; I am not going to pet you. I have a headache." Olympia said but the horse kept nuzzling her. At one point, she turned around, and the horse's mouth was in front of her. Runner gave a horse kiss to her face. Irritated, she heard Olsen laughing.

"Here, Miss Olympia." Olsen passed her a piece of cloth.

"What is wrong with that horse?" asked Olympia, as she wiped her face.

"Runner must like you. He doesn't let anyone near him. So, you must have something special for Runner to want to kiss you," and Olsen laughed again.

When Lord Wolfson mounted his horse, all the others were ready and the company set off. Like every day, she was riding with 'the Boss', but on this day, the movement of the horse was making her headache worse. The day was cloudy, and the glare made her eyes hurt.

She tried to look down, but keeping her head down made her neck hurt, compounding her pain. They stopped to rest the horses and eat their midday meal at noon. Olympia took the opportunity to ask Olsen for a piece of cloth, which he found and gave to her.

Needing some relief from the pain, she sat down and tied the piece of cloth over her eyes. The sounds bothered her even more than they had that morning, and the stench of the men was making her want to be sick. She covered her face and nose, and tried to take deep breaths, but nothing helped her pain.

"What is wrong with you?" asked Matteo. Olympia could not answer. She stood up, ran away, and when she was far enough, she vomited all she had eaten at noon. Her head felt a little better once she'd vomited.

"Here, take this." Matteo gave her another cloth to wipe her mouth.

"Does your stomach hurt?" asked Matteo.

"My head hurts. It feels like it's going to burst."

"How long have you had the pain?" asked Matteo.

"It started last night," she said weakly.

Matteo stepped away, and a few minutes later, he returned with Tony, the healer.

"Miss Olympia, you look green. What's wrong with you?" asked Tony.

"I have a nasty headache. My eyes hurt, and the pain radiates over my head," said Olympia.

"How often do you get these headaches?" asked the healer.

"Probably once or twice per month." Tony rubbed his hands and closed his eyes, turning his hands green, then yellow. He reopened his eyes, then placed his hands over Olympia's head. Olympia felt the pain subside; even her eyes hurt less. Tony's healing magic made the pain disappear from her eyes, but it still remained at the top of her head.

“Do these headaches come when you eat something in particular?” asked Tony.

“They usually come when I am outside on a cloudy day or a day or two before my curses.”

“Here, add this powder to your tea. You had it before. Stir it well, add sugar, but make sure you drink it all. It will help with your headache,” said Tony. The healer gave her a small pouch with the powder, similar to the one he gave her on the first day at camp.

“You may still feel pain on the top of your head, but it will slowly go away. I’ll tell Olsen to get you a hat. It might help with this hazy light. It would be best if you had dark glasses. I’ll suggest to Lord Wolfson to buy you a pair once we reach a town in Yakuta. I can’t do anything about your curses.” Tony patted her shoulder in a brotherly way.

Later, Olsen brought her some bread, cheese, tea, and a wide-brimmed hat. She ate some food, drank her cup of tea, and reclined against a tree. She closed her eyes, trying to sleep a little. She got up, feeling a little better when it was time to mount the horses.

They traveled for about an hour. Olympia still had her headache, but it wasn’t as severe. The hat helped. The horses were walking along a narrow pass through a thick forest. Olympia could hear the clanging of Cook’s pots and other metals, the sound of the horses along the path, and the conversation of a few men as they walked along the trail. Matteo kept quiet the entire time, as he often did.

Olympia’s headache lessened as the day went on and by evening, she didn’t have it at all. Matteo didn’t talk to her much the entire day—they had found an amicable understanding. That night, the men erected a larger tent. At bed time, Matteo lay next to her, turning his back to her, but in the early morning she woke up with his arm over her waist, holding her close.

The light shined through a gap at the entrance of the tent, striking her face. Matteo, still asleep, was breathing in and out calmly. Olympia smiled, having him with her made her feel safe and warm, especially as the nights were getting colder. Later that morning, as happened every other day, Matteo woke, moved away from her, said his prayers, got dressed, and left the tent quietly, not knowing she was already awake, and watching him dress.

They made camp and stayed for a day, giving the horses a chance to rest. That evening, Olympia's back hurt and she had gone to sleep early. Two days had passed since the day she had her severe headache.

She woke at dawn with a stabbing backache. Standing up, she found blood between her legs and on her covers. Her curses had arrived. Olympia thought she must be the unluckiest woman in the world. How did women deal with this issue while traveling by horse? Matteo was still sleeping, and she was a mess.

Olympia found a pair of clean pants she had among her things. She took the one extra shirt Olsen had given her and managed to tear it into pieces. She put on a pair of dirty pants and stepped out of the tent. As always, a soldier stood guard.

"Go back inside," said the soldier.

"I need help," said Olympia.

"What ye need?" asked the blue-eyed man with a long beard.

"I have a problem, and I can't wait for Olsen to come get me later. Can you help me, please? I need you to go find either Miss Lorna, Beni, or Willow. And do we have a creek nearby? I need to wash," Olympia said, her cheeks turning warm. The guard looked from one side to the other, then down at her bloodied pants, and smirked at her.

"Wait here. I'll be back soon." The young man left. Olympia waited for about five minutes when the guard returned with Beni.

"Let's go. Warren told me what happened," said Beni.

"I am mortified."

"Why? We get our curses too. You'll get used to it," said Beni.

“Come with me,” said Warren. They followed Warren who was holding a torch to light the way. They walked for about five minutes just beyond the edge of camp, where they found a creek. He planted the torch in the ground, and stepped away behind some bushes.

“Clean yourself fast. I’ll stay here keeping watch,” said Beni. Olympia caught Warren looking at her from where he was hiding. She undressed from the waist down, walked in the cold creek, and washed. Olympia cleaned herself fast. The years as an Exotic had made her lose her apprehension at men looking at her naked, but having Warren watching her bothered her.

She stepped out of the water, put on a pair of Matteo’s underpants, and used the strips of cloth she had made from her shirt. She tried to wash her nightshirt and pants, but in the distance, something rustled the bushes. She stared at the area on the other side of the creek. She could swear she had seen a man, but it was still dark.

“Beni, look over where the tall bushes are, past the woods; something moved,” said Olympia.

“It could be a wolf or a bear. Let me help you wash your things. I have extra cloths I will send you. You need to some closer-fitting underpants to keep everything in place. I’ll send you a clean pair,” said Beni. They hurried. Once Olympia was done, they called out and Warren returned from behind the bushes, and picked up the torch.

“Let’s go. Soon, it will be time to muster. You both need to be back in your tents by then,” said the soldier.

They walked back to camp. Beni left to return to her tent, and after laying her wet pants to dry on top of a pile of wood outside the tent, Olympia entered hers. Lord Wolfson was still sleeping. She was feeling bone tired, and quickly went back to sleep.

Later when she awoke, she told Olsen she had her curses and had destroyed her spare shirt, so needed an extra one. He provided her with a new shirt and extra cloths for her menses.

After Olympia broke her fast, Beni appeared with a pail. "I asked Timo to get me a pail for you. It has salt and water. Put your bloodied clothes in the salted water. You can clean them later. I told Sheldon you would put the pail on the back of the cart carrying Lord Wolfson's things. He said he would find a place for it. Willow, Lorna, and I place our pails in it," said Beni. Olympia rubbed her face.

"I am embarrassed." She hated that so many men knew of her private cycle, but this was going to be life while traveling with those men.

"Don't think about this." Beni held her shoulder and shook her a little. "It is our natural way. The men don't care."

It was time to move on so, they mounted their horses and Lord Wolfson gave the order to march. While having her cycle, Olympia hated having to share a horse with Matteo. She disliked the waft of herself and wanted to wash every time, she had to relieve herself. Her back hurt, and her legs felt like lead, but she could not say anything. Olympia missed being in her home back in Palermo. They traveled through a forested area. Olympia kept looking around for signs of cities, but there were none.

In the afternoon, the scouts had found a place to spend the night; they even found a large, fallen tree, dry enough it could be chopped up for firewood. While the men were making camp, Olympia asked Olsen to take her to speak with Tony. She needed some things from the healer. Olsen obliged and led Olympia to Tony's cart.

"Yo Tony, where are you?" called Olsen.

"Hey Olsen, how yu doing?" asked Tony in his Parshtishi accent.

"I'm fine. I'm here with Miss Olympia," said Olsen.

"Yo, Miss Olympia, what yu doing here? Ye'r sick?" asked Tony.

"Hi Tony, no, I am not sick. I need you to make me a lotion if you can," said Olympia.

"What kind of lotion?" asked Tony.

“I need something to put on my hair to make it soft and not smell like a horse, please.” Olympia smiled.

“Not smell like a horse, ha! That miracle I can’t do. While we are traveling, that is all we stink like, but I can make you a lavender pomace, with a little aloe. It can make your hair soft. Will a pomace work? I make it for my wife and she loves it,” said Tony.

“Yes, that will work,” said Olympia.

“Come back in six or seven days, I’ll have it ready by then,” said Tony.

Olsen led Olympia back to Lord Wolfson’s tent. Earlier in the day, the men had found a creek near where they made camp, and Olsen took Olympia to get a quick wash, but she remembered she also needed to do her laundry. Olsen could not spare the time to take her back, but said he might be able to later in the day. While Olympia waited in the tent, Matteo popped his head in and startled her.

“Come with me, Olympia. Olsen said you needed to wash some of your clothing. The men said they found a creek nearby.”

“What do you mean? Maybe Beni or Willow could come with me?” asked Olympia.

“Olsen is busy, and each of the women are busy with many of their own tasks. Let’s go. Take what you are going to wash. I must wash my clothing too,” said Matteo. Olympia hated the idea of Matteo knowing about her private matters. She didn’t want him watching her wash her personal bloodied clothes. He entered the tent and took a bundle of his things, a bar of soap, and a basket. Olympia had no other choice, so she took her clothing and her bucket of personal clothes in salted water. They walked together to the creek in silence.

Once they reached the creek, Olympia went downstream from where Matteo was washing his clothing. She didn’t want him looking at what she was washing. While she washed her clothing, she sang. Olympia liked to sing. While living in the brothel, she used to do it often. Half an hour had passed, and she still wasn’t done. Upon finishing his own clothes, Matteo approached her with a friendly smile. She stopped and looked at him.

"I like the way you sing," said Matteo.

"Thank you, I enjoy singing," said Olympia. Matteo came and knelt next to her.

"Do you need help? It is getting dark. I don't want us to be this far from camp after dark," he said. Olympia kept her face low over what she was doing.

"No, thank you, I'm almost done. I'm sorry, I had a lot to wash." Olympia said.

"I understand, but please hurry," he said. Olympia could not look at him. Her embarrassment made her want to disappear. She finished what she was doing, and they headed back to camp. Olympia heard a sound a short distance away.

"Matteo, I think someone is watching us." He stopped to listen, then left Olympia where she stood to check around. The sun had recently set and only a little light shined through the trees on the horizon.

"I don't see anything. Let's go," Matteo said, sounding a little concerned. Once they reached camp, Olympia found some low branches and guy ropes to hang her things to dry. After she ate her supper, she returned to her tent and sat by the entrance. A few minutes later, Matteo came and sat beside her.

"Could you sing some more?" he asked.

"What do you want me to sing?"

"Do you know Starry Night?" asked Matteo.

Olympia nodded, and she began to sing the song in a soft voice. Other men turned to listen to her sing as voice grew stronger. One of the men took out a guitar and played along with her. Once she finished her song, Matteo smiled.

"Will you sing another?" asked Matteo. Olympia nodded again.

"How about Queen of the Night?" asked Matteo.

"You like Albrian songs?" Olympia asked.

"Yes, I do," said Matteo.

Part way through the song, another man with a wooden flute began to play, followed by an older man with a three-string instrument, and Olympia sang. When she finished singing, everyone applauded including Matteo.

"Alright, all of you, go to sleep. We will be rising early tomorrow," said Lord Wolfson.

"This was the first time I've ever sang by a campfire," said Olympia.

"Thank you for your songs," said Matteo.

"You are welcome. You are the first person who has ever thanked me for singing."

"You sing with a beautiful voice. It makes me want to dance." He smiled again, lost in his thoughts. "But now it is late. We have a long day tomorrow. Have a good night." He stood up and went to give orders to his men. Olympia smiled, thinking of him dancing to her songs. She entered the tent still smiling, and lay down to sleep. Later, Matteo entered and lay down next to her. Soon afterward, his arm came across and rested over her waist, helping her relax and fall fast asleep.

Matteo's mind wandered. He knew he should focus on returning to Yakuta safely, and yet he could not stop himself. They traveled for twelve more days, and every day he looked forward to having her near him on his horse. He liked the feel of her by his side. And after riding all day, the medium size tent meant they slept in close proximity each night. He tried to ensure she had fallen asleep by coming to the tent late in the night, and he gave her as much space as he could during the day. He liked that she wasn't boastful. Olympia had a gentle way to her. She never raised her voice, and she always had a smile for everyone.

After they had left the battalion, she did what he ordered. She stayed with Olsen or next to him. She spent her time, when not riding, working with Flint sharpening swords or any other object, or she would mend his clothing.

The best thing he liked about her was that she wasn't vainglorious or conceited. She could speak both Tony's and Flint's languages. The two men loved to chat with her. She cared for those around her.

Matteo kept a close eye on Olympia's actions and words. He would not have a self-centered, haughty woman trying to distract his men of his camp. They were in enemy territory, and he wanted to bring all his men home alive, or at least, as many as he could keep alive. They had stopped and he was planning a two day stay to give the horses rest.

On this night, she had asked Olsen to take her to the creek for a bath and wash her clothing, as they had done several times before, but Olsen said he couldn't because he had the third watch of the night and needed to go to bed early. The other women had already taken a bath. So Matteo, who kept a constant eye on Olympia and had seen this unfold, volunteered as he had done once before.

He was looking forward to taking Olympia to the creek to wash. It was a time to have her to himself. He could enjoy looking at her curves without anyone around him. He watched as Olympia piled her belongings high and transferred them to a bag. She added some soap and took an extra towel. He recalled she had said she wanted to wash her hair.

They walked to the creek. Matteo had his own bag, and held a torch. The stream was not too far, and the firelight from the camp was still visible. They soon reached the creek and Matteo thought the light from the torch made the water sparkle. But then he realized something in the water didn't just reflect the torchlight, it made it glow. Matteo touched the water; it had magic. He drank from it. It was fresh and almost sweet. Magic was in the water, in the air, and in the very ground they stood on, but Matteo could not tell where it was coming from or going to—it was all around. But when he saw Olympia near the water, she took his breath away and he forgot about the magic. He admired Olympia's beautiful black hair.

"I have a lot of clothing to wash. I hope you don't mind," said Matteo, lying.

“I don’t mind waiting for you.”

Matteo delighted in the view as Olympia removed her boots, her pants and undergarments. She folded them neatly and placed them on the side before taking off her shirt, and shivering. He undressed too, trying not to look at her naked body, but when she entered the water, and her nipples perked, he could not stop himself. He got excited. The water reached her knees, and she knelt to splash water over her body. She quickly lathered with her soap, rinsed well, and then tried to wet her hair without lying down in the cold water.

Lord Wolfson could not take his eyes off from Olympia as she struggled to wet her hair. He lifted his hands a little, and a flow of water rose up from the stream. It slowly fell like a rain shower over Olympia’s head. She watched with astonishment as Matteo worked his magic.

“Thank you.” Olympia said as she took on the task of washing her hair.

“What a wonderful sight!” whispered Matteo. The roundness of her breast was accentuated when she lifted her arms to wash her hair. The sparkling water left glimmering rivulets cascading down over her body. Matteo’s eyes seemed glued to her breasts, but then a soft light rose from the water and surrounded her. It was as if her body was absorbing and emitting light.

She seemed oblivious to the light show of her own body and that of an equally naked man who could not stop looking at her. It didn’t take long for her to finish, and as soon as she was done, Matteo released the water to let it run its natural course again. She ran to retrieve her towel, making her buttocks bounce slightly with the movement. He noticed a strawberry birthmark, shaped like a four-leaf clover on one of her buttocks. She bent over, and Matteo’s desire overwhelmed him.

Olympia dried her body and hair, combed it through. Once dry, she smoothed something over her body from a small container. From his distance, it smelled like an oil with the aroma of lavender. She turned. Matteo took in all of her and he enjoyed every minute.

Matteo stepped out of the water, the glimmering droplets of water remaining on his body, but he barely noticed. He stood stock still, wet, not minding the chill of the night—simply beholding all her soft curves and her glow. He did not bother to hide his erection.

Olympia stopped what she was doing and looked at him without any expression on her face. Then their eyes met. Not wanting to make her feel uncomfortable, he turned his back to her, but when he heard footsteps over the dry leaves he had to smile. A soft hand held his. She made him look at her. She gave his hand a gentle tug, encouraging him to sit on the ground and then recline against a log. Olympia went to her knees, slowly approaching Matteo's lips.

"Let me help you. You said I am not a prostitute anymore. You said I'm your mistress; you call me your woman. Then let me be your woman." She gave him soft kisses. He held her arm, as she kissed him. He returned her kisses, and as they were tasting each other, Olympia wrapped her knees around his hips and started lowering herself on him. Matteo held her waist, pulling her toward him. One hand still slid down to her hip, the other rose up to hold on to a breast. They kissed and Olympia set the pace.

Matteo had only one woman in his life, his wife. She had died three years earlier, so he had lived three lonely years after her death. Each time Olympia moved, Matteo marveled at how their wet bodies glowed, a light blue that turned to soft violet as they moved.

Now in the forest, surrounded by nature, he found a moment of happiness and release with Olympia. She took him to a land of happiness. After a few moments, he came back to his senses. Olympia was breathing hard. At some point during their coupling, they had lain on the ground with Olympia on top of him. Her head rested on his shoulder, and her small hands held his arms. He reached around her back and held her close to his chest.

“Thank you. You didn’t have to do this,” said Matteo. He sat up, but continued to hold Olympia close as he did. Olympia’s expression softened. She touched his face with gentle fingers, and smiled sweetly at him.

“You desired this, and I had my own needs I wanted to satisfy,” Olympia said, giving him another kiss. She tried to lift herself up and away from him, but he held on to her.

“You smell like lavender. I love the scent of lavender. Please, stay in my arms for a little while longer,” said Matteo. Olympia nodded. He continued to hold her, each losing themself in each other’s arms for a long while. Finally, they moved apart and started talking. They talked about the war, and Olympia asked him about his mage training. An hour later, they had to bathe again before washing their clothing and returning to camp.

Matteo had Olympia in his arms for the next three nights. They would walk away from camp, and Olympia only had to kiss him for Matteo to get aroused. They would kiss and kissing progressed until they both were satisfied. From that night on, Matteo never let Olympia sleep alone in their tent.

CHAPTER 8

The Mercenaries and the Krapens Leader

Olympia found comfort in Matteo's arms. She liked the way her Matteo made her feel. They made love every night following the first time by the creek. He was a generous lover, which she liked about him.

Four days later, Olympia realized with disbelief that they had traveled for so many days and had not crossed paths with any other travelers. The day went on as usual, but things changed as the afternoon progressed. Near dusk, they were still searching for a place to make camp when a strange feeling crept up on Olympia.

"The forest feels strange," said Olympia.

"What do you mean?" asked Matteo.

"I am not sure. It's too quiet. What time is it?" she asked.

Matteo took out his pocket watch. "We will stop and make camp soon. It's ten past five," he said, just as a brown and green orc demon landed on him and Olympia, and threw them off the horse. Lord Wolfson quickly stood up, drew his sword, and fought the orc, but had to use his magic to kill it. Olympia lay on the ground where she fell for a second or two, while trying to clear her head, but the horse reared. She had to roll away fast so it wouldn't step on her.

From both sides of the road orc demons descended. The grotesque creatures reeked like rotten eggs and their teeth protruded from their mouth in sharp points. The monsters jumped down from the nearby trees, forcing the soldiers in the caravan to jump into battle with whatever they had at hand.

Olympia got up fast. She took Matteo's rifle from the horse's saddle holster. She shot at one of the orc demons between his eyes. Olympia knew how to shoot rifles, but not how to fight. She shot the one and only bullet. She tried to reload the gun, but a mercenary who attacked with the orc demons, captured her from behind and abducted her from the battle.

"Aaahhh, let me go. Help me, help me!" Olympia shouted, but the tall mercenary had a firm grip on her and pulled her far into the forest. He stopped, slapped her, and tossed her over his shoulder. She moved, kicked, and shouted, trying to get off, but the man holding her didn't budge.

"Help me, help me! Matteo, Olsen, come find me. Help me, Matteo, help me!" Twigs and branches hit her, grazing her skin and clothing as the burly man kept jogging deeper into the forest. He ran through labyrinthian paths and tracks, between and around bushes and trees, until he reached a camp. In the camp, creatures she had never seen before in her life roamed and worked. They had bulging eyes, broad noses, and long canine teeth. These monsters' bodies were very muscular, but their dark gray skin sagged from their bodies. Several stood next to a brawny green man who didn't appear fully human. The mercenary dropped Olympia at his feet.

"Look what I found traveling with the Yakutan soldiers," said the mercenary. He was dressed in black with a dark-blue bandana around his head. His beard covered his face, and his bushy eyebrows almost covered his eyes.

"She's so pretty," said one of the dark gray men.

"This is the one I watched bathing well over a fortnight ago. I could almost taste her blood in the water. The intoxicating smell made me cum in my pants. I have me a delightful piece of ass for tonight." The monster grabbed Olympia by the hair, pulling her to the side.

"You guided the company out of our way just to catch this one female?" asked a red demon with black eyes, who was standing by the fire. The demon's two big horns curled to the sides. The sight made Olympia tremble.

"Sobo, remember who you are talking to," said the leader.

"Ha, I know who you are—Foller. But remember this. You will soon die. I see it in the fire," said Sobo.

"You are my slayer, not my oracle. Now find me my next target," said Foller, and Sobo, the red slayer demon with horns, sneered, but left in a run.

"Yaka! Yaka, where are you?" A mercenary dressed all in black with a red bandana appeared.

"I'm here, master."

"Take her to my tent and guard her."

"Yes, master," said Yaka. The second mercenary took Olympia by the arm, yanking her hard.

"Come, walk fast," said Yaka, as he pulled her away. They walked through the camp consisting of fur tents and empty cages wherever she looked.

"What are those gray-looking monsters? I've never seen anything like them, not even in books," Olympia asked.

"Stupid woman, those are dullahans," said Yaka. He pushed her into a smelly tent. Olympia almost landed on a pallet of furs, but managed to remain on her feet. She turned back to the entrance to look for escape, but when she glanced outside, she saw Yaka standing just outside. Olympia ran to the opposite corner from the tent's entrance and tried to pry up the edges from the ground. They had planted the tent with stakes in the ground, but Olympia managed to lift one edge. It was no use. Once she lifted it enough, she saw several dullahans walking about, weapons in hand. Olympia could not escape that way, not yet, at least.

She kept looking as darkness fell, and more dullahans walked about. Olympia sat on the pallet made of furs. How could this happen? She was in a camp of Behuian demons, monsters, and mercenaries. These … these things were not part of a general or a noble's army. There were no knights to behave honorably. These monsters were at the fringe of the battalion. Behui claimed they were not using demons in their battalions, but clearly, they lied. Here she was, in a Behuian camp from hell.

Her life was shit. Matteo was most likely dead, and she was in the possession of a man in the body of a devil. She had thought her life could not get any worse. Hunger and thirst were growing, and she also needed to relieve herself. What a moment to need to answer the call of nature. Olympia searched the tent for something to eat or drink, but found nothing. Nor could she find anything she could use to relieve herself. She resolved to ask Yaka.

"Excuse me, Mister Yaka," called Olympia, from inside the tent. She stuck her head outside the tent, where she spotted a huge fire at the center of the camp. There were a few tents dotted around made of furs, but she didn't see any carts aside from the cages. No sooner had she stuck her head out and called to him, Yaka pushed her back inside.

"What you want?" asked Yaka.

"I am hungry and thirsty too. I also need to relieve myself. Can you let me out?" asked Olympia.

"NO!" was all Yaka said.

Olympia stepped back, away from the tent door. She didn't want Yaka to come inside the tent and hurt her. She sat down on the pallet of furs, thinking of the horrid night that awaited her at the hands of the giant man, the owner of the tent. Nevertheless, a few minutes later, a man dressed in black with a red bandana entered the tent carrying a plate of food—some bread, a piece of meat, and a tankard. Shortly afterward, another man entered with a bucket. Olympia accepted the plate of food and the tankard. No utensils were provided, so she placed the meat inside the bread and ate it. It tasted like some type of bird flesh.

After she ate and drank her ale, she placed the plate aside and cleaned her hands on the tent since nothing was provided for the purpose. She had become accustomed to such rudimentary habits since traveling in the woods that she had lost her inhibitions of good manners. She used the bucket to do her natural business, and she waited.

"It appears I attract problems. Just when I marveled that we had had no incidents on the road, these bastards jumped down, like birds falling from the sky. I hope Matteo is alive. I don't believe in any god, but if there is a heaven and a god, let Matteo be alive," thought Olympia. The last time she saw Matteo, he was fighting an orc demon.

Olympia paced the tent and carried on thinking aloud, whispering to herself. "He must be dead by now. I hate my life. I got kidnapped just when I started to enjoy being with a man. Damn all to hell. Why me, why this, why now? I can't believe this." She wasn't one to cry. She had not cried since she was a young woman and her husband sold her to Chicho, but her eyes were wet with unshed tears.

Olympia's mind returned to that fretful morning when her husband found her in bed with his best friend. It wasn't her fault. She had not cheated on her husband. The entire ordeal was a nightmare she wanted to forget.

"Aaaaahhhhhh, Damn you all. I'll figure out a way to return to Palermo," shouted Olympia. She took a deep breath and calmed herself.

An hour later, Foller, the leader of the Behuian group, entered the tent. "Woman, take off yer clothes. I want ya now," said Foller from the tent entrance.

He took off his armor and his shirt. Olympia stood motionless. Foller was a giant, with bulging muscles covered by puffed up veins swelling out. Dirt and sweat covered him, making him even more hideous.

"You don't look human," said Olympia.

"I'm a Krapens. Now take yer clothing off, or I'll take it off for ya," growled Foller. Olympia swallowed hard. She closed her eyes and removed her pants and shirt as slowly as possible. She stood naked. Olympia would not employ any of her Exotic skills with the miscreation from hell. She didn't want this and hated her current circumstances; she was about to be raped and wanted to die.

“I see you have the Exotic mark on your breast. I am going to enjoy you.” Foller grabbed Olympia’s arm, pushing her to her hands and knees. He took off his pants and tossed them over, landing before Olympia. A few seconds later, he grabbed her hips and thrust himself hard into her.

“Aaaahhh!” screamed Olympia.

“What? I’m too large for ya?” said the Krapens with a chuckle.

“I wasn’t ready.” Olympia winced. She closed her eyes. In her mind, she recited the first and middle names of Chicho’s sons and daughters by birth order, followed by Chicho’s grandchildren’s names, also in birth order.

ᴕᴕᴕ

The battle following the ambush continued for about an hour before Lord Wolfson’s men killed all the mercenaries and orc demons. Wolfson killed a significant number of men, including dullahans and a few Krapens. This wasn’t an ordinary group of combatants. They were a well-organized group, and considering how they fought it was likely they were traveling to fight in the war.

“My Lord, we captured some mercenaries. Do you want to question any of them?” asked Olsen.

“Yes, but first, where is Olympia? I lost sight of her when we were first attacked.”

“I don’t see her,” said Olsen.

“Ask around to see if she is among the dead,” ordered Lord Wolfson. He started looking around for Olympia. Olsen came back to his master a few minutes later accompanied by Logan.

“My Lord, she is not among the dead,” said Logan. Flint came over to join them too.

“My Lord, I’m afraid I saw one mercenary abduct the little lassy,” said Flint.

“Why didn’t you follow her?” asked Wolfson.

“I am sorry, m’ Lord. I was being attacked by an orc,” said old Flint.

Willow approached, having overhead the conversation. “A mercenary took her due north. I was fighting an orc myself, so I could not help either.”

Lord Wolfson marched over to where the mercenaries were held. Drawing his sword, he stood in front of one of the mercenaries and pointed at the prisoner’s neck.

“Where have they taken the woman that was traveling with me?”

“Go to hell,” said the mercenary. He spat at Lord Wolfson’s boots. Matteo stared sternly at the mercenary, briefly considering his options. Without much hesitation he speared the mercenary through his heart, then sliced his throat for good measure. He moved to stand in front of the next mercenary, immediately next to the one Matteo had just killed.

“One more time, where is the woman that was traveling with me?”

“I don’t know.”

“What?” demanded Lord Wolfson.

“Go fuck yourself,” said the mercenary.

Lord Wolfson swung his sword without mercy. The head of the mercenary rolled to Olsen’s feet, and he kicked it.

“Wrong answer. I am going to keep asking the same question from each of you, and if I get an ‘I don’t know’ as an answer, you will forfeit your lives. I will continue asking until I get the answer I want or none of you are left alive. So, who is next?” asked Lord Wolfson. The men stood silent, but one young man stepped forward.

“They took her to our camp,” said the young mercenary.

“What did you say?” said Lord Wolfson.

“We have been following you for days. Our master spotted your woman bathing in a creek over a fortnight ago, and he wanted her,” said another of the men.

"Where is your camp?" asked Lord Wolfson. All the men looked at each other and said nothing. Lord Wolfson took his sword and swung one more time, cutting another man's head from his shoulders.

"Where is your camp? Must I repeat myself? I will keep cutting off heads until one of you tells me, or none of you are left."

"Will you let me tickle them with lightning first? Maybe a slower death will inspire them," asked Olsen, lightning skimming around his fingers.

The youngest man stepped forward again.

"I'll take you to the camp, but promise me you will not kill me or leave me behind. I want to defect to Yakuta. I am a telekinetic slave mage," said the young man.

"You have my promise. If you survive the attack, I will not leave you behind." He turned to Olsen. "Olsen, untie the young man and give him something to drink."

The young mage gulped down some water, then told them the camp's location.

Lord Wolfson gagged all the other prisoners, and arranged for his Arcane Mage to place a spell on them. They could not move a muscle. Lord Wolfson left a few soldiers behind, but took all his mages with him. It was late in the night by the time the young mercenary who was defecting brought Lord Wolfson and his men to the enemy's camp.

"Where do you think they placed my woman?"

"She'll be in the largest tent, the leader's tent," said the young telekinetic mage.

The mercenary base was in a clearing, so Lord Wolfson stood hidden in the brush while he organized his attach. He surrounded the camp with his fire and lightning mages, and positioned his archers behind the mages. It took them a while to surround the camp. Close to midnight, they were all in position.

"Watch for Olympia," was all Lord Wolfson commanded his men.

ᏛᏛᏛ

Olympia had remained lying for a few minutes next to the Krapens leader, curled up like a newborn. Tears slid down the side of her face. He had taken possession of her body and caused excessive pain. During the ordeal, she had wanted to shout many times while he abused her, but she didn't give him the satisfaction of hearing her scream—aside from the first time he entered her. She had had many brutes in her life, but in the brothel Chicho enforced the rule that none were allowed to leave any marks on her Exotic body. This time she knew her body would be badly bruised in the morning and for many days.

Olympia stood up, finally free of the Krapens brute who slept soundly. Listening to the sounds of the camp, she let her tears flow. As a norm, she never cried, but now her life was in peril. She knew this man was going to kill her once he tired of her. Maybe I can escape. Ha! What am I thinking? I am in a mercenary camp. Oh, how far away from the safety of the brothel I have come! Oh, Lord of The Morai, I know I will die at the hands of this animal, but please let me die without further pain. I just hope Matteo is alive. He was a good man. Matteo never hurt me, and he always provided me with what I needed. He needs to be alive.

The Krapens leader had a lantern in the tent, making the monster's face visible. He looked like a demon when awake, but like a man when asleep. By the way he moved, he was having a nightmare. Olympia moved away from him. She didn't want to be in the path of his fists if he was the type to throw punches as he woke. Olympia took a deep breath and dressed. She cleaned the tears from her face, wishing for death.

"I wish I were back with Matteo. At least with him, I had the possibility of being free," whispered Olympia.

Olympia was deep in her musings when a loud shout came from outside. She opened her eyes and saw the tent was on fire, the fur hide being rapidly consumed. Olympia screamed and Foller woke up. He shoved on his pants, grabbed his sword and Olympia's hand, and left the tent. He dragged her out as if she was a rag doll. For each step he took, Olympia had to take two. The pandemonium in the camp made Olympia think she might pull away from the Krapens and run into the forest.

"Master, they have fire mages," shouted a mercenary.

"I thought you killed all their lighting mages? Watch out for the arrows. They're raining down everywhere," shouted Foller. A scarlet cloud rose from the fires around the camp. Shouts of men and screams of dullahans came from the depths of the camp on fire.

The mercenaries ran in all directions. Water mages were trying to dowse the flames, but lighting would strike, killing the mages. Followed by more flaming bolts, re-igniting the fires everywhere. Dullahans could be seen running to the edges of the camp, trying to escape the inferno; flaming arrows flew overhead, hitting the fur tents. The Krapens leader, still holding Olympia's arm, also ran like a coward. But when he reached the edge of the camp, they found a wall of fire blocking the way to the forest, and they could not cross over.

"I am going to die," shouted Olympia. Foller pulled her, running to the other side of the camp, but another wall of flames barred their way. He ran to yet another side of the camp, and found an opening in the firewall. He ran out, crossing the wall of fire through the opening, swinging his sword. There he found a group of mercenaries already engaged in fighting mages and Yakutan soldiers.

Olympia tried to pull her hand from Foller, but he kept a firm grasp on her. She kept pulling, but the Krapens fought a Yakutan soldier with one arm. He deftly swung his sword, making the Yakutan soldier move, trying to evade the strikes. They lunged, and parried, back and forth, but throughout, Foller did not release his hold on Olympia. That was, until someone approached from behind and sliced the arm holding Olympia.

"ARRRRRR, damn you," shouted Foller, as a stream of black blood gushed out of him and bathed Olympia. She landed on the ground from where someone pulled her out of the way. She was about to scream, when it locked in her throat as she looked back; it was Flint.

"Flint!" shouted Olympia; she was so happy to see the older man, she forgot she needed to run away.

"Let's get you out of the way."

Flint ran, holding her hand. A dullahan ran out through the ring of fire and chased Olympia and Flint, but when Flint turned his head and saw the dullahan chasing them, he spoke the words: "Sutegi bat sortu!"

The dullahan stepped on a red ring on the ground and he exploded in a burst of blue fire. They kept running. Flint reached Logan who took her the rest of the way, as Flint returned to the fight. Olympia looked over her shoulder as they were running away. She saw Matteo fighting the Krapens leader. Just as she looked, the horrific animal of a man, tried to hit Matteo in the head. In the process, the blood from his stump showered over Matteo.

They stepped left and right, looking for an opening. Then, in one clean swing, Matteo cut off the head of the Krapens leader. Once the leader was dead, the fire mages closed the one remaining escape route through the ring of flames, enclosing all the monsters inside the camp, killing them with fire. Lord Wolfson's men decapitated all the remaining orc demons, dullahans, and mercenaries who had escaped the flames.

When the noise and activity lulled, Logan took her back to Lord Wolfson.

"You came for me!" Olympia beamed.

"I told you before. You are part of my family; you are my Olympia. I don't leave my people behind. Come, it's late. I am tired," said Matteo. Olympia could not believe her ears. Why risk the lives of all his men to save hers? She was just an Exotic. She was a nobody in the hierarchy of trades compared to him. He made no sense to her.

Holding her hand, they walked away together; he showed her the way back through the forest. They walked for about an hour. It was well past midnight when they arrived on the site of the original ambush, where Lord Wolfson had left the rest of his men. When they arrived at the site, they found that the men had already set up camp, and had lit a fire near the edge. Several men kept watch, most of them warriors. They had erected Lord Wolfson's largest tent. Olympia felt sticky. She had been bathed in a shower of black blood when Flint cut Foller's arm.

"Did you find a creek or a river nearby?" asked Lord Wolfson, when they arrived at camp.

"We found a river not too far from camp, my Lord," said Logan.

"Tell me where it is."

Olympia felt like she had run a thousand miles. Her body ached. Thinking of her kidnapping made her want to curl up and die, Matteo's rescue gave her strength and a new desire to keep on living—despite the chill of the night making her pine for indoor living. She observed how well-organized the group worked together, each knowing his or her own task. Olympia felt better, knowing they would fight for each other, even for her. After a few minutes, someone held her hand.

"Come, Olympia," said Matteo. He had taken her gently by the hand, making Olympia look down at their joined hands. She didn't say a word; she walked after him in silence.

"Take the torch," said Matteo, as a man passed a torch to Olympia. They walked away from camp for a few minutes until they found the river. He took the torch from Olympia and stuck the wood in the ground.

"The water must be cold, but we both need to wash. Here, take this soap and wash off all the caked blood. Please hurry, I haven't eaten anything, I'm exhausted, and you need to warm up." Matteo went to the side of the river, where he removed his armor. Olympia stared at him. She had seen him gloriously naked before, but this time he carried visible injuries. He had one large bruise on his chest and a deep cut on his back.

"Oh no, you have a cut on your back."

“I know. I can feel it. I’ll have Tony heal it later. You first, bathe fast please,” said Wolfson, looking at her with tired eyes.

Olympia undressed and entered the water.

“Ah, this water is freezing.”

“I’m not surprised. Hurry so we can go,” said Matteo.

Olympia scrubbed the blood from her body. When she washed between her legs, she winced. It hurt in every way. Olympia carried the evidence of the Krapens’ assault. She closed her eyes and washed as best she could. She climbed out of the creek with shaking legs, and hurried to dress. As she was putting on the last of her clothes, she turned to find Matteo watching with the saddest of looks on his face.

“Did that man hurt you tonight?” asked Matteo.

“He didn’t do anything I haven’t experienced before,” Olympia said. She collected her dirty clothes and washed them as fast as possible.

“I am sorry I took so long to find to you,” he said as he washed his own clothes. Olympia nodded.

Matteo picked up the torch and smile at Olympia, fatigue showing in every line on his face. “Are you ready?”

She nodded and followed him back to camp. They walked to where Cook was preparing a hearty soup, where they took some bread with a bowl of soup, and ate. Olympia had eaten already, but she was thankful for the soup. Later, Matteo accompanied with her to his tent.

“What time is it?” asked Olympia.

“I don’t know. I lost my pocket watch when the fighting started.”

“Oh no! Can we go look for it? I can help,” said Olympia.

“I’ll ask some of my men to help me search for it tomorrow. I asked the men to set up the largest tent, and I had them make your pallet with extra furs. Go to sleep, Olympia. I still have a lot to do; you rest,” said Matteo, leaving her in the tent. Olympia was sad about the watch. The beautiful thing was supposed to go to his son. Olympia laid down on the furs. She tried to sleep, but one thought above all others would not go away. She still could not believe Matteo had come to her rescue.

ଓଓଓ

Lord Wolfson went looking for Olsen. He found him sitting by the fire, drinking some tea. After the battle with the mercenaries, most of the men had not gone to sleep. Some tossed the bodies on a pyre they had made beyond the edge of the camp, while others cleaned equipment. Lord Wolfson went and sat next to Olsen.

"How is Miss Olympia?" asked Olsen.

"She was hurt badly. I don't know what I'm going to do with her," said Lord Wolfson.

"My Lord, you should train Miss Olympia to defend herself. We may encounter more of these ambushes. It is hard to fight and guard her at the same time," said Olsen.

"I know. It's just that she's been through so much pain, and putting her into fighter training is harsh."

"You don't have to train her to be a killer soldier. She just needs to know enough to keep alive; enough to give us time to come help her," said Olsen, finishing his tea.

"Let's hope we don't have any more incidents," said Matteo, getting up to serve himself some tea, then sitting down again.

CHAPTER 9

After the Fight

They traveled for another four and a half weeks; rain fell for many days making their progress slow. The ambush carried out by the Behui mercenary group left the company with fifteen fewer men, but Lord Wolfson spread the remaining company out as far as he could, dispersing the mages throughout the caravan. He had several men scouting the areas ahead in different directions. He wanted to avoid another ambush and unnecessary loss of life. Some mages from the Behui mercenary group defected to Lord Wolfson's company, so he gained seven new mages.

Still needing to make the best progress they could, Lord Wolfson made them ride most of each day, with only a minimal camp in the evenings. Every fourth day they stopped and made camp for an entire day to allow the horses some rest.

ଓଓଓ

Olympia woke early most days with an aching body. She had not slept in an actual bed for over two months. She felt tired all the time. Her stress levels were killing her. At least Matteo didn't ask her for anything, which was good.

One morning, after everything was packed, she stood by Runner, Matteo's stallion. The horse kept nibbling her ear. Olympia kept shooing the horse, but each time he resumed standing next to her. The horse placed his head over Olympia's shoulder. She relented and petted the massive black stallion.

"Alright, alright, I'll pet you, but I don't have anything to give you as a treat. You truly are a beautiful horse," said Olympia. She petted the horse while waiting for Matteo. Soon he appeared and they mounted the massive horse, leaving the camp behind. They had ridden for some time, when a thought struck her.

“Matteo, where are you from? I have no idea where we are heading,” said Olympia.

“I am from the town of Kalbaka in Yakuta. My father’s castle is at the top of Kalbaka Island in the middle of the Sindu Lake,” said Matteo.

“You own an island?” asked Olympia.

“My family owns an island, yes, and now that my uncle is deceased, I own some of the land around the lake,” said Matteo. Olympia kept asking questions and he kept answering. They talked for over three hours. She was glad Matteo had saved her life, but she still yearned to return to Palermo. Matteo freed her from prostitution, but Chicho had promised her total freedom. He had said he would buy her a new trade and give her coin to start a new life.

“I read your map. We are close to the town of Binty. It would only take two days to travel from here. They have a train station. Will you reconsider letting me return home to Palermo?” asked Olympia.

“I can’t deviate from my path. I must reach Highcove to take possession of my land. I must pay my taxes in less than six months, or there will be severe repercussions. We have already crossed the border into Yakuta, but we must still travel quickly to reach my destination. When we get home, I promise we’ll talk about this,” said Lord Wolfson. So, Olympia changed the subject and asked about Kalbaka.

He was good to her. He had placed his men on the line to rescue her from the Krapens demon. He said she was free, but now she had to live under his rule. She didn’t want men or women in her life. She wanted to live her life in solitude, and Chicho had promised her that kind of freedom.

According to the map, in another day they would reach a fork in the road—one direction would take her to the town of Binty. She could steal the gold from Lord Wolfson’s trunk, take one of the horses, and ride to the town of Binty. She could make it on her own. She just needed to hold on for two days. She could survive without food or water for two days.

They made camp for the night, not far from the fork in the road. It was late at night, so she encouraged the men to set up the smallest tent for Lord Wolfson. That way, he would sleep outside. She also asked Sheldon to bring down Lord Wolfson's trunk with the excuse that he needed a fresh pair of pants. She had made up her mind. She would escape and make it back to Palermo on her own. Everything was as she arranged, the tent and the trunk.

Lord Wolfson arrived late, and as always, when they set up the smallest tent, he lay on a pallet at the entrance. She waited until she heard him snoring. She had gone to bed fully dressed. Fumbling around in Lord Wolfson's trunk, she found his gold. Donning her coat, she slowly stepped out of the tent. She looked side to side; all was quiet. The men were sleeping. Only the night guards stirred. Two of the guards sat by the central fire, keeping warm. Two others were standing watch by the food cart, but the last two were missing.

She listened for sounds of anyone nearby, but she could only hear the sounds of the night forest. She figured all she had to do was follow the road and make a left turn when she encountered the fork in the road. According to the map, that road would take her to Binty. Olympia crept as quietly as she could, avoiding the guards, but when she reached the corral, Olympia was faced with a dilemma. Which horse would she take?

Where is Runner?

No, she could not take his horse. She passed by the Takapian stallion, but Runner neighed when she neared him. Olympia touched his snout and stood still until the horse calmed.

"Runner, you need to be quiet," whispered Olympia in the horse's ear. Runner calmed down a little. Then she found Olsen's horse.

Now, where are the saddles?

She could not find them. Olympia kept looking around, but Runner walked to her side and neighed again, louder this time. Taking the horse would surely make a ruckus.

"This is not a good idea," said Olympia. She would have to wait until they reached Lord Wolfson's land. So, she exited the horses' corral, trying not to make as much noise as the horses. Olympia walked back to her tent on tip-toe, when a rough hand grabbed her arm.

"What are ye doing up so late?" whispered a beady-eyed man.

"I wasn't sleepy and wanted to take a walk. Let me pass." Lust shined in the man's beady eyes.

"So, what were ye doing in the horses' corral?" asked another man with a long beard.

"I like horses. Let go of my arm," Olympia talked a little louder to draw attention from others in the camp. But without warning, a younger man grabbed her around the waist and tried to cover her mouth, but she bit his hand.

"Help! Help me, I need help!" shouted Olympia. The second man with the long beard, punched her in the face, making her lose consciousness. Moments later, she woke—hands tied and with a gag in her mouth. She was being carried over someone's shoulder. The men were running through the dark, but after a while their pace slowed to a walk. Shortly after stopping, the beady-eyed man who had been carrying her, dropped Olympia hard on the ground and spared no time in unbuttoning his pants.

The younger man, the one with the long beard, was carrying a torch. He just stood there, scanning the area and looking scared. "You better hurry. Master Wolfson will appear at any moment," said the man. He was the same man who had taken Olympia to the creek when she had her curses and had watched her bathe. She recalled his name was Palov.

The beady-eyed man grabbed Olympia by her hair and ungagged her.

"Help, help me!" shouted Olympia again. The beady-eyed man slapped her hard in the same place where she had been punched in the face earlier. She landed on the ground sideways, hurting her shoulder.

"Shut yer cakehole. Yer gonna open yer mouth for only one thing," said the beady-eyed man. She kicked him square in his balls, making him hunch over, and scream like a little girl. Olympia took the opportunity to shout loudly over the mewling of the man she had just kicked.

"HELP," she screamed at the top of her lungs. "THIS BASTARD IS GOING TO HURT ME. HELP!"

The beady-eyed man stood back up, with a look of hatred. He was about to grab Olympia, when a flash of lightning struck him in the back. The beady-eyed man flew up into the air and landed five feet away. Olsen appeared, manipulating blue lighting around his fingers and hands in every direction. Olympia raised her eyes, looking up at Palov, just as a sword came out of his chest.

"No, wait, it was all her fault," said Palov, still holding the torch. He tried to turn his head, but a second sword also impaled him through his neck. He fell to his knees, and the blade slid out slowly as he fell forward, leaving Lord Wolfson standing behind him with the bloodied swords.

"Come, let's go." Matteo reached out his hand to help Olympia up with shaking legs. He untied her hands. She walked ahead of him, happy she was alive and remorseful at having taken Lord Wolfson's coin.

The men were awake and waiting for Lord Wolfson when they reached the camp. Matteo stood in the middle of the camp.

"Come near, all of you. I want you to listen and I don't want to have to shout."

Once all the men surrounded him, he raised his bloodied sword for all to see. "I just killed Palov and Warren. They kidnapped my mistress. I don't know what they were thinking. If any of you ever even think of hurting her, I will not hesitate to kill you. Stay away from my woman. This is my second and final warning." Lord Wolfson took Olympia's hand and went to their tent.

"I don't want to know what you were doing outside your tent. I just killed two of my men because of you. Good fighting men."

"I did nothing. The men found me walking about and took me." Olympia tried not to lie to him.

"You were supposed to be sleeping."

"I had to pee." This time Olympia lied.

"Next time you need to pee, wake me. Now go to sleep. I'll return to the tent in a few minutes," said Lord Wolfson. Olympia climbed inside the tent, closing the tent door behind her. She went to Lord Wolfson's trunk and replaced the bag of gold coins she had stolen. Her face hurt, but she finally realized she had to remain with Lord Wolfson. Olympia lay on her pallet. Filled with anxiety, she could not fall asleep.

ᴄᴐᴄᴐᴄᴐ

The following day when she woke, she could not see through her right eye. Her face hurt badly and her eye had swollen shut. She touched her face, which made it hurt even more. She stepped out of the tent, but it was Logan waiting for her instead of Olsen.

"Oh no, we need to take you to the healer. Your eye has completely closed," said Logan. He led Olympia to the healer's cart.

"Tony, come out. Hurry, Miss Olympia needs your help." Tony stuck his head out of the cart, then jumped down fast.

"Those bastards did that to her last night?" asked Tony in his Parshtishi accent.

"Yes, they roughed her up really bad," said Logan.

"Come, Miss, sit by the cart and let me take your pain away." Tony's hands turned yellow, and then green. His hands hovered over Olympia's face.

"Did they hurt you anyplace else?" asked the healer.

"No, just my face. But my shoulder hurts a little because I fell after being struck." Olympia smiled sadly at the healer. Tony used his magic for a few minutes, during which time Olsen arrived and Logan left.

"I mended your eye and shoulder. They should feel better, but the skin around your eye will remain bruised for a few days. Olsen, bring her back if she's in pain."

"I will. Thank you, Tony." Olsen started leading her away. "I am sorry Miss Olympia. Sheldon needed help this morning and Lord Wolfson said it was fine for Logan to take you to break your fast." Olympia nodded.

He took her to find some food. All the men stared at her as she walked by, making her feel self-conscious. She never cared when people looked or stared at her before, but this time, it bothered her.

"Olsen, the men are all staring at me," said Olympia.

"Lord Wolfson killed two of his men last night. Now they are wary of you."

"But I did nothing wrong. All this time, I have kept to myself. It has been lonely for me and highly stressful."

"I know, but the men know you were a prostitute. I am sure some of them have wanted to know if they could purchase your time ever since you arrived here." Olsen rarely spoke his mind, but he shared his thoughts this time.

"But they know I am Lord Wolfson's woman. Also, Exotics are *exceedingly* expensive." Olympia stressed the point.

"They don't know you were an Exotic. These men haven't had a woman in almost two years," said Olsen.

"How about you? You don't seem bothered."

"I have a lover. He and I share a tent, and we keep our friendship to ourselves. I trust you can keep that to yourself," said Olsen.

"What you do in your tent is none of my business." Olympia said and Olsen nodded.

She walked back to the tent, and collected the few things she had, ready to move out. Olympia sat in the tent waiting and trying to hide from the men, but a short while later Lord Wolfson stuck his head in and startled her.

“Come outside; we are not leaving today.”

“Why? I thought we were moving out in a few minutes.”

“No, I decided we will stay here today to give the horses more rest. Also, we must bury Palov and Warren. But for now, I want you to follow me.” Lord Wolfson withdrew his head, giving Olympia space to step out. She found him holding his scabbard with his sword sheathed.

“Follow me,” was all Lord Wolfson said to Olympia.

Oh no, he is going to kill me for sure!

She followed him with her head bowed low, hands shaking, and sweating heavily. Her eyes watered.

Maybe he noticed I had taken the gold from his trunk. He punishes thieves with death. But I returned the gold. Why is he taking me out of camp? Is he going to kill me? I know he will because he had to kill two of his men. He told me, ‘If you make any of my men step out of their way and I find them alone with you, I will kill the man, and I will kill you.’ Oh god of Lord Wolfson, don’t let him kill me. I want to live.

Lord Wolfson stopped walking once they reached a clearing. He turned to face her. She was sobbing by the time they stopped walking. Olympia knew this handsome man had a strict way of dealing with his people. She knew she had done a few things wrong, but nothing worthy of death. Head bowed with hands on her face, she fell to her knees and cried.

“What is wrong with you?” asked Lord Wolfson.

“Please don’t kill me. I don’t want to die. I have done nothing worthy of death. I have kept to myself. I have never enticed any of your men. I swear on my life; I only talk to the women, Olsen, Tony, Logan, and Flint. Please don’t kill me.” Olympia said between sobs.

“Wait, why do you think I am going to kill you?” Olympia looked up at him.

“Because the first day we met, you told me that if I made any of your men step out of line and you found them alone with me, you were going to kill both the man and me. I swear I didn't entice the men. Please, I want to live." Olympia lowered her head and stared at her hands. Lord Wolfson knelt beside her. He took her hands with his calloused ones.

"I am not going to kill you. I have observed you the entire time you have been with us, and know you have followed what I asked of you."

"Really? Then w-why are we h-here?" asked Olympia between sobs, gasps, and pants.

"What I am going to do is teach you how to fight. You need to learn how to defend yourself. I don't want to worry about having you defenseless." He cleaned the tears from her face.

"I was so afraid. I h-hate living my life in fear. I can't live like this." Olympia said, her speech returning to normal.

"When my mind is in turmoil, I meditate and pray. It helps me regain my peace. I feel my g-d close to me."

"I don't believe in any god."

"A lot of people don't believe, but it doesn't mean my g-d is not real, or he is not with them. I believe that if you pray with an open heart, he will listen. In my faith, we believe that people have a direct connection to g-d through their spirit, and sincere prayer is the conduit to g-d," said Lord Wolfson.

"I don't know how to pray," said Olympia.

"Oh, there is nothing to it. You just need to get your thoughts together and talk like you are talking to your best friend. You can close your eyes or leave them open. You can say your prayer out loud or in your mind. I like to say mine out loud when I am alone. It helps me to remain focused. There is no right or wrong way to say a prayer," said Lord Wolfson. He took her hand and kissed it, then stood up.

"Come, stand up. You have a lot to learn. From now on, I will teach you something new every day. After the lesson we will practice for about an hour in the morning before we saddle up and move on," said Lord Wolfson.

"Good! I want to learn how to fight." Olympia stood up and the lesson commenced. He taught her a few moves and made her do some stretches and exercises to help her gain strength. They trained for about two hours. When they were done, they walked back to camp, chatting about the moves Lord Wolfson had just taught her and what would be next. Olympia went to Flint's section of the camp. He didn't have any work for her. So, she went to Timo, to the enclosure where the horses were corralled. She liked to pet Runner.

As it had many mornings, constant rain had turned the ground to thick, slippery mud in places. Olympia stepped on one of those patches of wet mud when she reached the corral, making her slip and fall, sliding under the lowest bar of the corral and landing on a pile of horse manure. Her entire back, including her hair, was covered in manure. She stood up and walked back to camp with her pride in shambles.

"What happened to you?" Lord Wolfson asked, trying not to laugh when she reached him.

"I was going to give an apple to Runner, but I slipped in the mud and slid under bars of the corral. I need to wash. This stench is awful." Still chuckling he reached out and took Olympia into his arms.

"What are you doing?" screamed Olympia. Carrying her, he walked over to a barrel of water and without ceremony, dunked her in it.

"You need more than a wash. You need a bath," he said, laughing. Olympia stood up, all wet and angry.

"Yo, Boss, that's no way to treat a lady," said Timo, standing nearby.

"Hey, Boss, now you're all covered in manure too," said Bina. Lord Wolfson kept laughing. After a minute or two, he took her out of the barrel and held her in his arms.

"Bina, find me some clothing, soap, and towels. We're going to the river. We both need a bath. Hurry, please," said Lord Wolfson as they walked to the river.

"I am sorry, Olympia. My father did the same to me when I was young. I fell in manure on our paddock back home." Bina followed them with their things, leaving the essentials and the couple near the water's edge.

"Well, it wasn't funny," she said, taking her clothing off, looking all exasperated.

"It was my way of getting you naked and to myself." He had a wicked smile.

"If you wanted me naked, all you had to do was tell me, and I would have come to the river with you happily."

"Yeah, but this was a lot more fun," he said, holding her, as naked as the day he was born.

"To you, maybe. Now Timo will have to scrub that barrel with lye to get the manure off."

"Come, we need to wash. You have manure everywhere," Matteo said. He took the soap from her hands and lathered her, and they ended up loving each other after their bath.

❧❧❧

The next day, they woke early and started the new routine. While the men broke camp, Lord Wolfson took the time to train Olympia. When it was time to ride, Lord Wolfson led a new horse over to Olympia.

"He is your horse now." Mateo placed the reins of the horse in Olympia's hands.

"Where did you find him?" asked Olympia.

"I loaned this horse to Palov. His father is a Lord and the man paid for his son to have one of my horses. Palov is dead, so the horse is yours now." Matteo gave her a pat on her shoulder and stepped away. She admired the handsome black horse, she looked at Matteo with appreciation. She had got used to traveling with him, and now she had her own horse. Like Runner, he was majestic.

"The horse is mine, like as a gift, mine?"

"Yes, a gift, your horse," said Matteo.

"I have never, I don't know, I … Thank you. What is his name?"

"It's your horse now. You name him." Matteo went to get Runner.

"I don't know what to name you." Olympia looked at her horse, and he neighed.

She mounted her horse. Matteo was next to her in an instant. He guided her horse so it would ride next to his. A feeling of elation overtook her. No one had ever given her a gift this amazing. It was a Takapian horse, one of Matteo's.

"I will name you Arrow," Olympia said to the horse.

A fortnight more of traveling, and Lord Wolfson training Olympia each morning, had passed without event. One day Olsen was riding next to her, but he kept quiet while Olympia sang a song. The men that rode around her sang with her, which made her feel happy. Happiness was a weird feeling to have. She hadn't been joyful since she had been a young woman living in her parents' home. But here with these burly men, she had a modicum of happiness. Olympia smiled. When she finished her song, she took a drink of water from the canteen she carried on the side of her horse.

She was replacing the canteen when Tony's cart, reached her.

"Hello, Miss Olympia, how you doing?" asked Tony.

"Oh, hello, Master Tony. My face doesn't hurt at all, but I still have some bruises."

"It's only been a fortnight; the bruises will disappear eventually. How about those nasty headaches? You haven't had any of those in a while," said Tony.

"No, I haven't." Olympia said with a smile.

"We've had many cloudy and rainy days," he said, almost as a question.

"You are right," Olympia's smile went away as she considered his words.

"Anyway, I am glad you feel better," said Tony. The cart rode past her, just as Olympia remembered the last time she had one of the nasty headaches. It had been over eight weeks ago, and so were her curses.

Oh no, I might be with child.

Olympia's heart jumped into her throat. Pain pierced her heart, and her stomach started doing somersaults. She turned her head and vomited everything she had eaten. Olsen pulled her horse to the side.

Olympia almost fell off her horse in her rush to dismount. She fell to her knees and then sat on the ground. Her world turned precariously. She placed her head between her legs for a few minutes, but she stumbled when she stood up and tried to walk toward her horse. Having dismounted his horse when she did, Olsen stood next to her, making sure she stayed upright.

"What is wrong? Do you have pain in your stomach?" Olympia shook her head.

"Tony, come back here!" Olsen shouted, holding Olympia's horse by the reins in one hand, and Olympia in the other.

It can't be. I'm with child again. I don't want this thing. It might be from that monster.

"What am I going to do?" Olympia said out loud. She stumbled again, so she sat back down against a tree.

"What are you talking about, Miss Olympia?" asked Olsen. He told one soldier to get Tony and Lord Wolfson. Olympia didn't want to think. She was being a nuisance to Lord Wolfson, and soon he would kill her for sure. Lord Wolfson rode back to where Olympia and Olsen were.

"What happened to her?" asked Lord Wolfson.

"Miss Olympia vomited, and she looks like she may faint," said Olsen.

"Call the healer. Let's stop here for a while and give the horses a rest." Lord Wolfson rode away. Tony, came and sat next to Olympia.

“I am a senior healer, but I can only treat you up to a point. I would need you naked to figure out your ailments. That is not possible, here. So, I need you to tell me what’s wrong?” asked Tony, the healer. Olympia looked up at Tony when Olsen had stepped away.

“Please, this must stay between the two of us,” Olympia pleaded.

“There are a few things I am obligated to tell Lord Wolfson, but for the most part, what you tell me stays with us.” Olympia regarded Tony.

“I think I am with child,” Olympia whispered her words.

“Then Lord Wolfson needs to know he’s going to be a father,” Tony whispered.

“You don’t understand. Lord Wolfson may not be the father. Around the same time I was with Lord Wolfson, I was kidnapped and forced by the Behui Krapens leader. It may be from the Krapens monster,” said Olympia.

“Oh. You still need to tell Lord Wolfson,” said Tony.

“I don’t want him to know.”

“You don’t understand. He must know. You’re his mistress,” said Tony.

“He will kill me. Please, Tony, my first husband, made me an Exotic because he found one of his friends forcing himself on me. You saw what he did to his men for betraying him. He will kill me,” said Olympia.

“It wasn’t your fault. Lord Wolfson will not kill ya,” said Tony.

“Tony, please, do the procedure and take it out of me. Lord Wolfson doesn’t need to know,” Olympia pleaded, her palms together as though in prayer.

“I can’t,” said Tony.

“Tony, he will kill me. He said he kills those who betray him. I don’t want to die. Do the procedure, please,” begged Olympia.

“What is happening? What procedure? Of what is she dying? Talk, Tony,” said Lord Wolfson. He had approached, unnoticed.

“I am sorry, m’lady. The law binds me. My Lord Olympia has a problem. When your woman was taken by the mercenaries, the animal that took her, raped her. Now she’s with child, and there is no telling if the child is yours or the mercenary’s,” said Tony, his glowing hands resting on her shoulder.

“What? This can’t be. Exotics are sterile,” said Lord Wolfson.

“Not so; only those trained from childhood are made sterile. The ones that come to the trade as adults are often left intact,” said Tony.

“How did you come to the trade?” asked Lord Wolfson.

“My husband sold me into prostitution,” said Olympia.

“So, what procedure were you talking about?” asked Lord Wolfson.

“She wants me to take her child out of her now. She doesn’t want to carry him to term,” said Tony.

“What? You want to do what?” said Lord Wolfson.

“My Lord, I can only do the procedure if you give me permission,” said Tony.

“What? No, why can’t I get one?” asked Olympia.

“The law is simple. A woman bonded to a nobleman can only have the procedure if the noble permits it,” said Tony.

“Well, this is the end of the conversation. I don’t permit it. Is she ready to travel?” asked Lord Wolfson and his ice-blue eyes were on Olympia.

“Wait a minute. It’s my body. Don’t I have a say?” asked Olympia.

“This is an option all free women have, and their husbands can’t interfere, but women bonded to nobles are ruled by the laws of the peerage. In Yakuta, our laws state that a mistress’s child may have rights to inherit the lesser titles. The oldest son inherits the higher title, while the younger children inherit the lower ones—if the fathers choose so. In this case, your child may inherit some of Lord Wolfson's titles," said Tony.

"But this may not be his child."

"There will be no procedure. My child will be born on my land, just like all my other children. You will be traveling in a cart with Tony. So, mount the cart. Hey Liko, Tony will drive the cart from here on, so you will be riding my woman's horse. Let's go," Lord Wolfson said, as he strode away.

"He can't do that," said Olympia.

"Well, he just did. I told you he wouldn't kill ya."

"This can't be happening," said Olympia. She started pacing. This was all Chicho's fault. His avarice made him stupid. Chicho had left her intact since she made a lot of coin from the moment she came to his brothel. If he had made her sterile, she would have had to rest for three months. The greedy man left her as she was.

She had fallen pregnant four times, and each time he had the child removed, with only two weeks to recover. Olympia always wanted a child, but now that she was an Exotic, all she ever wanted was her freedom. Chicho promised her a way out of prostitution. He was going to buy her freedom. She would live her life in a quiet village, teaching languages or history, her favorite subjects.

Olympia walked away thinking about all the other times she had been with child. In all those times, she had never known the child's father's identity, and it was no different this time. It could be Lord Wolfson's, or it could be the child of the monstrous Krapens. She wouldn't know until the child was born. She didn't want to know what Lord Wolfson would do to her if the child was turned out not to be his.

CHAPTER 10

The Inns and Outs

They had traveled for another seven weeks, and Olympia wanted to cry every other minute. One moment she was happy, the next she was teary-eyed. And the moment after that she was snappy. Her back hurt, her stomach churned, and she wanted to sleep late. But what puzzled her was that she wanted sex. Her body yearned for a man's touch, but she could not understand why. In all her years as an Exotic, she had never desired sex. She didn't care for sex. Now, it was a need that came and bothered her.

They had crossed the border between Behui and Yakuta several weeks earlier. Now, they reached the small town of Salgado along the way. Lord Wolfson had stopped and purchased provisions. He also decided to stay at the local inn.

The town only had three inns, a few taverns, no hotels, and no train station. The best inn in town was so small it only had six rooms, of which only two rooms available. So, he rented a room for himself and Olympia, and bathing options too. Olsen rented the second room for him and Logan. Olympia walked into the room, and smiled. It had a large enough bed for the two of them. The rest of the men stayed in the camp outside the town.

They had dinner, and Olympia went to sleep. She left Lord Wolfson talking with Olsen and Logan. Once in the room, she undressed and went to bed. Olympia didn't have her nightshirt, so she went to bed naked. She didn't notice when Lord Wolfson came into the room or when he climbed into bed. They had stopped having sex once he found out she was with child, and she missed his touch. Lord Wolfson slept outside the tent every night after he discovered she was increasing.

The following morning, she woke up an hour before dawn with a warm arm wrapped around her waist. She could feel Matteo breathing calmly at her back. He smelled clean, like he had taken a bath. She inhaled deeply and allowed herself the simple enjoyment of having him close. Matteo wasn't like all the other men that had purchased her time. Matteo made her feel wanted and needed.

She went back to sleep, to awake two hours later with Matteo still sleeping next to her and her back still turned to him. Slowly, she turned and faced him. Matteo had a few wrinkles at the corners of his eyes, which made him look severe when angry, but he also had a distinguished nose. She touched his rugged eyebrows, and his cheeks. She had rarely gone to bed with a man and subsequently woken with him. Lord Wolfson was aroused, and Olympia smiled.

His eyes opened and he gazed directly at her, but remained stock still as she touched his face. The arm that lay over her waist did not even twitch as Olympia continued to explore the side of his face and his hair. He opened his eyes but still, he did not move.

"Good morning," said Olympia. In reply Lord Wolfson reached up to touched her face and leaned in to give her a soft kiss. It was Olympia's turn to stay still. No man had ever kissed her with such gentle lips. He moved back and tried to stand up, but she held his arm. Olympia wanted to caress his body, to gently trace the scars on his back. She found Matteo's water-mage body markings made him look sexy. She wanted to kiss him. He turned to look at her.

"We have time before we need to leave. Come back to me, please, Matteo, love me," said Olympia.

"Do you really want me?" asked Matteo. She nodded, and pulled him to her.

He laid next to her, giving her kisses from her face to her neck, to her breasts. This time, he took his time loving her until Olympia shouted in pleasure before he found his own release.

He lay next to her for a while, then gave her a quick kiss and said "Thank you," as he got up a few moments later. He dressed, then returned to her, sitting back down on the bed, he kissed Olympia again.

“Take your time, and when you are ready, come down. I’ll have food waiting for you to break your fast.” He got up, took his coat, and left. He closed the door behind him softly.

Olympia got up and dressed. This man kept surprising her. She left the room only a few minutes after Matteo left her. He was on the first floor, breaking his fast with Olsen. She sat next to the men, and quietly ate a bowl of porridge, some bread, and tea. They all finished eating, but as they were about to leave, a man dressed as a Trade Official stopped them. The sniveling man had long, greasy blond hair and was dressed entirely in black. He had come from a table across from theirs.

“Gentlemen, my name is Mr. Agson. I am one of the Trade Officials in town. It was brought to our attention that you have a prostitute in your company, and when you arrived yesterday, she didn’t register in our office,” he said.

“We arrived late yesterday. We are here only passing through, on our way to my land,” said Lord Wolfson.

“When are you going to register her?” said the official, Mr. Agson.

“We are leaving now. There is no need to register,” said Lord Wolfson.

“Oh, there is. I was told the prostitute provided services last night, and should have stayed in one of our brothels.”

“She provided no services last night,” said Lord Wolfson. In an instant, Mr. Agson grabbed Olympia’s right arm and tried to look at her tattoos, but Olympia snatched it back.

“She is a high-ranking courtesan. Let me see your breast. I saw your Exotic-tattoo when you stood up.”

“You are not showing him anything,” said Lord Wolfson.

“Are you, her employer?” asked the Trade Official. Olympia stayed quiet. She didn’t want to get in the way of the law.

“She is my mistress. I am the Earl of Wolfson and have just inherited the title of Duke of Trenton.” Lord Wolfson showed him her burn mark with his name tattooed on her left arm. The Trade Official stood back, his eyes opened wide.

“We will be leaving your town now,” said Olsen. Lord Wolfson took Olympia’s hand, but as they walked past Mr. Agson, Olympia noticed he was fuming with hatred.

They left the town in a hurry; Lord Wolfson making Olympia ride with him and Logan rode Arrow back to the camp pulling his horse behind him.

“I was supposed to have stayed at a brothel last night,” said Olympia.

“No! You are my mistress and carrying my child. You are not staying in any brothel. No one touches you but me.”

ଔଔଔ

As soon as they reached the camp, Olsen gave orders to move out. They would leave as soon as possible. In future, they would not stay in the vicinity of any other town.

The men broke camp fast and moved away from the town that same day. Olympia rode with Tony on the cart. For the rest of the day, she kept thinking of the weird Trade Official. She realized the man would have been a problem if they stayed in the town for much longer. They rode as fast as they could until it grew dark, when they had to stop and pitch their tents. Standing in her tent, Olympia thought about her childhood, which inevitably led her to thoughts about the child she carried, and tears fell. She could not help it. She cried a lot lately. Lord Wolfson entered the tent and found her crying.

“Why are you crying? Are you hurt?”

“I am just sad and lonely. I am fine,” Olympia said, cleaning her tears away with the back of her hand.

Lord Wolfson looked a little perplexed and stepped back out of the tent, leaving Olympia behind as she tried to calm herself down. A few minutes later, Willow poked her head through the tent entrance.

"Hello Willow. It's nice to see you again. Do you need me for anything?" asked Olympia.

"Hi dear. Olsen went out with the scouts. He asked me to take you to get your meal today." Olympia smiled, stepping out of the tent. Both women walked toward the fire where Cook had his pots. They got their food and then sat together to eat their meal. Lorna and Beni joined them.

"We haven't talked to you in ages. We heard you're with child. How are you feeling?" asked Willow. Olympia looked from one woman to the other.

"It appears there are no secrets in this place," Olympia said.

"I'm afraid not," said Lorna.

"I feel well one day and awful the next." Olympia took a big bite of her food.

"I thought Exotics were sterile," said Beni.

"Most of them are, but the ones that come into the trade as adults are often left intact. My master is a greedy bastard and didn't want to spare the time that I would need to rest after the procedure, so my slave master put me on a schedule. But even on the schedule, I've got pregnant four times," Olympia said in between bites of food.

"So, your children are waiting for you in Palermo? What will happen to them now that you are Lord Wolfson's mistress?" asked Lorna.

"I don't have any living children," said Olympia.

"What? What happened?" asked Beni.

"My master had all four of them removed before the second month of pregnancy." Olympia said with a weak smile.

"Did you want them removed?" asked Lorna.

"It didn't matter what I wanted. I was a slave. My master wanted them removed. I had no choice in the matter," said Olympia.

"Oh, how sad," said Lorna.

"What about this one? Do you want it? I heard it may be from the bastard that kidnapped you," said Beni.

"When I first found out, I didn't want it. But now, I don't know. There is the possibility of the child being Lord Wolfson's. I always wanted to be a mother and have someone to love," said Olympia.

"Children are a big responsibility, but if Lord Wolfson intends to make you have him or her, then he should provide for the child regardless of the father," said Willow.

"I have three children, and they are a pain in my ass. But I love them no end," said Lorna.

"Now that you are here, who is taking care of them?" asked Olympia.

"My mother-in-law and father-in-law are taking care of them for my husband and me. We both had to come on this campaign."

"I have one little girl, but my mother is taking care of her. My husband and I are both here as well. You know my crazy husband," said Beni.

"Is your husband one of the mages?" asked Olympia.

"My crazy husband is none other than Tony, the healer. He is a pain in my neck, but I adore him," said Beni, and all the women laughed.

"If you decide to keep the little bean, like Tony used to call our daughter, just make sure you drink a lot of water and stay away from all hard liquor, including ale. Tony says it is not good for the child," said Beni.

"Are you done with your plate?" asked Willow.

"Yes, I am done. I ate it all. I was hungrier than I thought," said Olympia.

"Let's walk back to your tent," said Willow.

"Have a good night," said Lorna.

"Sleep well," said Beni.

Willow walked with Olympia back to her tent, making sure no one bothered her. But in truth it was unnecessary, all the men seemed to ignore her.

Once she returned to her tent, Olympia sat by the entrance and as she had done every night after her rescue, she started singing. One man accompanied her on his flute, and another played a guitar. The rest of the men listened to her sing, until Lord Wolfson came to sit by Olympia's side. He too listened to her songs, but after the second or third tune he sent everyone to sleep. Afterward, she went to her pallet and tried to sleep, but lately, memories of her old life made her sad. The thought of having a child that may not be human made her cry every time.

ଓଓଓ

True to his word, Lord Wolfson didn't enter, or even approach, any town or city along the way until two weeks later when they reached the city of Highcove. He arranged for his men to make camp outside the city. Taking Olsen, Logan, Tony, Beni, and Olympia with him, they entered the center of the city. Lord Wolfson and the others rode their horses to the largest general store, where they tied their horses. He took Olympia by the hand, and they entered the merchant together.

"Olympia, pick a dress fast and a pair of shoes. Get whatever you need to look like a lady, and do it fast. You only have twenty minutes. You need to be presentable where we are going," said Lord Wolfson.

Olympia nodded. She hurried around the store, looking for what she needed. She took the opportunity to buy scented soaps, a lotion for her skin, and another for her face. Beni helped Olympia find a lovely dark-blue dress with a low cut that would reveal her Exotic-tattoo. She was obligated to always show her Exotic-tattoo. Matteo said to hurry, so she picked shoes that matched her dress. She bought undergarments, some makeup, and stockings.

Once she had what she needed, he paid for her things, and they rode to the best hotel in town. They walked in like they owned the place, but all the people they encountered stared at them with disgust. They stank like horse manure.

A hotel attendant was about to kick Lord Wolfson out of the hotel until he showed them his house's crest on his left arm. Lord Wolfson rented four rooms—one for Olympia, one for him, one for Olsen and Logan, and one for Tony and Beni.

"I don't want any problems with the Trade Office in this town. So, you will have your own room tonight. I will have the hotel bring your dinner to your room. Tomorrow, at half-past nine, I want you in the lobby, dressed and ready to go," said Lord Wolfson. Before he left, he kissed her.

Olympia opened the door to her room, and was welcomed by a white room with exquisitely carved ceilings, an impressively decorated table, and an inviting bed. She went straight to the bathroom, where she found running water, and scented oils and salts. She drew a bath. Once the tub was full, Olympia quickly removed her clothing and sunk in to the delightful water.

She wanted to relax in the tub for hours. She scrubbed all the grime and washed her hair, and used the soaps and lotions she had purchased. After her bath, she combed her black hair until it was dry. Lord Wolfson was true to his word. They brought food to her bedroom, and she had the best night's sleep in months.

The next day, she woke up early. She took her time to do her hair and makeup. If she was going to be around polite company, she wanted to look her best. Her morning meal came to her room just as she was getting dressed. She ate and left the room to meet the men in the lobby.

Olympia stood looking out of the hotel lobby through the grand glass window when she heard a voice speak just behind her.

"I haven't seen a more beautiful woman than you in all my life." Olympia turned around. It was a man dressed in a dark gray coat with a dark-blue pair of pants. His black hair made him look as Exotic as she was.

"Thank you, and who may I have the pleasure of such gallant company?" asked Olympia.

“I am the Duke of Levany, and this is my town. I have never seen you around. Who are you and who is your family? And where is your Lady’s companion?” The Duke took Olympia’s right hand, kissed it. Then his eyes went up to her left breast where her Exotic-tattoo was.

“I am Olympia Corona Takatsu. I am here with my benefactor, the Earl of Wolfson,” said Olympia.

“Ah, a gorgeous Exotic; he should not leave you here by yourself unattended,” said the gentleman.

“Hello, my Lord, I am the Earl of Wolfson, here to claim my Dukedom of Trenton. And who may I ask are you,” said Lord Wolfson, stepping in and taking Olympia’s hand. When Olympia heard the man was going to be a duke, she had to do a double take. She knew he was an earl, but she hadn’t known the new title of nobility he was inheriting.

“Hello, Earl of Wolfson. I am the Duke of Levany. Once you become the Duke of Trenton, we will be neighbors. My land borders with yours. Now, I must ask you, from which brothel did you hire this lovely Exotic? I want to purchase her time,” said the Duke.

“She doesn’t work in any of the brothels in this city. She is my mistress. We arrived late last night, and we are leaving today,” said Lord Wolfson.

“You are a lucky man. She is an exquisite woman. I am sure we will talk some other time. Will you excuse me,” said the Duke of Levany. He nodded politely at Lord Wolfson, took Olympia’s hand and kissed it, then left.

“Why did you have to buy a dress that shows that tattoo?” Matteo asked pointing at her Exotic-tattoo.

“Because it’s a legal requirement of my trade. If I don’t do it and I am found out, I can go to jail,” said Olympia.

“I hate your trade,” said Lord Wolfson.

“Yes, as do I, and I don’t like that man,” said Olympia.

“You will never have to deal with him again. Now, let’s go and try to hide that … thing,” said Lord Wolfson, pointing at her breast.

Olsen, Logan, Beni, and Tony arrived soon after. They rode to the Halls of Commerce. The office was almost empty when they arrived, with only three people waiting. Lord Wolfson approached one of the free attendants. He asked for the Director of Lands and Customs. Olympia didn't know what to think. She wondered why Matteo had taken her with him. In truth, he never left her alone with anyone aside from Flint, Timo, Logan, Tony, Olsen, or the women in camp. Perhaps, she mused, that was why.

They waited for about five minutes, and a young man with an ink-stained apron appeared. He saluted after he introduced himself as the assistant to the Director. He led them to the second floor of the building, where they waited outside an office for about an hour until a white-haired older man in a gray suit arrived. The official opened the door to a small office.

"Hello, Lord Wolfson, I am Master Reiner Klaster. Please come in. I am sorry it took me so long to get here, but I had a problem with two mages disputing ownership of a piece of land. One of them burned down my office, so I am attending you in my assistant's office."

"Hello, Master Klaster; I understand your situation. I am here to set claim to my title and lands which my Uncle the Duke of Trenton left me as an inheritance," said Lord Wolfson.

"I have the Duke's will and the order from King George. Two months ago, we received the Duke's ring and his seals, along with his three other titles, crest, rings, and seals. I need to confirm your family affiliation-tattoo. After that, the paperwork for the transfer of jurisdiction won't take long. Since you also inherited your uncle's three lesser titles aside from the Dukedom, you might want to choose which one you will want to give to your eldest son," said Master Klaster.

"My son Ivan will be the Marchese of Kleinberg on his twelfth birthday," said Lord Wolfson.

The rest of the day went by in a turmoil of walking from one office to another. Lord Wolfson signed a plethora of papers, and after several hours of legal procedure, Master Klaster passed to him a case with four rings. After that, they had to walk to the offices of the Trades Officials, where Lord Wolfson had to receive a tattoo on his right wrist, making him a member of the House of Dukes.

This time, they didn't have to wait. An official was waiting for them. They were led into a private office where a young official had a cabinet full of different seals and paraphernalia to make tattoos. The young man asked Lord Wolfson to sit on the chair in front of the table laid out with the needles and ink.

The Trade Official first made the Duke's tattoo on Matteo's left wrist. Then he made the tattoos of the lower titles. Finally, the official took the ducal ring from Lord Wolfson and heated it. A few minutes later, he burned the seal of the Dukedom on Lord Wolfson's left arm.

"I want to add the crest of the Duke of Trenton to her arm," said Lord Wolfson. The Trade Official looked at Olympia unmoving.

"Where would your wife want the Duchess' signet to be placed?" asked the Trade Official.

"She is not my wife. She is my mistress. She has the Earl of Wolfson's crest on her arm. I want to add the Duke of Trenton's crest to her," said Lord Wolfson. The Trade Official said nothing. He reheated the ring. Olympia's face lost all its color, and sweat beaded on her forehead.

"Since we are adding a mark, this time, it has to be done by one of us. We must be careful not to cover the crest that was already created," said the young man, ignoring Olympia.

"Don't worry, Olympia; Tony is here to give you healing right away and Beni is here to help you if you need anything more private as a woman." Matteo held her hand while he reassured her.

The official took Olympia's left arm and carefully branded the ducal crest next to the Earl of Wolfson's mark. The brand was done to the right side of the mark of the

Earl. Olympia didn't make a sound, but she recoiled. Tony took her arm and gave her healing at the same moment.

The Trades Official gave him Olympia's registration papers, and they left the office. When they stepped out of the office Logan was conversing with the Duke of Levany. A few minutes later, Logan hurried back toward them.

"My Lord, we need to leave now. The gentleman you were talking to this morning is asking for Miss Olympia's registry as an Exotic," said Logan. They hurried and left through a side door. Once outside, they mounted their horses.

"It is time to go. I will not register Olympia in this city. Tony, Logan, go back to the hotel and pick up our things. Olsen, and Beni you two are leaving with me and Olympia." They galloped away as fast as the horses could move.

CHAPTER 11

Olympia Got to Fight

They reached the camp late in the afternoon, and Lord Wolfson prepared the men to be ready to leave at dawn the next day. As Olympia dismounted, still dressed in her finery, all the men around looked at her. Head held high, she walked to Lord Wolfson's tent. There, she undressed and put on an old pair of pants and a blue shirt that she buttoned high up to her neck. But she had left her serviceable boots back at the hotel. She waited in her tent almost two hours until Olsen arrived, bringing a bag with all the things she had left in the hotel room. All the lotions, makeup, and scented soaps, along with her old clothing, that the hotel staff had laundered, and her boots.

After she put away her things, Olympia left the tent and went to find Flint. She found him sharpening swords on a whetstone. Olympia joined him, picking up some of Cook's knives that were waiting to be sharpened, and working them on a second whetstone. She worked for about an hour until Olsen came to find her. Like every evening, they went to get supper. She walked quietly alongside Olsen, her mind dwelling on the new brand on her arm. What impact would the brand have on her standing as an Exotic? She didn't know.

They approached the area where Cook had set up, and Olympia sat by the fire while Olsen went to get them food which he brought back to where she sat.

Unexpectedly, Flint came to sit beside her. "Miss Olympia, you did a nice job sharpening Cook's knives. Dino is quite happy with your job on his ax as well. Little lassy, you are getting good at your job, you know."

"Thank you, Flint,"

"Now eat; ye need your strength for yer bairn," said Flint. Olympia almost choked on her drink.

"How do you know I'm increasing?" asked Olympia.

"Olsen told us. We are all to make sure ye and the bairn stay safe," said Flint. And Olympia shook her head, and chuckled.

They were eating their meal when twenty men on horseback arrived at the camp. Olympia almost choked when she saw the Duke of Levany had arrived with the group of men. Olympia froze. Flint stood up in front of her. He was as wide and tall as the mountains, a boulder of a man.

"Where is the Duke of Trenton?" asked the Duke of Levany.

"I am here. What is your business at this late an hour?" asked Lord Wolfson. Three of the men jumped from their horses, and one approached.

"I am Trade Official Kona. We have Mr. Agson, a Trade Official from the town of Salgado who says you have a high-ranking prostitute in the middle of your camp of men. She must be making an exorbitant amount of coin servicing the men of his camp. She must pay taxes on the wages she's been earning since joining your camp."

"She is not making any coin. She has serviced none of my men," said Lord Wolfson.

"It is hard to believe you have a prostitute woman in a camp of over seventy men, and she has made no coin," said the Duke of Levany.

"The Duke of Levany told us that the woman was an Exotic. She must be in a brothel," said one of the twenty men in the group.

"None of my men would dare approach her because she is my mistress," said Lord Wolfson.

"How did an Exotic agree to travel in a company of military men?" demanded the Duke of Levany.

"I must see all of her tattoos, including the ducal crest," said Trade Official Kona.

“Olympia, where are you? Come here, please,” said Lord Wolfson. Flint stepped aside. Olympia walked to where Lord Wolfson was standing.

“I need to inspect all of your tattoos,” said Official Kona. Olympia showed him all her tattoos and brands, including her Exotic-tattoo on her left breast.

“She has the ducal crest of the Duke of Trenton and the crest of the Earl of Wolfson, which makes her the duke’s mistress,” said Official Kona.

“HAS SHE BEEN WORKING?” shouted Trade Official Kona. All the men in the camp shook their heads, and Tony stepped forward.

“Hello, gentlemen. I am the senior healer in this camp. I can attest that Miss Olympia hasn’t worked in her trade since the day she arrived with us. Added to this, Miss Olympia is carrying the duke’s child. All the men in this camp protect her and her child,” said Tony.

“That is impossible. We all know Exotics are sterilized,” said Mr. Agson. That was when Tony stood next to Olympia. He activated his gift and his hands shined green. Then he placed his hands over Olympia’s belly; his hands shined white and the shape of the life forming inside her appeared hovering in front of her belly.

“Your Grace, Duke of Levany, we can do nothing in this case. The woman is the mistress of a duke and is carrying a child. However, Duke of Trenton, once she gives birth and you are living in your manor, she needs to find a brothel where she can work and that will house her, or you must give her a home in which to live. Do you understand?” said Official Kona.

“Yes, I understand,” said Lord Wolfson.

“I am sorry for the interruption, Your Grace. Men, let’s go!” said Trade Official Kona. The Duke of Levany mounted his horse, giving Lord Wolfson a hateful stare. The twenty men left following the Trade Official and the duke.

“Olsen, I want two fire mages and two lightning mages standing guard on each quarter of the night’s watch around this camp tonight. Timo, I want you to have some men pitch a tent in the middle of camp, where Olympia will sleep. I will take the first watch tonight," said Lord Wolfson.

Despite all that happened, Olympia kept her counsel.

They woke early the next day and moved away from the city of Highcove. Lord Wolfson wanted to go the Trenton estates to carry out a general surveillance of the land and manor he had just inherited, but he knew better. The men needed to get paid, and he needed to reach his father's castle posthaste. They rode all day, during which time he considered Olympia. He had kept a constant eye on her and concluded she was more trouble than he had expected, but she had found a place in his heart.

He made sure not to touch her too often. He wanted to give her space. Olympia appeared like a fragile soul. He had seen people with such sadness in their souls, who ended broken forever. There had been fire in the girl when he'd first met her, but although Olympia kept to herself after they rescued her from the mercenaries, she seemed much sadder. He had found her crying in corners, and when he asked what happened, she would clean her tears and say she was just lonely.

He knew women liked to have other women around. He had two sisters who never stopped talking when they were young. He didn't know what to do with Olympia, aside from having the three female mages accompany her often. He didn't want her to practice her trade. He wanted her to forget her Exotic trade and be like any other woman. He wanted her to be free of being an Exotic in her body, mind, and soul.

They needed to get as far away from Highcove as it was possible. Later, he would figure out a way to save Olympia from having to live and work in a brothel once they moved to his manor among the Trenton estates. They rode for the entire day, only stopping to give the horses rest. Lord

Wolfson made sure to position his mages at the fringes of the company.

In the evening, they stopped to make camp in a clearing, and he ensured Olympia always stayed near to Olsen, Timo, Tony, or Flint. He'd had a bad feeling that stayed with him, ever since the Trades Officials had left the night before. Having a man following them all the way from the town of Salgado did not sit well with him.

All the men did as they were supposed to, setting up camp, the tents and watches. A routine had developed with Olympia answering the call of nature after supper, and then spending the evening sitting by the tent's entrance and singing for the men.

That night, Lord Wolfson went to tend to his stallion, but when he came back to his tent, Olympia wasn't there.

"Olsen! Where are you?" shouted Lord Wolfson, but Olsen was nowhere to be found.

"Where is Olsen?" demanded Lord Wolfson of one of his men on the first watch of the night.

"I don't know. I haven't seen him for a while."

Getting more upset by the minute, Lord Wolfson strode around camp looking for Olsen and Olympia, but no one had seen either of them after supper.

"Get everyone. I want Olsen and my woman found. NOW!" said Lord Wolfson.

Olympia got off the cart, where she had ridden all day next to Tony. She needed to stretch her legs. As happened every day of late, Olympia went to work with Flint, after helping Tony with his remedies, or she would help Timo. Later, once the men pitched her tent, Olsen would come to get her for supper.

On this evening, after she ate her supper, Olsen took her to relieve herself at the edge of camp, as usual. But while they were walking back, she heard a snap of twigs. It was faint, but it made her stop walking. Olsen was a little ahead of her. Another twig snapped. Olympia tried to listen, but a hand grabbed her around the neck from behind.

Olympia shouted, and Olsen turned. A flash of lightning passed by her, almost hitting Olsen, but he ducked. Olympia twisted and turned, and hit the man in the groin. He let go of her. But there was another, younger man behind her. He grabbed her arm; twisting around, she punched him in the neck and he fell back. Olsen used his lightning magic. He lifted a third man off his feet and tossed him away. Olympia grabbed a long stick and used it to strike at the legs of the hooded man who came after her. She remembered what Lord Wolfson had said to do.

"Olympia, keep your weapon close to your body until it is time to hit, and then you use all the strength of your body in the strike."

But his advice failed her. A second man, tall and hooded, held on to her stick, then grabbed her by both arms. She kicked and tried to punch, but he had her trapped.

"Help!" shouted Olympia. Olsen kept using his lightning magic. Olsen and Olympia had fought several men when Lord Wolfson arrived with Logan and several others. Logan used his telekinetic magic and he lifted Olympia and the assailant that held her.

"Let her go, or I'll crush your neck," said Logan.

The man let go of Olympia, and Logan brought everyone down. But once on the ground, he took out a knife and was about to stab Olympia, when from somewhere in her periphery came a spear made of ice. It passed her head, striking the man standing near her, impaling him with a spear of ice. Olympia looked up.

"Logan behind you!" she shouted. Logan turned to find a knife plunged into his heart. Olympia tried to scream again but couldn't.

"NO!" Olsen bellowed, as Logan fell to his knees.

Lightening came from Olsen's hands hitting the man who was holding the bloody knife, slamming him against a rock. The three men left alive stopped fighting. They ran away.

"LOGAN!" Olympia shouted and she ran to him.

"Go get Tony!" shouted Olsen to one of the men that had arrived with Lord Wolfson, as he ran to Logan's side.

"Did you see who they were?" asked Lord Wolfson.

"No, they had hoods and face coverings," Olsen cried.

"Logan's dead." Olympia cried and so did Olsen.

"I am so sorry my friend. Let's take his body back to camp," said Matteo. Olsen lifted Logan's body, carrying him like a babe, and Lord Wolfson walked beside him.

"You trained her well. She fought with skill considering she's only had lessons for less than two months," said Olsen.

"We will keep teaching her. But from now on, I want her to relieve herself in the tent. We will give Logan a warrior's send-off," said Lord Wolfson, as they walked away.

Olympia could not sleep that night until Lord Wolfson came to lie by the entrance of the tent.

"Will you come in here with me? I don't want to sleep alone," said Olympia. Still crying for Logan, her thoughts raced, not letting her relax. Before entering the tent, he removed his boots, armor, and shirt. He took Olympia in his arms, making her feel better, and at last, she was able to fall asleep.

The first order of the day was to create a funeral pyre. Logan was a battlemage—they would give him no less than a full warrior's farewell. After the warrior ceremony, they broke camp, and moved away fast.

Lord Wolfson had not received any instructions about how to proceed upon his return home, so he went directly to Fort Egan. It took them another week of travel to reach the fort.

As usual, Olympia rode on the healer's cart next to Tony. She would sing for Tony, and he would sing along with her. Olympia got the first glimpse of the fort as they rode along the road. The place stood on top of a hill overlooking a valley below. It had tall black walls, and she noticed the shadows of cannons on the ramparts.

"Tony, that is a massive structure. But why have a fort in the middle of Yakuta?" asked Olympia.

"This fort is a reminder of times when Yakuta was divided into provinces. Each province was ruled by a duke or earl. Many decades ago, when the Duke of Anshty killed an entire village of Morai to take ownership of the land, the Earl of Tonay, Lord Marcus Gardner, went to war against the duke. The surrounding nobles of the south sided with the duke, and the nobles of the north sided with Lord Marcus. It was a bloody time. In the end, Lord Marcus won the war, uniting Yakuta. He became the first king, King Marcus the First. I thought you were from Yakuta," said Tony.

"My father is from Yakuta, my mother is from Albria. I was born in Albria. My family moved to Yakuta when I was five. I know the history, but I didn't know we still had these forts in use," said Olympia.

"We have many still functioning, but now we use them as training facilities. We use smaller forts as warehouses."

Late that day, they reached Fort Egan. Olympia climbed down from the healers' cart. Lord Wolfson arranged for Olsen and Olympia to follow him. She stayed close to Matteo, despite wanting to go on a walk around the entire fort. Matteo had many tasks to take care of and she didn't want to get lost in the massive place.

First he went to the communications office and sent a message to the capital. He had to announce his return to the general who had recalled him. Soon after, he went to the fort's commander to relinquish command of his company to the fort's commander. Olympia was in awe of all the pageantry among the commanders, but she guessed it was tradition.

In the fort, everyone was busy and no one cared about her. Olympia had never been around so many female mages and soldiers. She was so busy looking around that she kept stumbling over her own feet as Matteo led her through the fort. They walked through a series of long walkways until they reached an office with ten tables arranged in two groups of five in a line.

Lord Wolfson received his pay, and afterward registered Olsen as a mage at the service of the King of Yakuta, but retained his services under the Ducal house of Trenton. While Lord Wolfson finished signing for the return of his equipment, Olsen took Olympia outside. The sun shined brightly, bringing warmth to her tired body.

There was a sense of urgency in everyone around her. Olympia stood aside against a wall, leaving enough space for the men and women to go about their tasks, when she saw some friends approaching.

"Miss Olympia, we must say goodbye," called Willow, from some distance away still. The three mage women hurried to where Olympia stood.

"I will miss all of you," said Olympia.

"I hope all goes well with you, your Little Bean, and Lord Wolfson," said Beni, making Olympia chuckle.

"You take care of yourself," said Lorna.

"I am sure Lord Wolfson will care for you well. Don't you worry, all will be fine. He will find a way, so you don't have to return to a brothel," said Willow. Each of the women hugged Olympia, and they left.

Once Lord Wolfson completed his business, he exited the building to find Olympia, and took her hand. "Let's go home," said Matteo.

They left the Fort with Olsen, Timo, and Flint following them. The four men made pallets out in the open, around a central fire. After supper, Olympia went to her pallet and tried to sleep. She had never slept out in the open, but once Lord Wolfson laid beside her and held her in his arms, she allowed herself to fall asleep.

The next day, they resumed their travels to Lord Wolfson's home. Flint had said they were still a week away from reaching Sindu Lake. But Olympia was happy Matteo made a point that they would find only small villages along the way, with no Trade Offices, for them to spend their nights.

CHAPTER 12

Wolfson Castle

As anticipated, it took them a week to reach Sindu Lake. When the island came into view, Olympia's first sight was of an enormous structure, built of huge white stones, standing on top of the tallest mountain. She had visited too many castles, keeps, abbeys, manors, and even the King of Palermo's palace. But she had never seen a castle that sat on a small island in the middle of a lake. The day was waning, and the afternoon light reflected on the lake's water. Overhead, pink and light-orange colors filled the sky, with lots of feathery clouds.

The group crossed a long, wide bridge separating the island from the mainland. Olympia could swear the bridge swayed. Broad columns, which were linked together and formed barriers to the lake, adorned the side of the bridge every ten or twelve feet, with torches fixed to each. The stone of the bridge was worn smooth, and when the horses walked over it, a loud clap, clap, clap of their shoes resounded. The sound kept time with Olympia's racing heart, reminding her that her life would soon change forever. Escaping this castle would be near impossible.

Once they crossed the bridge, the group entered the structure through the central gates of the imposing walls. Above, on the battlements, men stood tall, keeping watch. The entire island was part of the castle's lands surrounded by those great walls, but the small town inside the walls was quaint. It was the town of Kalbaka. The castle itself rested on top of the tall mountain at the center of the island, with many houses dotted along the road leading up to it. Olympia admired the people on the streets of this weird island castle as they waved to Lord Wolfson. They clearly loved their master. Olympia watched as children ran alongside the horses of Lord Wolfson's group. They kept going up and up the paved, hilly streets. They passed stores, hotels, inns, taverns, houses, stables, churches, and even a hospital.

They left the townspeople behind and continued going up the mountain. There were so many trees and bushes on both sides of the winding road. Olympia could swear a deer and her fawn ran from one tree to another hiding in between the brush. The magnitude of the place took Olympia's breath away. The cart had been left behind at the fort, so Olympia rode Arrow behind Runner, keeping her horse close to Matteo's.

Late in the afternoon, they reached another wall that surrounded the structure of the castle—Lord Wolfson's home. As they entered the gates, pandemonium greeted them. Three young children ran to Matteo, screaming.

"Father is home. Father is home. Aunt Katherine, Grandmother, come," said one child.

"It is, father. He is home," said another child.

"Mr. Andrews, it's father; he's home," said the children in chorus. Olympia knew the Lord had children, but she didn't know he had three. These were younglings of less than ten. The children surrounded the horse.

"Ivan, Axel, Viktor, hello, boys; I've missed you terribly," said Matteo. The three children in jubilation kept calling for Mr. Andrews. Olympia absorbed everything she saw as they reached the main entrance of the castle. Lord Wolfson dismounted his horse and a stable boy took his horse away.

Lord Wolfson lowered himself to one knee, and all three of his sons surrounded him, giving him hugs between joyful shouts of laughter. An austere-looking noblewoman waited by the door next to an even older noblewoman. The woman Olympia assumed was Matteo's mother had her gray hair swept up in a well-designed chignon. The older woman, wrapped all in black and could be Lord Wolfson's grandmother, stood with a cane. Her hair was completely white, but she stood as erect as a teacher's rod. The long, elegant yet practical dresses of both women made Olympia feel underdressed in her men's pants and shirt. Olympia had never been dressed in anything less than the best clothing when surrounded by nobility. Chicho ensured she had the best of the best. The women were accompanied by a man, dressed in what appeared to well-tailored servant's uniform, standing behind the women.

Olympia dismounted Arrow, and went to stand behind Lord Wolfson. She was overawed by Matteo's attitude. Every noble she had ever met did not care for their offspring. Once the children could read, they mostly sent them away to learn languages, history and philosophy, or to mage academies, but this man treated them differently.

She had never seen anything like it. Even her parents had hired tutors and a governess to care for her. She never saw her parents unless she got in trouble, when her father would discipline her. Her mother only called for her when she entertained friends at home, but Olympia had to sit primly and quietly. Her mother only wanted to show how well-behaved her daughter was.

"Matteo, son, welcome home. I am so glad to have you back with us. I thought you would be away longer," said the austere-looking woman. Lord Wolfson gave her a kiss, and another to his grandmother. The older woman touched his face with her fragile hands.

"Hello Mother, hello Grandmother, it is lovely to see you both doing so well. How is Father?"

"Your father is weak, but he is a stubborn man. Can you believe he is already walking about?"

"Where is Father?" asked Lord Wolfson.

"The cantankerous, old man is inside waiting for you," said his mother, holding her son's hand.

"I am so happy to have you back with us," said the grandmother.

"Where is Katherine?" asked Lord Wolfson.

"She is inside with your father," said the woman.

"Is she still smitten with that man from Palermo?" asked Lord Wolfson.

"Yes, we have been waiting for your return to marry Katherine. Her fiancé can't wait for your return," said the grandmother. Matteo nodded. Then he looked up at the butler by the door, and the older man bowed to him.

"Hello, Mr. Andrews!" said Wolfson.

"Hello, my Lord, it is so good to have you back with us," said Mr. Andrews.

"Thank you, Mr. Andrews. I am glad to be home. You look better than when I left."

"Healer Martina helped me recuperate faster. Thank you for getting her to me," said Mr. Andrews.

"No need to thank me; we care for our people," said Lord Wolfson. "In all the time I was in battle, I was relieved to know that my family had you with them."

"The young masters and ladies of the house have all been wonderful with the staff," said Mr. Andrews.

Just as he was finishing his observations to Lord Wolfson, a young servant came running out to the steps where they still stood.

"My Lady Agatha, Lord Findley fell," said the servant. Lord Wolfson was about to run up the steps to the front door, when Olympia stepped forward and held his arm.

"My Lord, wait, what would you do about me?" asked Olympia. Olympia feared what he would do since he was in a hurry.

"Mr. Andrews, this is Miss Olympia Takatsu. She will be living here with us. Please have Mrs. Andrews give her something to eat and assign her a place to sleep. Olympia, we'll talk later," Lord Wolfson said, as he ran inside the castle, still carrying the two smallest children in his arms, and the third following him not far behind. Lady Agatha turned toward Olympia and gave her a curious look.

"Miss Takatsu, follow me," said Mr. Andrews. He took Olympia around the outside of the castle, where she entered through a door that opened into the kitchen. She had never been in a kitchen before. So, this was another new thing for Olympia. Her surprise at being in a castle kitchen quickly changed to fear. The servants barged in and out, carrying plates of prepared food. Obviously, the servants were preparing the dining room for the family dinner.

Oh Lord in Heaven, this man is making me a common servant.

"Did Lord Wolfson look hurt? He must have been hurt to have returned from war so suddenly," said a gray-haired woman in the middle of the kitchen, who was leaving a pitcher on a table.

"He's fine. He didn't look hurt. I heard he's here because of his uncle's passing and the Marchese's poor health. You'll find out. What happened to Lord Findley?" said Mr. Andrews.

"When he found out Lord Wolfson was outside, he got up too fast, and Lord Findley fell onto his knees when he tried to stand from his chair. Lady Katherine was with him. I sent three servants to help," and, seemingly without taking breath, the woman who Olympia assumed was Mrs. Andrews, continued "But who is she?"

"I must go up to him," said Mr. Andrews, and as an afterthought, "Oh, this is Miss Olympia Takatsu. She arrived here with Lord Wolfson. He gave me orders for you to feed her and give her a place to stay."

"Is she a new servant? What is she here to do? Did you ask him?" Mrs. Andrews glowered at Olympia from head to toe.

"Lord Wolfson didn't say who she was aside from her name. He was in a rush to go to his father when he heard Lord Findley had fallen," said Mr. Andrews.

"Let me see your arm. I'll give you a job based on your trade," said Mrs. Andrews. Olympia hesitated. This woman would see her courtesan prostitute-tattoo, and she would make Mr. Andrews call a Trade Official and have her sent to the local brothel.

"Come on, I don't have all day. Show me your trade tattoo," said Mrs. Andrews. Olympia rolled her sleeve and showed her right wrist with her multiple tattoos.

“What’s all this? How many skills do you have? This is uncommon,” said Mr. Andrews.

“Look at her wrist. How many skills can a servant have?” asked the servant, helping the cook. Mrs. Andrews took Olympia’s right arm and looked at her tattoos.

“You are a prostitute!” said Mrs. Andrews. Olympia unbuttoned her shirt and showed her left breast tattoo.

“Oh, my Lord, what is Lord Wolfson doing with an Exotic?” asked Mrs. Andrews.

“I don’t know. Like I said, Lord Wolfson didn’t give me any information on her,” said Mr. Andrews.

“She is useless in this household,” said Mrs. Andrews, eyeing Mr. Andrews.

“Don’t look at me,” said Mr. Andrews.

“Where am I going to put her? I don’t want her with the other girls. I don’t want them learning bad habits from her,” said Mrs. Andrews, pointing at Olympia with her head. Olympia had kept quiet up to that moment.

“Listen, Mrs. Andrews, my training is … very specific. Since I am useless here, maybe you could suggest to Lord Wolfson to return me to my previous master,” proposed Olympia. But they clearly were not listening to her.

“I’ll see what I can do. Now, come, sit. I’ll give you something hearty to eat for your supper, and after you finish eating, I’ll take you to your room,” said Mrs. Andrews.

Mrs. Andrews served a bowl of a red stew, with meat and vegetables. She also gave Olympia a roll of bread. Olympia tasted the savory stew, and its beef and beats flavor was so tasty, she ate the entire contents of her bowl. Mrs. Andrews passed her a tankard of ale.

“I don’t mean to be a pest, but do you have something aside from ale?” asked Olympia.

“Why? You don’t like ale?” asked Mrs. Andrews.

“The healer said not to drink ale, that it is not good for me.” Olympia remembered what Bina had said about ale, and she didn’t want to hurt her child.

Wait, what? My child, I said I didn't want to hurt him. Should I keep him? Chicho is not here. The Little Bean is mine.

"Here, drink this. It's pomegranate juice," said the old woman. Olympia drank the juice, and she loved it. Cook gave her some cookies too, just as the housekeeper called her. Olympia took the cookies and wrapped them in a piece of cloth, and placed them in her pants pocket.

"Have you finished eating?" asked Mrs. Andrews.

"Yes, ma'am," said Olympia. She knew she best be polite with the woman who held her food.

"Excellent, then follow me."

Olympia stood from the kitchen table and thanked the cook, saying "Cook, your food was delicious. You make the best stew I have ever eaten." Olympia gave her a slight bow of her head, and then followed Mrs. Andrews up a few more stairs.

When they reached the main floor, they walked through a hallway and made a turn to the left at the end of the hallway. They took a second set of stairs, which took them to the second floor. They walked to the end of the second floor, made a left turn, walked to the end of the hall, and took another set of stairs. After walking around, and around, they arrived at the third floor of the house. Once there, the level divided into a mezzanine, with half a floor up and half down, separated by a short set stairs each way.

"The lower section is the nursery. The children of Lord Wolfson sleep there. You must stay away from the children's section. Let's go," said Mrs. Andrews, and they went up the short set of stairs, reaching a separate section of the third floor.

"Your room is on this floor. You will share a bathroom with the other servants on this floor. It will be the last room to your right. You must keep it as clean as you find it after every use," said the housekeeper.

The older woman walked ahead along yet another long hallway, finally opening the last door at the end. Olympia entered the small, cold room, which she found was sparsely furnished, with only a small bed, table, chair, and small dresser. It had a window with a curtain. Clearly, this room had an owner until recently; it had no visible dust. A maid appeared, carrying towels, bedsheets, and three blankets, which she left on the bed. A second maid entered with a basket. Olympia looked in the basket and in it she found soap, a comb, a chemise, a night dress, and some undergarments.

"We break our fast in the kitchen early in the morning before the family. Make sure you are down in the kitchen at dawn if you want to break your fast," said the old woman.

"This room is freezing." Olympia said while she peered inside the room, holding her arms together.

"It has no fireplace and no furnace."

"I can't stay here," said Olympia.

"I am sorry, but this is all I have to offer. It is why I gave you three blankets," said the older woman.

"Wait, I have one more request. I need to talk to Lord Wolfson. I need to make him aware of my situation. I can't live with the servants and without a job. I need to pay my taxes. You know, with an Exotic-tattoo, my taxes are—quite high," said Olympia.

"I understand your predicament. We all pay taxes. I'll talk to Mr. Andrews. He will talk to Lord Wolfson after the family's dinner," said Mrs. Andrews. She left and closed the door behind her. Olympia stayed in the cold room. She took the undergarments, soap, face cloth, towel, and night dress. She needed a bath, so she went to the bathroom. It was empty.

"How fortuitous," whispered Olympia under her breath. *The room is empty and I don't have to wait. I am exceedingly tired.* She walked in, and immediately felt claustrophobic, as if the walls were pressing in on her. Olympia spread her arms and she could touch each wall. There was no place to rest her things, so she placed them on the floor, hoping it was clean. She let the water run, and after some time, the hot water ran.

"Thank you, Lord Wolfson, for little favors," said Olympia. Once the tub was full, she bathed as quickly as possible, fearing she would get a cold in the freezing bathroom. By the time she walked back to her room; someone had brought up the few possessions she had.

She had the dress and shoes Lord Wolfson had bought for her in Highcove. She also had the extra pair of pants and an extra shirt Olsen had given her. The room felt colder than when Olympia left for her bath, so she decided to sleep with her coat on. It was the first time she had to sleep with so much clothing on, but the freezing room made it necessary.

It took some time to get warm, even with the three blankets Mrs. Andrews gave her. She huddled like a tiny kitten, and finally, after an hour of trying to get her feet warm, she fell asleep.

CHAPTER 13

The First Day in the Castle

Early in the morning, a knock at her door woke her, and without Olympia's bidding, the door opened. A young, happy-looking maid entered her room and opened the curtains as if she owned the place.

"Hello, I am Edith. You need to get up, get dressed, and go down to the kitchen if you want to eat," said Edith. Her smile was contagious.

"Hello Edith, yes, thank you. I'll be down in a few minutes," said Olympia. The young servant turned and left the room as unceremoniously as when she had entered. Olympia sat up in bed. Her room was as cold as it had been the night before. She took a towel and walked to the bathroom. It was occupied, so she waited outside. A few minutes passed, and an older, blond-haired servant walked out. She glowered at Olympia, looking at her from head to toe.

"So, you are the new Exotic-turned servant," said the older woman.

"Good morning to you. Are you done?" asked Olympia. The woman stepped aside, letting Olympia enter the bathroom.

She carried out her morning ablutions. Looking up into the mirror, Olympia sighed. A tired woman looked back at her, a shell of the Exotic she used to be. Her hair and skin needed care. She returned to her room and dressed in the clean pair of pants and shirt from her possessions they had brought up to her room the night before. She left her room and tried to remember how to return to the kitchen, but the night before was all a big blur. Olympia stood at the end of the hallway. She stood in front of what Mrs. Andrews called the nursery. She turned around but could not find the servants' stairs.

"You seem lost," said a voice coming from behind her.

Olympia turned around.

"Don't worry, you will get orientated soon enough," said Edith. Olympia smiled at the girl.

"It took me a while to figure out where everything was in this place. Follow me, I am headed to the kitchen. I am hungry and need to break my fast. By the way, the servant you bumped into before you went in the bathroom is Margo. She is the head maid on the second floor. She's mean," said Edith. Olympia made a mental note of Edith's comment.

Edith took Olympia down the labyrinth of hallways, down to the castle's kitchen. Olympia tried to make a mental map of the castle as they walked through the hallways and stairs. If she was going to be made to live with the servants, she needed to learn to navigate the maze and at least find the kitchen.

Olympia arrived in the kitchen and everyone stood still when they saw her. She smiled and walked, with elegant composure, to stand next to a chair.

"Good morning to all," was the only thing Olympia could think to say.

Mrs. Andrews stood by Cook. "Good morning to you. Mr. Andrews talked to Lord Wolfson last night, and he asked for you to be in his office at ten in the morning. Come, eat, and then you can return to your room. I don't want the other girls around you. I'll send someone to get you when it is time for your meeting with Lord Wolfson."

Olympia sat on the chair, and Mrs. Andrews passed her a plate with bread and goat's cheese. They served her a cup of tea, and Olympia felt nauseous.

"I am sorry, but do you have anything aside from goat's cheese to eat? The smell of goat's cheese combined with black tea makes me nauseous." Olympia looked up at Mrs. Andrews, who squinted back at her.

"Here, how about some porridge and jam for your bread? I drink coffee in the morning. Lady Agatha loves it, and so do I," said Mrs. Andrews. She served Olympia a hot cup of coffee. Olympia took the cup and inhaled the aroma.

"It smells delicious." Olympia took a sip. "Oh, what a glorious flavor." Olympia said. It was the first cup of coffee in her life. Mrs. Andrews smiled.

"I'm glad you like it."

After Olympia finished eating, she stood up slowly, making sure not to get dizzy, but she stumbled anyway. "Mrs. Andrews, can someone come with me to my room? I'm afraid I don't remember the way." Olympia crossed her arms while she talked. It was a chilly morning, and she had forgotten her coat.

"Come, I'll take you," said Mrs. Andrews. As they walked up the stairs and through the hallways to reach the third floor, Mrs. Andrews stopped and held Olympia's arm.

"Are you with child?" said the woman.

"What?"

"Are you with child?" asked the woman again.

"Yes," Olympia furrowed her brow.

"How far along are you?" asked the old woman.

"I think I am almost four months," said Olympia.

"I thought Exotics were sterile."

"Not the ones made Exotics as adults," said Olympia.

"Do you know who the father is?" asked Mr. Andrews.

"Yes!"

"Does Lord Wolfson know about your child?" asked Mrs. Andrews.

"He is my child's father." Olympia wasn't sure, but there was always the possibility. Mrs. Andrews continued walking to the third floor. They reached Olympia's room, and the housekeeper left. Olympia entered the cold room. She had nothing to do, so she went back to bed. She felt like the weight of the world was on her shoulders. If Chicho had not sent her to Prince Wallen's castle, she would be free by now. He promised if she agreed to increase the pain level and service Prince Wallen's pain request, he would pay for her to transfer to the teachers' trade and eliminate the Exotic trade. She would escape the trade of prostitution. Chicho didn't need to pay for her education, so he had made a lot of gold coin from her. But now, now she was stuck in the household of Lord Wolfson. She lay on her side and went back to sleep.

Several hours later, another knock woke her.

"Come in," said Olympia. It was Edith again.

"I'm here to get you. It's time for you to see Lord Wolfson," said Edith. Olympia got up from her bed. She tried to comb her hair and fix it back into one long braid. Olympia wished she had a mirror. She had been so long without her beauty products that she knew it was going to take weeks for her skin to return to its usual complexion. It was only a matter of time before she would have to start working again, to earn enough money to buy her own lotions and creams. She had the makeup she had bought at Highcove, but she figured it was best not to add much to her face. Olympia finished fixing her hair. She considered putting on her only dress, but it showed her Exotic mark, and she didn't want to show it. So, she went to see Lord Wolfson in her traveling clothing.

Edith took her down the stairs and around a set of hallways to what Olympia thought must be the front of the castle. They reached an open foyer of such grandeur, it took her breath away. To the right side, there was a sizable room, into which Olympia could see through the open doorway. It held the most magnificent, well-preserved library she had ever seen. She could live in that room. To each side of the room, there were rolling ladders giving access to the top shelves. Such an extensive library was Olympia's version of heaven. Edith knocked on the door frame.

"Come in," said the rough voice of Lord Wolfson. Olympia entered the room. He was alone.

"I was told you wanted to talk to me. What is the problem?" said the Lord. Olympia walked forward, to stand in front of Lord Wolfson.

"You said that once we reached your lands in Yakuta, you might return me to Palermo. Will you honor your promise? I mean—" Lord Wolfson didn't let Olympia finish.

"I figured that was what you wanted to talk about. You understand that here you can come and go as you please?" asked Lord Wolfson.

"I want to go home because my master promised me a deal I can't refuse," said Olympia.

"You are free in Yakuta. We don't have slaves. You are pregnant. If you return, they will make you give up the child."

"Yes, but if I stay here after I have the child, the Trade Official said I must return to work in a brothel. My master in Palermo made a bargain with me. I want to go home," said Olympia.

"I want you to stay, but I want you to be happy." He called out to the butler, "Mr. Andrews, send in the Trade Official and his people."

"What are you doing?" asked Olympia.

"Giving you what you want."

Three men entered the office. They all wore Trade Official's uniforms.

"Hello, Lord Wolfson. It is good to have you back at Wolfson Castle. My name is Tam Solis, and I am here at your service," said the official.

"Mr. Solis, this is Miss Olympia Corona Takatsu. She wants to go back to Palermo. I decided to grant her request. She is a high-ranking prostitute, an Exotic."

"What? How do you come to have an Exotic in your household?" asked the young Mr. Solis.

"It's a long story. Miss Olympia wishes to return to Palermo, but I can't deliver her personally. So how can I ensure she gets to Palermo safely and without any problems along the way? I don't want her staying in cheap brothels along her travels," said Wolfson.

"It will be hard to do," said the Trade Official.

“I realize that, which is why I’ve sought your expertise on the matter,” said Lord Wolfson.

“Show me all your tattoos. Start with your Exotic one,” said Mr. Solis. Olympia could not believe Matteo was actually going to send her back to Palermo. He wasn’t a liar like all the men she had met throughout her life. She had a master in Palermo who had promised her he would give her the gift of freedom. Now Lord Wolfson was sending her back. Lord Wolfson had treated her with respect, which made her want to stay with him, but she wanted freedom from everything more than anything in the world.

Olympia showed Tam Solis all her tattoos, including her Exotic mark.

“Wait a minute, she has quite a few skills. Ah, this is going to be difficult since she still has her owner’s trademark symbol. Do you have her registration papers?” asked Mr. Solis.

“Yes, I was asked to brand her wrist. Here are the papers,” said Lord Wolfson. Mr. Solis read the papers.

“The new Yakutan law stipulates that you can’t dismiss her or sell her. She is yours to keep,” said Mr. Solis, after he took a second look at Olympia’s brand.

“What do you mean? Why? How?” asked Lord Wolfson.

“You branded her left wrist with your house crest and gave her your name, thus making her your mistress forever. She is yours and yours alone. Despite her being, or having been, a sterilized Exotic, she was that when you branded her, so you can’t cast her away on the technicality of her not being able to give you children,” said the Trade Official.

“I don’t understand,” said Lord Wolfson.

“In Yakuta, the law says that if a nobleman brands any woman on the left wrist with their crest, that woman is bound to that man until death,” said Mr. Solis.

“But that is for our wives,” said Lord Wolfson.

"No, that is with all branded women. That is why you must be careful who you brand. Did any nobles witness the branding? Oh, never mind, I can see General Joshua Caleo, the Duke of Coldwell, his first Lieutenant Commander Lindell, and his man of business all signed your certificate," said Mr. Solis.

"Yes, the General witnessed the transaction since he was the one that asked me to brand her," said Lord Wolfson.

"I am sorry, my Lord, but this is the law of Yakuta. If she was from a noble family, she would have the option to leave you and return to her family. But she is a prostitute, and that right is not afforded to her. You can't send her to Palermo. She is officially your mistress for life," said Mr. Solis.

"We were told after she gave birth to my child, she would have to return to work in a brothel," said Lord Wolfson.

"Some Trade Officials say that, relying on everyone's ignorance, to get high-ranking prostitutes back in the trade. That way they make large profits and the Tax Officials can collect high revenue from them. But I can assure you, a mistress only works if their master allows it. You can't sell her or dismiss her from your home unless she is found to be an adulteress. You gave her the ducal crest and wrote your name on her wrist. In Yakutan society, she is as good as a second wife." Mr. Solis extracted some papers from his case and passed them to Lord Wolfson to read.

"The laws concerning Exotics in Yakuta changed because of Prince Otto Hightower, the nephew of King George. You can make her your—" Mr. Solis was interrupted before he finish his sentence.

"This is too much information," said Lord Wolfson.

"She is prohibited from working as an Exotic in your home or a brothel. You can't make any profit from her Exotic talents, ever. We will be back to check on her and her status in your household in a year from now. She can't be treated as a prostitute or a servant. Also, because of her many skills, we must keep tabs on whether she is working for wages in any other capacity," said the young Trade Official. "I am sorry to be the one to give you the news," said Mr. Solis.

"Are you sure I can't return to Palermo? I mean, Palermo is a different kingdom," said Olympia.

"The trade rules are almost the same in the five kingdoms. The only variants are things that rule mages. But, Miss, here in Yakuta, we abolished slavery long ago. Here, you are part of his family. You are Lord Wolfson's mistress, and under his house's protection. You have many liberties; in Yakuta, Tsestelago, and Alhambra, mistresses are equal to second wives with all the rights pertaining to the wifely status.

"As a mistress here, you are not a slave like you might be in Behui or Palermo. But since you do still have the trademark symbol, I suggest you stay away from Palermo until you get a mage to erase the trademark-tattoo, or your owner can recall you to his service," said the official.

"I want the trademark-tattoo erased," said Lord Wolfson.

"We can't do it. The Arcane Mage with the power to erase tattoos, only comes to town once every four months—but that won't be until three months from now. When he gets here, I'll make sure to send him to you."

"Yes, please, I want all these links to slavery erased from her skin," said Lord Wolfson.

"I understand." Turning to Lord Wolfson, Mr. Solis bowed and said "If you have no further need of my service, have an excellent day, Your Grace."

Olympia lowered her gaze, and sat down on a nearby chair. The Trades Official started to pack his things, but his papers fell all over the floor. He went on his knees to retrieve his documents.

"Olympia, you heard what the official said. I can't send you back to Palermo. You must learn to live in my home," said Lord Wolfson.

"Since I am registered as your mistress, what will happen to me? Will you keep me living with the servants?" asked Olympia.

"What did you say?"

"I slept in one of the servant's rooms last night. Are you keeping me with the servants?" Lord Wolfson got up from his chair and walked to his office door.

"Mr. Andrews, come in here now," shouted Lord Wolfson. Mr. Andrews walked into the office a few seconds later.

"Why did Mrs. Andrews place Miss Olympia in a room with the servants?"

"We didn't know who she was or what to do with her. You only gave me her name," said Mr. Andrews.

"I want you to tell Mrs. Andrews to assign a handmaid to Miss Olympia. She is my mistress. Also, tell Mrs. Andrews to move Miss Olympia to the bedroom to the right of my room," said Lord Wolfson.

"I am going to need dresses and shoes. I can't keep walking around in breeches and your old shirts." Olympia said in a soft voice.

"You will have all that you need. Andrews, call healer Martina. Miss Olympia and I will need the ministrations of a master healer. I want us both checked for everything. We were both exposed to many undesirable things in the wilderness. If we have any diseases, I don't want anyone in this home exposed to them any more than they have been already. Call a seamstress, a shoemaker, and a miller, and have them provide Miss Olympia with all she needs as a mistress in this home. You may leave," said Lord Wolfson.

Mr. Andrews left the room.

"And you," he turned to look at Olympia once they were alone, "I tried to send you back just as you wanted. Now you see it is impossible. If you want to be an Exotic so badly, then know this. I don't want you practicing your trade with anyone, not a guest, servants, or workers in this home. If you need anything, ask. I'd like to keep your trade out of your head and away from my children. Do you understand me?"

"Yes, but do you understand? I am a scholar. I have more education than most nobles. All I wanted was—"

"I know what Exotics are, and I don't care how much education you have. All I care about is that I gave you the option of being free in this house, and you wanted to return to be an Exotic. You wanted to go back to sleeping with half the aristocracy of Palermo. Is that what you want?"

"I—" Olympia was cut off before uttering another word.

"No, don't answer me; I think I know the answer. I tried to be a gentleman with you, but all you wanted was to return to your old life. I am not an uncaring man, but I must protect my children, family, and staff. You are pregnant, and it appears you don't even care for the child. By law, I must keep you here. I will care for you just like I care for any other member of my household. I will not sell you. But if I find you practicing your Exotic trade, you are out of here, do you hear me?" said Lord Wolfson.

"Yes, but you don't understand. I only wanted to go back because I wanted my freedom," said Olympia, almost shouting at the man who would not listen to her.

"What do you mean? You already have your freedom here," said Lord Wolfson.

"My master told me that if I accepted an increase to my pain level and go to Behui to service Prince Wallen and his friend, he would buy me the teacher's trade and erase the Exotic trade. I wanted to live in a place where no one knew me or my past. I wanted to start anew," said Olympia.

Official Solis lifted his head from his papers. "You do know that he lied to you?"

"No! What! How did he lie?" Olympia faced him.

"For all of us, trades are forever. We can only add skills to our trade. Prostitutes are the only ones who can escape their trade, and only through marriage can a prostitute leave the trade. We can purchase trades for our children, but once tattooed, they stay in their trade. Your old owner could never have purchased a trade for you as an adult. Increasing your level of pain can only happen if you agree. That is a choice given even to slaves in all five kingdoms. So, I guess he used the false promise of giving you a different trade as his way of controlling or coercing you," said Mr. Solis.

Olympia dropped back down onto the chair she had only recently stood up from. She wanted to be invisible.

"I only wanted to live free of my trade. I don't want this mark on my body." Olympia said, touching the Exotic mark.

"I understand now," whispered Lord Wolfson.

"In this kingdom, we only have one Exotic who managed to escape the trade. That is Lady Ultima Hightower, the wife of Prince Otto Hightower, the nephew of King George," said Tam.

"Olympia, don't give this anymore thought. Here, you are free. As long as you live in this home, you will never work as an Exotic. I will dismiss anyone who injures you. Now go find Mrs. Andrews," said Lord Wolfson, as he placed his hand on Olympia's shoulder and gave it a gentle squeeze. Olympia stood up and left the office.

At the opposite end of the hallway from the library, she saw an open door that led outdoors. Realizing it provided her an escape, she left running, straight out to the back gardens. As she ran, she passed some well-manicured gardens, finally reaching a family of trees at a good distance, just inside the castle's inner wall. A pine beckoned her, so she sat under it and cried. Not tears of sorrow, but those of anger. How could she be so stupid? That son of a bitch, Chicho, lied to her. Something told her Chicho was hiding something. The man had always been a greedy bastard.

Now, in this house, she was a mistress, only slightly better than a servant. Free, ha, this life wasn't freedom. She wanted to make her own decisions. She wanted to be loved. She never had loved, nor been loved. Neither her parents nor her ex-husband, Vincent, gave her any real affection, and now she was in a home with a man who was obliged to keep her due to a technicality.

"Aaaaahhhh, why me? All I ever wanted was to be myself, have my own home, and not have to answer to anyone," shouted Olympia to the sky. She sat on the grass with her eyes closed, reclining against the tree, still crying, but the tears had slowed. Chicho made her a promise he knew he could not, would not, keep. Now, here she was with the knowledge that Exotics were prostitutes forever.

Although Lord Wolfson said she would never work as an Exotic, she knew that was a promise he might not be able to keep. Once she had her child, the Trade Official from Highcove had said he would send her to live in a brothel. Olympia hated that tattoo. Her eyes were closed as she continued to consider her life, when a little hand tapped her on her shoulder.

"Why are you crying?" asked one of the boys.

"I am a little upset," Olympia said, cleaning her tears away with the back of her hand.

"So, you cry because you are upset?" said the youngest of the boys.

"Sometimes, yes," said Olympia.

"I cry when I am hurt," said the youngest boy. Olympia smiled.

"Do you want to play with us? If you play, you will feel better," said another boy, showing her a kite.

"I can't play now. I must return to the house. You go and have fun."

"We would all rather stay here with you," said the oldest boy.

"Yes, you seem like you need friends."

"What are your names?" asked Olympia.

"I am Axel. These are my brothers. Viktor is my youngest brother, and Ivan is the oldest. He's the one holding the kite." All three boys were blond with blue eyes.

"Here," said Ivan, as he gave Olympia a cookie he took out of his pants pocket.

"From where did you got this?" asked Olympia, taking the cookie the boy gave her.

"I stole it from the kitchen earlier today," said the little boy. Olympia smiled at the boy.

"Ivan, Axel, Viktor, get away from that woman. Come here at this moment," said a stern voice. It was the children's grandmother, Lady Agatha.

"Bye," said little Viktor. The children ran to their grandmother, and Olympia stood up from the ground. She cleaned her pants as best she could, and returned to the house.

Living with these people was going to be interesting. It appeared that Lord Wolfson's mother ran the house like Matteo ran his military company of mages, but there had to be a wife. Matteo had three children. What would Lord Wolfson's wife be like? Would she make her life miserable? What would Olympia's job be? Olympia worked her entire adult life. She needed something to do—anything.

CHAPTER 14

The New Mistress

Olympia walked back to the house. Once inside, she found Mrs. Andrews waiting for her in the foyer in front of the library. The housekeeper looked distressed, but at that moment Olympia did not care what the woman felt. She just wanted to sleep. Her body was travel weary after so many months on horseback and sleeping in tents. She did not want to deal with anyone or anything, but here was the housekeeper.

"Miss Takatsu, I was told that you are Lord Wolfson's mistress. Why didn't you say so last night? I got in trouble by placing you in one of the servants' rooms," said Mrs. Andrews.

"Please call me Olympia. I am sorry, Mrs. Andrews. I didn't think of showing you my mistress-tattoo. In the end, I didn't care much. It doesn't matter," said Olympia.

"It does matter, Miss Olympia. It matters a lot," said Mrs. Andrews.

"Will Lady Wolfson care that Lord Wolfson has a mistress in the house?" asked Olympia.

"There is no Lady Wolfson," said Mrs. Andrews. They walked through the hallway.

"Why? What happened?" asked Olympia.

"Lord Wolfson's wife died three years ago. We only have Lady Marina, Lady Agatha, and Lady Katherine in residence. Come, I prepared a room for you next to Lord Wolfson's," said the older woman. They went up the winding stairs that rose from the front of the reception hall until they reached the second floor, when they turned left. After they passed a few doors, they arrived at a set of tall doors.

"Lord Wolfson's bedroom is here at the end of the hallway, and yours is next to his," said Mrs. Andrews. She opened the door to the right of Lord Wolfson's, revealing a lovely room decorated in soft shades of peach, cream, and white. Olympia stepped in and felt the warmth in the room, very different from the cold room where she had stayed the previous night. A fire was going in the fireplace, and two maids were getting the room ready. One was making the bed, and the other came out of the adjacent bathroom.

The women hurried out of the room. Olympia sat on one of the lovely chairs with her arms on the armrests.

"I'll provide Edith as your maid. I believe you have already met Edith?" said Mrs. Andrews.

"Yes, Mrs. Andrews, I met her. Hmm, I would like to go back to sleep. Could my midday meal be brought to my room, please?"

"Yes, Miss Olympia and I'll have the seamstress, milliner, and shoemaker here tomorrow," said the white-haired Mrs. Andrews. She left a key on the table near where Olympia sat, and left the room soon after. Olympia remained seated, taking in the massive room. She loved the four-posted, mahogany bed that she could see would fit three people.

Olympia stood up. She had to touch the fireplace mantle. She had never seen such intricate carving on mahogany. There was a tall dresser as beautifully carved as the mantle, and a sofa with soft pillows. A lovely carved round table and two cushioned chairs were in the middle of the room, and candles in each of the sconces in every corner. This room was created for a close member of the family. A three-paned, floor-to-ceiling window with arches at the top overlooked the back gardens. The white sheer curtains obscured the view from outside, while heavy curtains were drawn to the sides.

Olympia walked into the bathroom and found a basket full of soaps and body lotions, many towels of different sizes and a folded white robe with slippers in the corner. She opened the robe to see that a W was embroidered on the left side.

I wonder if this belonged to Lord Wolfson's wife? She was tired of wearing men's clothing. Olympia turned on the water in the tub. She undressed while the tub was filling, then thankfully immersed herself in the warm waters. Finally, clean and soothed, and wearing the robe, she left the bathroom and went straight to bed. All she wanted to do was sleep.

Olympia slept all afternoon when a knock on her door startled her awake. She looked around and remembered where she was. She bid the person to enter, and Edith entered carrying something lacey. Olympia sat up in bed.

"Miss Takatsu, I am bringing you some new chemises. Mrs. Andrews sent a servant to town to get these for you. You need a lot more, but the seamstress will be here tomorrow. She will bring what you need," said Edith.

"Thank you, and call me Olympia. Please tell Mrs. Andrews I said thank you." Olympia tried to get out of bed, but the world turned. She almost fell, but Edith came running to help her stand.

"You need to take it easy when you stand. Mrs. Andrews said you are with child. I will make sure you are well taken care of," said Edith.

"Thank you, Edith. I'll be fine." Olympia smiled at Edith, taking any sting out of the words.

The seamstress, milliner, and shoemaker arrived together the following morning after Olympia broke her fast. They measured every part of her body. They brought a few things to fit Olympia while they made dresses and shoes. Mrs. Andrews also arranged for a hair stylist to visit the castle. Olympia loved having her hair done. It was one of the few things she liked about being an Exotic.

In the following days, Olympia ate all her meals in her bedroom. She spent her days either reading or sleeping.

"Miss Olympia, wake up," said Edith. She had fallen asleep on her favorite chair while reading her book.

“What is it?” asked Olympia. She squinted from the brilliance of the light shining through the window.

“It’s time for the midday meal. Come, you must eat,” said Edith. The young maid had brought a platter of chicken with vegetables, some bread, and jam. Olympia eyed her food, making a face.

“I am not hungry. Leave it on the table. I’ll eat later.”

“Oh no, not again. You hardly touched your morning meal, and last night, you didn’t eat at all. You must eat. It is not good for you or the child,” said Edith.

“I can’t eat. Most food makes me nauseous, and if I eat despite the nausea, I gag and end up vomiting. But, I’ll take a look …” Olympia stood up and went to the table. She tasted a tiny portion of the bread, then she took a bread roll, spread some jam on it, and took it with her as she walked away from the rest of the food.

“Tell me what foods don’t make you nauseous?” asked Edith.

“Bread, pastries, jams, some hard cheeses, turkey breast, chicken breast, ham, some vegetables, beef stews, soups, fruit … oh, and I love coffee and pomegranate juice. Please don’t bring me any fish, shrimp, muscles, clams, oysters, things that have a strong scent, or cured meats, ale, or tea. Soft eggs make me gag horribly,” said Olympia.

“I’ll tell Cook, so she can avoid what makes you sick and cook the things you can eat.” Edith hurried out of the room. Olympia stretched her back and decided to go out for a walk. She needed to get some fresh air. She had rested in her room for a week. Although she had needed the rest, it was time to move about. She had to find something to do, a job. She could not live her life, stuck in her room.

Before leaving, she ate her bread, some of the fruit tart, and drank the pomegranate juice. She waited a little to make sure her stomach would sit well, then she took the warmest shawl she had and left her room.

Olympia exited the castle through the side door she’d found before when she ran from the library to the gardens. Gardens always gave her peace. But she had only seen a section of the castle then. Now she walked around all of it. The castle was beautiful. It was a perfect blend of rustic masonry and well-crafted woods.

There was a well-maintained lawn, and the cherry trees looked impressive. She walked around until she found a gazebo with four chairs. As she sat listening to the soft breeze moving the leaves and branches of the trees for a while, her mind and body began to relax. Olympia closed her eyes and remembered when she was a little girl in her grandfather's land. They had a tall tree with a swing. Olympia had sat and swung for hours. She was reminiscing about times past, when someone cleared her throat, breaking the enchantment.

"Ahem!" Olympia opened her eyes, and in front of her stood Lady Agatha and Matteo's grandmother. Lady Agatha wore her usual stern visage, but the grandmother reminded her of her own grandmother. The small, older woman had an elegant beauty with a cloud around the iris of her loving brown eyes. Olympia thought her smile looked sad. Olympia stood up, then curtsied.

"You have been in my castle for over a week, and we haven't been formally introduced. I am Lady Agatha, the Marchioness of Findley. And this is my mother, Lady Marina, the Countess Dowager of Langlade, and you are?"

"I was Exotic Courtesan Olympia Corona Takatsu. Now, I am Lord Wolfson's bonded mistress."

"My son told me how you came to be his mistress. Our men don't partake of prostitutes. Having said that, I was alarmed when he came home with an Exotic as a bonded mistress. But we are Benanti, which means we are hospitable to all," said Lady Agatha. Lady Marina sat and kept her counsel.

"Yes, Matteo told me you follow the Morai religion and tradition," said Olympia.

"Yes, we do. Since you will now be living in this castle, you need to understand our traditions and customs. I hope you understand that part of that requires you to forget your old life. I will not tolerate you practicing your trade in this home." The woman remained standing at some distance from Olympia, enabling her five-foot-almost-nothing inches to look imposing.

"I know." Olympia said taking a step back from the imposing older woman.

"Did you receive all you needed from the seamstress and shoemaker?" asked Lady Marina.

"Yes, they brought many things, and are making me more dresses and shoes," said Olympia.

"We called the best in town. We can't have you walking around looking like a farm boy. Another thing, you have yet to come down for dinner. Are you ill?" asked Lady Agatha.

"I, I, my stomach is not well. I'd rather eat in my room for now," said Olympia.

"That is rubbish. Unless you are ill, I expect you at the family dinner table," said the older woman.

"Ah, yes, I am ill," said Olympia.

"What do you have? If you needed a healer and my son has not arranged for one to visit you, that would be remiss of him, not to provide you with care," said Lady Agatha.

"What is your sickness? I'll have a talk with my grandson," said Lady Marina.

"No, I am sorry, my Ladies. It's complicated," Olympia's heart was beating fast, and her sweaty hands shook.

"What is complicated? Talk, young lady, now," said Lady Marina.

Oh no, here it was. The older woman was going to kick her out of the castle. This was going to be the end, but she had no say in the matter.

"While we were traveling here, I shared a bed with your son several times, but around the same time a group of mercenaries kidnapped me and one forced himself on me. Now I am pregnant, and—"

"This can't be. I must talk to my son." Lady Agatha left. Olympia turned to Lady Marina.

“It is not my fault. I have never been unfaithful to Lord Wolfson. I tried to get rid of the child, but your grandson would not let me.” Olympia didn’t want to look at the woman. Lady Marina came over to stand next to Olympia. She took her hand.

“And so, he shouldn’t. But in the end, it is your child, no one else’s. Do you want the child?” asked Lady Marina.

“I don’t know,” said Olympia.

“I love babies. So, when you have yours, I am going to have another great-grandbaby to spoil. I hope it is a girl. We have too many boys in this family.”

“Wait, this may not be Lord Wolfson’s child. You can’t accept me or him.” Olympia could not believe the woman.

“You don’t understand; there is a possibility that it is his child. That possibility makes the child a member of this family,” said Lady Marina.

“But what if it is not? What if I have a gray monster with red eyes? Will you accept him or me?” asked Olympia, with more gumption than she wanted to show.

“My darling girl, in our faith, we protect our own and those that are weaker and need the most help. My grandson marked you with his crest. You are part of this family. If the child is born with red eyes, then I will make her a little white hat to match her eyes,” said Lady Marina.

“You can’t be serious?”

“Yes, I am serious. Our faith is very important to some of us.’

“But what about Lady Agatha?” asked Olympia.

“Don’t worry about my daughter. I know she will not judge you,” said Lady Marina.

“I don’t know.”

“Now come with me. One of your tattoos on your wrist proclaims you a singer. I play the piano. Let’s go inside and have some fun,” said the older woman. Olympia smiled, and they returned together to the castle.

Two days later, Olympia was in the library, returning a book and looking for a new one, when Lord Wolfson entered the room. She had not seen him since their talk in the library, the day the Trade Officials visited. He looked stunning in his clean new pants and coat.

"Finally, you are out of your room. How are you feeling?" asked Lord Wolfson.

"I feel well. I'll be out of your way. I just came to get a book," said Olympia.

"Wait, Master Healer Martina will be here today. I want her to check you and the child. I gave her the permission to do whatever you wanted with the child. I want you to keep it, but it is your decision." Lord Wolfson turned around and left the room.

Olympia could not believe what he had just said. She could do whatever she wanted. This was too much. She had a choice. This time, nothing was imposed. Olympia felt like someone had poured a bucket of cold water over her, when Lady Marina's hand touched her arm.

"Olympia, I've been calling you. Are you feeling well?" asked Lady Marina.

"I feel fine. Lord Wolfson just said that Master Healer Martina will be here today."

"I know. My daughter said the healer was visiting to carry out her fortnightly exams of Lord Findley. But I've been looking for you. I want to show you something. Come with me." She took Olympia by the hand, and together they slowly walked to the parlor, where Olympia saw a knitting basket sitting next to Lady Marina's rocking chair.

"Look what I made for your baby. It's a hat and booties. I'll make a little coat next," said Lady Marina, as she pulled out a little white hat and a pair of tiny booties from the basket. Olympia noticed how fragile the woman's hands were when Lady Marina gave her the knitted things.

"They are beautiful," said Olympia.

"I need to go shopping for more yarn. You need to come with me to the local shops," said Lady Marina.

“I would love to go shopping,” said Olympia. That would be a novel experience. Chicho never let her leave the brothel alone, and never gave her any coin to go shopping. All that she owned was selected for her. The worst part was that she had no say in the matter.

“I’ll make arrangements for us to go later this week,” said Lady Marina.

“Will you excuse me? I must get ready for Master Healer Martina’s visit,” said Olympia.

“Yes, yes, go, we can talk later.”

Olympia left the room with her thoughts swirling She didn’t know what she wanted. Olympia had to decide, but what was the best decision for her? She had not given much thought to either the child or the circumstance. In the end, she was an Exotic, and sex was her trade. But in her case, the Krapens’ actions were forced. During her twelve years as an Exotic, all the sex had been imposed, but it was a business transaction based on her trade. What had happened with the Krapens was not a business transaction.

Lord Wolfson said he wanted the child. He didn’t care. In his mind, the child was his. Lady Marina was already making him clothing, and she admitted a feeling of attachment developing. She wandered outside to the gardens. Olympia could always think better when she was outside in cultivated gardens. She sat, contemplating the view. From where she sat, she could gaze up at the mountains. The days were getting colder as winter was drawing near. She recalled the days when she traveled with the men, and when she sat with Tony in the cart, singing songs with the crazy man.

She needed to calm her mind. Closing her eyes, she breathed deeply, then recited a nursery rhyme she had learned as a child. But then felt a presence of someone nearby.

She opened her eyes, and startled. There was a boy with big blue eyes, the exact color of like Lord Wolfson’s, right in front of her face. She recalled the three boys’ names were Ivan, Axel, and Victor, but she couldn't remember which was which.

"Are you sleepy?" asked the boy.

"No, I'm just thinking." Olympia said, pulling back from the boy's face.

"Ivan, come here," said the boy, calling to the one who had given her the cookie last time.

"Is she alive?" asked Ivan.

"She said she's thinking," said the first boy. Olympia figured he must be Axel, because she remembered the youngest was Viktor.

"I'm Viktor," he reminded her, "and I am a healer mage. I can try to make you feel better if you hurt yourself. I am still little, but I can try to make your pain go away," said the youngest boy.

"You are so sweet. No darling, I feel fine."

"What's your name?" asked Ivan.

"My name is Olympia."

"I am Axel, and I am a fire mage. Ivan is a telekinetic mage," said the boy, looking proud.

"Well, hello again, to all three of you mighty mages," Olympia said in a grandiose voice.

"Ha, ha, ha, ha, you are funny," said Viktor.

"Are you going to live with us forever?" asked Axel, putting his hands in his pants pockets.

"I think so. That is what the law says." Olympia looked around for any adult to come get the children.

"Do you want to play with us?" asked Viktor.

"I think I should go back inside. I am waiting for the master healer." Olympia stood up.

"We will accompany you inside," said Axel, the little gentleman. All three boys walked with her inside the house.

CHAPTER 15

The Great-grandfather's Story

Olympia reached the house being followed by the three boys and Mrs. Andrews waited for her by the door. She appeared irritated.

"Miss Olympia, Master Healer Martina is here. I showed her to your room. She's been waiting for you," said Mrs. Andrews.

"Thank you, Mrs. Andrews," said Olympia.

"Boys, I need to go. I'll play with you some other time," said Olympia.

"You promise?" asked Viktor.

"I promise." The boys left, running back outside. She went to her room, thinking about her decision. Olympia opened the door to her room expecting to see an older woman, but she found a young woman waiting for her, looking out the window. Master Healer Martina looked as if Olsen had zapped her with lightning. Her wirey brown hair made Olympia want to laugh, but she didn't. The woman had an oversized brown bag on the table, with several vials already out next to the bag.

"Hello, you must be Master Healer Martina." Olympia said, holding back a chuckle.

"Hello, Miss Olympia; I was called here to give you a full checkup and cure any illnesses you may have acquired in the wilds. Lord Wolfson also said you are with child. You look pale and tired. I have some herbs that can help with that." Martina rummaged inside her bag, her head almost disappearing inside it. When her head popped back up, she triumphantly held out some herbs.

"Yes, what do you want me to do?" asked Olympia.

"These herbs will be good to give you energy in the morning. Have the servant make your morning hot beverage with them. But for now, please, undress and stand under the light. I need to see all of your skin," said Martina. Olympia did what the woman asked of her. She walked to the end of her bed, undressing slowly. Martina checked her body. The healer rubbed her hands together, making her hands shine with a yellow glow. She held her hands just above Olympia's skin, hovering and moving slowly over her entire body, from her head to her toes. As Martina's hands moved over Olympia's body, the light in her hands changed at times, from a pale yellow to a dark ochre at certain points over her chest and abdomen.

"You need to lie down on the bed, please," said Martina. Olympia did what the woman asked. Martina stood beside the bed and spoke a few words in an ancient language Olympia didn't recognize. Martina's hands hovered over her chest. At first, her hands changed to a pale green, then she turned her hands so they faced each other and she moved them from side to side, as if she played with a ball. From her hands, a green orb started to form, beginning small, but quickly growing until it was as wide and long as Olympia.

Lowering the orb, Martina made it engulf Olympia. The orb encased Olympia from head to toe. It felt warm, and as though many fingers were touching her skin. The process lasted a few minutes, during which time it changed color from blue to green, back to blue, to red, to yellow, to green, to orange, to pink, to purple, and back to green. Finally, the healer's hands stopped glowing, so Olympia assumed she was finished. Martina helped Olympia stand up. She passed Olympia a robe, and shook her hands many times. Olympia went to stand by the table. She picked up a glass of water and drank some.

"Is there anything I should worry about?" asked Olympia.

"You had a bad infection that, if left untreated, would have caused your death. I cured it. Your child was also sick. I cured her as well. She should be fine," said Martina.

"How do you know it is a girl?"

"Because when I was healing her, my magic turned purple once I finished. If it's a boy the light turns brown. But the magic only turns to a particular color, if the child will be a mage. The first color was blue. So, I think the child is a water mage like Lord Wolfson, but the multitude of colors we saw is something I have never experienced. All I can say with certainty is that the child will be a girl," said Martina, cleaning her hands with a cloth she had brought with her.

"The child is a water mage!" Olympia said.

"Apparently, a powerful little thing. I haven't seen a little life so full of power. Most people get their magic when they are one or two years old and come to full power when they are about twelve to fourteen. But this little one already has her magic within her, although the multitude of colors may be that her magic has not fully established yet, or maybe the child might have several types of magic, or you are going to have three or four little ones, but I only detected one. And no Wolfson woman has ever had more than one child at a time," said Martina.

"I can't believe it," whispered Olympia.

"Lord Wolfson said that you may want to remove her. If you want to do the procedure, it must be done now. If you wait, it will be too late. I can't do the procedure after the fourth month, or it will kill you in the process, and you are late into your fourth month," said Martina.

"I don't know." Olympia closed her eyes.

"It's your choice, but you must make it now. The child is quite large, and you will die if we wait any longer. I am running a risk as it is," said Martina.

"I always wanted to be a mother." Olympia said to herself.

"Then have your child. In the end, it is yours. All children belong to their mothers. That is why you have the choice of being a mother or not," said Martina. Olympia walked to her bed, sat down, and thought for a moment. She had been pregnant four times, and all four times, her owner had those pregnancies terminated. She didn't have a choice in the matter. They were all taken from her. Now, she had a choice, and she took it.

"I will keep her. She is my water mage," said Olympia.

"Well, it is congratulations to you. I will come back in a month to check on you both. But if you feel you need me for whatever reason, you call me," said Martina. She took her bag of things and left the room.

Olympia stayed behind in her room, sitting on a chair. After a few minutes, she went to look in the mirror. She appeared to herself the same as always. Olympia removed her robe off and gazed at herself sideways.

Oh, my stars, there it is, a not-so-little bump on my lower belly.

She chose to keep the Little Bean, the name she had got used to calling her child. Olympia dressed and went to the library. She wanted to get a new book, but when she arrived, Matteo stood in the middle of the library. She was about to turn away when Matteo spotted her.

"Olympia, wait a minute. Come back, please." Olympia walked back into the room and faced Matteo.

"Yes?"

"So, what did you decide?" he asked.

"I chose to keep her," Olympia said, crossing her arms.

"Excellent! Now wait; how do you know is going to be a girl?" asked Lord Wolfson.

"Master healer Martina told me." Olympia was about to leave the room when a man entered.

"Son, what is going on?" An older man entered, walking with a cane. His eyes were the same color as Matteo's, but his hair had mostly turned white.

"Hello, father, you haven't met Olympia. Let me introduce you to her," said Lord Wolfson. The older man walked with slow steps, limping on his right leg.

"Father, this is Miss Olympia Corona Takatsu Wolfson, my mistress."

"Olympia, this is the Marchese of Findley, Lord Arnold Ivan Hanno Fernand Wolfson, my father," said Lord Wolfson.

"It is an honor, my Lord," Olympia said, curtsying deeply.

"So, this is the Exotic you took for your bonded mistress." The older man walked slowly to a chair. He sat, put on his glasses that hung around his neck, peered at Olympia. "She is beautiful."

"Thank you, my Lord," said Olympia.

"My son told me how you came to be his bonded mistress, and he said you used to be a slave Exotic. But he never mentioned whether you came to be a slave Exotic as a child or an adult?" asked the Marchese of Findley.

"That is not important, father," said Lord Wolfson.

"Yes, it is very important," said the old man. Olympia's stomach made a somersault. Here it was—the dreaded question.

"I came to be an Exotic as an adult." Olympia said, looking down.

"A dishonored woman is the kind you brought into our home?" said the old man to his son. "Were you an adulteress, or were you found by your father disgracing the family name?" Olympia looked up at the older man, and furrowed her brow. She had enough with people thinking the worst of her.

"Father, you must stop," said Lord Wolfson.

"I was never disloyal to my husband," Olympia said, looking up at the old man.

"Then how did you end up as an Exotic?" asked Lord Findley.

"Olympia, you don't have to answer that," said Lord Wolfson.

"No, I think you both need to know my story." Olympia paused for a second. She didn't know where to start, but it was best to tell the entire story.

"My father is the Earl of Lorenz, Lord Allen Okano Barton Tanner, from the northern lands of Yakuta. He married my mother, a Lady from the house of Skylar from Otao in Albria. He owned gold mines in Albria. We escaped to Yakuta when the revolution came to Albria. Most of my mother's family were killed. I was five years old when all this happened. We lived in the city of Goli, near the capital, where my father had his business. Twelve years ago, I had a sizable dowry, and my father married me to his best friend's son, from Palermo, Mage Vincent Takatsu. A week after our wedding, my husband moved us to Palermo."

"He didn't let me socialize unless it was with his friends. We were married for three months, when one night, my husband invited one of his friends over for dinner. All I remember was that after dinner, my husband was called to go help a sick person. Vincent is a Healer-Mage. My husband's friend stayed in the house talking with me. He gave me a drink. After a few minutes, I felt dizzy, and lost consciousness. The next thing I remember was waking up naked in my bed, my husband's friend taking advantage of me, and a few minutes later, Vincent entered the room with two servants.

"My husband accused me of being unfaithful. His friend lied and told him I had started the entire thing. We argued; I tried to talk to Vincent. He hit me, I yelled, and they both left the house. A few days later, Vincent returned to the house he had bought with my dowry. He had divorce papers.

"He took me to the Trades Office with his two servants, and without any further preamble, sold me to Chicho di Roberti. But because of my education, I ended up serving as an Exotic in the Il Palazzo di Roberti brothel. That is how I ended up becoming an Exotic twelve years ago," Olympia finished, looking from one man to the other.

"Since you were the daughter of an Earl, your family had the option of taking you back," said the old man.

"My family disowned me. They believed Vincent's lies. I don't care what you think of me. I had never met a man worthy of my respect until I met your son. Thus far, your son has saved my life three times. That is something I can never repay," said Olympia.

"Hum, do you know what happened to your ex-husband?" asked the old man.

"Yes, one of my clients told me he had a pregnant mistress when he divorced me. So, after he sold me, he married his mistress, and they live with his lover, Darren, in the same house he bought with my dowry."

"That is a horrible story," said Lord Findley.

"It is the truth." After Olympia finished her story, the older man slowly stood up from his chair and walked toward the door.

"I will stay away from the family if that is what you want," said Olympia.

"That is not what I want. When are you going to join us for dinner?" asked the Marchese of Findley.

"I don't know," said Olympia.

"Young lady, I expect you down for dinner with the family today," said the Marchese of Findley as he was leaving the room.

"I don't understand your family."

"We are a different kind of people," said Lord Wolfson.

"I have never been around any noble family like yours. How come you are so different? Is it your religion?" asked Olympia.

"We have vowed to honor our g-d through our faith for generations. We believe we are so blessed and successful in all we do because of our vows. We are also blessed to have mages throughout all our generations," said Lord Wolfson.

"I need to know why you believe what you believe. It is incomprehensible to me."

"It's a long story, and many who hear it don't believe it, while others think we're crazy," said Matteo.

"Tell me the story; let me be the judge." Olympia sat, and Lord Wolfson chose the chair opposite her.

"About three hundred and seventy years ago, my many-greats-grandfather, Horace Wolfson, was on his way back to his lands from helping the King of Yakuta in his war against Behui, but he was mortally wounded. The enemy shot him in the leg with a poisonous arrow. Great-grandfather's healer removed the arrow and tried his best to cure him, but he couldn't. All my great-grandfather's men thought he was going to die.

"Horace Wolfson kept traveling even though he was wounded, all because he wanted to die in his own land. But on the way, he fell off his horse. The men made camp in the land near a Morai village. That night, a Morai man came to camp. He asked if the men needed help, but when he found out my great-grandfather was dying, the Morai entered his tent and gave him healing. Great-grandfather's men said that the Morai man spoke a prayer to his g-d in a language no one knew.

"My great-grandfather said that when the Morai man was praying, an angel taller than a house, with wings made of gold, came to him. The angel said her name was Adria and he had been chosen to be a warrior for g-d. She placed her hand over his head and anointed him. My great-grandfather slept for three days, but he woke up feeling better. After a few days, he recuperated completely. When Horace was ready to leave, he went to the Morai village looking for the healer, but the villagers said no man fitting his description lived among them. My great-grandfather never saw the Morai man again, but from that moment, my great-grandfather always healed fast from any ailment. Lord Wolfson stood up and went to his bookshelf. He extracted a book and sat back in his chair. Then he continued the story.

"After that, my great-grandfather took a vow of fealty. He adopted the Morai religion, and he promised that all the members of his family would serve the Morai g-d. That is my family's story and why I follow the Morai religion," said Lord Wolfson.

“That is an interesting story. Are you sure your great-grandfather wasn’t hallucinating about the angel? He was in the arms of death when that happened.”

“I don’t know what was happening to him. All I know is what was told to me. We have taken the vows of the Morai and have followed their laws. Our doors are always open to any Morai. But I can tell you that the direct descendants of my great-grandfather Horace have an uncanny ability to heal really fast,” said Lord Wolfson.

“I have never met any man who cared so much for faith,” said Olympia.

“In this family, we teach our young people our history and their value among the family. As part of this family, you need to know our history, traditions, and what is expected of you. Do you understand?” asked Matteo.

“Yes, my Lord.”

“Here, take this book; this is the history of our family. Read it and learn. We dress for dinner, so you will need to allow time later to get ready. We eat at seven. A little earlier than most families, but my grandmother goes to bed early.”

“Thank you, my Lord, if you’ll excuse me.” Olympia took the book, stood up, and went to leave the room.

“Wait, what is this with *my Lord*?”

“Yes, Matteo.” Olympia chuckled and left the room. When she reached her room, she left the book on her night table, and changed into comfortable outdoor shoes. After hearing the story about the family, she felt out of place. If what she had learned was true, this family had a deep-rooted belief system, yet she believed in nothing but her skills. She wondered if she could learn to live among them.

Olympia knew she could not stay in her room. She wanted to walk the grounds of the castle. Earlier, she had seen the outline of the stables from one of the windows on the second floor and wanted to check them out. After everything that happened that day, Olympia needed some fresh air. She found the exit at the back of the castle. She soon passed through the gardens, and then she saw the most enormous stables she had ever come across.

Olympia had been on many hunts, parties, and soirées in gardens, on patios, and in the grounds of nobility, but nothing compared. There were three huge buildings, side-by-side. From the castle wall, she followed a rocky path to the stables.

"How many horses are in this place?" Olympia said out loud. As she got closer to the stables, at the far end she saw a familiar face. Olympia didn't hesitate to approach the man.

"Hello Olsen, what are you doing here?" Olympia's heart leaped with happiness. She hurried to reach her one-time bodyguard.

"Oh hello, Miss Olympia. I work here with Lord Wolfson. I train his horses and I teach his sons magic. It is good to see you. What are you doing here?"

"I am just walking around. These are amazing stables. I have only seen similar stables at the King of Palermo's winter castle," said Olympia.

"Would you like me to show you around?" asked Olsen.

"Yes, I would love to. I also want to ride Arrow." Olympia spotted Runner, and the horse neighed when he noticed her.

"I must go and say hello to Runner. By the way, where is my horse? Where is Arrow?" asked Olympia.

"Arrow is in the back pasture."

She went to pet Runner as a stable boy was brushing him. "How many horses are in this place?" asked Olympia.

"Counting the fillies and the colts, Lord Wolfson has twenty-six horses at the moment," said Olsen.

"What? Why so many?" asked Olympia.

"He trains some of the King's knights' horses for war, others for hunting, and others for show. Horses come and go. Five horses are leaving for Alhambra in a week, and three are headed to King George's Army. We will sell two at an auction. So, in less than two weeks, we will be down to sixteen horses. But two weeks after that, we will receive ten more from the mayor of the town of Vallego," said Olsen.

Olsen took her to each stable and showed her the stallions, the prized mare called Pearl, and all the other horses. He told her the names. She asked him about the breeds and for what purpose each was being trained. Olsen responded to all her questions. They ended up in an area with several closed paddocks and training rings. Olympia marveled at how the two horses being trained moved so gracefully. Olsen kept explaining the difference between each breed of horse and the training they endured. As they walked back to the largest stable, she saw another familiar face drawing up on a cart. She smiled when she recognized the smile with the gappy teeth.

"Miss Olympia, how are ye, little lassy?" said Flint. He parked his cart, jumped off it and rushed over to her. She couldn't stop smiling at the sight of the big man.

"I am fine. How are you doing, Flint? It has been a long time. What are you doing here?" asked Olympia.

"I am fine. I am here to re-shoe three of Lord Wolfson's horses," said the boulder of a man.

"I miss working with you," said Olympia.

"Well, go change into some breeches and come back. I'll teach ye how to shoe a horse," said Flint. Olympia's eyes opened wide.

"Really! Where are you going to be?" asked Olympia.

"In the largest of barns," said Flint.

"Wait for me. I'll be back in a few minutes. Olsen, thank you for the tour," said Olympia. She ran back to the castle and hurried up to her room. She searched for her old pants and shirt, and found her old traveling coat and boots. She changed. The pants didn't fit her. So, she left all the buttons unbuttoned and used a belt. She put on her boots; leaving in a hurry soon after. As she opened the door to her room, she encountered Margo, the servant, and Lady Agatha.

“Miss Olympia, the mistress of the house, should not look like a common boy. Where are you going looking like that?” asked Lady Agatha. Olympia gave a curtsy to the woman.

“Hello, my Lady, I am going to the stables, and this is all I have. I don’t want to dirty my dresses,” said Olympia.

“What are you going to be doing looking like a peasant in our stables?” asked Lady Agatha.

“I will be working with the horses. Will you excuse me, Lady Agatha?” Olympia darted around the austere-looking woman, leaving in a hurry.

Olympia didn’t give a second thought to Lady Agatha. She was going to learn something new with people she had grown to love. She found Flint and Olsen getting the metal ready in the furnace housed in the largest stable. Olsen gave her a pair of gloves while Flint heated the metal.

Olsen taught her how to prepare the horse’s foot, getting it ready for the shoe. Flint explained how he would shape a metal rod to fit the horse and measure the horse’s toe. They were re-shoeing the first horse when Lord Wolfson arrived.

“Olympia, what are you doing here?” shouted Lord Wolfson from afar. She looked up, and her smile went away. He was frowning, and his voice was domineering.

“I am learning how to shoe a horse,” Olympia said sheepishly when he arrived.

“Why? The mistress of the house should not be in the stables working as a commoner,” said Lord Wolfson.

“I am bored, so I thought I could come here and help.”

“My mother went looking for me and told me you ran out of the castle looking like a farm boy.”

“Listen, I’ve just about had it, being in this place and not having anything to do. All I do is sleep and read in my room. I need a job to do, or I will go crazy,” said Olympia. He remained quiet for a moment.

“You are pregnant, woman,” said Lord Wolfson.

“Please don’t start calling me *woman* again. I feel fine. If I get tired, I’ll rest. I promise.”

“Alright, alright, fine, but you are only to come to the stables while I am working here. Olsen and I will teach you how to work with the horses. We need someone small to ride the older ones, anyway. Olsen, do you have any problem teaching her?”

“No problems at all,” said Olsen.

“My Lord, I didn’t think it was going to be a problem since, she learned to sharpen swords,” said Flint.

“It’s all right, old man, I’m just an overprotective husband,” said Lord Wolfson, and Olympia smiled.

“Well, if you are going to learn how to shoe a horse, you need to pay attention to Flint. He is the best. I expect you here tomorrow after you break your fast. If you are going to work with my horses, you have a thing or two to learn,” said Lord Wolfson. Olympia nodded, with a smile.

Lord Wolfson returned to the castle, but she remained with Olsen and Flint. After Olympia helped to re-shoe one horse, she went back to her room, feeling tired but accomplished. She took a bath and then a nap. She had to go to dinner with the family that evening.

CHAPTER 16

The Lady of the House

Earlier, the Marchese had said he expected Olympia at dinner later that day. In the beginning, she didn't want to socialize with the family, but after living for so long in the castle, it was inevitable. Now that Olympia was the bonded mistress of the son of the marchese, she must have certain responsibilities; whatever those were, she needed to find out.

Now, at least, she had a job. At the start of her travels with Lord Wolfson, being around the dirty men of his military company bothered her, but after living among them for so many months, she learned to respect them. Some had even endeared themselves to her, especially Flint.

Lord Wolfson's stallion, Runner, became attached to her. She loved Runner and her own horse, Arrow. Her horse needed more training since he was still a young horse. It was fantastic that she would learn how to train him. But as a bonded mistress, in a house where Lady Agatha seemed to dislike her, no task could be found for her to do. The circumstances were unusual.

It was time for dinner, and by the appointed time, Olympia had already taken a bath, fixed her hair, done her makeup, and changed her clothing. She walked down to the dining room early, but found no one in the parlor. Nevertheless, she entered and sat on the chair nearest to the fireplace. One of the many skills she was supposed to have was patience. She tried to wait, but waiting disturbed her. She closed her eyes, and as she did every other time she was irritated, she recited the names of Chicho's grandchildren by birth order. Afterward, she recited a few poems she had learned as a child. She was deep in thought, whispering a poem in Palermian when someone cleared his throat.

“Olympia, you are early,” said Lord Wolfson. She stood up fast, but she felt dizzy. Losing her footing, she had to hold on to the chair. Lord Wolfson stepped in fast and held her hand.

“Stay seated. I’ll sit here next to you. Have you been waiting long?” asked Lord Wolfson.

“No, only a few minutes. I didn’t want to be late,” said Olympia.

“My mother, grandmother, and father will be here shortly. I still need to introduce you to my younger sister, Katherine.” At that moment, Lady Marina, and Lord and Lady Findley appeared in the antechamber to the room. He walked slowly with his cane, but with his back straight. Both ladies looked radiant in their frocks.

Lord Wolfson stood up. He bowed his head to his father and went to take his grandmother’s hand, whom he escorted into the room. Olympia stood up slowly, and she curtsied.

“Hello, Miss Olympia, I see you are finally joining us for dinner,” said Lady Agatha.

“Father told Olympia he wanted all the family together at dinner,” said Lord Wolfson.

“I am glad you are here with us,” said Lord Findley.

“Son, the boys are not in the house tonight,” said Lady Agatha.

“Why? Where are my sons?” asked Lord Wolfson.

“Vicar Martell and his mother invited the boys to stay for dinner. They bade me to allow the children to stay overnight with his niece and nephew. You were not around, so I gave them permission. They will be here early tomorrow,” said Lady Agatha.

“I want my sons at the stables and ready to learn with Olsen at the appointed time,” said Lord Wolfson.

“They will be,” said Lady Agatha.

“I hope Miss Olympia can stay with us after dinner,” said Lady Marina, giving Olympia a wink.

As inconsequential bantering was exchanged, a young lady Olympia assumed was Katherine entered the room. Her appearance was the total opposite of Lord Wolfson; where he was tall, she was short; where he was sturdily built, she was petite; and his hair was dark brown, while hers was flaming red. Olympia wondered who had red hair in the family.

"Katherine, dear, we have been waiting for you. Why must you always be late?" asked Lady Agatha.

"I am sorry, mother, I just couldn't decide which dress to wear," said Katherine.

"Dear sister, I must introduce you to Miss Olympia Takatsu," said Lord Wolfson.

"Finally, she came out of her room," said Katherine.

"Katherine, mind your manners," said her father.

"I am sorry, father. It is lovely to meet you, Miss Olympia," said Katherine.

"It is lovely to meet you." Olympia said with a smile.

"Mr. Andrews, is dinner ready?" asked Lord Findley.

"Yes, my Lord," said Mr. Andrews. Lord and Lady Findley entered the dining room first, followed by Matteo, who escorted his grandmother, and Olympia and Katherine brought up the tail. Lord Findley sat at the head of the table with Lady Findley to his left and his son to his right. Olympia sat on Matteo's right, and Katherine sat by her grandmother's side.

Dinner proceeded with quiet conversation. Olympia ate and listened to the family's conversation. Mr. Andrews served her a different meal than the rest of the family.

"Mother, why is she eating something different from us?" asked Katherine.

"She has a sensitive stomach; mind your food, Katherine," said Lady Agatha.

"So, Miss Olympia, I like to play the piano after dinner. It would be lovely if you would sing for us," said Lady Marina.

“Yes, I enjoy singing,” said Olympia. They finished dinner, and Lord Findley and Matteo joined the women in the music room. As Lady Marina approached the piano, and searched for some sheet music, Lady Katherine grabbed Olympia’s right hand.

“Oh, my lord, how many trades you have? Mother, have you looked at her wrist?”

“Yes, yes, she has many,” said her mother.

“I don’t understand,” she said. “Noble women don’t have trades. What are you?” asked Katherine.

“Matteo, I think you should tell her,” said Lord Findley. Olympia lost her smile. She knew this would not end well. It never did with the young women.

“She was an Exotic,” said Lord Wolfson.

“What? You brought a prostitute into this home! You know our faith and our traditions. Father, what is going on?” said Katherine. Olympia kept quiet. She didn’t want to be part of the family discussion.

“Now is not the time. It is a long story. I’ll tell it to you later,” said Lord Wolfson.

“How could you do this? We don’t condone or partake in prostitution. You need to explain this now, brother,” said Katherine.

“I don’t owe you any explanations. Olympia is my bonded mistress. She is here to stay,” said Lord Wolfson.

“I can’t believe you. I don’t want to think about what Lord Teddy and his family will say. This is shameful.” Katherine stood up in a huff, and left the room.

“Katherine, come back here. I told you she wasn’t going to take this well,” said Lady Agatha, giving her son a hard look, as she followed her daughter out of the room.

“I am going to retire. It was a lovely dinner: goodnight, gentlemen, Lady Marina. I’ll sing for you some other time.” Olympia also left the room, soon after the other two.

In the next few days, Olympia woke early, broke her fast, then went with Matteo to the stables. It had been fascinating to learn about the horses. As the days went by, she memorized the names of all the horses, colts, and fillies. She worked mainly with Arrow, Runner, and the prized mare, Pearl. Lord Wolfson wanted to mate them. He wanted to have a new colt, or filly, from Runner and Pearl. Olympia was learning how to train the young colts. She loved her new job. One morning, while Olympia was brushing Larleea, Arrow's sister, a voice startled her.

"I think I will have to give you a new trade tattoo. You are becoming quite adept with my horses," said Lord Wolfson, and Olympia jumped.

"You scared me," said Olympia.

"I'm sorry. I came to tell you that my grandmother arranged for you and her to go shopping today. I missed you at breakfast, so I am telling you now. You need to leave and change if you are planning to go shopping. I don't think you want to be around the stores smelling like a horse," said Lord Wolfson, with a smile.

"I must bathe. What time is she leaving?" asked Olympia, getting out of the stall.

"Grandmother is leaving in another hour. You have time if you hurry. But if you're going with Grandmother, I had better send two servants with you. I am afraid you two will buy the town," said Lord Wolfson, chuckling at his own joke.

"Oh, I said I would go with her, but I don't have any coin," Olympia said in a sad voice.

"Yes, you do have coin. I opened an account for you. Didn't my mother tell you?"

"No, your mother doesn't talk much," said Olympia.

"You have an expense account in all the stores in town. All you have to do is tell them you are Miss Olympia, show them your Duke of Trenton crest, and they will charge everything to our account. Be wise with the gift I am giving you," said Lord Wolfson with a smile.

"I have never had any coin of my own. Even when I lived with my parents, I never went shopping. My mother bought everything for me. When I married Vincent, I never had an account. He bought everything," said Olympia.

"Come here," said Lord Wolfson. Olympia hesitated, but she went to him. He gave her a hug and a kiss on her head.

"You have your own coin with me. Here, this is some pocket gold. For all the work you did while traveling here and all you have done with my horses. You have much more in the accounts I opened for you. Now go and get ready." He gave her five gold coins he had in his pockets and let her go.

"Thank you," said Olympia. She kissed him, took the coins, and she left the stables in a hurry.

She got back to the castle in minutes, and went straight to her room as fast as she could. Edith was already waiting for her. Olympia took a quick bath. She did her hair and applied a little makeup. Olympia dressed in a warm, light-brown and teal dress. She found comfortable shoes and a matching reticule. She took her five gold coins, placed them in her reticule, and hurried down to the first floor. Olympia arrived at the front door short of breath. Lady Marina was already putting on her hat and gloves.

"I am sorry I am late." Olympia said, out of breath.

"Nonsense, I just got here myself. Are you ready?" said Lady Marina.

"Yes, my Lady." Olympia said, putting on her hat. A large carriage waited for them. Two servants were going with them. Olympia could barely remember the last time she went shopping. It was over twelve years ago when she was eighteen, when her mother and Olympia went shopping for her wedding dress. She remembered going to the seamstress for her wedding dress and the milliner for a hat. The memories made her sad, so Olympia shook her head. She didn't want to remember her wedding to Vincent or her past life.

The carriage went through the streets of the town of Kalbaka, and Olympia could not believe the beauty of the town. All the stores were decorated in honor of the harvest fall celebration. She could almost taste the seasonal change in the air, and the trees were changing color. Olympia loved the yellow ochre, red, and orange leaves on the trees. In rural Palermo, they celebrated the harvest, but in the city of Nolia, the shops remained unchanging unless there was a national celebration. Chicho seldom let her out of the brothel during the day unless she was going to entertain someone or be an escort for an aristocrat.

The carriage stopped in front of a store that had a display of handheld fans and parasols. Lady Marina held Olympia's hand.

"Olympia, I am taking you to *Lace Le Blanc*, my favorite store in the city. They make candles, perfumes, and handkerchiefs made of local textiles by local craftsmen. They also sell parasols, fans, gloves, and cosmetic products. They have an extensive variety of lotions. I like their hair pomade and lip balm. Next to them, you will find *Lambert and Jones*, the best watchmakers in the entire kingdom. And across from them is the *Sweet Fairy*, the best bakery in town," said Lady Marina.

"That is excellent. I have five gold coins. I want to buy Matteo a new pocket watch with my own coins," said Olympia.

"You will find what you need in *Lambert and Jones*, of that I am sure," said the older woman. The two women left the carriage, and they entered the first store. When the servant opened the door, the pungent smell of scented candles gave Olympia an instant headache.

The plethora of competing aromas permeated every corner of the shop, and her senses. Lady Marina made her way to the front counter, her cane causing a small thud every other footfall. A matronly attendant stood at the counter, clucking and issuing joyous banter when the old lady came into her view. Olympia walked behind her and tried not to breathe. The mélange of aromas made her want to run out of the store, but she had to stay with Lady

Marina. The older woman introduced her to the shop's owner, Mrs. Le Blanc. Olympia said hello and politely stepped away with the excuse of wanting to find a new fan to match a new dress she had just got.

Lady Marina stood talking to Mrs. Le Blanc. Olympia walked around. She found a white and pink fan that had orange blossom trees on it, which reminded her of a fan her grandmother used to have. Olympia didn't look at the price. She took it to the front desk, where Lady Marina was still talking to Mrs. Le Blanc.

"Excuse me, my Lady, I found something I like here, but I know you are not done. I am eager to find a gift for Lord Wolfson," said Olympia.

"We have a vast selection of men's cologne you can give as a gift," said the matronly woman.

"He lost his watch in his last travels because of me. Lady Marina, you can stay here while I go and see to the gift. I'll come back once I am done," said Olympia.

"Go shop for your gift. I'll meet you there. Mrs. Le Blanc, charge her fan to my grandson's account," said Lady Marina.

Olympia paid for her fan. She spent ten pieces of silver for it and charged it to Matteo's account. Olympia didn't know if that was a reasonable price, but she made a point to find out what would be a decent price for a fan later. She needed to leave the odorous store.

She took her fan and walked with as much grace out of the store as she could. Once she was outside, she had to take a few steps away from the front door to get fresh air. Her head felt like it was about to explode. She held on to the light post and took several deep breaths.

"Miss Olympia, are you feeling well?" asked the servant that came with her.

"I have a terrible headache."

"I bet it was because of the waft of that candle store. I get a headache every time I take Lady Marina into that store," said the young servant, his smile lighting up his eyes.

“Let’s go to the watchmaker. I am sure the air in that store will be better, fresher,” said Olympia.

There was a glass pane in the black door of the watchmaker, through which Olympia could peep inside. The front window had a showcase with several timepieces and small clocks. She could see a well-lit establishment with two gentlemen, two workers, and a staircase. At the top of the door, the letters L&J were engraved in silver, and a sign that said *Lambert and Jones est.* A sign with the number 3419 swung with the breeze.

“Cling, cling,” tinkled a bell when Olympia opened the door to *Lambert and Jones Watchmakers*, and a coolness welcomed her, instantly relieving the pain in her head. The crisp air felt like soft fingers caressing her face, but unlike *Lace Le Blanc’s* candle store, this place felt like magic hung in the air. Olympia could tell a mage was using magic in the store. She knew when a magic caster was working. She had traveled with a company of over fifty mages for over three months, and when they used their magic, the air felt different. Olympia smiled when she walked in.

Tick, tick, tick, tick was the sound all around. She admired a classic Yakutan clock sounding its tick-tock in a corner. Inspecting the counters, she marveled at how many pocket watches and clocks were on display and how different they all were. To the right of the entrance, a set of stairs went up to a second floor, but it was cordoned off with red velvet rope, preventing guests from going up.

She walked further into the store and discovered counters on the left full of clocks of all kinds, and counters on the right with smaller clocks of different designs. She marveled at the round, golden ones with tiny numbers, and the square, silver ones with no numbers at all. They had clocks in the shapes of animals carved from various types of wood. Between the counters there were two shelves of wooden clocks. Olympia kept looking around, but then she remembered why she was there, and walked back to the front of the store to look at the pocket watches. She knew what she wanted. Olympia had a picture of Lord Wolfson’s watch engraved in her memory. She knew it was going to be hard to replace something so unique, but she had to find a similar watch. She kept looking, and distractedly took off her gloves.

"Excuse me, Miss, but you are going to have to leave," said the young store attendant. The young man had to be in his early twenties.

"Why? Are you closing?" asked Olympia

"We don't service prostitutes," said the young man. Olympia's smile disappeared.

"I am Miss Olympia Takatsu of the Wolfson household. I believe Lord Wolfson opened an account for me."

"You mean, as the Marchese of Findley and Earl of Wolfson?" asked the young man.

"No, as the Duke of Trenton and Earl of Wolfson," said Olympia. The young man took a step back.

"Wait one moment, Miss." The young man left in a hurry. Two gentlemen shoppers looked at Olympia when she said her name, but she tried to ignore them.

"Hello, Miss Wolfson. I am Octavio Jones, one of the owners. May I see the Earl's crest?" Olympia lifted her left sleeve and showed both of Lord Wolfson's seals.

"Thank you, Miss Wolfson. Now, what can I do for you? Is there anything in particular that you might have liked?" asked Mr. Jones.

"I am from Palermo, and I was told you are the best watchmakers in the kingdom. Was that an exaggeration?" asked Olympia.

"We established our reputation many years ago and have kept and warrantied our quality," said Mr. Jones.

"I am looking for something very specific. However, what I want you don't have. But maybe you can make it for me?" asked Olympia.

"What do you have in mind?"

"Lord Wolfson had a pocket watch that belonged to the family for generations, and he lost it in his last military campaign," said Olympia.

“If you are referring to the Wolfson’s Crest, watch, then you came to the right place because we made that watch for Lord Horace Wolfson,” said Mr. Jones. And Olympia’s heart leaped with joy.

“Lovely, will it be possible for you to make a copy of that watch?” asked Olympia.

“I can’t make an exact replica. Our timepieces are one of a kind. We never make two alike; that is what makes us different from the competition.”

“But can you make one similar? I want to give Lord Wolfson a replacement for the one he lost,” said Olympia.

“That I can do. Let me get pen and paper. Let’s design something unique for him,” said Mr. Jones. For the next twenty minutes, Mr. Jones and Olympia designed a new watch for Matteo. After the design was done, Olympia asked for the price.

“This will be six pieces of gold and ten silver,” said Mr. Jones. Olympia had five in her reticule. Her heart sank. She wanted to pay with coins earned by her.

“Did you find what you were looking for?” asked Lady Marina. While Olympia was working on the design of the watch, the elderly woman must have entered the establishment unnoticed.

“Ah, my Lady, I didn’t notice when you entered. No, I need to have the watch custom-made, but it’s six gold pieces and ten silver. I only have five,” said Olympia.

“Let me see what you commissioned,” said Lady Marina. The woman inspected the design, and afterward she studied the invoice carefully.

“Octavio Jones, you should be ashamed of yourself. I never knew the Joneses were extortionists. Six pieces of gold and ten silver for a pocket watch? And you know we will provide whatever gems the watch will need!” said Lady Marina.

“Lady Marina, how could you say that to me?” Mr. Jones took a step back as though in shock.

An older man's voice floated down from the second floor. "Because she's been a client of ours since before you and your father were born, that is why!"

"Jonathan, how are you, old man? I thought you were dead," called Lady Marina up the stairwell.

"Keep it up, Lady Marina, and I'll cast a spell on your gloves. You will not be able to take them off for a week," said old man Jonathan, with a chuckle as he descended the stairs. When the older man came into view, Olympia could see that he was completely bald. He bowed his head to Lady Marina, then raised her hand and kissed it.

"Grandson, let me see that design. What is it you are selling to this beautiful young lady?" said Jonathan. His dark brown eyes were as clear as the morning sky.

"It is a pocket watch for my grandson, and he is overcharging my granddaughter. He wants six gold pieces and ten silver. My family bought the first watch your family ever made, and we only paid one silver piece," said Lady Marina.

"That was over 370 years ago," said Octavio Jones.

"Grandson, be quiet. Lady Marina's family are our best and oldest clients. My Lady, I'll make the watch myself; I'll place a charm and a ward to guard against demons on it, and it will only be five gold pieces, but you must provide me the jewels for the eyes," said Jonathan.

"Deal! I'll send you the jewels later today when I get home," said Lady Marina.

"I'll bring the watch over to the castle myself once I'm done. I have a few other commissions before yours. It will take me about three months to make the watch," said the old man.

"My dear, pay for the watch in full. Jonathan Jones is honest about his work," said Lady Marina, eyeing the younger Octavio Jones. Olympia paid, and they left the store. Olympia watched the interaction with appreciation. Lady Marina and Olympia said their goodbye's and left the store.

Olympia could still not believe what had just happened. Once they were out walking to their carriage, she had to ask.

"How did you do that?" asked Olympia.

"That is called haggling. You never pay what they ask for at first if the price seems inflated," said Lady Marina.

"I've never seen that in my life," said Olympia.

"Come shopping with me more often and you will learn how to do it. Let's go. I am tired. I need a nap," said Lady Marina. They mounted the carriage and left for the castle.

CHAPTER 17

The Children

Five days later it was raining, and Olympia decided not to go down to the stables. She wasn't feeling well. She dressed in a warm blue dress and went down to break her fast with the family. When she arrived at the breakfast parlor, the only person present was Matteo. He was reading a newspaper and had a cup of what smelled like coffee. He also had a plate of half-eaten eggs.

"Good morning, Your Grace," Olympia curtsied. Lord Wolfson stood and went to accompany her from the doorway. He held the chair for her as she sat down.

"Olympia, please stop the pageantry. I'm Matteo."

"Ha, ha, ha, ha, I know, dear. I am just playing with you." Olympia said, smiling at him.

"You cheeky woman. Come sit next to me."

Mr. Andrews came and served her a cup of coffee, followed by a plate of fruit, hot bread, and cheese, and presented her with jam. Olympia added sugar and some cream to her coffee, and like every morning, she inhaled the aroma before taking the first sip.

"Today, Katherine's fiancé will be here for dinner. I haven't met him yet."

"Do you know how they met?" asked Olympia. She drank some of her coffee.

"Mother said they met at a dinner party at one of the neighboring Earls' estates. They quickly became friends. Two months later, he proposed. Father said he would only give his full blessing if I approve of him," said Lord Wolfson.

"Is he from around here?"

"Father said he was from Palermo and older than her."

"How much older?" asked Olympia while eating her fruit.

"She is only eighteen, and he is thirty-three," said Lord Wolfson.

"Matteo, he is fifteen years older than her. Doesn't that bother you?" asked Olympia.

"It does bother me. We are looking into this man's present and past life. I want to know why he hasn't married yet. Also, I want to know how he is planning to support my sister."

"I know many people in Palermo. Do you know which part of Palermo he is from?" asked Olympia.

"I don't know. Mother said he told Katherine that his father is an Earl in Palermo, and he is the third son."

"Unlike here, where the younger sons can inherit the lesser titles, in Palermo, only the eldest son inherits all the titles. Does he have a trade or a business? How does he plan to support a wife?" asked Olympia.

"We don't know anything. That is why Father wanted to wait until my return to give the final say. I must find out as much information about this man. My father is a marchese, and now I am a duke. He wanted at least an earl for Katherine."

"What is his name? I know all the nobility in the capital of Palermo. I have many acquaintances in Nolia. I can ask about his family. If they are not from the capital, I can ask people who have titled properties in the country. You just need to let me know his last name and let me contact my people," said Olympia.

"I am not sure if it is Lord Vardi or Lord Serdi," said Lord Wolfson.

"The name doesn't sound familiar. They could be from the northern country," said Olympia.

"Father is the one that knows well. I am going to meet him for the first time today. Over a month ago, father had his man of business inquire about all this man's business dealings—in Palermo, Yakuta, and Alhambra. I am eager to know what he discovered," said Lord Wolfson. They continued talking about trivialities when Lady Agatha arrived, and their conversation changed. They finished their morning meal, and Olympia went to find a book at the library.

ଔଔଔ

It rained all day, and Olympia was feeling tired, so she read in her room for a bit and afterwards, she took a nap. Later, when she awoke, she tried reading the book Matteo had given her, but the script was small. So she went to the parlor to read in the brighter room. She had been reading for about half an hour when little Axel entered and hid behind one of the larger chairs. She had not seen the children in many days.

"Hello, Miss Olympia," said Axel in a whisper, and his brothers came in behind him. The other two boys also tried to hide behind chairs.

"Hello, little ones. What are you doing here?" Olympia whispered her question.

"We are hiding," said little Viktor.

"I notice, but you are hiding from whom?" asked Olympia.

"Our teacher, we don't like him," said Ivan.

"Why don't you like him?" asked Olympia, looking at the little blond-haired boy.

"He is mean to us," said little Viktor, with his hands hiding his face—like that would hide his body. Viktor raised his head, and peeked out from behind his hands. The boy's big eyes hid behind round glasses. He looked at her with a tilted head.

"How is he mean to you?" asked Olympia.

"He hits our hands when we fidget, or when we answer a question wrong, or if we talk out of place," said the oldest child, Ivan.

“Look!” and little Viktor unbuttoned his sleeve and showed her his arm, and a welt from his elbow to his wrist marked his little arm.

Olympia took the arm, and kissed it. “This is awful,” Olympia said, but Lady Agatha walked into the parlor like a whirlwind, being followed by Mrs. Andrews.

“Where are those boys?” asked the imposing lady.

“Lady Agatha, wait a minute. What is happening?” asked Olympia.

“The boys ran away from Mr. Lemine. They can’t disrespect their tutor that way. They must go back to their instructor now. Oh, there you are. Come here now?” Lady Agatha went over and held Axel’s arm.

“Lady Agatha, wait one moment, please. The children said they are hiding from their teacher because the man is hitting them,” said Olympia.

“Ivan, Axel, Viktor, front and center now,” said Lady Agatha. The children came and stood in front of their grandmother.

“What did you do for your teacher to punish you?” asked Lady Agatha. The boys held their heads bowed, and none dared speak.

“The children told me their teacher hits their hands when they fidget, or when they answer a question wrong, or if they talk out of place. Look at Viktor’s arm. Look at the welt on his arm,” said Olympia.

“Mr. Lemine told me he fell on a desk,” said Lady Agatha with a frown. Olympia stood back at the woman’s response.

“He hits us,” said Axel.

“You have said that before, and when I ask him, he denies it. Now come, you need to apologize to Mr. Lemine for running away,” said Lady Agatha.

“No, they are not going to apologize to anyone. No one should hit a child for such a trivial reason as not knowing an answer to a question. And this welt looks like it was done with a rod,” said Olympia.

"And how do you know that?"

"Because I've experienced it myself."

"I am sorry to hear that, my dear. I really am. But what do you know about children's education?" said Lady Agatha.

"I have been a slave for over twelve years; I know abuse when I see it. Come, you three, we are going to talk to your father." Olympia said and she left the parlor holding Axel's and Viktor's hands. Ivan walked behind her, leaving Lady Agatha open-mouthed.

Olympia went toward the front rooms of the castle, where she found Mr. Andrews. But Lady Agatha had recovered her surprise and had almost caught up with them.

"Miss Olympia, leave those children to me. I am their grandmother. They must return to their classroom. Miss Olympia, STOP!" shouted Lady Agatha.

"Mr. Andrews, where is Lord Wolfson?" asked Olympia. Lady Agatha was approaching fast behind her.

"He is in his study on the east side of the castle," said Mr. Andrews, looking quite surprised.

"Thank you," said Olympia. She did not wait for Lady Agatha, but rather she took off with the boys to look for Lord Wolfson.

When Olympia arrived at the study, she didn't even knock on the door; she just entered. Lord Wolfson sat at his desk with two enormous books open.

"What is going on? Olympia, I am busy. I can't talk right now," said Lord Wolfson.

"Your children have a problem, and you need to solve it now," said Olympia. Lady Agatha rushed in behind her.

"Son, you don't need to worry about anything. I can deal with the problem. Come, children, let's take you back to your schoolroom," said Lady Agatha.

"No, you need to know that the children's teacher is abusing them," said Olympia.

"What do you mean, he is abusing them?" asked Lord Wolfson, standing from his chair.

"Ivan told me their teacher hits their hands when they fidget, or when they answer a question wrong, or if they talk out of place. I am sorry, but those reasons are not qualifiers to hit a child. There is no reason to hit a child. Viktor, show your father your arm. You see that welt? That was done with a rod," said Olympia.

"Ivan, Axel, Viktor, come here, boys," said Lord Wolfson. He knelt to be at the same level as his sons.

"Viktor, show me your arm," said Lord Wolfson. The little boy showed his father his arm. Upon seeing the angry welt, Matteo's face turned red.

"Mr. Lemine told me he fell on a chair," said Lady Agatha.

"Boys, I need you to tell me what your teacher is doing," said Lord Wolfson. All the boys looked down.

"Son, I'll take care of this. I'll have a talk with Mr. Lemine," said Lady Agatha.

"Mother, no. Viktor, did you fall on a chair? Son, did you invent that your tutor is hitting you? You know we are not liars in this home," said Lord Wolfson.

"We are men of honor, like our many-times-great-grandfather Horace. We don't lie. Tell him, Viktor," said Ivan, and he touched his brother's hand.

"Mr. Lemine hit my arm with his rod when I said seven times three was twenty-two. I am sorry, father. I truly didn't know," said little Viktor.

"Wait a minute. He is five. Do you know how to add seven plus three?" asked Olympia. Viktor lowered his head. "No," said the boy.

"How is this teacher going to teach a five-year-old how to multiply when he doesn't know how to add? What kind of teacher is he?" asked Olympia. Lord Wolfson looked up at Olympia, his lips had thinned to nothing almost and his hands were already drawn into fists.

"Why didn't you tell your teacher you didn't know?" asked Lord Wolfson, looking at his son.

"Because it would have been worse," said Axel.

“Why worse?” asked Olympia.

“He would have hit him twice on his back,” said the oldest child, Ivan, looking scared. Lord Wolfson stood up. He looked at Olympia and then at his mother.

“Every one of you, come with me now,” said Lord Wolfson. They all left the studio and went to the children’s classroom on the other side of the castle. They reached the classroom in a few minutes; once there, they found Mr. Lemine sitting behind the desk with many papers in his hands. Mr. Lemine was dressed like one of the teachers Olympia had when she was a child. He wore a black suit and white shirt. He was an older man and with a girth greater than he was tall. When he saw Lord Wolfson enter the room, he stood and gave him a slight bow.

“Hello, Your Grace, how are you doing?” said Mr. Lemine.

“I am doing well. But I have several questions for you,” said Lord Wolfson.

“I am a teacher. I hope I have the answer to your many questions, my Lord,” he said in a hoarse voice.

“My five-year-old son just told me you hit his arm because he didn’t know the answer to seven times three. Is that correct?” asked Lord Wolfson.

“I surely did. I don’t coddle my students,” said the teacher. Sitting on the side of the tutor’s desk was a rod. Lord Wolfson strode over, took the rod, hit the man five times on his back with it, and then broke the rod against the desk.

“You will leave this castle now. You are lucky you are leaving this place with your life. I will not give you a letter of reference. You are not a teacher; you are an arrogant beast,” said Lord Wolfson.

“Oh, my Lord, what have I done?” said Lady Agatha.

“No one hits my children,” said Lord Wolfson.

Mr. Lemine took his bag and left running from the room, throwing a dirty look over his shoulder at the children.

“Son, I am so sorry,” said Lady Agatha.

“Mother, when you hired him, did he have any references?”

“He came well recommended. His qualifications were extensive,” said Lady Agatha.

“Did you bother to have our man of business make an inquiry into those references?”

“I, hum, no, I assumed they were legitimate. They had the seal of the previous family,” said Lady Agatha.

“Mother, just because it had a seal doesn’t mean it was legitimate,” said Lord Wolfson.

Olympia stood to the side, watching everything that was happening. She knew Matteo loved his children, and he would not let anyone hurt them. That endeared him even more to her.

“You three come here.” Lord Wolfson hugged each of his children. “Now, go to your room and play with every toy you have and just have fun today. I promise your next tutor will be better. Viktor, I’ll have a healer come and take a look at your arm,” said Lord Wolfson. The boys hugged their father back upon hearing his declaration that they could go and play. And as they were leaving the room, they each hugged Olympia too.

“Olympia, from the sheer number of skills you have on your arm, you have more education than I do. I would like you to help find tutors for the children,” said Lord Wolfson.

“I will, don’t worry. In the meantime, I intend to teach them myself,” said Olympia.

“Thank you,” Lord Wolfson kissed Olympia, then walked out of the classroom.

Olympia left the room with Mrs. Andrews following behind her, leaving Lady Agatha looking out the classroom window.

“Miss Olympia, will you be wanting to place an advertisement in the local newspaper?” asked the housekeeper.

"No, I want to place advertisements in all the best newspapers in the Yakutan capital of Namina. I want the best tutors for the boys. Ivan is going to be a Duke, and the others will have titles of their own according to Yakutan laws, so we must prepare them well. I've been working in the stables in the mornings, but I am going to teach the children instead. I want to have them ready to learn by eight tomorrow. We will go to the stables after the midday meal for their magic training," said Olympia.
Mrs. Andrews nodded her acquiescence.

CHAPTER 18

The Fiancé

Later that afternoon, while getting ready for dinner, Olympia changed her dress three times. Her dresses all fit her a little too snugly. She needed to call the seamstress. Her body was increasing faster than she thought possible. She was dressed in a pale-blue dress that made her hazel eyes look brighter. Olympia was sitting in front of her vanity while Edith helped with her hair, when a knock sounded at the door.

"Edith, be a dear and open the door," said Olympia. Edith placed the brush on the vanity, and did what she was asked. It was Lady Marina. She entered, all ready for dinner. Her white hair was in a well-designed bun behind her neck, and her black dress made her look elegant. Lady Marina held a maroon box in her hands. Olympia stood up, facing the woman, and curtsied.

"My Lady, I'll be down for dinner in a few minutes," said Olympia.

"Ha, darling, take your time. The men will wait for us. I heard what you did today for the children," said the old lady.

"All I did was care for them. I can't stand aside while children are being abused," said Olympia.

"I feel horrible. Agatha rarely lets the children near me. It is though she thinks they will break me," the old woman chuckled.

"They *are* boisterous, but they are good boys," said Olympia.

"That they are, but I am here to bring you a gift. Here, open it,' said Lady Marina. Olympia opened the box, and in it, a necklace with rubies and matching earrings lay in all their glory.

"They are beautiful," said Olympia.

"They are some of my personal jewels, not linked to any title. I want you to have them and wear them tonight," said the woman.

"Are you sure? I don't think your daughter will approve," said Olympia.

"My daughter has no say in this matter. These jewels were a gift from my late husband. He gave them to me, and I will give them to whomever I please. They are not linked to a title."

"I don't know what to say, aside from thank you," said Olympia.

"You are welcome. Let me help you put them on," said the older woman.

Once Olympia completed her preparations, she went down to the parlor where the family gathered before dinner. Matteo and his father were already waiting, and when she entered, Matteo smiled at her and stood from his chair. She curtsied and he took her hand. Matteo was dressed in a three-piece black suit.

Olympia particularly enjoyed looking at him when he smiled. She smiled in turn, and thought of maybe going to his room that night. They had not shared a bed in many weeks, and she missed him. Soon afterwards, Ladies Agatha and Marina entered the room, but like every day, they waited for Katherine. Half an hour later, Katherine arrived in a light-blue dress with a shawl over her arms.

Olympia smiled at the young woman, but Katherine ignored Olympia and didn't even give her a salutation. Olympia did not care; she was used to dealing with arrogant people. The young woman entered the room and sat with her mother. After a few minutes, Katherine stood up and raised her voice.

"What is she doing with Grandma's ruby necklace? Grandma, that is supposed to be Sairah's or mine when you pass on," said Katherine.

"Young lady, you lower your tone with me. It is my jewelry, and I give it to whomever I choose," said Lady Marina.

"Mother, you should not have given away father's first wedding gift to Olympia. She is not family," said Lady Agatha.

"She is family. She is my grandson's bonded mistress. She is the same as a second wife," said the older woman.

"Mother, enough. I am going to take Olympia and my children to my ducal house. We will go to stay at Livingston Manor for a few months," said Lord Wolfson.

"Don't over-exaggerate everything. No one is pushing you out," said Lady Agatha.

"I'm not reacting to the pettiness here. I simply want Olympia and the boys to get to know the property. Plus, I need to survey my land," said Lord Wolfson.

"So, now you are leaving us because of HER!" said Katherine.

"Enough, I want silence," said Lord Findley. And all stayed quiet. A few seconds later, Mr. Andrews entered the parlor.

"Is dinner ready?" asked Lord Findley.

"Not yet, but Lord Verdi has arrived," said Mr. Andrews.

"Show him in," said Lord Findley. Olympia's surprise when she heard the last name was evident by the change in her demeanor.

It cannot be my ex-husband's friend Mr. Verdi. How in the world is he in this castle?

A few minutes later, a tall, slim man entered the room. Teddy Verdi had blond hair, and his white teeth made Olympia want to regurgitate.

That mouth had been over hers and her body. He was Vincent's friend. The one that raped her and told all the lies that got Vincent to divorce her.

"Hello darling, I must introduce you to my brother. He is now the Duke of Trenton, Lord Matteo Wolfson. Matteo, this is Lord Teddy Verdi, my fiancé," said Katherine.

No, that is Todd Verdi. What is she doing with that animal?

"Hello, Your Grace, I was looking forward to meeting you." Todd said, bowing and extending his hand to Matteo for a handshake.

"Lovely to meet you, Lord Verdi."

"I've been eagerly awaiting your return," said Todd. Todd entered the room and greeted the rest of the family, but his smile disappeared when he stood in front of Olympia.

"Exotic Olympia Takatsu, what are you doing here so far away from Palermo?" asked Todd, in his deep Parshtishi accent.

"I am now the bonded mistress of the Duke of Trenton, Lord Matteo Wolfson," said Olympia.

"Is that so? Well, good for you, darling. I have no idea how you got Chicho to sell you, but I am happy for you," said Todd.

"You seem to know Miss Olympia," said Katherine.

"Yes, I do. It was before she became an Exotic, but that is a long story," said Todd. Mr. Andrews walked into the parlor and announced that dinner was ready, and they moved to the dining room. Olympia was dazed. Dinner came and went, and she could not believe she survived it without shouting. They moved back to the parlor, but when the men were about to go talk in the library, Olympia stirred from her lethargy. She had to speak to Matteo. They left the room, and Olympia followed the men. She caught up with Matteo, and pulled him aside.

"I need to talk to you in private. Please don't make any arrangements with that man. His real name is Todd Verdi. He is a dangerous man."

"What do you mean?" asked Lord Wolfson, but Todd and Lord Findley appeared, and she didn't want to make a scene.

"Please, I know what I am talking about. He is not a Lord. Can we talk later?" whispered Olympia.

"Come to my room later tonight. We will talk in private then." Mateo whispered back. She nodded, turned, and left for the parlor.

Once she returned to the parlor, she found Lady Agatha holding a notebook, making notes of all that would be required for Katherine's wedding. Katherine was twittering on and on about her preferences for colors and flower decorations. Olympia drank some tea, waiting to speak with Matteo. After two hours of the women's discussion about which seamstress they would hire to make the dress and where Katherine wanted to hold the wedding, Lord Wolfson entered the room.

"Where is Todd? Did you come to an agreement about my dowery?" said Katherine.

"No, I asked him to return in two days," said Lord Wolfson.

"Why? We waited months to have you back to arrange my dowery. Father wanted you to deal with that part of the arrangement," said Katherine.

"I need to find out who this Lord Verdi is. I do not know that man. For all we know, he could be a mercenary."

"Really, brother! You see shadows in every corner. Lord Teddy has businesses all over Palermo. He showed me his business seal, and I met his best friend, Mage Paecci. He assured me Lord Teddy had many holdings," said Katherine.

When Olympia heard Todd's friend's name, she almost choked with her tea. They all looked at her, and she took a napkin to her mouth.

"I am sorry." Olympia took a napkin and cleaned her mouth. "I must retire. You all have a good night," said Olympia. She stood up, leaving the parlor in haste. She rushed up to her room. Olympia removed her dress and changed into her nightdress and robe. Lord Wolfson had said to go to his room later that night. She wanted to talk to him that same night. It could not wait. So, she left her room and went inside Lord Wolfson's room. She sat on a chair, and after an hour of waiting, the door opened.

"You seemed distressed earlier. What is wrong?" asked Matteo. He entered, closed the door behind him, and took off his coat.

"It is vital for you to listen to me," said Olympia.

"You seem nervous. Calm down and tell me what's on your mind."

"That man, Teddy, is my ex-husband's best friend. He is the one who gave me the adulterated drink and later took advantage of me. His name is Todd Verdi and he is not a Lord. He lied to my husband, saying that we were having an affair when I never even had a conversation with him outside of general greetings. Later, when I was an Exotic, I discovered Todd was married in Alhambra. One of my clients who did business with him told me his pregnant wife ran away from him. I don't know what happened to his wife. You must believe me. Todd is not a man to be trusted," said Olympia.

"Lord Verdi told me and my father that you and he were lovers and that his friend found you two together. He said he tried to stop his friend from making you an Exotic, but his friend would not listen, which is why you ended up as an Exotic," said Lord Wolfson.

"He lies; I was never his lover. Todd is a wicked man. Matteo, please don't dismiss my words. The friend Katherine is talking about is Vincent Paecci Takatsu, my ex-husband. I don't want any other woman to end up as an Exotic like me because of sniveling rats like Vincent and Todd. They are evil men. You must believe me," pleaded Olympia.

"I love my sister, and I am not going to let her marry a man I don't know. Father told me he had our man of business investigating the business dealings of Lord Teddy Verdi. Today, I sent a message to a friend I have in Palermo. He is the head of the Commerce Commission of the kingdom. If Lord Verdi has any businesses, they will be registered. I will hear from Lord Hardon in a day or two, so for now, just rest. I will not make any harsh decisions." He took Olympia's hand and kissed it.

"I have something else entirely, that I need to bring to your attention," said Olympia.

"Tell me," Lord Wolfson said, still holding Olympia's hand.

"Your servants sleep in rooms that have no heat. They are loyal to you and your family. They need to have a good night's sleep," said Olympia.

"I didn't know that. How do you know?"

"I know because the first night I was here, I slept in a freezing room with only three blankets."

"That is unacceptable. I'll talk to my father. That is a large undertaking to add heat to all those rooms, but it will get done," said Lord Wolfson, kissing Olympia.

"May I stay here with you tonight?" asked Olympia. And Lord Wolfson nodded. He kissed her again and held her in his arms.

"I missed you in my bed," said Lord Wolfson.

"Why didn't you come and get me? You know where I sleep," Olympia said, her voice a little muffled against his chest.

"I wanted to give you time to get used to living here," he said. Olympia looked up, then slowly unbuttoned his shirt and kissed him as she exposed his chest. He looked at her and caressed her arms. Little by little, she removed his shirt. She kissed his lips with soft kisses.

"I want you tonight. Do you mind having sex with a woman like me?" asked Olympia.

"What do you mean, a woman like you?" asked Matteo, holding Olympia by her arms.

"You know, large with child. My body is no longer perfect," said Olympia.

"Ha, ha, ha, ha, what are you talking about? Your body is perfect. I slept with my wife many times when she was expecting my boys. It was a joy for me to see her round belly." He held Olympia and untied the knot that held her robe together.

"But this child may not be yours," said Olympia.

"Nope, I had you first and several times. We Wolfson's are fertile. This little girl is mine; besides, she is a water-mage just like her daddy," he said, kissing each breast while removing her robe.

"The best part of a pregnant woman is that her breasts get bigger with every pregnancy," said Lord Wolfson with a chuckle.

"You love a big-breasted woman, huh!" Olympia smiled as he touched her.

"No, I love the woman I have with me." He kissed her. He took off his pants, and they both climbed onto his bed.

CHAPTER 19

The Love Chase

After they loved each other, Olympia fell asleep in Matteo's arms. He kept her warm all night. In the middle of the night, they woke and loved each other some more. Olympia stayed awake after that, watching Matteo sleep. Being next to him made her feel safe. In the morning, her ache for sex was gone. She got up and walked back to her room. Once in her room, she locked her door, climbed into bed, and returned to sleep. Lately, she needed more sleep than usual. Olympia still had some nausea, but it was not too terrible.

A knock at her door made Olympia lift her head off her pillow.

"I locked the door," she said out loud. She got out of bed, put on a robe, and opened the door. It was Edith with her morning tea.

"Edith, I need to bathe before I start my day," said Olympia. Edith helped her prepare and get ready for the day. Her mind was on the lessons she had for the boys that morning and the chores she had in the stables afterward. So, she dressed in pants and a short coat and walked down to the breakfast parlor, where Lady Agatha and Matteo sat having their meal.

"Good morning." Olympia said when she entered. Matteo stood up and showed her to a chair.

"Good morning. Come sit down and break your fast. We have a new mare I want you to ride this afternoon," he said.

"Good morning, Miss Olympia. Did you sleep well?" asked Lady Agatha.

"Yes, I did. How about you?"

"As well as could be expected at my age," said the older woman. The servants served Olympia a portion of fruit, porridge, and bread, with coffee. She ate everything before her. Her appetite had returned. After she finished eating, Olympia looked up and the manifestation of evil walked into the parlor. Todd Verdi, the man that raped her. She felt like someone had slapped her. He was supposed to have left the night before. She almost fainted.

“Good morning to all,” said Todd.

“I thought you had left last night,” said Lord Wolfson.

“I asked him to stay. We have a lot to decide about the wedding. It will be ideal for him to stay here rather than having him make so many trips from the city,” said Lady Agatha. Katherine entered the room; she became jubilant when she saw Todd.

“Will you excuse me.” Olympia said hurrying to stand up.

“Oh, my dear Olympia, would you give us a show later with your singing and dancing abilities? I used to pay good coin to see her sing and do her Exotic dancing,” said Todd.

“She will do no such thing. Olympia, let’s go. We will talk later.” Lord Wolfson stood up and waited for Olympia to join him.

“I meant no disrespect. Olympia is the best singer and dancer in the entire capital of Nolia. People travel for many miles just to see her perform,” said Todd.

“I must go about my day. Excuse me, Lady Agatha.” Olympia got up and left the room.

“I am right behind you,” said Lord Wolfson.

Olympia wanted to scream. As she passed by a mirror, her reflection gave her pause. Her face had turned red and her ears rang so loud she could no longer hear anything around her. That only happened when she was so furious she was about to lash out or when she was about to faint. Knowing that Todd would be in the house for two days, she resolved to work in the stables, then hurry back to her room for the rest of each day.

Olympia did not want to have any encounters with Todd, neither alone nor accompanied. She had just about reached her limits. As Olympia was walking down to the stables, Matteo caught up with her.

"Olympia, wait," he said.

"I'm aware that man infuriates you, and I've already told him to stay away from you. After your lessons with the boys, I'll remain with you all afternoon. Forget about him. The children are waiting for you. And later, I'll be waiting for you and the boys so I can show you the new mare."

"What is her name?"

"Her name is Lily of the Valley," said Lord Wolfson.

"You named the mare after a flower?" asked Olympia with a smile.

"You need to see her. This horse is as beautiful as a Lily," he said. Olympia smiled, and she left for the children's classroom.

Olympia taught the children all morning, and they appeared happy with their new teacher. After the midday meal, all four of them went down to the stables together—they all wanted to meet Lily of the Valley. Olympia surreptitiously taught the children some science without them even realizing, while they were in the stables. Olsen taught the children their magic lessons while Matteo spent the afternoon with Olympia training Arrow. Once their chores were done, all five of them went up to the castle. Olympia went to her room and took a nap.

Olympia would have preferred to have dinner in her room, but the family was expecting her for dinner. Edith came to arrange her hair, after she put on a gray and peach dress. Olympia had placed her ruby necklace in Matteo's safe box, in his room. So that night, she didn't have any jewelry on, nor did she wear much makeup. Olympia left her room, but as she walked down the stairs, Todd cornered her.

"I don't know what you have told the old man and Lord Wolfson, but know this: if you mess this marriage up for me, you will pay dearly. I'll make sure of that. I'll have Vincent come here, just to tell your Lord Wolfson how much of a harlot you are," said Todd, holding Olympia by the arm, none too gently.

"As before, you are lying, but Lord Wolfson will never believe your lies," said Olympia. Todd smiled wickedly, and released her arm. He descended the stairs, leaving Olympia behind trying to calm her breathing.

Olympia arrived in the parlor, where Matteo and Lord Findley were seated by the fire, having a drink. Todd was already in the room, chatting away with Lady Agatha and Katherine. The men stood up, and Olympia curtsied. Matteo went to her and offered his hand. Lady Agatha gave her a dirty look, and Katherine ignored her completely. Lord Wolfson lent in close to her and whispered in her ear.

"What is wrong?"

"Nothing is wrong." Olympia said.

It appeared that he did not believe her, because he took Olympia aside and carried on an almost whispered conversation. "I know that is not true. Your cheeks are red, and you look like you're ready to kill someone." Olympia turned her head and studied his face for a few seconds. How could he know her so well?

"Todd found me on the stairs and threatened me," whispered Olympia.

"How did he threaten you?" asked Lord Wolfson.

"He said if I mess this marriage up for him, he will have my ex-husband Vincent come here and have a talk with you," said Olympia.

"Matteo, what are you doing, whispering in a corner? We have a guest. It is poor manners to ignore our guest," said Lady Agatha.

"We'll talk later," said Lord Wolfson, and he rejoined the group.

"Where is Lady Marina?" asked Olympia.

"Mother is not feeling well. She is having her dinner in her room," said Lady Agatha.

At that moment, Mr. Andrews entered and declared that dinner was ready. They went into the dining room, and each sat in their respective seats. During dinner, Todd talked about his business endeavors. He also said he needed to return to Alhambra soon. Lord Findley said little, and Matteo kept asking business questions. Katherine kept singing Todd's praises, and Olympia wanted to leave the table. It was a farce. Soon, dinner was over, and they moved back to the parlor adjacent to the dining room.

Todd requested a private conversation with Matteo and Lord Findley, so the women stayed behind as the men moved on to the library. Olympia wanted to leave soon after, but Lady Agatha spoke before Olympia could excuse herself.

"Miss Olympia, today Lord Teddy told us he knew you from Palermo. He confessed to us that you pursued him, and he relented and had an affair with you. Lord Teddy told us your ex-husband and two witnesses found you in bed with him. He said that adultery was the reason your ex-husband divorced you," said Lady Agatha. Her eyes blazed as though she could throw daggers from them.

"This is the kind of woman Matteo brought to this house. I want her gone," said Katherine, pushing her red curls behind her back.

"His real name is Todd and he lied to you. I didn't have an affair with him. I was never unfaithful to my ex-husband," said Olympia.

"The one lying is you. How did you end up as an Exotic then?" said Katherine.

"Todd forced me, and my ex-husband found him. He lied about the affair," said Olympia.

"I don't believe you. You have the Exotic-tattoo. You are a loose woman," said Katherine. She stood up, and Olympia took a step back. Her hands shook, and she felt an oily drop of sweat sliding down her spine.

"Nothing I say will convince you. I speak the truth. Todd is not to be trusted. You should not have that man in your home," said Olympia.

"It is Lord Teddy. Stop disrespecting my fiancé. We will have him in this castle for as long as he needs to be here," said Katherine.

"You both have a good night," she said, not wishing to be berated any longer. Olympia turned and left the parlor. She ran up the stairs and locked herself in her room. Olympia didn't want to open the door, not even to Edith. After waiting for about an hour, she changed into her nightdress, put on a robe, and went to wait for Matteo in his room. She didn't have to wait long. He entered a short while later, in a bad mood.

"Olympia, it is late. You should be sleeping."

"I am afraid. If that man Todd is in the castle, I don't want to be in a room by myself," said Olympia.

"He brought convincing evidence to his story. He even knew of your birthmark on your buttocks." Matteo said. Olympia sighed. Her eyes watered, and her shoulders slumped. She could not believe it. The one man she thought might be different.

"I told you he forced me!" said Olympia. He frowned, and his lips disappeared under his mustache and beard.

"Good night!" Olympia tried to exit the room, but Matteo reached for her hand and held it.

"Olympia, wait! I know you told me what he did to you, and I believe you. But there is an emergency which requires me to leave the castle. I don't know what time I'll be back. If you are so afraid, I don't want you alone in my room or yours, so please call Edith and have her stay with you through the night and—lock the door. I don't trust that man Verdi," said Lord Wolfson. He kissed her and hugged her. Olympia smiled, and soon left the room in a hurry. She found a servant in the hallway, and asked him to go find Edith for her. Once back in her room, she locked the door.

A few minutes later, there was a knock at her door.

"Who is it?" asked Olympia.

"It's Edith, Miss Olympia." She opened the door and let the maid enter. Edith was wearing a thick robe over her bedtime attire. “Miss Olympia, do you need anything?” asked Edith.

“Yes, I am afraid. Please sleep in my room tonight. I don’t want to be alone,” said Olympia. Edith nodded. Olympia gave one of her pillows and a blanket to Edith, who went to sleep on the sofa near the fireplace.

“This is nice. I will not be cold tonight,” said Edith. Edith’s remark saddened Olympia.

“Edith, I talked to Lord Wolfson about the servants’ rooms and the lack of heat. I hope they do something about it.”

“Thank you, Miss Olympia,” said Edith. Olympia went to bed and relieved, she fell asleep almost immediately. Several hours later, Olympia woke to the sound of someone trying to open her door. Edith got up off her sofa, and both Olympia and Edith went to the door.

“Who is it? Miss Olympia is sleeping,” said Edith. No one responded, but Olympia could hear steps walking away.

ઉઉઉ

Early the following day, Olympia woke and found Edith folding her blanket. Olympia got up slowly having a dizzy spell. Edith rushed to her side, but Olympia put up a brave front. The young maid helped her mistress to dress, before leaving for the kitchen in search of her morning meal. Olympia had woken with a headache, so she remained in her room until she knew the family were likely to be down in the parlor, breaking their fast.

Walking downstairs fast, she reached the parlor without incident. Lord Findley was breaking his fast alone. He stood up with difficulty, and Olympia curtsied. She walked in and sat across from the older man. A servant came and served her some coffee, bread, and fruit.

“Good morning, my Lord,” said Olympia.

“Good morning, my dear. Did you sleep well?" asked the older man.

"I did, how about you?"

"I didn't sleep at all, thinking about this Lord Verdi issue. But now that I have you here by yourself, I have something I need to talk to you about in private," said Lord Findley.

"I think I know what's on your mind," said Olympia.

"You do! Lord Verdi told us a story about you. He gave us his version of the events that brought you to the brothel. But I have a nagging feeling he is lying to us. A few weeks before Matteo arrived here, I sent my man of business on a quest to inquire about the dealings of Lord Todd Verdi, not only in Yakuta and Palermo, but also in Alhambra. If his business is so prosperous as he claims, he must have some dealings in Alhambra," said the old man.

"That was a wise decision on your part," said Olympia.

"I have my moments." And the old man chuckled. "You need to eat. A woman with child needs plenty of food," said Lord Findley. Olympia ate her food, and the old man looked at her over the rim of his cup between sips.

"My son is smitten with you. He told me many things you said about Lord Todd, which are distressing. If my man of business corroborates what you said, we will have a lot to thank you. But if Lord Todd turns out to be a respected man, you will have much to answer to us. We don't like liars," said Lord Findley. Olympia lowered her head. Her headache moved to her neck.

"I am not a liar. I have never been. Please excuse me, I don't feel well," said Olympia. Lord Findley nodded. She got up and left the room. On her way to her room, she found Mrs. Andrews.

"Please have the children play in their room today. I don't feel well."

"Yes, Miss Olympia," said Mrs. Andrews. Once she reached her room, Olympia locked her door, and returned to bed.

Two hours later, Edith called from the outside her door. Olympia let her in.

“Miss Olympia, Lord Wolfson, and Lord Findley want you to come down to the library,” said Edith.

These men are going to send me away. Todd must have found a way to make them believe his lies. Poor Katherine, she will have a horrid life with that bastard Todd as her husband. I hope they send me to a clean brothel.

Olympia left her room and down to the library without hurrying. She had accepted her fate. What would happen to her child if they sent her to a brothel? Maybe they would send the little girl to an orphanage. The Little Bean was a mage. She would be well protected, unless she was born part-Krapens. Olympia entered the room with the worst expectations. A man dressed in gray, with a severe haircut, sat in a chair by the desk opposite Lord Findley, while Matteo was by the window.

“Olympia, this is Mr. Madden. He is my man of business. He has just arrived with information about Lord Verdi. I wanted you to be here when we received the report,” said Lord Findley. Matteo turned and faced Olympia. He smiled at her.

“We are ready. So, Mr. Madden, if you will. What did you find out?” said the old man.

“At first glance, I didn’t find much about Lord Teddy Verdi aside from a real estate business in Palermo, but after digging, I found numerous things about Mr. Verdi. First, he is not a Lord. He is the illegitimate son of a Baron from the southern part of Palermo. His real name is Todd Verdi in Palermo and known as Toro Vako in Albria. He has several aliases in Palermo, Yakuta, and Alhambra. He goes by Lord Todd Verdi, Mr. Tobias Verdino, Lord Teddy Verdi, Sir Thomas Veradi, Mr. Toro Vaka, and Lord Toro Caskel.

“I found many things associated with all the other aliases, but I’m only going to give you the information related to Mr. Todd Verdi since that is his legal name, and how that information concerns our laws here in Yakuta. To start, Mr. Todd Verdi has several business dealings in Alhambra, but according to my sources, he owes money to several banks—he is bankrupt. Mr. Todd Verdi owns three brothels in Palermo, all staffed with slaves, and they are of low reputation," said Mr. Madden.

"Is that all?" asked Lord Findley.

"Oh no, there is a lot more. We found a Mr. Todd Verdi involved in several scams involving swindling money from unsuspecting small business owners in our capital in Namina." Mr. Madden looked through his papers and found one with some pictures on it.

"Also, in the town of Talbert in Alhambra, there is a Mr. Todd Verdi, who has a warrant out for his arrest for the attempted murder of Madam Calixta Harlow Carlyle. But the most important thing, in my opinion, is that he is technically married to Mrs. Isalia Verdi. There is an additional warrant out for the arrest of Mr. Todd Verdi for the attempted murder of his pregnant wife, Mrs. Isalia Verdi. But I say technically, because the woman has disappeared. She is believed to have died in a fire in the home of Madame Carlyle, but Mrs. Verdi's body has never been recovered," said Mr. Madden.

"It sounds as though we have dodged a swindler and possibly a murderer," said Lord Findley.

"I can keep looking for more, but this was as thorough as I could make it for only having had a little over a month to search."

"How many copies of this report do you have?" asked Lord Findley.

"I have three copies," said the man of business.

"Thank you, Mr. Madden. Please, would you take a copy of this report to the local constable? Please also leave a copy of your report on my desk. We will be in contact with you," said Lord Wolfson.

"Good day, my Lord, Your Grace. If you need anything else, don't hesitate to call on me," said Mr. Madden, and he left the library.

"Olympia, you've been vindicated. This man wasn't to be trusted," said Lord Findley.

"What are you going to do now?" asked Olympia.

"Matteo, I want him out of my home today," said Lord Findley.

"I will take care of it, Father." On his way out, he placed a hand on Olympia's shoulder, kissed the top of her head, and left the library. Olympia stayed behind.

"Olympia, I owe you an apology," said the old man.

"Why?" Olympia furrowed her brow.

"I should have believed you from the start," said the old man.

"Don't worry unduly. I am used to men dismissing me. Will you excuse me?" Olympia left the library and walked out into the gardens looking for fresh air.

Olympia was sitting in the gazebo, contemplating what had just happened. Her life had changed drastically from when she lived in the brothel to what it was now, here in the castle. Although Katherine hated her, that didn't bother her much. Most of the time, women didn't like her. The only one she cared about was Matteo. He said he didn't believe she was an unfaithful woman. And now, after hearing the report from Mr. Madden, she was sure he would understand the type of man Todd really was.

She did have Lady Marina, Olsen, Flint, the children, and Edith. They made her happy. But once her child arrived, Olympia wondered how things would fare for her and the child. Maybe Lady Agatha would mistreat them both. The child might be a monster. Olympia could not live in a place where her child might be mistreated.

Initially, Lady Agatha wouldn't even allow the children near her. But after the incident with the tutor, things had changed, and now she was the instructor. Olympia had arranged for several people to come for interviews for the position of tutor, so a decision would soon be required.

Olympia felt better thinking that Todd was finally going to be put out of the house. That wretched man was the reason her life went to hell twelve years ago. Todd brought a kind of death to her life—she died when Vincent sold her to Chicho. But now, here in Wolfson Castle, her life started anew. All the years she had been in the brothel, she had people who talked to her. She even received adoration from some of her clients, but she wanted freedom and respect.

Olympia continued to contemplate her life, taking deep, cleansing breaths. She was thanking Lord Wolfson's g-d for the blessing of a house free of Todd when Lady Katherine came stomping toward where she was sitting, clearly ready for an argument.

"You stupid woman. What did you do? It had to be you," said Katherine.

"What are you talking about?" asked Olympia.

"My brother broke my engagement to Lord Teddy, and I know it was because of you," said Katherine, pointing a finger at Olympia.

"I had nothing to do with this," Olympia stood up and faced Katherine.

"It was because you had an affair with him. What happened? You wanted him back. You tried your Exotic ways, and my brother found you? He can't get rid of you, so he got rid of poor Lord Teddy," said Katherine.

"I did no such thing. Todd is a married man in Alhambra. He is bankrupt, and he is not a Lord. He lied to you all," said Olympia.

"I don't want to hear you. You are the liar," said Katherine running back to the castle.

"Katherine, wait!" Olympia went after her, but she couldn't run as fast. Katherine could not be left believing the lies Todd told her, but once Olympia reached the castle, she could not find Katherine. Her headache had not yet abated, and she wished Tony was there to take it away as he did when they traveled. She walked to the library hoping find a cooler, darker area in which to sit. She would talk to Lord Findley or Matteo later. They needed to let the young woman know what Mr. Madden had discovered.

She'd been sitting there for a while when Lady Marina entered the library, as fast as her old legs allowed her.

“The servants are never around when you need them. Olympia, you must find Matteo. I just witnessed that despicable man Teddy open the family safe, with Katherine by his side. They took several pieces of the family’s jewelry and left the house. I tried to stop her, but she said she was going to leave with Lord Teddy. Please go find Matteo. That stupid, stupid girl,” said Lady Marina.

“I’ll go get him, don’t worry,” said Olympia.

She went to the one place where she knew she could find Matteo—the stables. Olympia raced to the back of the castle, as fast as she could now move. Running was becoming hard for her. Once she reached the stables, she searched around and found Matteo out in the pasture with Grace of the Stars and her colt. She tried to run out to the far end of the pasture.

“Matteo … Matteo, I need— I need to talk to you … Katherine … Katherine … left with Todd,” Olympia said, huffing and puffing.

“What are you talking about, woman? Calm down and breathe.” Lord Wolfson held Olympia by the arms.

“I was out sitting at the gazebo when Katherine came. She was in a rage. She accused me of breaking her engagement. Katherine left, and I followed her but lost her. I went to sit in the library, thinking she would have gone to her room. An hour later, Lady Marina came to me. Your grandmother said she watched Katherine and Todd open the family safe, and extract several of the family jewels before leaving the castle. Lady Marina said the exchanged some words, but that Katherine left with Todd. You need to find her.”

Olympia related the story to Matteo, as Olsen stood by in the paddock listening. A look of comprehension appeared on his face.

“Lady Katherine was here about an hour ago. She had a large bag and ordered one of the boys to saddle her horse. Then she left in a hurry,” said Olsen.

“Olympia, please go to the castle and tell my father,” said Lord Wolfson. “Are you with me Olsen?” He and

Olsen saddled two horses, and left. Olympia returned to the castle as fast as she could go, when she came across Mrs. Andrews.

"Mrs. Andrews, I need to talk to Lord Findley. Do you know where he is?" asked Olympia.

"He is in his bedroom, taking a nap. You can talk to Lady Agatha. She is in the blue parlor."

"Thank you."

Olympia located the blue parlor; once more, arriving breathless. She found the woman was knitting. Lady Agatha looked up at her, over the top of her wire glasses.

"What is wrong?" asked Lady Agatha.

"Lady Katherine just left with Todd."

"What! That can't be. After all the information we got about him from our man of business, she should be happy he is gone," said Lady Agatha.

"She came to me and said I invented everything the man of business said. Later, Lady Marina said she witnessed Katherine and Todd taking several jewels from the safe. She told Lady Marina, she was leaving with Todd," said Olympia. Lady Agatha stood up, and her knitting fell to the ground.

"We need to tell Matteo."

"He already knows and went after her," said Olympia.

"Mr. Andrews, where are you?" Lady Agatha left the parlor calling for the butler. Olympia didn't know what else to do. So, she went to her room and tried to rest, but she could not fall asleep. She felt tired, but she couldn't calm her mind. Time passed and she heard nothing. She picked at some dinner that had been brought to her room, but she wasn't feeling well. Her child had been moving, and she had a sharp pain in her back. Olympia took a long bath and tried to read until she fell asleep.

Three days later, Matteo and Olsen had not returned to the castle. Olympia feared the worst. Todd was a despicable man. Those types of men would do anything for money. Todd also didn't have anything to lose. At this point, if he could find a Master Arcane mage without scruples, he would open a portal, and Todd could take Katherine far away. Heavens only knew what he would do to her. Olympia didn't want to see any of the members of the family. She kept thinking of Matteo. Olympia had feelings for him and wanted to believe that he loved her, but men were all alike.

CHAPTER 20

The Old Boss

Two more days had passed, and Matteo had still not returned to the castle. The family feared the worst, but Olympia worried the most perhaps because she knew what Todd was capable of doing. If Katherine made the mistake of sleeping with Todd, she would disgrace the family, and they could take her to a brothel. She hoped the Marchese of Findley would not do that to her. As much as the girl was uppity and selfish, that would destroy her.

Olympia finished reading the book Lord Wolfson had given her, about the family's history. They were an honorable family with a long history of mages, of all types, serving the King. She wanted to learn more about the family's traditions and history, so after she broke her fast she went to the library to search for more books on the subject. That morning, she was due to interview a possible tutor for the children. Olympia had arranged for the children to work on their reading, and afterward they had riding lessons. With the busy day planned out, she went to the library to look for a book on the local traditions. She found one a few minutes later, just as Lord Findley entered.

"Olympia, we have a problem, and I need to talk to you," said the old man.

Olympia turned around to face Lord Findley, then Mr. Tam Solis and the man she thought she would never, ever see again, Chicho di Roberti joined them. Two of Chicho's bodyguards entered the room behind her old boss. Olympia lost all feeling in her hands, and the book she had been holding fell to the floor.

"What is going on?" asked Olympia.

"We have here, Mr. Chicho di Roberti from Nolia, Palermo. He claims you were stolen from him. He is here to claim his property," said Mr. Solis.

"How did you know I was here?" asked Olympia.

"Your old friend Todd Verdi sent me a message letting me know of your whereabouts," said Chicho.

"I don't understand. The last time you were here, you said since the officials of Highcove branded me with the Duke of Trenton's crest, that made me his mistress forever," said Olympia.

"The problem lies in that you still have the trademark seal on your right arm. That seal wasn't erased; thus, according to Palermo's laws, that makes you the property of Mr. di Roberti for life regardless of your brand," said Mr. Solis. Chicho stood in a corner with a greedy smile.

"Olympia, you look like mierda with that dress, and you are not showing your Exotic mark. That's against the law. You know that, my little golden Exotic," said Chicho.

"I don't leave the house with this dress," said Olympia.

"Let's hurry. I want to take my property now. I have a train to catch," said Chicho.

"Wait, she is pregnant with my son's daughter. You can't take her. My son is a duke, and the child has the right to inherit according to our laws," said Lord Findley.

"I am taking her and removing the child. She is an Exotic. Her body must be perfect," said Chicho. Olympia had been standing behind a tall-backed chair. She walked out from behind the chair and stood in front of Chicho.

"You can't remove my daughter. I am six months pregnant. If you have the procedure done, I will die. The child is too big." Olympia said with nervous words.

"Maldita sea," said Chicho in Palermian.

"There has to be a way we could keep Olympia with us?" said Lord Findley.

"If the duke had married her and erased the trademark, Mr. di Roberti would not have had any claim on her."

"Did you tell him that he could marry her?" asked Lord Findley.

"I didn't have time to do it," said Mr. Solis.

"It doesn't matter. She is mine. I'll let her have the child. Once the child is born, the Duke can come and claim his child," said Chicho. Olympia's heart skipped a beat. She placed her hands on her growing belly.

"Let's go. You don't need to take anything from here. I brought some of your things with me," said Chicho.

"I must take my dresses from here. Nothing that I used to wear would fit me. Look at me," said Olympia.

"Go, have the servants pack a trunk for you," said Chicho.

"You can't take her. We have rights in Yakuta," said Lord Findley.

"He can do it. Our treaties with Palermo specify that we will uphold their laws," said Mr. Solis. Olympia's legs didn't want to move. She didn't want to go with Chicho. According to the Trade Official, she would be an Exotic for life. Olympia walked to the door and asked a servant to have Edith pack her dresses.

An awkward silence fell on the library while Olympia's trunk was being packed. That was when Lady Agatha came running. "What is happening here? Mr. Andrews said that the Trade Officials are here to take Olympia," said the lady. Lord Findley explained what had happened to his wife. Lady Agatha held Olympia's arm.

"You can't take her. She is my son's mistress. She is carrying my granddaughter," said Lady Agatha. A servant knocked on the door, informing them that Olympia's trunk had been brought down. Chicho went and grabbed Olympia by the arm, pulling her away from Lady Agatha, and virtually dragging her out the front door of the castle. Olympia struggled behind him, with her head down. She was going back into prostitution again. Chicho had two carriages waiting for them, one for him and one for his bodyguards.

The rest happened as in a dream, or perhaps best described as a nightmare. One of Chicho's bodyguards took Olympia by the arm, and forced her to climb into the carriage with them. The horses pulled out of the castle grounds. Olympia looked out the window and saw the three children running out of the castle. Little Axel ran after them with his little hands pointing at the carriage. He sent fire streaming from his hands.

"Let her go," shouted Axel.

His brother Ivan also held up his hands, just as Olympia felt the carriage jolt left and right, and it jumped as if they hit a pothole on the ground.

She sat back. She didn't want to see the boys. She couldn't even say goodbye to them. Olympia sighed, and the men sitting on either side of started sliding their hands up her legs. She shoved their hands away.

"I am an expensive Exotic. If you want to touch me, you must pay," said Olympia. She stood up and sat on the seat across from the men. Her eyes watered as the carriage made its way across the island. They traveled down the mountain, along the main road where they passed the bakery Lady Marina had taken her for chocolates, and the seamstress's store where her dresses had been made. The city was decorated for the winter festival, but then she remembered the pocket watch she had commissioned for Matteo. She had wanted to give it to him during the festivities.

They traveled beyond the town and over the causeway back to the mainland and to the nearest town of Clearsky. They reached the town late that afternoon where there was a train station. Chicho had purchased tickets for a compartment, one for him and one reserved for Olympia. It was the last train leaving the town. Once she entered the compartment, she found a trunk with her old dresses, shoes, lotions, oils, makeup, and creams. None of her old dresses fit her, but she could use the rest.

They train was a fast one, taking only two weeks to reach Nolia. Chicho didn't talk to her the entire trip. The wretched man entertained himself with a very young courtesan. He preferred young little girls. Olympia's pregnant body moved slowly, and she had an idea of what would happen to her now she was in Chicho's clutches.

The train pulled into Nolia station early in the morning. When Olympia stepped off the train, the stench of urine and filth hit her. Nausea made her want to vomit, but she managed to avoid doing so. The group walked briskly, evading people, carts, luggage, and many other things along the way. They rented carriages, and she traveled with the bodyguards again.

Upon reaching the brothel, Olympia looked at the building she had called home for twelve years. It was as she remembered, but now it seemed horrid to her. The white walls were an ironic contrast to all the socially accepted but morally depraved activities done behind the walls. Olympia didn't want to think of the little girls being used for Chicho's pleasure. The carriage door opened, and if one of Chicho's men had not been holding her, she would have run away. They entered through the solid mahogany doors, after which Chicho ignored her. He walked to his office, but her old slave master received her.

"Olympia, what happened to you? You look like a cow," said Nancy, the redheaded woman with a dozen bangles on her left wrist.

"I am almost seven months pregnant. That's what happened to me," said Olympia.

"What? No, no, no, no, no, Chicho didn't say you were ruined. It is too late; we can't get rid of that parasite now. You can't entertain most of your regular clients looking like this," said Nancy.

"I am tired. I've been on a train for two weeks. I wonder how Chicho got to Yakuta so fast?"

"He told me he was going to pay Arcane Mages to open portals for him. Chicho wanted you back badly," said Nancy.

"I hate that man. Be a dear and walk with me to my room. I need a bath and a bed," said Olympia.

"I'll send a maid with some food. I honestly don't know what I can do with you looking as you do now," said the woman, accompanying Olympia to her room.

“Maybe I can teach the prospective Exotic girls, or sing in one of the plays. I can converse or be a companion.” Olympia said, walking with her head held high.

“There are always those men that like to sleep with pregnant women. We could never provide that service before. But with you here, now we can,” said Nancy. Olympia’s heart sank. She didn’t want to share her body with anyone. She had grown accustomed to only being with Matteo.

They reached her bedroom, and it was as she left it, nice and cold. It was a medium-sized room with a fireplace and a private bathroom. She had a comfortable bed and a wardrobe of clothes that would not fit in her current condition. The small sofa in front of her fireplace, a vanity, chair, and a corner table were in the exact places she left them.

She hadn’t missed her brothel bedroom while living at Wolfson Castle. There in the castle she had felt safe. A man had walked behind them with her trunk. He placed the trunk by her bed, and left.

“I think I know who you could service. I am going to contact him, he might want you. You might have your first client in two or three days, depending on the client. If he wants you, you may end up with a regular client. Try to rest.” Nancy left the room, closing the door behind her.

Olympia undressed. She took out one of her chemises from her trunk and went to her bathroom. Olympia took a quick bath, changed into her chemise, and went to bed. Her child had been moving a lot. She hoped her little girl would look like Matteo.

ଔଔଔ

The next day, Olympia woke early. As her eyes adjusted to the light, her nightmare came back to her. She cried. She was back in Il Palazzo di Roberti. She got up and went to her bathroom. She dressed and combed her wavy black hair.

A few minutes later, a young woman entered the room with her morning meal. She left her room in equal silence. She missed Edith and her cheerful chatter. As the day passed, a team of hairdressers, beauty assistants, and a masseuse came to her room. Two women tried to give her a massage, but they did not know how to deal with her growing belly. Afterward, the hairdresser fixed her hair, and a seamstress came to measure her for new dresses. Other women came and removed all her body hair, then another gave her a facial. The last to arrive was a healer. She assessed her child and confirmed the child could not be removed without taking Olympia's life.

Chicho didn't let her out of her room for two days until the day Olympia had to work. Olympia had to wear a red, shear robe with nothing else under it. The client she was to entertain wanted to bed a pregnant Exotic. Her expression didn't change throughout the day. Her mind was in Wolfson Castle with Lord Wolfson and his family. She even missed Lady Agatha.

"I wonder if they found Katherine," whispered Olympia while she waited in Lord Armand's favorite room. Her client was supposed to arrive by 8:00 that night. It was already thirty minutes past the hour, and Olympia wanted to go to sleep. Pregnancy made her need to sleep more than usual. She yawned and stood looking out the window. The busy street contrasted wildly with the streets of Kalbaka. She sat on the sofa by the fireplace when the door opened.

"Lord Armand, it is lovely to see you. How are you?" Olympia curtsied.

"Oh, my, my, my, my, my, what a beautiful sight. You look stunning," said Lord Armand.

"Thank you, but how can you say that? My body is not perfect as you are accustomed to seeing me," said Olympia.

"I love to gaze upon women's pregnant bodies. Come, let me see you under a better light," said Lord Armand. Olympia walked as slowly as she could. He took her hand and slid her sheer robe off to the side of her body, exposing one breast and her belly. Olympia closed her eyes and took a deep breath.

Lord Armand touched her, down her breast, from her face to her neck. He squeezed her breast tight, and Olympia stood still. In Chicho's brothel, they trained her to experience pain. He moved his hands to the roundness of her belly touching every inch of it, but when he pressed and poked her belly hard, Olympia pushed him away from her with so much strength he stumbled.

"Don't touch me. You are hurting my child." Olympia said, covering her body with her robe. Her daughter kicked. She felt the need to run out of the room.

"What is wrong with you? I paid good money for tonight. Come here right now!" said Lord Armand.

"NO! You will not hurt my child. She is the daughter of the Duke of Trenton from the Kingdom of Yakuta, and you will not do anything that will hurt her," said Olympia.

"What are you talking about? The Duke of Trenton is dead and left no heir."

"The King of Yakuta named the old Duke of Trenton's nephew, the Earl of Wolfson, the new Duke. The Earl of Wolfson marked me as his mistress. Take a look at my left arm," said Olympia. Lord Armand took Olympia's left arm.

"You should not be here. I know the Earl of Wolfson. He is a good man. Why are you here?" asked Lord Armand.

"Chicho has a hold on me because of the trademark symbol on my wrist. I was living in Yakuta with Lord Wolfson when Chicho came and got me," said Olympia.

"Oh darling, come and sit down. I don't touch the women of other nobles. I may have my kinks, but I have my limits. But tell me, I need to know how you became Lord Wolfson's mistress and how he got you with child. I have never seen a pregnant Exotic," said Lord Armand. Olympia sat on the sofa, and Lord Armand sat beside her.

"It's a long story," said Olympia.

"I have plenty of time to hear it. I paid for an hour of your time, and you know Chicho's policy. No refunds!" said Armand, and he chuckled.

Olympia told Lord Armand how she came to be Lord Wolfson's mistress. She did leave out the encounter with the Krapens. Lord Armand asked a few questions, and Olympia answered.

"That is an incredible story."

"It is all true. Would you like something to drink?" asked Olympia.

"No, thank you. My hour is done. I wish you the best. You are beautiful, my dear." Lord Armand took Olympia's hand, and he kissed it.

"Have a good night, my darling girl." Lord Armand left the room, throwing his coat over his shoulder. Olympia took a deep breath. She had dodged having to have sex with him, but she knew it was only a matter of time before one of the aggressive clients would buy her time.

ઙઙઙ

An hour after Lord Armand left, Olympia waited for her second client. Nancy had said they were two gentlemen who wanted to have her at the same time. Olympia decided she was going to fight. She didn't care what Chicho would do to her. She wasn't going to let anyone treat her like an Exotic anymore. Lord Wolfson had taken her out of the trade so she would never sexually entertain anyone again. She had her daughter to think about. When the men entered the room, Olympia looked at both of them. She knew she had to use whatever fighting skills Matteo and Olsen had taught her. Olympia didn't smile or welcome them. She had never seen the men in her life. They were new clients.

"Oh, Clive, look at her. She is perfect," said one of the men.

"Come to me, my little Exotic. We paid a substantial sum of gold for you," said Clive.

"What would you like me to do? I can sing for you and dance, but that will be it," said Olympia.

"You must be crazy. I want your ass," said Clive.

"And I want your mouth," said the other man.

"I will do no such thing. I am pregnant, and doing any of those services will hurt my child," said Olympia.

"That is mierda. My wife did it for me all the time when she was pregnant," said Clive.

"I don't know if you have any diseases. I do not want them," said Olympia. The men laughed, and Clive came and tried to hold Olympia by the arm. She pulled him closer and kneed him as hard as she could in his groin.

"You little bitch, you are going to pay," said the other man, and he came at her, but Olympia lifted a chair and struck him with it. He fell to the floor, and Olympia left the room running. Nancy came out of the door next to the room.

"ARE YOU OUT OF YOUR EVER LIVING MIND?" shouted Nancy.

"I will not have sex with anyone. I already told Chicho. I will entertain by singing, dancing, or talking, and that will be it until my daughter is born," said Olympia. She stormed back to her room.

ঙঙঙ

Upon returning to her room, all she wanted was her bed. Her legs and arms hurt. She had kicked the man with all her might with the tip of her foot, and it landed well between his legs, hard. She wondered if hitting the second man with a chair had hurt her daughter. The man who brought a friend deserved what she did to him after what he said to her. She had entertained two men at the same time before, but she would not do it anymore.

"Chicho is going to have to kill me."

Olympia felt defiled, though nothing had actually happened that first night. She went to her bathroom and bathed quickly. It was well past midnight, and her body hurt all over. If she had to do this every night for the next three nights before her next free night, Olympia would definitely end up losing her child. But no, she would be smarter. She had to talk to Chicho. He had to understand her child was the daughter of a duke. She lay on her bed, and soon fell asleep happy with herself. But moments later, her door was slammed open.

"Olympia Takatsu, are you crazy? You almost castrated one of my clients. Mr. Glass and Mr. Hens said they were going to sue me. What do you have to say for yourself?" said Chicho. He walked in dressed in a three-piece suit, smelling like an expensive cigar.

Olympia shot out of bed, and almost fell down again, but stood her ground. "I told you. The only thing I would do is teach, sing, or be a companion. I will not let any harm come to my daughter."

"You will do everything I tell you to do," said Chicho.

"No, I will not have sex with anyone. Not until I have my daughter," said Olympia.

"You will do what I say, or you will not have any food. NANCY, where are you?" Chicho's face was about to burst.

"I am here." Nancy came running into the room.

"Do not bring any food or water to Olympia until she reconsiders her new policy about entertaining her clients," said Chicho.

"But she is pregnant," said Nancy.

"Then let her starve. That way, we can get rid of the parasite." Chicho left the room, taking with him the tobacco aroma.

"Now, look at what you have done. You did more harm than good to your child," said Nancy.

"If I die, I die, but I will not have sex with anyone. Please, Nancy, don't set me up with anyone who wants to lie with me," begged Olympia. Nancy said nothing, and she left the room.

Olympia was well aware of what Nancy was doing. For the following three days, she set her up with men who wanted to hear her sing or with women who wished to have dinner with Olympia and converse with them. Olympia knew Chicho had lost a lot of coin because of her, but she didn't care.

As Chicho ordered, they didn't even bring her water, but she drank from the bathroom faucet. For the first two days, she could not stand the pains in her stomach, but on the second night, Nancy scheduled a client who wanted Olympia to have dinner with her. She ate to satiation and took some bread and pastries to her room, hidden in her robe pockets.

The next morning, Olympia woke late. After taking a bath, she walked into her room and checked her robe pockets. She still had the food from the night before. Olympia ate it and sat on her sofa. She didn't want to think how things could get worse, because then it would. She cried while looking out her window. Freedom was something she had had with Matteo, and Chicho had taken away. Her heart hurt. She wanted to be back in Matteo's arms. She wanted to be back teaching the children.

She stood, walked to her bathroom, but then she saw a razor blade on the floor under the corner of her vanity. The woman who had removed her body hair the day before must have dropped it. She took it. Contemplating her options, she looked at her wrists. The left one had Matteo's crest and name burned into her skin, but even those marks did not help her avoid the brothel. But then her daughter made herself known. She kicked her mother so hard under her side it made Olympia drop the blade to the floor.

What am I going to do? I can't carry on like this. Olympia got back in bed, crying some more and rubbing her fast-growing belly. She sat and did what she had never done in her life.

"Oh, g-d of Matteo. He said you would listen if I talked to you with an open heart. He serves you faithfully. It is possible that I am carrying his daughter. Could you please help me keep his daughter safe? I can't do this alone. I can’t live like an Exotic anymore. Help me escape. One way or another, I must leave this place. I need your help.” Olympia prayed for the first time ever. She lay on her bed and, repeating the names of all of Matteo’s horses, she fell asleep.

CHAPTER 21

Kidnapped

That night, she had only one client, and he paid for two hours of her time. Olympia dreaded what the new client wanted her to do in those two hours. Her nerves made her vomit twice, but she had nothing in her stomach. Nancy sneaked a calming tea in her room. Olympia wanted to run. Chicho kept her isolated. Only Nancy and one maid who came to help her dress had access to her. She got dressed in a long red dress with a black sleeved overgarment.

It had embroidered dragons, in gold and silver thread, on both sides of the dress. There was also an intricate wave design, also embroidered with gold and silver threads, on white strips that edged the sleeves of the garment and along the opening of the dress. The black collar of her dress fell a little down her back.

The dress had four tiny golden buttons, and a satin belt that kept the dress in place over a white under garment that was also made of satin and lace. The total ensemble accentuated Olympia's pregnancy-enlarged breasts. The hairdresser had arranged her hair in a series of buns and flairs. She had heightened the design with a black and red kanzashi with white flowers. The final touch of the hair ornament made Olympia want to cry. In the past, she had been proud to wear clothing that represented Albria, but now she didn't want to dress for strangers.

She picked up her fan and took her time walking to the room where she was to work that night. Once inside the room, she went to sit on a chair by the window. She waited about ten minutes, when the door opened and servants entered to set up a table for dinner. At least she was to have dinner with her client. Olympia waited for another half hour before the door opened again. Hope sprung in her heart as she saw who the guest was.

"What are you doing here? You can't possibly be my client for the night," said Olympia.

"Hello, Miss Olympia, I am here to …" Olympia stopped Olsen from talking. She went to a small table by a wall, took a piece of paper, ink, and a pen, and wrote a note.

We must be careful what we say. I am being listened to and watched. I'll talk in your native Catalagac. The person who is listening doesn't understand your language fully. Please do not mention Lord Wolfson's name."

She let Olsen read the note. He nodded, then hid the note in the inside pocket of his coat.

"It is good to see you, m'lady. My master paid for my time here with you. I have much to tell you," said Olsen in Catalagac.

"Oh, I'm so glad you are here, but come sit down and have dinner. I haven't eaten anything in many hours." Olympia took his hand and brought it to her chest. They sat at the dinner table beside the bed. Olympia called the servants to bring dinner to the room. Once the food was served, the servants left.

"I hope you don't mind if I eat while we talk. I am famished," said Olympia.

"Please eat, m'lady," said Olsen. Olympia ate her food with as much delicacy as she could muster.

"What happened after the brothel owner took me from the castle? Did your master find his sister?"

"We found Lady Katherine four days after we left. Like we thought, she had run away with that piece of human excrement, Todd. He had convinced her to give him the family jewels," said Olsen.

"Where did you find them?" asked Olympia.

"They were in the town of Polar. By the time we found her, he had ruined her and was trying to sell the family jewels. He is alive because the young lady would not step aside when we found them," said Olsen.

“That is horrible. What happened to Todd? What happened to the young lady?” asked Olympia.

“We found them staying at a local inn. My master accused him of stealing the family jewels. So, we took the constable with us, and he arrested Todd. We found him with some of the family jewels. He had sold a few of them. Lady Katherine tried to get him out of jail by saying she took the jewelry, but my master contested that as Lady Marina had seen Todd opening the safe. He also told the constable that Lady Katherine didn’t know the combination of the safe and she didn’t have the skills to open the box.

“I can’t believe Katherine would do such a thing.”

“After Todd was in custody, my master took her home. He showed her the full report from Mr. Madden. She left the room crying. I don’t know what happened to her after that,” said Olsen.

“I am happy she is safe,” said Olympia.

“By the time we arrived back, you were gone. Your weasel of a boss had already taken you three days before we returned to the castle. My master lost it. He gave chase the very same day. When I heard what happened, I volunteered to accompany him. Flint went into a rage, the likes of which I’ve never seen, and packed his bags. He is here with us as well. We arrived this morning on the first train. How are you feeling? How’s the little one?” asked Olsen.

“She is fine, but I need to escape. I can’t do this for much longer. I’m being starved when not dining with a client, in punishment for not allowing myself to be physically abused,” said Olympia. Her eyes watered as she talked to Olsen. She had eaten a good portion of her meal but still felt hungry.

“We went to the Trade Office as soon as we arrived in town. My master has been trying to negotiate with the Trade Officials, but the laws here are stringent regarding slaves and trademarks. We purchased two hours of your time tonight because there is much to discuss. We have an idea of how to get you out,” said Olsen.

“What is he trying to negotiate? I am the property of Chi… the brothel owner. Lord Findley tried to step in and point out that his son had given me his ducal crest, when he went to get me. He stressed the point that I was the mistress in the house, but the officials said that the trademark supersedes the crest,” said Olympia.

“My master’s father told us what happened and what your boss said about the child. My master is trying to get you out on account of the child. He will not let anything happen to you or the little one,” said Olsen.

“I don’t know what he can do for me,” said Olympia.

“We found a way we can get you out of your trade, but first we need to get you out of the brothel,” said Olsen.

“That will not be possible. The brothel owner does not even let me out of my room, other than to practice my trade on this side of the brothel. Once finished, I return to my room—no food or water, except what I drink from the bathroom faucet.” Olympia said, then she took several bites of her food.

“Why? You would think he would want to keep his Exotics healthy.”

“It’s because I refuse to provide sexual services. Anyway, how does your master think he can free me from the trade? Mr. Solis told me Exotics are the one class of prostitution that are bound forever,” said Olympia.

“Don’t worry about that. We will explain everything later. Now, I need you to make a detailed drawing of the brothel—both business and private sides of the house. I need to know exactly where your room is in this building.”

“Why?”

“I can’t tell you why, but trust me. Please, make the drawing. We don’t have much time left.”

Olympia went to a side table, took another fresh piece of paper and returned to the dinner table. She drew a picture of the brothel, making sure to add as much detail as she could remember.

"I am trying to give you as much detail as I can, but I don't understand what this picture will do for you," said Olympia.

"What time are you returning to your room tonight?" asked Olsen.

"You are my only client tonight. After I'm finish with you, I'll be returning to my room. I will stay locked in my room alone until a maid comes to help me get dressed, around six o'clock tomorrow afternoon. Since they are not feeding me, no one visits me during the day. How will you get me out?" asked Olympia.

"You shouldn't worry about that," said Olsen. He took the picture of the brothel, folded it, and put it in his coat pocket.

"I think my two hours are up. M'lady do not fret, you will be out of this place soon." Olsen took Olympia's hand, kissed it, turned, and left. After Olsen left the room, Olympia opened the door, and Nancy stepped out of the small room next to it.

"What happened in there? I could barely understand what he said. He spoke so softly, almost like a murmur," said Nancy.

"He just wanted to talk about his history and the war of Alhambra. I had little to say aside from agreeing or asking a question or passing a little comment," said Olympia.

"He seemed happy," said Nancy as they returned to Olympia's room.

"That is good. At least the client will not be asking for his coin back. Not that Chicho would give him any," said Olympia.

Life was good; she was happier than she had been in a long time. Her Matteo had come for her. He had talked to the Trade Officials. What would that do? Maybe he found a hidden law. Olympia didn't know what Matteo could do, but knowing he was in town gave her hope.

It was two hours till midnight when Olympia was getting ready for bed. She had removed her shoes and had laid her night shift over her bed. Olympia sat on her favorite chair by her table, writing in her diary. She had left her diary when she departed for Prince Wallen's castle. She was jotting down the final notes when she felt a kick on one side of her body and then another on the other side.

"You need to calm down, Little Bean. It's nighttime." Olympia said to her baby. The dark room was lit only by a lantern on her table and the fire in her fireplace. She was almost done when a spark of light appeared over her sofa. It made her jump up and run away, to stand near her bedside. Then she watched as the spark grew into a suspended ball of light. It was made of lightning, and it continued to grow and grow. She rushed to push the sofa out of the way, not wanting it to burn. She didn't want to die in a fire. She looked around for an escape, but then realized she could see inside the ring. She could see a room through the ring, and from the middle of the ring, Lord Wolfson's foot appeared as though taking a step. He reached out to her.

"Take my hand; I am getting you out of here. Let's go," said Lord Wolfson. Olympia smiled. She grabbed her diary, put on her shoes, and waddled as fast as she could to Lord Wolfson. She took his hand, and they stepped back through the portal made of lightning. When they reached the other side, the ring closed.

"I must be dreaming," said Olympia.

"No, you are not dreaming," said Lord Wolfson, then he hugged and kissed her.

"How did you create a portal? I know you are not an Arcane Mage," said Olympia. Her legs were shaky, so she sat on the sofa before she fell.

"No, but I am," said Flint, sitting on a chair, wheezing.

"You must remember to breath when you use your magic Flint. Anyway, We must leave Nolia as soon as possible," said Olsen.

"Wait a minute, it is cold outside. I am not dressed for the cold weather. Where are we?" asked Olympia.

“We are at my friend’s town house, Lord Jake Hardon. He is letting me use his Nolian home while holidaying with his family on the Alegria coast. They just left this morning when we arrived, and they won’t be returning until the week’s end. I brought you a pair of breeches made for a portly man. Since no one is due to visit your room until late tomorrow afternoon, we will have time to run. We will leave at dawn tomorrow, travel by carriage out of the capital, head to the nearest town with a train station outside of Nolia, and head east to Yakuta,” said Lord Wolfson.

“We have a problem. I can’t enter any city or town with a Trade Office. I would have to show myself and register. All will be over when they see my Exotic-tattoo. I would have to stay in a brothel,” said Olympia.

“We *are* making a stop, but it will be fine. We must reach the town of Cilisa,” said Lord Wolfson.

“That is a Morai town. Why are we—”

“You two should talk by yourselves. We’ll give you some privacy. Let’s go, Flint,” said Olsen. Flint rose so slowly that Olympia thought he would fall at any moment. Olsen helped Flint stand up, and they left the living room. Olympia stood alone with Matteo. He was as handsome as the first day she had met him. He sat down next to her.

“Olympia, listen. I don’t know how to do this, but here goes. Will you marry me?” asked Lord Wolfson.

“What did you just ask me? You want to marry me?” Olympia’s surprise left her speechless.

“When I returned from searching for Kathrine to find you were not home, I went mad. Father told me your old owner had come and taken you. You are my Olympia. I didn’t know how to get you back. The first thing I did was go to the Trade Office to talk to Mr. Solis. He said the only way to get you back and out of the trade was to marry you. I want you back. I fell in love with you along our travels. My children adore you. Please marry me. I need you forever. Will you be my duchess?” Lord Wolfson had a bracelet and a matching necklace in his hands.

“I, I don’t know what to say,” said Olympia.

"Say yes, I want you to never worry about Chicho coming after you," said Lord Wolfson.

"But how are you going to marry me? I have the trademark on my wrist. No Trade Official will remove that tattoo from my arm, and no one will marry us. I am an Exotic at the service of Chicho," said Olympia.

"I have it all planned out. I am going to take you to a Morai village. We are going to get married by a Benanti priest, and afterward I will have you registered in the Morai village Trade Office. Mr. Solis said Prince Otto Hightower from Yakuta married an Exotic in Tsestelago. Before coming here, I asked how he did it. Mr. Solis said that the Exotic had a twelve-year-old daughter with him; he claimed her as his and thus was able to marry the Exotic. So, I will do the same," said Lord Wolfson.

"You thought of almost everything. But I'll still have the trademark-tattoo. That still binds me to Chicho," said Olympia.

"I've thought about that already. Flint, come here," said Lord Wolfson. Flint entered the room. The old man still looked pale, but he held himself upright.

"It is time. Are you ready?" asked Lord Wolfson.

"Yes, m'Lord, I feel a little better, but I can only do this once. I'm only a level five Arcane Mage," said Flint.

"It will be fine," said Olsen. Flint took a chair and sat in front of Olympia.

"M'lady, please show me yer right wrist," said Flint.

"What are you going to do?" asked Olympia.

"Don't you worry, little lassy; it'll not hurt at all," said Flint. Olympia gave the old man her right arm. Flint took her wrist in his beefy hands, closed his eyes, and his lips moved. Olympia tried to listen to Flint, but she could not hear what he was saying.

"What is he doing?" asked Olympia.

"Don't worry about it; just relax and watch," said Lord Wolfson, still sitting next to her. As Flint mumbled, a faint orange light surrounded his hands, and hovered over

Olympia's wrist for a minute, then two, three minutes, four, and nothing happened. Five minutes passed, and her wrist stayed the same. Perspiration covered Flint's forehead, his hands shook, but the light remained stable over Olympia's wrist.

Flint trembled as time passed, but he did not let her wrist go nor let the light diminish, and the incantations he made continued to be whispered. After about an hour, the trademark-tattoo started to fade. The tattoo ink became lighter and lighter, but the union of the trademark with the rest of the tattoos became an open gap. Two hours of intense magic casting passed and the tattoo was gone entirely, but Flint fell to the ground.

"Flint," said Olympia. She tried to catch him, but the boulder of a man was too much for her. Olsen stepped in and helped Flint to his feet.

The gap between the skills made her a little nervous. What would that mean? Should they insert something in the gap? She didn't know.

"What did you do? I mean I am happy I don't have the trademark-tattoo, but now there is a gap between my set of skills," said Olympia.

"We will fix that when we reach the Morai village," said Lord Wolfson.

"I don't understand." Olympia kept looking at her wrist.

"Olympia, I need to know. Will you marry me?" asked Lord Wolfson again.

"What will you do if my child is born a Krapens, and she has gray skin? Will you get rid of us? Will you send me back to be an Exotic? Because if you are going to do that, then what will be the point of me marrying you?" asked Olympia.

"I don't care if the child is born gray, green, or orange. She is my little girl. She will be Lady Emma Wolfson. I already have a name for her," said Matteo.

"How can you accept her? I don't understand you," said Olympia.

“Sit down with me,” he said. Olympia sat back down next to Matteo. “Let me tell you a story. In my family, I have three siblings, but what you don’t know is that Katherine is not my father’s daughter by birth.”

“What? I don’t follow,” said Olympia.

“I am the firstborn. I had three brothers, Par, Hanno, and Liam. They all died soon after birth. My parents were devastated by each death. When I was ten, my parents had my brother, Ivan. You don’t know him. He teaches magic at the Warwick Academy in Namina. Later, when I was fourteen, my parents had my sister, Sairah. My father was happy beyond measure to have a daughter. Five years later, my mother and father were invited to the wedding of a friend’s son in Alhambra. They went to the wedding and left Ivan and Sairah with Grandfather Matteo and Grandmother Marina. I was at the Warwick Mages’ Academy in the capital by then. At the wedding party, one of my father’s oldest rivals drugged my mother, took her to one of the rooms, and took advantage of her.

“The housekeeper caught the man hurting my mother. She went and told her master and my father, but in the end, all was kept quiet. My father took my mother home, but six weeks later, she found she was with child. My father wanted her to keep the child in the hopes the child was his. However, when Katherine was born with red hair, we knew she wasn’t father’s daughter, but he didn’t care.

“Katherine has been his baby girl all her life. Father loves her the same as he loves me, Ivan, and Sairah. I will love Emma as I love Ivan, Axel, and Viktor,” said Lord Wolfson. Olympia sighed.

“Wait, Emma, who is Emma?”

“That is our daughter’s name. Emma is one of Sairah’s middle names.”

“Emma, I like the name. But Matteo, are you sure you want to marry me? I am an Exotic. I come with a lot of baggage.”

“I am sure. Will you answer me?” Olympia stayed quiet for a few minutes.

"Fine, I'll marry you, but I want it in writing you will not dunk me in a barrel of water if I get covered by horse manure." He smiled at Olympia, then he kissed her.

"You've got it. I give you my most solemn promise: I will not dunk you in a barrel if you get covered with manure. Olsen, Flint, she said yes. We need to get everything ready. We are leaving tomorrow."

ଓଓଓ

Olympia woke with Matteo's arm over her swollen midsection. Moments later, he kissed the side of her face. She had her back to him, but when she turned, she found him gazing at her, smiling. The bed was so comfortable Olympia didn't want to get up.

"Good morning, beautiful," said Matteo, touching Olympia's face.

"Good morning. When are we leaving?" asked Olympia.

"We must go now. If what you said is true and no one visits your room until late afternoon, we only have a few hours to get out of this city." Matteo got up, got dressed, and put on his boots.

"I'll wait for you downstairs. Don't take long. We must be out of this place before dawn. In the bag on the chair by the bed you will find clothing. Get dressed and tie your hair back. You are going to wear men's clothing. If anyone sees us leave, they need to see four men moving out," said Lord Wolfson. He left the room, leaving Olympia still in bed. She got up, went to the adjacent lavatory, and did her morning ablutions. Inside the bag, she found a pair of pants made for a portly man, a shirt and a coat to fit such a rotund man, a belt, warm socks, and a pair of traveling boots.

Olympia dressed, noticing that the pair of pants fit her with room to spare. She used the belt to keep everything in place, but not so tight it would press on her little girl. Once dressed, she went down to the first floor, where the three men were ready to leave.

"Come this way, Miss Olympia. We have some food for you to break your fast, but you must eat quickly," said Olsen. The men had prepared bread with butter, a boiled egg, some cheese, and a cup of Olympia's favorite drink, coffee. She ate it all. After she was done, the men cleaned everything. They picked up all their belongings, ensuring they left the house as they found it. At the door, Lord Wolfson wrapped a scarf around Olympia that covered the lower part of her face. He gave her a heavy traveling coat and popped a man's traveling hat onto her head.

"Let's go," said Olsen. They had a carriage waiting for them outside. It was still dark, and the street was deserted. The men packed the bags on top of the carriage. When they climbed into the carriage, they made sure Olympia was in the middle and out of sight from a casual passerby.

"Do not talk. I don't want anyone hearing your voice," whispered Lord Wolfson in Olympia's ear.

The carriage moved. Olympia's nerves made her stomach turn somersaults, as they left the city behind. An hour later, the sun was rising as they left the city behind. They reached the neighboring town of Folia, where the carriage took them directly to the train station.

"Wait, I can't go to the train station. They are going to ask to see my trade tattoo. They will notice the black space where the trademark used to be," said Olympia.

"Do not worry. I need you to do your hair the best you can and use this different hat." Lord Wolfson pulled a wide-rimmed traveling hat out of his enormous bag. Olympia didn't question him; she did what Matteo asked. She did her hair the best she could and put on the hat. They got off the carriage onto a street that was getting busy. The train station had an enormous ticket area. They walked through the station as fast as they could, evading the few people walking about. No one paid any attention to them, which delighted Olympia.

The station had four platforms and several trains waiting. Olsen went to get the tickets and while the others waited on the platforms. Olympia kept her face down since each platform had three guards. All of a sudden, Flint disappeared.

"Where is Flint?" asked Olympia.

"Don't worry about him. He has a task to do," said Lord Wolfson.

Olsen came back with the tickets, and the three of them waited for the time of their departure. They were going to take the first train out of Folia, going east. The guard was walking through the waiting group of people. Lord Wolfson and Olympia stood where the first-class carriage doors would open. The guards were asking to see people's trade tattoos.

The guard was getting nearer to them. Olympia's sweaty hands held on tightly to her bag. The guards finished checking most of the common people, and were now walking toward the noblemen's area, just as the train doors opened. Matteo did not hesitate, he pushed Olympia through the first-class carriage doors in a rush. They sped down the aisle of the train, looking for their compartment. Once found, they entered and locked the door.

"Give me your right wrist," said Lord Wolfson. She did, and Matteo put on a thick diamond bracelet that covered all the skills tattoos. He also put on her matching necklace and earrings.

"I want you to get completely naked," said Lord Wolfson.

"WHAT? Are you crazy?" Olympia could not believe him.

"Please, do what I say. Hurry."

Olympia got undressed. He took a woman's dress out of his bag and tossed it on the side of the compartment. He took off his coat along with his shirt, and unbuttoned his pants.

"This is not the time to have sex," said Olympia.

"Don't worry, make believe you are having a good time, but don't be loud," said Lord Wolfson. He passed his shirt to Olympia.

"Put it on, but do not button it." Matteo pulled her naked body to his chest, ensuring the sides of the shirt covered her belly. She made some noises, and he kissed her forehead.

"I love you," said Matteo. Olympia touched his face and kissed him.

A knock on the compartment door interrupted the kiss.

"Tickets," said the conductor.

"One moment," said Matteo in a raspy voice. He cracked open his door.

"Someone opened the train's door before I could check everyone's tattoos and give the order of all clear. I saw some people entering the train, and I didn't have time to check their trade tattoos. I must check for runaway slaves," said the guard.

"This is the noblemen's section. What does that have to do with us?" asked Lord Wolfson.

"I need to see inside the compartment," said a guard. "And I need to see your tickets," said the conductor.

"Here are our tickets, but you caught us indisposed at the moment," said Lord Wolfson. He opened the door a little more.

"Let me see your nobility-tattoos," said the guard. Lord Wolfson showed him his ducal crest on his left arm and his right arm with his mage-tattoo.

"I'm sorry, sweetheart." Matteo kept Olympia facing him, giving the conductor and the guard her back. He made her show the ducal crest on her left wrist to the guard by bringing her left arm to her back.

"She is my duchess."

"I am so embarrassed." Olympia said, hiding her face in Matteo's neck, and placing her right hand over his shoulder, deftly showing her thick diamond bracelet. Lord Wolfson opened the door a little more, just so the guard could see inside. The guard took a step inside the cabin. He did not touch either Olympia or Matteo. He left, chuckling and shaking his head.

"I am sorry, Your Grace. Now I know you are busy with your wife. I will not bother you again," said the conductor. Matteo closed the door, taking a deep breath.

Olympia was trembling in Matteo's arms; he held her tightly.

"Get dressed. It's cold in this compartment. I don't want you getting sick on my account."

"That was a stroke of genius," whispered Olympia as she dressed.

"I have my moments," he said, putting his shirt back on.

Once dressed, Olympia sat next to Matteo, and she fell asleep, but he woke her for her midday meal. Olsen had brought them food from the dinner car, and they ate in the cabin. They stayed together all afternoon, playing cards, talking, and Olympia sang a few quiet songs for him, but she soon fell asleep again. Half an hour before dusk, Lord Wolfson woke Olympia.

"Olympia, you must wake up. We are a few minutes away from our stop. I think by now, they have found out you are gone, and Chicho has contacted the authorities. We must get off the train and travel by horseback. This train only made two stops from Folia to Pasha. It took us far enough," said Lord Wolfson.

Olympia woke up. Her things were ready, so she had nothing to worry about. Lord Wolfson had a huge bag. He had ensured all was well packed away since their encounter with the conductor and the guard. The conductor went through the hall outside, calling out the next stop: Pasha, and Matteo waited until the conductor had passed before leaving their compartment. When the train stopped, they alighted from the train, hastily moving along the platform and out of the station, with Olsen and Flint following behind.

They walked out to the streets of Pasha, so Olsen called for a carriage. Pasha was a small town, but Olympia had visited some time ago with one of her clients. Pasha had vast grain fields and many famous vineyards. Many Nolia people would visit the town to sample the wines and enjoy the scenery.

They traveled beyond the central town square toward the outskirts, and soon arrived at a smith's shop. Olsen knocked on the door to the house, at the side of the shop, while the others waited outside.

"My shop is closed for the night. What do you want?" asked a man. He opened the door with a ball of fire around his fist.

"Hey—stop Lewis, it's me, Olsen."

"You're late," said the balding man. What little hair he had grew only on the sides of his head.

"The train was delayed," said Olsen.

"Come in, you're letting the heat out," said Lewis. The warm house made Olympia feel cozy. It had an inviting fire in the large common area.

"Thank you, my friend," said Olsen.

"Sure, anything for an Academy brother," said Lewis.

"Do you have the horses?" asked Olsen.

"Yes, but this lot ain't cheap. Takapian traveling horses and their mounts are hard to find in these parts. They generally only sell working horses in these parts. But I got them. They're waiting out back in my barn," said Lewis.

"Thank you, I owe you one," said Olsen.

"I don't want to know who your friends are. By the look of them, y'all are running from something or someone," said Lewis.

"Stop using your mental magic on them. They are mages, too," said Olsen.

"Yeah, that silent tower of a guy is an Arcane Mage, and the tall blue-eyed bodyguard of the girl is a water mage, I know."

"He's good. He knows all our magic," said Flint.

"Not all of you are mages; that little pregnant girl in breeches is not. You all need to hide her better. Her face gives her away," said Lewis.

"You never change," said Olsen.

"Is that Olsen I hear?" said a woman from the kitchen.

"Cali, how are you?" asked Olsen. The woman came out of the kitchen wearing an apron dusted with white flour. Olsen went and picked her up in a bear hug. She had soft, happy brown eyes.

"I haven't seen you in ages. When Lewis said you were coming to get the horses, I knew you were going to come hungry. I cooked enough for all of us," said Cali.

"Thank you, love; I sure am hungry," said Olsen.

"You're always hungry," said Lewis. They had dinner in the kitchen while Lewis and Cali talked about their lives in Pasha. Olympia discovered that Lewis and Cali were mages who trained at the same Academy as Olsen. They had defected to Palermo when they found out their Mage master in Alhambra was planning to steal their son and give him to another family, just because the boy wasn't a mage. Now, their son was older and doing an apprenticeship with a carpenter. He was staying at his master's house that night.

Olympia ate all her food, but her back started to hurt afterward. Cali gave her a cup of tea.

"Here, it will help you with your backache," said Cali.

"How do you know I have a backache?" asked Olympia.

"I'm a healer mage with a few other gifts," said Cali, winking at Olympia.

Lewis provided them a room to stay in, for which Olympia was grateful. She really didn't want to sleep on the floor in her state. The next morning, they were breaking their fast when Lewis rush into the house.

"You four need to leave right now," said Lewis.

"Why? What happened?" asked Olsen.

"I went to town early this morning. Cali wanted fresh eggs and bread. In the bakery, I encountered the constable. He asked me if I had seen two people matching the description of your woman and the big water mage here. Apparently, someone stole a prized Exotic slave from a brothel. How can anyone steal an Exotic from under the nose of the slave masters?" asked Lewis, looking at Flint with a sly, yet knowing glance.

"I thank you for your hospitality. Here is the gold for the horses and a little extra for the inconvenience. We must leave now," said Lord Wolfson.

Cali packed a large bag of food. The four left the house via the backdoor, directly into the barn. They saddled, packed, and mounted the horses.

"Olsen, my friend, I wish you good travels. If the constable is looking for your friends, I suggest you stay away from any towns large enough to have Trade Offices. News travels fast. If they're for searching for an Exotic slave, we're talking about an expensive piece of property with a high bounty on her head."

"Thank you for your help; I owe you one," said Olsen, shaking hands with his friend. They rode eastward at a fast trot for a while, until it was time to give the horses some rest. Olympia wasn't feeling well. Her growing belly didn't let her sit comfortably on her saddle. It took almost two weeks by train to get from Wolfson's castle to Nolia. She didn't want to think how long it would take on a horse.

CHAPTER 22

The Wedding

"How long will it be until we reach the border of Yakuta?" asked Olympia. She dismounted the horse and walked around a little, stretched her back, and drank some water.

"It will take us about two weeks by horse to reach the border," said Lord Wolfson.

"Oh no, I won't last on horseback for that long. My back is already excruciating," said Olympia.

"I allowed for many stops, but once we are married, we will be able to take a train. We just need to be on the road for a little longer. I promise it will be fast," said Lord Wolfson.

They rode on for the rest of the day until it grew dark when they made camp for the night. Flint made a fire. That evening he cooked two hares he had caught earlier in the day. They had no tents, and the nights were very cold. Lord Wolfson prepared two pallets next to each other. He took the first watch of the night. Olsen had the second watch, and Flint had the third. Happiness overwhelmed her for the first time in a long while. It was cold, but she didn't care. She was with people who loved her.

The following day, at the first rays of light, Olympia woke up cuddled in Lord Wolfson's arms. She got up and walked away a little distance to answer the call of nature, when she realized they were sleeping very close to a village's limits. She ran back to camp and found all three men getting ready to leave.

"I am afraid we traveled too close to a town. Please assure me we are not going to that town."

"Yes, we are going to the village. It's too small to be a town. Calm down, all will be fine. It's a Morai village," said Lord Wolfson.

They finished packing the horses, and traveled to the village. The inhabitants looked at them with an inquisitive glare. The four companions rode into the village and past the local market, going directly to the church. The building was the tallest in the village. The imposing stone structure stood in the center of a humble building that surrounded it. The church had multicolored stained-glass windows on each side of the front door, depicting some type of divine scenery that Olympia didn't recognize. They entered, and the priest was sweeping around the front pews.

"Hello and welcome, stranger," said the Morai priest.

Olympia looked at the man as the others talked. He wore a dark-blue, long-sleeved shirt under a long white coat. His gray eyes were striking against his dark skin.

"Hello, pastor, I am here to ask for one of your benedictions," asked Lord Wolfson.

"I am sorry, but you know this is a Benanti church," said the priest.

"I know. I am a Benanti believer. I've been a follower since my birth," said Lord Wolfson.

"I am not one to deny others' beliefs, but I have never seen a human follow the Morai faith," said the priest.

"Ask something of me that only one of the faithful would know," said Lord Wolfson.

"Say the morning prayer of protection," said the priest.

"I pray for Your protection, oh Lord of the heavens above, and the land I step upon, as I begin this day. You are my hiding place, and my fortress. Under your wings, I can always find refuge every day of my life. Protect me from trouble wherever I go and keep evil far from me on this day and always," said Lord Wolfson.

"Welcome to our parish. I am the pastor of the church, Bishop Linwood. Who are you? And which benediction are you seeking?" asked the priest.

"I am Lord Wolfson, the Duke of Trenton from the land of Yakuta, and I wish to marry this woman," said Lord Wolfson.

"Your Grace, are you sure you want such a humble wedding? We can't give you the celebration a man of your station would require, but we can put together a small party if you give us a few days," said the priest.

"Bishop Linwood, I don't need a celebration. I just want to marry my woman." The priest looked at Olympia, still dressed in her oversized breeches and overcoat.

"When would you like to have the ceremony? I assume the lady will want to change into a wedding dress," said Bishop Linwood.

"No, Bishop, I don't need to change. Could you conduct the ceremony now, please?" Olympia opened her coat and revealed her belly to the priest.

"I want my child to have her father's protection as soon as possible," said Olympia.

"Oh, I understand. Wait here a few minutes. I'll be right back," said the clergy man, hurrying away with a smile on his face. He exited through a door at the back of the church, closing the door behind him. Olsen remained by the church entrance, and Flint stayed outside with the horses. After waiting about fifteen minutes, Bishop Linwood returned dressed in a royal blue robe with a yellow ochre sash around his neck. A Morai woman walked in behind him, also dressed in royal blue, with a light blue tunic over her arms.

"This is my wife, Violet. Miss, would you go with her to the back of the sanctuary? She will get you ready for the ceremony," said Bishop Linwood. Olympia nodded. She followed the tall Morai woman, who towered over Olympia by almost a head and a half. Her straight black hair with braids around her face gave her a sense of authority, but her brown skin and pale-blue eyes made her seem ethereal. Olympia followed her to the back of the sanctuary, to a small room.

"Hello, Miss. In our religion, men and women marry in a light-blue garments, wearing no shoes. We are all supposed to be barefoot while in our church. Here, I brought this dress for you to wear at your wedding. I hope it will suit you. My husband said you are large with child, but you are a little thing of a woman," said Violet.

Olympia took her coat, shirt, and pants off, and stood in her underclothes. Violet helped her get into the long A-line dress. It had a V-neck with a lace infill over the chest and lace sleeves. Both the sleeves and the dress itself, were too long, but Violet spoke an incantation, and the dress shrunk with the magic to fit Olympia.

"What kind of mage are you?" asked Olympia.

"I am not a mage. I am a Magus. I use the energy from the mountains, trees, earth, air, water, and fire to protect, fight, and heal," said Violet.

"I have never heard of Magus," said Olympia.

"Only Morai have Maguses. There are few of us, but I sense something special within you. May I touch your belly?" asked Violet. Olympia nodded. Violet gently touched Olympia then her hands glowed purple.

"Oh, you have a gift within you. You are a blessed woman. All your children will be Maguses." Violet smiled, and reaching around Olympia, she held her in her arms. Olympia opened her eyes wide.

"Children?

"Every single child you give birth to, all of them will be Maguses," said Violet.

"Every one?"

"It doesn't matter how often you give birth; all your children will be Maguses." Olympia smiled, and she closed her eyes.

"The year your children turn thirteen, you must bring them to a Morai village for training," said Violet.

"How can that be?" asked Olympia.

"I don't know. I have never seen a non-Morai with such a blessing, but let's do your hair; your man is waiting," said Violet. The Morai woman released Olympia's hair, letting it hang loose. She combed it and then arranged Olympia's long hair in an intricate cascade down the back of her head. As the final touch, she placed a white silk sash around Olympia's neck, leaving it to fall over her shoulders.

"Now you're ready to marry under a Morai benediction." The two women returned to the church.

ଓଓଓ

When Matteo saw Olympia re-enter the main church in her blue dress, he was lost for words. A ray of light shined through the glass window in the back wall of the sanctuary, falling onto Olympia, making her light up. She came to stand next to him.

"My wife will be your woman's companion, but do you have a witness of your own for the union?" asked Bishop Linwood.

"Olsen, please come here. Would you be our witness?" asked Lord Wolfson. Olsen came into the church and stood next to Matteo.

"My Lord, I have no faith. Is this even legal?" said Olsen.

"You don't have to believe in our g-d for our g-d to love you. Before we start, the two of you must take off your shoes," said Bishop Linwood, smiling at both men. They took off their shoes, and Olympia, already barefoot, stood next to Matteo. Bishop Linwood started the ceremony.

Matteo could not believe the woman looked even more beautiful than before. She shined with an inner light, in a way that had not been there when she went into the back room. The bishop gave them a cup of wine to drink. They both drank a sip. Bishop Linwood had Olympia and Matteo keep their hands together, as he poured water over their hands. To end the ceremony, he spoke a prayer in the Morai language.

"You have your wife, Lord Wolfson, and you have your husband, Lady Olympia," said the bishop. They kissed for a few seconds, then separated to go sign the registry at a side table. Bishop Linwood gave them their marriage certificate after all the signatures were done.

"Take this certificate and go to the Trades Office and have your tattoos made," said the bishop.

“Your Grace, before you go,” said Violet, “I’ve already told your wife, but you should also know. Your wife is the bearer of a gift. All your children will be Maguses,” said Violet.

“That can’t be; only Morai have Magus,” said Lord Wolfson.

“I don’t know how it happened, but she has been blessed. The year your children turn thirteen, you must find them a Morai Magus to teach them how to use their magic,” said Violet.

“My Lord, I don’t want to interrupt your conversation, but we must go. You must get your new wife registered before the day is over,” said Olsen. Lord Wolfson gave the bishop one gold piece while Olympia went to the back room to take off her dress and change back to her traveling clothes.

ଔଔଔ

They left the church and hurried to the local Trade Office, as fast as they could. The Department of Trade and Commerce was nothing more than three rooms on the first floor of the village’s town hall. Matteo and Olympia entered the office expecting a crowd, but no one was waiting. Only a single Morai man sat behind a desk.

“Hello, friend. I need to register my new wife. She already has my ducal crest,” said Lord Wolfson.

“Hello, my Lord, did you marry her in a church or a clerical office?” asked the young man.

“Your local pastor, Bishop Linwood, just married us,” said Lord Wolfson.

“My uncle married you today?” asked the young man.

“Here is our marriage certificate,” said Lord Wolfson. He gave the young Morai man the certificate, which he inspected with a frown.

“That’s my uncle’s signature. You know my uncle is a high priest and the second bishop of the Palermo Benanti.

“No, I didn’t know.”

"Come and sit down. If someone already branded her with your ducal crest, all she needs is the wife-tattoo," said the young man.

"She used to be a prostitute," said Lord Wolfson. The young man gave him a double look.

"Then you must brand the wife's symbol over her prostitute-tattoo," said the young man. Olympia hated the thought of another brand on her body. Lord Wolfson whispered in Olympia's ear while the young man heated the small wife brand.

"I need you to unbutton your shirt. I found out I must also brand you over the Exotic mark on your breast. I am not going to tell him you are an Exotic until after I've obliterated that tattoo with the new brand," said Lord Wolfson. Olympia looked at him, clearly frightened, but she unbuttoned her shirt discretely.

When the young man passed the brand to Lord Wolfson, he didn't hesitate to open Olympia's shirt and brand her breast first. The man was not watching and did not see. Olympia closed her eyes and didn't scream, but the pain made her pull back. Lord Wolfson took her arm, used the wife mark brand, and burned over her prostitute-tattoo on her wrist next. Once all was done, Olympia pulled back her arm and held it to her body.

"Here, my Lady, put this salve over your burn. It will alleviate your pain," said the young man.

Olympia took the salve and applied it to both burns.

"Where on your wrist do you want to add her name?" asked the Morai clerk.

"At the base on front. Also, I want you to link the marks of the Duke of Trenton's crest and the Earl of Wolfson," said Lord Wolfson. The young man inked the tattoos on Matteo first, but when he reached for Olympia's arm, he stopped.

"Wait, why is there an empty space in her skill ring? What happened here?" asked the young Trade Official.

"She was supposed to get a new trade, but her instructor never arrived to certify the trade," said Lord Wolfson.

“Which was the trade?” asked the Trade Official.

“She is a Takapian horse rider for shows,” said Olsen behind Lord Wolfson. “I am her instructor and didn’t make it for the certification,” said Olsen.

“Do you want to do the certification now? I need to see your master-tattoo first,” said the Trades Official. Olsen showed his tattoo, and Olympia received a new trade in her skills ring, where the trademark used to be. Once all was done, they signed the papers and left the office. Olympia wrapped a piece of clean linen around her wrist to cover her wife’s brand and new tattoo.

“Can we travel by train now?” asked Olympia.

“No, not yet; we must travel a little bit further east and give your tattoos and brands some time to heal before we can take a train. I don’t want any questions when we board.”

They found Flint, mounted their horses and galloped away, headed due east. Mateo wanted to get as much distance as possible from the village as fast as they could. They traveled all day but Olympia was feeling sick and her back hurt, so when they reached a small village, they looked for an inn to stay the night. The village only had one inn. Olympia could not believe changing her tattoo was so easy.

She didn’t have her prostitute-tattoo any longer, and that made her happy. They tried to blend in with the population. Matteo even let his long hair loose, allowing it to cover his face, while Olympia hid her face under the hood of her cloak.

Matteo went to rent a room in the inn, leaving Olympia to order some food. She made sure her right wrist remained hidden as she talked to the tavern owner. Olsen and Flint opted to stay in the barn protecting the horses. Olympia was happy that they would be sleeping under a roof that night.

After renting their room, they sat at the table to eat their supper. The tavern owner serving them himself, and eyeing Olympia all the while. But Matteo sat next to her, and tried to shield her from view. They had an early dinner and went to sleep soon afterward.

The following day, Olympia woke dizzy, but it soon went away. She stood by the window looking out when dawn broke the horizon. As she looked down at the street, she was startled to see a constable carriage from Pasha parked outside the inn. Her heart leaped, and she ran back to her bed.

"Matteo, you must wake. Wake up, please." Olympia shook him. He woke abruptly.

"What happened?" He sat and blinked several times.

"There is a constable carriage from Pasha outside. Why would a constable carriage be out here?" asked Olympia.

"I don't know. Stay in the room; I'm going to get Olsen and Flint. We'll leave directly," said Lord Wolfson. He dressed in a hurry and left the room. Olympia dressed in her oversized pants, making sure to tie her belt tight enough to keep up the pants. She waited in the room for over an hour. She got more nervous as the minutes went by and since Matteo had not returned for her, she kept looking out the window. By then, a second Pasha police carriage arrived. Her heartbeat started racing. Why would they be there? They had been so careful. She jumped at a loud knock.

"This is the Pasha sheriff. Open the door," said a man. Olympia's eyes watered. The sheriff found her. How? They had taken so many precautions. Olympia opened the door, and an older man grabbed her by the arm, pulling her out of the room.

"What are you doing? Let me go."

"Be quiet, Exotic," said the sheriff. He almost dragged Olympia down the stairs. When she reached the first floor of the tavern, neither Matteo, Olsen, nor Flint were there.

What would have happened to them?

"Where are you taking me? Who are you?" asked Olympia.

"The tavern's owner sent for us yesterday. You are the escaped prized Exotic Olympia Corona Takatsu. We are here to take you back to your owner," said the sheriff.

"No, I am not an Exotic. I am a married woman. I am carrying the Duke of Trenton's child. Let me go."

"We arrested the Duke of Trenton for suspected theft of a highly prized Exotic, a piece of property owned by Mr. Chicho di Roberti. The tavern owner saw the duke come in here with you," said the constable.

The constable paid the owner of the tavern three pieces of gold then he dragged her forcefully by the arm. Once outside, she saw Olsen and Flint looking out from a nearby church's window. The constable dragged Olympia to one of the carriages. He mounted the carriage with her and quickly drove away.

CHAPTER 23

In the Worst Den of Wolves

Three days after the sheriff captured Olympia, they reached Nolia by train. The carriage rode through the streets of Nolia and Olympia couldn't care less. The constable from Pasha ensured that Olympia sat next to him at all times. The sheriff had placed a metal collar around Olympia's neck, and only he had the keys. She didn't say a word to the man except to let him know when she needed to use the commode or when she was hungry or thirsty. Olympia worried about Lord Wolfson. She had not seen him since he left her in the room at the inn.

Olympia looked out the window at the dirty streets of Nolia packed with horse-drawn carriages, people riding horseback, horseless carriages, and so many people milling about. She wondered why she ever wanted to come back to that city. It had snowed, but instead of a lovely snow scene, everything was mired under gray and brown slush.

Nolia didn't look anything like Kalbaka. She missed the little town on the island in the middle of the lake. Olympia dreaded going back to the brothel. Il Palazzo di Roberti had been her home for over twelve years, but she knew Chicho would make her pay dearly for escaping. He would probably not feed her for a month, or maybe he would beat her. She wouldn't put it past him.

When the carriage arrived at the brothel, Olympia's was close to tears. Here she was again. The constable opened the carriage door and pulled her out of the carriage like a rag doll. The snow blanketed the front of the brothel, making it look beautiful. The clean snow in the front yard showed up little prints, possibly or a squirrel or maybe a bunny. But the sheriff dragged her to the door by the arm and rang the bell to the brothel, bringing her back into the moment. The door opened, and Norman, the porter, opened the door. The constable entered with Olympia. Norman gave Olympia a sad smile.

"I am here to see Mr. di Roberti. I found his kidnapped Exotic," said the sheriff.

"Wait here," said Norman, slowly walking away. A few minutes later, Chicho arrived in the front gallery, reeking as always of cheap cologne and expensive cigar, his fingers all adorned in gold rings. He entered in a hurry, and Nancy walked in behind him, her red hair coming loose from a bun.

"And here she is. Thank you for bringing her back to me." Chicho gave Olympia an odious glare.

"I found her in—"

"No, I don't want to know where you found her. Here is your reward." Chicho gave the sheriff a bag of coins. The constable gave Chicho a slight bow, removed the collar from Olympia, and left.

"You keep costing me more coin than you make, Olympia. I've had it with you. I've decided to sell you to a lesser brothel. They want to have an Exotic in their ranks," said Chicho.

"When is the sale going to happen?" asked Olympia.

"Your new owner will be here tomorrow. But tonight, you will have three clients. I need to recover some of the gold I lost. Nancy, take her away. I don't want to see her face," said Chicho as he left.

Nancy didn't say anything. She took Olympia's arm and walked with her to her bedroom. Olympia kept quiet. She didn't have anything to say. She was overwhelmed with all that was happening. No one ever listened to her, anyway. Once they reached her room, Nancy unlocked the door and stood aside.

"I'll send someone later with some food and water. You have no idea the trouble you caused me," said Nancy.

"I am not an Exotic anymore,' said Olympia.

"You will forever be an Exotic," said Nancy, as she closed and locked the door. Olympia took off her shoes, collected a clean robe, and went to her bathing room to take a bath. She rubbed in some oils and lotions, and combed her hair. Her baby had been moving a lot lately.

Sitting by her vanity, she was rubbing her belly when a servant opened the door and brought in a tray of food. Olympia ate, then she went to bed. She didn't care if she had a million clients that night. She would never be an Exotic again. After an hour, a group of women arrived to prepare her for the night's clients.

Olympia wore a silk-red dress with black shoes. She wrapped a scarf around her neck and draped it over her breasts. Nancy came to get her when her first client arrived. The women said nothing to each other. They walked silently to the room where Olympia was to work through the night. Once inside the room, Olympia sat by a table, waiting alone. A few minutes passed, and a man entered and closed the door behind him.

"Ah, the exclusive Exotic Olympia Takatsu. An anonymous benefactor paid me for thirty minutes of your time. I don't know why I am so lucky," said the gentleman.

"I have never seen you before, who are you?" Olympia didn't care to be polite.

"I am Mr. Lawrence Heart, Esquire, one of the partners of *Kenner, Kenner, and Heart*, the law firm."

"I'm afraid you will not have me. I am not an Exotic anymore. I am with child. I was taken away from my husband, the Duke of Trenton, Lord Matteo Wolfson. I married to the duke. He is from the Kingdom of Yakuta. I am the Duchess of Trenton, and I appeal to King Antonio, to the law of this land, and I also want to call the Ambassador of Yakuta," said Olympia.

"That is impossible. Exotics can't marry," said Mr. Heart. Olympia removed her scarf and showed him her wife branding where her Exotic-tattoo used to be. Olympia also showed him the Duke's crest on her wrist.

"Ah, now I see why I am here. You have appealed to the King; by law, I am obliged to help you," said Mr. Heart.

“I am desperate. I am pregnant with my Duke’s child. I am not supposed to be here.”

“Sit down, Your Grace, and tell me all that has happened,” said Mr. Heart. Olympia told the lawyer a condensed story since she only had thirty minutes.

“They are forcing me to take another two clients after you tonight.”

“I’ll take your case and bring your appeal to King Antonio’s court; as for tonight, you should not be taking any clients. Your husband is a member of the Yakutan nobility, so based on our treaties, that makes you a high-ranking Lady not only in Yakuta but in Palermo.”

“My husband is in jail. He needs representation.”

“What did he do? What were his charges? Do you know which jail the authorities took him?” asked Mr. Heart.

“I don’t know the answer to any of those questions. All I know is that when I was taken, the constable separated us. I only know he was arrested,” said Olympia. There was a knock on the door. Nancy entered.

“Your time has ended,” said Nancy.

“I will be here tomorrow. For now, I need to talk to the owner of this establishment,” said Mr. Heart.

“You need to be here early; Mr. di Roberti is selling me to another brothel tomorrow morning.”

“I don’t think so.”

“Mr. Heart, you need to leave. Your thirty minutes are done,” said Nancy with authority.

“I need to talk to your boss,” said Mr. Heart, leaving the room as dignified as he entered.

“What was that all about? You think you are not an Exotic anymore? Chicho will be furious if that man asks for a refund. Olympia, you need to stop these flights of fancy. I’ll be back with your next client in half an hour. Fix your thinking, fast!”

Nancy left the room and Olympia took a deep breath. Who would have paid Olympia’s rate for that lawyer to visit her? It had to be Olsen or Flint. Who else was in

Palermo that would want to help her? She had clients, but no one she would call a close friend. She sat on the sofa in front of the fireplace and waited. Half an hour later, the door opened with a snap.

"What is all this about? I was told that you don't have the Exotic-tattoos anymore. What have you done?" shouted Chicho. Olympia stepped closer to him and showed him her left breast, where the tattoo used to be, and where she now had the wife branding.

"¿Maldita sea, quien te hiso eso? Tell me, bitch. Who did that?" Chicho spat his words.

"I got married to Lord Wolfson. I am the Duchess of Trenton. Look at all my tattoos and markings on my left arm," said Olympia, showing him her left arm.

"That lawyer said he is representing you, and you appealed to the King's court. Is that true?" asked Chicho.

"Yes, I did, and I will not take any clients tonight. I am a duchess. I will have my husband sue you if you hurt me or our child."

"You will pay for this. You hear me? Forget me selling you to another brothel. I am going to sell you tomorrow to a slave trader. Let him take you from Palermo and do whatever he wants with you elsewhere. Take her to her room," Chicho's face had turned a violent scarlet color, and his eyes blazed. He left the room, slamming the door.

"Let's go, Olympia," said Nancy. They walked to Olympia's room, again in silence. Once they reached Olympia's bedroom, she entered and Nancy followed her inside. She closed and locked the door behind her.

"How did you do it?" asked Nancy.

"How did I do what?

"Get out of the Exotic trade. There is no way for an Exotic to escape the trade." Nancy held one of Olympia's arms, appearing agitated.

"Lord Wolfson got me with child, and he married me."

"Now I understand why Chicho prevented you from keeping any of your children," said Nancy.

"No, you don't understand. I didn't know the identity of the fathers of any of my children. The child's father must claim the child and he must also marry you. At least that is what happened to the woman who married the nephew of King George in Yakuta."

"I don't quite understand it all, but it gives hope to Exotics," said Nancy.

"I need a miracle tomorrow if Chicho is planning to sell me to a slave trader." Nancy took a deep breath and held Olympia's hand.

"Try to sleep tonight. Let tomorrow bring its own problems. Sleep is the greatest equalizer," said Nancy, leaving Olympia in her room. Olympia changed into a clean chemise, went to bed, and prayed.

"g-d of the Morai. I am in big trouble. I am back in Chicho's brothel. I am not an Exotic anymore. I need to get out of here. Please help Mr. Heart. Please help me. I want to go home with my husband.

"I don't have much to give you in exchange for your help. I hope my fealty will be enough. With all my heart, I pray. So, it may be."

She lay on her bed and tried to sleep. She would gain nothing by worrying.

ഽഽഽ

The door snapped open, and one of the burly bouncers strode into Olympia's room. She sat up in bed pulling the covers with her. She had slept little the previous night, and had a headache. The bouncer walked in, grabbed her by the arm, and pulled her from bed.

"Wait, where are you taking me?" Olympia pulled her arm away from the man.

"Chicho wants you in his office now." He grabbed Olympia's arm again.

"I must dress. I can't go to Chicho's office in my chemise," said Olympia, trying to pull her arm from the tight grip a second time.

“Fine, get dressed and do it fast.” Olympia looked for a dress. She combed her hair and tied it back. She found comfortable shoes, and when she went to get a shawl, the bouncer grabbed her once more and dragged her from the room. They sped through the hallways, despite Olympia trying to lag behind, down the stairs, and passed the hall. Chicho’s office door was open when they reached it. Olympia entered. She saw a man dressed like a gentleman first, but with the appearance of a weasel, then she spotted a scruffy-looking man standing at the back. Chicho was behind his desk, counting gold coins.

“Is this the pregnant Exotic?” asked the man dressed as a gentleman.

“This is her. You will have a well-trained bitch with this one,” said Chicho.

“Are you sure she can sing and dance?”

“Yes, yes, this one came with many skills.” Chicho didn’t look up from his coins.

“I hope the child is a girl. I want to gain a new Exotic out of her,” said the man.

“No, you can’t sell me. I am not an Exotic. I am a wife and a duchess.”

“I know that. I will have a healer cut out the wife mark and we’ll reapply the slave- and prostitute-tattoos,” said the well-dressed man.

“No, I am the wife of a duke. Chicho, you can’t sell me. I have a lawyer.”

“Chicho, we’ll talk again. Come, sweet thing; we must take you to the Trades Office to reapply the slave-tattoo. We have a long way to go. You will be working in Alhambra now. Barra, take her,” said the man in the gentleman’s suit. Barra went and grabbed Olympia by her arm, but when he tried to tie her arms together, Olympia kicked Barra in the groin. She tried to run out of Chicho’s office, but the bouncer who stood outside the office caught her.

“Oh no, you don’t. Give me the cuffs. I’ll restrain her,” said the bouncer. Olympia tried to get herself away, but the bouncer overpowered her.

“You just sold me a wildcat.”

“Marcelo, you know I only have the best stock,” said Chicho. Barra, the scruffy-looking man, slapped Olympia.

“That’s for kickin’ me nuts,” said Barra.

“Don’t damage my goods,” shouted Marcelo, and he hit Barra’s head.

“I’ll walk with you to your carriage. I want to watch the bitch’s face when you take her away,” said Chicho.

They walked through the reception hall while the bouncer held Olympia by her cuffed hands. Norman, the butler, held the front door open for them. He stood aside the door, but when he noticed Olympia with them, he gave her a sad look and honored her with a slight bow.

The moment Olympia stepped outside she shivered, all the way to her soul. It had snowed the night before and she didn’t have a coat. A carriage waited for them in front of the building. She felt a tightness in her chest, unlike anything she had ever felt before. But as they descended the stairs to the street, a carriage pulled up in front of Marcelo’s carriage, blocking its path, and a second carriage parked close behind.

A man wearing a black coat and top hat stepped out from the front carriage, accompanied by four other men. They greeted Marcelo, Barra, and Chicho as the group approached, but did not appear friendly.

“Which one of you is Chicho di Roberti?” asked the gentleman in the top hat.

“That is I,” said Chicho, raising his voice.

“I am the Ambassador of Yakuta, Lord Allen Melvin Beckford.”

“You know me. We met last night,” said Mr. Heart.

“And I am Sheriff Santo Galan. We are here to collect the Duchess of Trenton, Lady Olympia Takatsu Wolfson. I hope you don’t make things difficult for yourselves.”

"I am the Duchess of Trenton, Lady Olympia." She spoke loudly for the men to hear. The sheriff pushed all the men aside and went to stand next to Olympia.

"Why is the Duchess in handcuffs?" asked Sheriff Galan.

"Chicho sold me to his friend, Marcelo," said Olympia.

"How can you sell a free woman, the wife of a Duke, *and* a citizen of Yakuta?" asked the Ambassador of Yakuta.

"She is not free. She is mine. She has my trademark. You know the trademark laws between Yakuta and Palermo—besides, Exotics are not wives," said Chicho.

"She is mine now. I just purchased her. We are going to the Trades Office for her slave-tattoo," said Marcelo.

"Let me see your right arm. Remove the handcuffs," said the sheriff. Barra complied, and Olympia, rubbed her hands and wrists, then pulled back her right sleeve.

"She doesn't have the trademark-tattoo, but she does have a wife's brand," said the sheriff.

"What?" Chicho grabbed Olympia's wrist. Disbelieving, he turned it from one side to the other.

"What did you do with my trademark? I want a Trade Official to come and verify my property. I had her registered as my property. She is an Exotic trained by my people," said Chicho.

"She doesn't have the tattoo, but she does have the Duchess mark. We are taking her to the embassy. You are free to go to the Trades Office and file a claim."

"Stand aside! Your Grace, here, take my coat. You must be freezing. Officers, escort Lady Olympia to our carriage," said the sheriff. One officer came forward and helped Olympia climb into the carriage.

Once inside, the officer with her gave her a blanket. She smiled, then she laughed. She couldn't stop laughing. Her prayer had been heard and answered. She was free and going to the Yakutan Embassy.

CHAPTER 24

The King

Olympia sat in the carriage, looking at her hands the entire way to the Yakutan Ambassador's mansion, keeping her gleeful thoughts to herself from the men she rode with. Mr. Heart saved her from Chicho's malevolence and the hands of that slave master, Marcelo. But would she see her husband again? Undoubtedly, the Ambassador and Mr. Heart would help Matteo, just as they had helped her. Olympia's heart filled with joy. She was going to return to Yakuta.

In her musings, she barely noticed her surroundings. When they reached the Ambassador's mansion, Olympia stepped down from the carriage, and looked up for the first time since leaving the brothel. The mansion took her breath away. Fifteen-foot-high iron gates protected the mansion, which sat amidst perfectly manicured grounds.

The grandeur of its hexastyle portico made Olympia want to stay outside and just look at the red brick and white stucco in front of the entrance. A tall double door made the entrance look magnificent. The first floor of the mansion had many floor-to-ceiling windows, and up above, there were four chimneys—*a warm building*, she thought.

The Ambassador held out his arm to Olympia and led her through the front door. Olympia knew she was safe when they entered the foyer, and passed a reception room full of people working. They continued down a hallway, and after passing several doors to the left, they arrived at and entered a grand parlor, all decorated in gold colors.

"Your Grace, we located your husband in a jail not far from here, and managed to get him released some time earlier this morning. He will be joining you shortly. Your Grace, please wait here," said the Ambassador.

He stepped out of the room, leaving Olympia alone with her thoughts. She had nothing to eat that morning; her stomach made embarrassing noises. She sat on one of the many chairs and waited, reciting a poem in her mind. After waiting for about fifteen minutes, she heard a familiar voice.

"My dear, you are a sight to behold," said Lord Wolfson.

Olympia stood up and raced to her husband, as fast as her pregnant body allowed. She didn't care who was around. She kissed him thoroughly. He still wore the same clothes as he had at the Morai village; his hair was a mess, and he stank, but Olympia didn't care. He was with her.

"What happened to you back at the Morai village?" asked Olympia.

"The sheriff arrested me outside the inn when I went to get Olsen and Flint. He placed me in one of the carriages, which was a cage that rendered my magic inert. I tried to talk my way out, but he had a warrant for my arrest. I had no choice but to go with them.

"When we reached Nolia, they wouldn't permit me to contact a lawyer or the Yakutan Ambassador. I was due to go before a judge in another two days. I thought I was going to have to use my magic to get out of jail, but today, a lawyer named Mr. Kenner came. He talked to the authorities, and they let me out. Mr. Kenner said they represented both of us now.

"How about you? How did you manage to get a lawyer to help you?" Lord Wolfson took Olympia by the hand. He sat her on a chair while he knelt by her side.

"I think Olsen and Flint anonymously paid for one of Mr. Kenner's business partners to be one of my clients for thirty minutes last night. That is how I met Mr. Heart, of the law firm *Kenner, Kenner, and Heart*."

Matteo stood up and started pacing around the golden room. "I need a bath and I am hungry." Fortunately, the Ambassador chose that moment to enter the room.

“Your Grace, I had my servants prepare rooms for you and the Duchess. I had my butler call a tailor to come here today and bring some pieces for you. I also had my housekeeper summons a seamstress urgently for your Duchess,” said the Ambassador.

“Thank you, Lord Beckford; I appreciate all you have done for us,” said Lord Wolfson.

“I’ll have the servants bring food to your rooms. I am sure you both may want to rest. We can talk later,” said Ambassador Beckford.

A servant escorted Olympia and Matteo to their rooms on the second floor. Olympia’s happiness overflowed. She was out of Chicho’s brothel. The room was small, but just as beautiful as her room in Wolfson Castle.

A few minutes later, a servant arrived bearing a tray with a corn porridge, a selection of fruits, cheeses, bread, jams, and tea. She ate until she was sated, and afterward undressed and took a nap. She wanted to sleep, but a knock at her door woke her. Olympia found a robe in the room, so she put it on and opened the door. It was the seamstress and a shoemaker. They spent the next two hours measuring her for clothing and shoes. The seamstress had brought a few pieces of clothing with her that were suitable for a pregnant woman. The dresses only had to be taken in a little and fixed at the hem. Olympia didn’t care about the style or color—she just wanted to go to sleep.

A few hours later, a maid came with the midday meal. Olympia was famished, so she ate until she was replete. Not a moment after she finished eating, there was another knock at her door. She went and opened it.

“My dear, you look so beautiful. May I come in?” Matteo was at her door, looking clean and well-dressed. Olympia took his hand and pulled him into her room.

“Have you heard about Olsen and Flint?”

“They are here. And you were right. I found out they were, indeed, the ones that contacted the lawyers,” he said.

Olympia went into her husband’s arms, and he held her tight. Talking into his chest somewhere because she didn't want to let go, she asked him if he'd had his midday meal yet.

"Yes, dear, I have."

They finally released each other and sat at the table.

"Matteo, when can we leave for Yakuta?"

"Ambassador Beckford told me that your former boss made a claim at the Trades Office, and he's called his lawyers. He is suing me for tampering with a trademark-tattoo. We can't leave the country until a judge adjudicates the case," said Matteo.

"This can't be happening."

"My Love, Mr. Kerner told me you appealed to King Antonio. That may be what saves us. Mr. Heart took your appeal to the King today. Ambassador Beckford said he is going to push for an early audience, sometime in the next week. Only in Palermo, do they have these crazy laws of putting trademarks on people. How can a person place a trademark on another person?"

"It is only done to slaves, ones with specialty training, such as Exotics. I hate our laws." Olympia closed her eyes.

"Why don't you put on a coat, and come have a stroll outside with me? It's a beautiful day. It is cold, but sunny. We can breathe fresh air and try to forget these things for a little while," said Lord Wolfson. Olympia smiled at her husband. She stood up, picked up the coat the seamstress had just brought her, and they went outside for a walk.

ଓଓଓ

Two weeks later, Olympia and Lord Wolfson had an audience with the King of Palermo. Mr. Heart filed a claim in two departments: one with the Department of Foreign Relations and another with the Department of Commerce. The lawsuits were filed in the name of the Duchess of Trenton, Olympia Corona Takatsu Wolfson, of Yakuta, to the King of Palermo.

Lord Wolfson and Lady Olympia traveled from the Ambassador's mansion to the Palace of the Lions at the center of Nolia. The Palace of the Lions was where all the legalities of the kingdom of Palermo were managed.

Arriving at the palace brought back unwelcome memories for Olympia. The first time she had visited that place was the day Chicho had made her entertain the Minister of Commerce in his office.

Olsen and Flint did not go with them, so instead, the Ambassador arranged for three embassy guards to accompany them in another carriage. As Lady Olympia and Lord Wolfson climbed out of the carriage, she noticed four of Chicho's roughest bouncers lounging about. She grip tightened on Matteo's arm, discreetly pointing out the men to him. He squeezed her hand in acknowledgment, and they hurried into the building.

They entered the building through a side door that opened into an immense reception hall. Unlike the King's residence, where Olympia had also been several times, this palace was more of an oversized office building. They were walking through the receiving hall when Olympia saw Mr. Heart and another man, whom she assumed was Mr. Kenner.

"Your Graces, it is good to see you both. I am Mr. Scott Heart," he said to Lord Wolfson, and turning to Olympia he continued, "and this is one of my associates, Mr. Harrold Kenner."

"Thank you. It is a pleasure to meet you. I am grateful for all the help you have given to my wife so far," said Lord Wolfson.

"It was and is my pleasure. Please follow me." They followed Mr. Heart and his associate through the enormous reception hall and several corridors to reach the antechamber where Mr. Heart said they would meet King Antonio and his ministers. Olympia hoped Chicho would not be at the hearing, but knowing the greed of her previous owner, he probably had filed a request to be present at the proceedings.

They waited for about an hour when the doors opened. Lady Olympia and the Duke of Trenton were escorted into the room. The lavishly decorated chamber had four rows of benches on each side and a walkway in the middle, with a red, black, and white carpet with green accents that led all the way from the door to the edge of the first step of the raised dais where the throne sat. The benches along the sides were cushioned in green velvet, and the room was illuminated well from natural light that came through the tall windows on each side, east and west. Upon the dais at the front sat not only the King's throne, but also two smaller thrones to either side.

Although the King sat on his throne, Olympia could see it was a majestic chair, gilded, with purple cushioned arms, seat, and back. On the smaller, navy-blue upholstered throne, to the right and slightly behind that of the King, sat the Archimage of Palermo. Ten other severe looking men were sitting on the chairs on each side of the room.

Olympia, Matteo, Ambassador Beckford, and the two lawyers stood by the door waiting to be called forward. Olympia's hands shook. She had been at parties where Kind Antonio had been in attendance and a client introduced her to the King some years ago, but she had never had a conversation with him.

"Your Royal Highness, now we have the Duke of Trenton, Marchese of Kleinberg, Marchese of Kalia, Earl of Mair, Earl of Wolfson, and Viscount of Berna, from the land of Yakuta, and his wife, the Duchess of Trenton, also known as the famous Exotic Courtesan and Prostitute Olympia Corona Takatsu," said the steward. Olympia and her group walked up to the area cordoned off at the front of the room, where King Antonio sat on his throne. When they reached the cordoned area, the men bowed and Olympia curtsied.

"Your Highness, the Duchess has appealed to the King's court. The Duchess used to be a slave with the trademark of Mr. Chicho di Roberti's Exotics market training facility. The Duchess of Trenton alleges that since the Duke of Trenton married her and she is carrying his child, she is no longer a slave. As her husband and a member of the Yakutan peerage, the Duke of Trenton removed the trademark from her," said the steward in the room.

"I know Exotic Olympia. I have listened to her sing and seen her dance many times. I remember the Earl of Marta introduced us a few years ago. I see you are large with child. I thought Exotics were sterile," said King Antonio.

"Not all, Your Highness, Mr. di Roberti left her intact," said Mr. Heart.

"You look as lovely as ever."

"Your Highness, Mr. di Roberti is here, and he has sued the Duke of Trenton for stealing his trademarked property," said the steward.

"Is Mr. di Roberti in the building?" asked King Antonio.

"Yes, Your Highness," said the steward.

"Let him in. He needs to be here also," said the King. One of the young pages opened a side door and ushered Chicho and another gentleman into the room.

"Duke of Trenton, I need to know how Exotic Olympia came to be in your household?" asked King Antonio.

Lord Wolfson went on to tell the story of the raid on Prince Wallen's castle and how General Joshua Caleo, Duke of Caldwell, had gifted him with Olympia. He continued explaining why he marked her with his Lord's crest. Lord Wolfson clarified that if he had kept her a slave, he would have broken Yakutan law. So, he changed Olympia's status to that of a free mistress under his house.

Lord Wolfson pointed out that he was an adherent of the Benanti religion and always wanted to be married by a Morai bishop, so he found one and arranged the marriage. Lord Wolfson said she was carrying his child, and he wanted his child to be born in his home and with his name. Mr. Heart presented the King's steward with a copy of their marriage certificate. King Antonio listened to all they said with interest.

"Fine, let's hear what Mr. Landry needs to say on behalf of Mr. di Roberti.

"Your Highness and members of the court, my client, Mr. Chicho di Roberti, is the owner of the most prestigious brothels and Exotic training school in all of Nolia. He purchased Exotic Olympia as a slave twelve years ago. Once his instructors had fully trained her, he gave his trademark seal. Mr. di Roberti sent her to do a simple job in Behui. There, she was stolen as a prize of war. Palermo has nothing to do with the war between Alhambra and Behui and may never be. The Duke marked her as his mistress, and later, when he kidnaped her from Mr. di Roberti's establishment, the Duke married the Exotic in a Morai village. This marriage is a farce. Mr. di Roberti seeks the return of his property and remuneration for lost wages during her absence. She is his property by Palermo law," said Mr. Landry.

"By the laws and treaties between Behui, Alhambra, and Yakuta, all that is found in a war raid belongs to the winning side, including slaves. The Alhambran battalion won the battle, so all within the castle belonged to General Caleo, Duke of Caldwell, and he could do with his loot whatever he wished," said Mr. Heart.

"Palermo is not part of that treaty. Thus, that law doesn't apply to us," said Mr. Landry.

"She was not in Palermo. She was in Behui territory without a Palermian official to make the claim," said Mr. Heart.

"The problem is the trademark. Mr. di Roberti marked Exotic Olympia with his trademark, which made her Mr. di Roberti's exclusive property in all the kingdoms," said Mr. Landry.

"The Duchess is expecting the Duke's child, and he wants his child to be born in Yakuta," said Mr. Heart.

A man sitting on the lower seats, on the chair closest to the King stood up and clapped his hands twice, requesting a turn to speak. Olympia frowned. It was Prince Andres, the King's younger brother and one of her regular clients.

"Trademark laws must be honored, or why do we have propriety marks?" said the King's brother.

"I know about proprietary laws. I don't need to be reminded," said King Antonio.

"Please forgive me, Your Highness. I meant no disrespect. I only want for our merchants to have a fair outcome when it comes to slave trademark property," said the King's brother.

“My dear brother, I know you have high stakes in the slave trade, but even a royal prince must think of the good of all the citizens,” said the King.

“What does the Duke want?” asked the King.

“The Duke of Trenton asks for the King’s help in this matter. He only wants to take his pregnant wife home,” said Mr. Heart.

“The Duke is not a Palermian noble. We are talking about a valuable Exotic slave. We can wait until the Exotic gives birth. Afterwards, the duke can take his heir home, and the Exotic can be returned to her owner,” said Prince Andres. Chicho grabbed Mr. Landry’s arm and said a few things in his ear. Mr. Landry turned to address the court.

“Mr. di Roberti likes those terms, and he is willing to drop the lawsuit and allow for the Exotic to have visits with the Duke of Trenton as long as she can continue to work as a teacher in his establishment.”

“I have heard enough for now. What an unprecedented case. We have never had a high-ranking aristocrat from an allied kingdom challenging our trademark laws.

“Mr. di Roberti has a right as a merchant with a registered trademark Exotic. He can’t be denied under our law, but neither can I forget the legal marriage of the Duke. I release the Duchess to her husband for now, but they are to stay in Nolia. They are to present themselves when the crown calls them in the next few weeks,” said King Antonio.

“Your Highness, we would like for the Secretary of Slave Affairs and the Guild of Merchants to be part of the proceedings,” said Mr. Landry.

“Your Highness, the Guild of Merchants does not need to be part of these proceedings. They have no say in the royal crown’s enactments,” said one of the ten judges sitting on the left side of the King.

“Letting the Exotic loose will benefit no one, and it will give others the false idea that goods with trademarks can be released or stolen. This will be detrimental in the exchange of slave goods between merchants," said a Lord at the far end of the room.

"I am invoking my royal executive action with this one. The Exotic is to stay with her husband until such a time we call her back to appear before this body for a final ruling. Lord Tunner, did you write the entire enactment as I spoke it?" asked King Antonio.

"Yes, Your Highness."

"Lord Garland, I am not passing any laws at the moment. I am simply gathering as much information on this matter as possible. Need I remind you we are dealing with diplomats of an allied kingdom and a request from one of our citizens. She was a slave at one point, but now she is the wife of a duke, and carrying the Duke's heir. He can't be denied his progeny," said King Antonio.

"I support our King's decision," said one of the Benanti bishops, standing to the right of the room. And a few others voiced their agreement.

"Mr. di Roberti, your appeal is on hold, contingent on my decisions. Duke of Trenton, you may take your wife. I am going to miss listening to the Duchess's beautiful voice at the coming festival of lights next week," said King Antonio.

"Thank you, Your Highness." Olympia said to King Antonio giving him another curtsy. As she walked out, Prince Andres gave Olympia a most disrespectful look, but she stayed on her husband's arm and her head held high. Those in the room left, ensuring they did not turn their backs to King Antonio. Once outside the throne room, Olympia let her tears flow.

"I can't believe what just happened," Olympia said. Matteo passed her his handkerchief.

"We haven't won this case. I suggest you take your Duchess to the Ambassador's house, which is considered Yakutan territory. No one can enter and kidnap your wife from the Ambassador's mansion, since it has magic wards," said Mr. Heart. Prince Andres came out of the throne room and approached the group.

"My brother doesn't understand the error in letting propriety goods walk free. If I were King, I would have sent you back to your legitimate owner," said Prince Andres.

"We will wait for the King's ruling on this matter," said Mr. Heart.

Prince Andres turned to address Olympia. "You will be returned to your rightful place, be sure of that. I will not lose my favorite Exotic." The prince walked away not giving her a second look.

Olympia stared after the prince. Anger made her want to slap him. Mateo held her arm and kissed her hand.

"You will never be an Exotic again. I promise you that, my Lady," said Mr. Heart.

Olympia nodded, and they left the building. She had her time in front of the King. She didn't have to be an Exotic for now, which made her happy. They needed to go back to the Ambassador's mansion. On their way back, Olympia felt tired. It was as though the weight of the world was on her shoulders, but she was with Matteo.

Once they arrived at the mansion, Olympia went to her room and changed her clothing. She wanted to rest. It had been a stressful day. Although, for now, she and her baby were safe.

Chapter 25

Run!

Days turned into weeks, and Olympia had not heard anything from the King's court. She was getting nervous, but Matteo kept saying no news was good news. She wanted to leave Palermo and put as much distance between Chicho and herself as possible, but they had to wait. On a Lunarx day, late at night, Olympia could not sleep. So she went to the blue parlor to read a book. She had not been there long when Matteo and Ambassador Beckford entered in a frenzy; she stood up as fast as her belly allowed.

"I've been looking for you everywhere. We must leave," said Lord Wolfson.

"Why? What is going on?" asked Olympia.

"Mr. Heart was just here. He brought bad news. He told us that an assassin has just killed King Antonio," said the Ambassador.

"What?"

"His brother Prince Andres is next in line for the throne. Mr. Heart said there is a big chance that when Prince Andres is recognized as the new king, he will side with Behui, bringing Palermo into the war," said the Ambassador.

"When did this happen?"

"It happened earlier today. We must leave Nolia tonight. If we stay, with all this commotion, I know that our case will be lost in the new administration. And if Palermo joins Behui, we are in danger. Go to your room and change into traveling clothing," said Matteo.

"I must pack," said Olympia.

"Forget about packing it all. Just get the essentials for traveling light. Hurry, we don't have much time." Olympia left the men behind, rushing back to her room where she found a maid already packing a bag for her. She changed into traveling clothing when Matteo entered her room.

"Are you ready? Flint and Olsen are waiting for us."

"Where are we going? There are no trains leaving this late."

"Mr. Heart arranged safe passage for us, but we must leave now. We are going to travel by carriage to the town of Banta. From there we will take a train to the port city of Vero, then catch the first boat headed to Yakuta." Matteo took Olympia's hand and led her out of the room.

They reached the receiving hall, and Ambassador Beckford was waiting for them. Servants were coming and going, packing things around the manor. Olsen and Flint stood by the door with bags by their feet.

"Are you sure you want to leave this late at night?" asked Ambassador Beckford.

"Yes, they must. All is prepared for them," said a man in a traveler's hat.

"Olympia, this is Mr. Quoken. He is our travel guide. Mr. Heart hired him for us. He agrees we must leave tonight.

"Hello, Mr. Quoken. Thank you for helping us. But could we not leave tomorrow morning?" asked Olympia.

"I am sorry, my Lady, but you must leave now."

"My dear, I don't want to be here in case Chicho attempts to kidnap you among all the chaos, or if our kingdoms enter the war the officials may try to make me leave you behind. I don't want to run the risk," said Matteo.

"What about you? What do you think, Ambassador Beckford?" asked Olympia.

"That is not up to me; I am not going to stop you. I may even be joining you in a day or two if Palermo and Yakuta become enemies. I must stay here until the new king formally enters the fray alongside Behui—*if* he joins with Behui," said Ambassador Beckford.

"My Lady, before we leave, put on this old cloak, use this purse, and change into these old boots. Your Grace, I need you to change your shoes and coat too. I need you both to appear like common folk," said Mr.

Quoken. Olympia changed, giving her new shoes to a maid. Matteo did the same.

Matteo and Olympia said their goodbyes; they climbed into the carriage waiting in front of the manor's front door with Olsen and Flint and without further ado left the embassy. They rode for two hours until they reached the town of Banta and stopped in front of a shady tavern.

"Tonight, you are staying at the Poppy Seed Tavern and Inn. The town has three hotels. If Chicho tries to track you, a Duke is less likely to stay in the poorest inn when there are hotels in town," said Mr. Quoken.

"That makes sense," said Olsen.

"Lady Olympia, please, would you raise your hood? I need you to hide your midsection as far as possible, and cover your head, and face. Try to keep your head down. Your Albrian looks make you stand out like a red pimple on the middle of my crooked nose. Your Grace, you need to button the sleeve of the old coat I provided you, to hide the ducal crest on your left arm. We intend to pass you off as a mage traveling with your sister," said Mr. Quoken. Olympia chuckled, but she did what he asked. Olsen and Flint entered first; after twenty minutes, Matteo and Olympia followed. She stood quietly next to her husband while Mr. Quoken rented them rooms.

They walked through a hallway to the far end of the first floor, and found their room which was more like a closet with a small bed. Olympia was tired to the core, but Matteo took the covers from the bed and tossed them on the floor. He took a clean blanket from one of their three bags and gave it to his wife, and then left the room. Olympia went to bed and quickly fell asleep.

Olympia woke up being shaken. She opened her eyes to a dark room.

"Matteo, it is still dark. What is it?"

"It is dawn. You must get up and dress fast. We are leaving on the first train out of this town. We must get to the train station to get our tickets before anyone else arrives. Mr. Quoken doesn't want us to attract any attention."

"What do you mean?" asked Olympia.

"Mr. Quoken said he would purchase our tickets for us, but we must remain hidden while waiting for the train. He doesn't want anyone looking at you," said Lord Wolfson. He was dressed in a simple shirt and pants. Once Olympia's eyes cleared up and fully saw him, she could barely recognize him.

"What did you do to your beard?"

"I shaved it all off last night. Olsen gave me a haircut," said Lord Wolfson. He didn't look like her Matteo. He didn't look like a duke, but she didn't look like a duchess in the dress Mr. Quoken sent for her to wear. They left the room soon after dawn and walked to the station. Once they arrived, Mr. Quoken appeared from the middle of the crowd dressed as a soldier. He gave them some bread and pastries he'd bought from a bakery that morning, to break their fast.

"Matteo, why is Mr. Quoken—" Olympia was stopped before finishing her question.

"We need to get on the train without a real guard looking at your many skills around your branded wife mark," said Olsen from behind Olympia. She wanted to laugh, but equally, the thought of being found and sent back to the brothel made her shudder. After a two-hour wait, they walked to the train platform. Olympia kept her hood over her head and held a big bag in front of her, hiding her midsection. A guard was walking along the platform checking the trade tattoos of all the passengers when Mr. Quoken came around checking the tattoos of the people near Olympia. Flint stood in front of Olympia and Matteo was next to her, shielding her from people's view. After a few minutes, Mr. Quoken came to stand in front of them and asked to see their trade tattoos. When the official guard came to them, Olympia held her breath. This was it.

"Hey! Who are you? I was told I was to work on this side of the platform," said the guard.

"And I was told to come help," said Mr. Quoken in a thick, typical Nolian accent.

Flint stood tall, in all his six-feet-five-inch glory, towering over Matteo and Olympia. He couldn't hide.

"Fine, you finish this side. I'll go to the nobles' area," said the guard, and left.

Mr. Quoken checked the tattoos of the four of them, and moved along checking the tattoos of the people around them.

The conductor opened the train doors and shouted.

"All aboard!"

Olympia and Matteo entered the train through the nearest door. They moved quickly through the train to an empty compartment, followed by Olsen and Flint. Once inside Matteo whispered some instructions.

"Olympia, lean your head on the window and make believe you are sleeping with your hood over your face."

The conductor knocked on the door. "Tickets!"

Matteo opened the door and gave the tickets to the conductor. He left as soon as he saw the tickets. A few minutes later, the train whistle sounded, and the train jerked. As it moved forward, gaining speed, Olympia took a deep breath.

In the week they traveled, the train made many stops, but early in the morning of the sixth day, the train stopped and a new group of people boarded.

Matteo, Olsen, and Flint were in the dining car for the midday meal when a man in gentleman's garments sat next to Olsen and passed him the newspaper. It was Mr. Quoken. "Hello, gentlemen, be quiet and read the paper."

Matteo could not believe what he read.

"Olsen, read this."

"Oh, this is bad," said Olsen.

Matteo hurried out of the dining car, returning directly to the compartment he shared with Olympia. He entered and without preamble announced: "Palermo has officially joined Behui in the war against Alhambra and Yakuta."

"What?" Olympia's hand shot up to cover her mouth. Matteo gave her the paper.

"Oh no, King Andres is giving citizens of Alhambra and Yakuta only two weeks to leave the kingdom." Olympia looked up from the paper in surprise.

"King Andres knows exactly what he is doing," said Lord Wolfson.

"All the people that have businesses and homes here will now be destitute. How are they going to leave it all behind?" Olympia asked just as a knock sounded at the door. Matteo opened the door; it was Olsen and Flint.

"My Lord, after you left, Mr. Quoken advised we must be ready to get off this train soon."

"What is happening?" asked Lord Wolfson.

"The paper you read is yesterday's. Mr. Quoken gave us another newspaper from this morning. Here, read this,"

"The authorities are looking for Exotic Olympia Takatsu and her kidnapper, Mr. Matteo Wolfson. The authorities issued a warrant for the arrest of Mr. Wolfson and a bounty to anyone providing information about the whereabouts of the kidnapper and the Exotic. If you happened to…"

Olympia looked from one man to the other, her heart sinking. Her back had been hurting for the last two days, but the previous night had been the worst. She slept little, with a sharp pain that came and went.

There was a knock on their door. Olsen opened it. Mr. Quoken stood outside, with an angry look on his face.

"You people don't listen. I told you to return for further instructions."

"We need this as much as we need a boil on our arse. What are we going to do?" Flint asked, two worry lines appearing above the bridge of his nose.

"I have no idea," said Olsen.

"We only have one more day of travel, and tomorrow by supper, we will be at the border port of Vero, and we can board a ship," said Flint.

"Yes, but I'd bet my last coin that the constables will be waiting at the port of Vero to try and catch 'the Exotic and her kidnapper' while trying to cross the border to Yakuta," said Olsen.

"Why don't we get off at the first station in the morning and cross the border via the port of Louda?" suggested Flint.

"The constable at the port of Louda will be checking the trains arriving as well," Olympia said.

"Do none of you plan to listen to me? We have already arranged your escape. You must do what Mr. Flint said. Tomorrow, you'll get off at the little town of Prima. It is the first stop in the morning. I have disguises for all of you, and there will be horses ready. You must travel by horseback to the outskirts of Louda, where I will meet you and give you your next set of instructions." The men continued talking. Mr. Quoken explained where to go on a map, and they made plans for the morning. Olympia sat by the window, trying not to think of her pain and the idea of traveling by horse.

ଓଓଓ

They woke early and waited while the train slowed as it approached the town. Olympia's brow prickled with sweat and her hands were shaking. Here she was again, running for her life. A gagging sensation filled her throat and stomach as the train slowed down and the town came into view. She closed her eyes and held onto Matteo's arm. They stood by the door, ready to disembark quickly.

The train reached the platform. Flint exited first as soon as the train stopped and the porter opened the doors. Matteo was next, followed by Olympia. Olsen had the rear. They each carried a bag, moving fast among the people leaving the train. The train station was small, with only two platforms, one for trains going and one for trains coming. Olympia wore a hat that Mr. Quoken had provided, making her dress like a man with a gentleman's suit and wearing dark glasses. She had used her makeup to make her face look ashen. It was good that her face had gained some weight with her pregnancy.

As expected, two deputies walked about on the platform with flyers in their hands. Contrarily, Mr. Quoken had Matteo dress in a woman's outfit. He wore one of Olympia's hats, and Olympia had made up his face with her makeup—even giving him a mole on his chin. He walked hunched over, holding his bag tightly across his chest. Flint and Olsen had cut their hair really short, and Olympia had made their faces red, just like the Morai people. They hid their hands so as not to give away that they had five fingers instead of four. Flint used his magic, changing the color of everyone's eyes. The four walked spread apart, but not too far from one another. Flint needed them reasonably close by for his magic to work.

Mr. Quoken specified that Olympia should keep her hands in her pockets. Her small hands would give away that she wasn't a portly man. They had concealed her slender neck under a scarf.

They had left the platform behind and were in the crowded station. "*We are almost out onto the street. A few more steps, and we are by the door,*" thought Olympia.

A young-looking deputy started approaching them, and Olympia's heart leaped. The deputy looked at the picture on the flyer in his hands and up at the people passing him by. A sharp pain struck her in the lower parts of her abdomen, and as a reflex, Olympia's hand went to her belly. She walked a few steps aside from the other men. She turned her head to Matteo, swallowed hard, and placed her hand back in her pocket, and kept walking.

Olympia stepped out, into the streets, with tears falling down her face. Pain and more pain in her back and lower belly made her falter and hunch over. People continued going in and out of the station, but Olympia stood by the entrance. Mr. Quoken came and held her by her elbow.

"Sir, are you well? I'll get a carriage," said Mr. Quoken. He walked with her, without touching her any further. Olympia smiled, but said nothing. Standing near her, Mr. Quoken called for a carriage. The carriage arrived, he opened the door and Olympia entered alone. Mr. Quoken gave instructions to the driver, and the carriage left with Olympia.

Her heart was in her mouth. What had just happened? She was alone in the carriage. The driver had moved along. Another pain came in her side, and a headache started forming in the center of her head. She breathed deeply and closed her eyes, but her heart was beating fast; she could not think straight. Where was she going? Olympia had no idea. She was in agony. The carriage suddenly stopped. Olympia opened her eyes. The driver opened the door.

"Here we are, sir," said the driver.

"Where are we?" asked Olympia in a raspy voice.

"We are at Javer's Mart," said the driver.

"What is this place?"

"The man that hired me told me to take you to the nearest horse trading market," said the driver.

"How much do I owe you?" asked Olympia.

"The man already paid me."

Olympia nodded, and when she stepped down from the carriage, another carriage pulled up just behind. Matteo, Flint, and Olsen stepped out of the second carriage that had parked behind hers and quickly walked over to where Olympia was standing.

"You don't look well," said Lord Wolfson when he reached her.

"I am fine. It is a little pain in my back, but it is nothing to be worry about."

"Have you been in pain for long?" asked Matteo.

"For a day or so," Olympia said, not wanting to add to the stress of the situation.

"Olsen, go—here, take the coins, and get us four horses. Get the best horses you can buy," said Lord Wolfson, passing a bag of coins to Olsen. Matteo was still dressed as an old woman. The other three walked away from the horse trading market. Flint went to the general store, but Matteo and Olympia waited in a nearby park. An hour later, Olsen returned with four horses, and Flint arrived with supplies.

"Good, Flint is here," said Olsen, and the group went to meet Flint.

"We must leave town now. Mr. Quoken showed us the route on the map. He said he will wait for us there, on the outskirts of Louda, in a day or so," said Flint.

They packed the horses with the supplies Flint had bought. Olsen helped Olympia mount her horse, and the group left the town at noon. After about two hours traveling, they stopped. Matteo changed from the dress to pants, and Olympia changed into a warm riding dress. The pants were constricting her belly. The cold of the day made Olympia want to cry, but the ache in her back and the fluctuating pain in her middle, kept her mind from her stiff hands. The group continued traveling east until late that afternoon, stopping for the day when Olsen and Flint returned from scouting. They found an area with fewer trees and made camp for the night.

Snow covered it all, ground, trees, bushes, even the top of rocks. So Matteo used his magic to clear the snow from the area they chose to make camp. Flint built a small fire to keep them warm through the night. Matteo made up his pallet next to Olympia's, and the other two men curled up beside each other.

Chapter 26

Birth

Olympia could not sleep. Throughout the entire night, sharp, throbbing pain came in waves across her lower abdomen. The pain kept jerking her awake, just as she started to drift—until someone stabbed her in her back, or at least that's how it felt.

"Matteo, please wake," whined Olympia.

He woke with a startle. "What's going on?"

"I am in pain," said Olympia.

"Where?"

"On my back and lower abdomen."

"How long have you been feeling this way?" asked Matteo.

"For a few days, but it wasn't until today that the pain became unbearable."

"Why didn't you say something when I asked about your pain in the town?

"I didn't want you to worry."

"Do you think the child is coming?" asked Matteo.

"I don't know," said Olympia.

"Try to rest."

"I need to relieve myself," said Olympia. Matteo stood up and helped her up from her pallet. They moved a few yards away from the men for her needs, but on the way back, they heard a noise making them stop where they were.

"Did you hear that?" Olympia whispered, holding Matteo's arm. He placed one finger to his lips, and they waited. The noise became louder. It was dogs running and barking. Matteo took Olympia's hand, and they ran back to camp.

"Wake up, you two. We must get a move on. I hear dogs coming this way. Let's go." Olsen and Flint got up, then POW!

The sound of a shotgun came from nearby.

Spooked, the horses galloped away.

"Let's go; we must run," said Lord Wolfson. They grabbed their bags and left as fast as they could through the thick of the night.

"I can't see where we're going," said Olsen. Flint whispered an incantation and a green ward projected from his hands, illuminating the path in front of them.

"It is not much light, but it is the best I can do. We don't want to attract anyone's attention," said Flint.

The sound of dogs barking was getting nearer, accompanied by the shouts of men—making Olympia's heart pump even faster. Matteo pulled Olympia by her hand, encouraging speed, but then Olympia felt it. Water came from between her legs. Olympia pulled her hand from Matteo and stopped.

"Matteo, we need to stop."

"My dear, we can't stop. They will catch us. Flint, can you make that light brighter?" The light became a little brighter.

"Yer dress is all wet," said Flint

"I didn't urinate on myself, I swear," said Olympia.

"We need to get out of these woods. The child is coming. We must move faster," said Olsen. Matteo took Olympia's hand, and he pulled her. They tried to walk, but Olympia held her belly and cried with every step. Her entire body hurt; it felt like her insides wanted to come out.

"Look, a river," shouted Olsen. They reach the edge of a flowing river. The rapid water made a roaring sound.

"We must cross it. That will put space between those blasted dogs and us," said Flint.

"How deep is it?" asked Olympia.

"We won't know until we try," said Flint.

The group of four stood together, contemplating their options. Dogs barked, men shouted, and Olympia's ears rung, but she could hear their words now.

“Follow their footprints on the snow,” said one man’s voice in the distance.

“They are running toward the river! Do they have the Exotic with them?”

“I don’t know,” another man shouted.

Flint and Olsen waded into the water. Lord Wolfson stepped in behind his friends, holding Olympia’s hand, drawing Olympia into the freezing water behind him. It made her body shiver, and may have even increased the constant spasms in her abdomen. The water reached up to her thighs, and higher as she followed Matteo, holding onto his hand, but then—BAAM!—a shot.

Olympia flinched and stumbled. The water dragged her, and she released Matteo’s hand. Water covered her entirely as the current towed her under. The last thing Olympia saw, before she was entirely submerged, was a moonless night with a sky full of stars. Darkness and panic, arms flailing, water entered her lungs, more panic. The water moved swiftly, but a hand grabbed her arm. She broke the water’s surface, coughing and gasping for air. Olympia held onto the hand that pulled her. It was Matteo. He raised her so she floated on the water, and he used his magic to make the water push her to shore.

They crossed the river. Olympia was on her hands and knees, coughing water and shivering. Matteo took a blanket from his bag and wrapped her with it. Unlike Olympia’s, his bag was dry.

“You must stand. If we stop, we will die,” said Matteo, helping Olympia stand. The sound of dogs barking and men shouting continued unmercifully.

They looked back to the other side of the river, and a sizable group of men with several dogs were breaking the forest’s edge. On this side, the four of them ran to the line of trees, and deep into the woods. Once hidden by the trees, Flint regenerated a circular green ward, as large as a house, lighting their path again. The group tried to race on, but Olympia could not keep up. Behind them, the men shouted.

“Catch them!”

“I see them running!”

The dogs barking behind her made Olympia keep looking back.

"AH!" She stumbled and fell on her knees onto the snow.

"Love, I've got you," Matteo said, as he helped her stand. Olympia grabbed Matteo's hand and squeezed it hard. Pain overwhelmed her as she hunched over and held on to her belly.

"Breath, take deep breaths. Olsen, please take her. I must cover our tracks." Olsen took Olympia in his arms, and they continued their rapid escape. Lord Wolfson used his magic to obscure their footprints in the snow by shifting the snow to cover their tracks. The forest opened to a grassy valley, covered in a thin layer of snow. They sped down the hillside until Flint stopped them in the middle of a field.

"We have cow patties everywhere. Take them and rub the manure all over yer body, even on the bottom of yer feet. That should mask our scent," said Flint. Olsen stood Olympia down. Matteo reached down to a cow pat and rubbed some all over himself and Olympia. She didn't object as she was busy trying to catch her breath, trembling, and trying to stay warm. After her swim in the glacial water, her teeth kept chattering.

"We have been running east. Why don't we run north this time?" said Olympia.

"Yes, that may throw them off," said Matteo. Olsen took her in his arms again after they finished slathering themselves with manure. They kept moving until they reached a barn at the bottom of the hill.

"No, we can't hide there. The first thing the constable and his men will do is go into the barn looking for us," said Olsen.

The group walked past the barn, with Flint lighting their path with his magic. They crossed the field and entered another set of woods on the far side. They continued for a further hour until they reached an old abandoned shack.

"Ah," Olympia shouted. "The child is coming. We must stop. Matteo, I can feel her almost out."

“I think all this running has made the child come faster,” said Flint.

“I am so sorry,” said Olympia.

They stopped and scouted the shack. Matteo opened the door for Olsen to enter with Olympia still held in his arms. The hut had two windows on either side of the door that opened onto the only room. It had a fireplace, a kitchen area, and ample space in front of the fireplace. There was a table and two chairs. Olsen found two buckets, two blankets, some dry wood to the side of the fireplace and candles on the mantel.

Olsen lowered Olympia to her feet, and she went to lie by the side of the fireplace. Her wet clothing stuck to her like a second skin.

“I will try to create a ward of protection around the shack. It will give us cover in the darkness, but it will do nothing for us come morning and it is almost dawn now,” said Flint. He left the shack, leaving the other three inside.

Olympia could still hear dogs barking in the distance when another contraction hit her. The contractions came in constant waves. Matteo removed Olympia’s clothing and boots and laid them to dry near a chair. He covered her with one of the blankets they found in the shack.

Matteo knelt down beside her, and started rubbing her legs, arms, and body. “You need to get warm,” he said, and continued his ministrations.

Flint hurried inside the shack and kneeled down next to his friends to whisper.

“The men are nearby. We need position ourselves under the windows and behind the door. Ye all need to be quiet.”

“Make an incantation to lock the door,” said Olsen.

Flint turned his hands from one side to the other, generating a yellow light around his hands. He sent the light toward the door, creating the ward, and then the light disappeared. Meanwhile, Olsen barricaded the door with the bags they had been carrying. They moved to squat under the windows, and Flint sat in front of the door.

A scream was locked in Olympia’s throat. A pressure and pain in her back and lower belly developed that was so intense it gave her a headache. She opened her mouth, but nothing came out. The guards would catch them if she made a sound.

A contraction hit her like a slap in the face. At that exact moment a bright light shined in through the windows. Sweat covered her brow. Another contraction came, she had to push. She felt the child's head making its way down. She felt like she was being torn apart. Perspiration of birthing warred with shivers from the cold of the night. Dogs barked outside, and the doorknob jiggled.

"Oh no..." thought Olympia, biting the inside of her cheek to stop herself from screaming.

"Look through the windows," she heard one man say.

"I don't see anything aside from a table and a chair. The dogs are going crazy."

"It smells like manure."

"There are cattle all over these parts," said a female voice.

More contractions hit Olympia. She had to push. She closed her eyes and held onto Matteo's hand trying not to make a sound.

"There's nowhere else. They must be inside the shack."

A loud thump on the door, made the hinges creak. Olympia opened her eyes; she looked at the door, and squeezed Matteo's hand tight. Another contraction. She had to push, so she did.

"The door has an enchantment on it. The shack's owner must be an Arcane Mage."

"The Exotic is not a mage, and her kidnapper is a water mage so they can't be inside." The female voice said irritated.

"Let's keep moving. I think the dogs lost the scent after the river, but the Exotic and her kidnapper can't be too far ahead," said a man.

The light moved away from the window. Olympia opened her mouth when an almost inaudible, soft whistle came out. Matteo looked between Olympia's legs.

"Oh, my stars, I can see her head. Listen, dearest. I've delivered many colts and fillies. I know it is not the same but not that different either. Stay calm—we can do this," whispered Matteo. Several contractions hit one after another. Olympia beard down. With an intense pain, she pushed hard, and the baby's head came out. Matteo gently moved the baby's head left and right and touched under the little one's neck.

The lights outside were gone. Olympia took a deep breath, and another contraction took over her body. She pushed again and the baby's body came out. Matteo received her in one of the other blankets when, with one loud cry, the little girl made her presence known. However, Matteo quickly took the little girl and hid her inside his coat.

From the distance they heard: "What was that noise?"

"It sounds like a small animal," said the female guard.

They waited silently for a few seconds.

"I hear nothing. Let's go and find the others. I am old, tired, hungry, and it's almost dawn," said a grumpy sounding man.

The guards moved off with the barking dogs, and after a few minutes—silence. Matteo took the baby out of his coat, cleaned her mouth, and held her close to his chest. Olsen used his magic, making lightning come to his fingers, giving them a little green light in the shack.

"She is so beautiful. Look at her. Her head is bald, but she has my blue eyes," said the proud father. After cleaning her with a shirt from his bag, he passed the baby to her mother. Olympia took her baby, gave her many kisses, and cried. Flint let out a loud sigh. He took off his boots and clothing. The tired man tried to warm up in a blanket he had in his bag.

The first light of dawn appeared through the windows when another wave of pain came to her. She held Matteo's hand.

"There's something wrong. I'm in so much pain. Oh no, I am having another contraction," said Olympia. Matteo touched her forehead.

"She might be having twins," said Flint. Matteo took the baby from Olympia and gave it to Olsen.

"You must push with every contraction," said Matteo. Three minutes later, a second baby, smaller than the first, made her way into the world. This one had a head full of black hair. Matteo found a piece of cloth from his bag to clean her mouth and face, and gave the second baby to her mother.

"See, neither one has red eyes or grey skin. They are pure-blooded Wolfson. This one has her Momma's hair and eyes." Matteo chuckled.

"You need to keep them both warm," said Olsen. Matteo took care of the afterbirth. Olympia was able to relax for the first time since they left Nolia. Olsen waited an hour before he took some of the wood from the corner to make a fire in the fireplace. They huddled next to it, falling asleep for a few hours. Olympia woke at the sound of the girls crying.

"I think our daughters are hungry," said Lord Wolfson.

"What are their names?" asked Olsen.

"I like Emma and Elaria," said Olympia.

"Our Emma is beautiful, but her sister is just as lovely. Elaria is the second one. Look at that beautiful black hair. They look just like their mother," said Lord Wolfson.

"Emma and Elaria are strong names," said Flint.

"Their names are Emma Corona Katherine Agatha Wolfson and Elaria Olympia Marina Nívea Wolfson," said Lord Wolfson.

"We have hungry mouths to feed. I'm going out to find something to eat," said Flint. They had laid out their pants on the chairs to dry. Flint dressed, took one bucket, and left. Matteo helped Olympia to sit up and lean back against the wall of the shack. She took one girl in each arm.

"I don't know what to do," said Olympia.

"I saw my wife feed my boys plenty of times so I'll show you what to do," said Lord Wolfson. After a few minutes, Olympia had each girl firmly latched to a breast. She rested her head on the wall and let her mind wander. Olsen, too, left to look for food. About two hours later, the door opened.

"I went back to the farm and found a healthy cow. Here, fresh milk," said Flint. Moments later, Olsen walked in with a buck over his shoulders.

"How did you manage to catch that?" asked Olympia.

"My Lady, have you forgotten I'm a lightning mage? It didn't take me long to find him," said Olsen.

"Excellent; I found some tea leaves, a kettle, and two cups while you were out. Let's dress this animal, cook it, and eat it. We need to feed Olympia," said Lord Wolfson.

"Let's dry some of this meat," said Flint, "and after we'll need to douse the fire for a few hours as the smoke may be seen."

The men prepared the food. They cut the meat into thin slices. Matteo used his magic and extracted all the water from the meat, drying it. They roasted the rest. They ate, satiating their hunger. Olympia thought the meat tasted waxy and the milk like cream, but she wasn't going to complain. After the early dinner, Matteo went out and looked for more wood to relight the fire when it would be dark. Later, Olsen went out scouting and returned with a frown.

"We must leave as soon as possible. I spotted over eight guards spread over the eastern parts of the mountain. We must keep moving northeast. I say we wake before dawn and get an early start," said Olsen.

"How far do ye think we are from Tokasa Lake?" asked Flint.

"If we keep up a brisk pace all day tomorrow, we can make it by early afternoon," said Olsen.

"Matteo, my daughters can't be out in the cold."

"We will bundle them up and keep them close to your body. You must try to sleep. The girls will be waking every few hours to feed. I am going to help you all I can, but we must get moving before dawn," said Matteo, making Olympia's anxiety return ten-fold.

ଓଓଓ

The following day, all four plus the two girls woke before dawn. Olympia felt lucky—she had fed the girls just before midnight, and the girls slept until Matteo woke Olympia before dawn. Olympia changed the girls' swaddling clothes that she had made by cutting up a nightdress the maids had packed for her, then fed them again. Matteo was happy that everything they owned had now been dried by hanging them near the fire.

Olympia wrapped the girls in pieces of her own clothing. Matteo cut the sleeves of a shirt to make little scarves for their necks. He secured them in a jerry-rigged harness inside Olympia's blouse, and used socks for hats on the girls' heads. Olympia ensured they had easy access to her breasts before putting on her coat and buttoning it to her neck. It only just closed around the three of them.

They picked up their bags; Matteo carrying both his and Olympia's, and left the shelter of the shack, heading northeast. A gust of wind buffeted Olympia as she stepped outside, the cold cutting her to the bone. Her nose was runny, and her eyes watered, but she didn't falter as she held on to her girls. The two little beans, as once she called them, were cuddled against the warmth of their mother.

The first light of a new morning lit their way. They walked single file and in silence through the woods until Olympia heard the sounds of barking dogs in the distance.

"Do you hear that?" asked Olympia.

"Dogs, we must walk faster," said Olsen.

Matteo walked at the rear, erasing their tracks.

"We must stop. I need to change the girl's swaddling clothes. I also need rest," said Olympia.

"We can't stop. Those dogs sound closer than I would like them to be," said Olsen.

“She gave birth less than a day ago. We can’t make her walk at this pace all day,” said Flint. Matteo raised his hands, clearing an area of snow.

“Olympia dear, sit down and care for the girls. Gentlemen, between the three of us, we can send these bastards to hell with our magic. If we have to fight, we can take them. Our nations are at war now. No one will touch my family. Olsen, you take the right side, I’ll go on the left. Flint, you stay near Olympia in the middle and make a protection ward around her,” said Lord Wolfson. The other two men nodded, smiling their assent at Matteo.

“Finally, we get to use our magic. I’ve been itching to fight back,” said Olsen.

After Olympia had changed the girls, and had help strapping them in the harness against her chest, they started moving forward again. After a while they stopped for the midday meal, eating some of the meat they had dried earlier. But it began to snow, and a fog made it hard for them to see before they even got going. The wind rapidly started to whirl about them, slicing into any exposed skin. Matteo erected a wall made of ice and leaned it against two trees, that fortunately worked as expected, breaking the main force of the wind. He added two more walls of ice, tipping them together and creating an ice shelter. They found refuge from the freezing wind and falling snow. The four huddled together; the men surrounding Olympia and the girls.

They waited for about an hour. When the storm passed, they climbed out of the ice shelter. A layer of new powder covered the ground. They set off again walking through the snow with Matteo shifting the snow from in front of them, letting it fall back in place behind them. Thus, they continued until they reached Tokasa Lake. From the lake, the port city of Louda should only be an hour’s walk north.

“How will we cross to reach the other side? Soldiers will be looking for us at all the ports harboring ships leaving for Yakuta,” said Olympia.

“Mr. Quoken said he would meet us here, but I don’t see anyone,” said Olsen.

"I may be able to open a portal, but I don't have enough power to create a big one. It will only transport one, maybe two people," said Flint.

"That's all we need. The constable is not looking for you or me. The only ones that need to move through the portal are Lady Olympia, the girls, and Lord Wolfson," said Olsen.

Olympia's legs ached. She wanted to collapse; fall on the ground and sleep. She was so tired. The men were talking among themselves when up in the sky, on the distance, a glimmer of light attracted her attention and she looked up. She could not believe her eyes, a ball as round as the moon and larger than a horse hovered in the sky. It was a blue and green balloon. At first, it just hung in the sky, but the thing started moving toward them and coming down. As it got closer, it was much larger. The thing had a basket hanging down that seemed like it could fit at least five people, and a man inside the basket was looking down at them.

She had never seen anything like it.

Olympia grabbed Matteo's arm. "Oh, Matteo, look up. You need to look up."

He looked up. Startled, he jumped back a little.

"What the hell is that?" Lord Wolfson pointed at the blue-green balloon floating down from the sky. When the enormous balloon landed an acre away from them, Mr. Quoken jumped out from the balloon's basket. He had two ropes with hooks that he used, one on each side of the basket, to anchor the balloon to the ground. Once secured, he came running toward the group. In the meantime, inside the basket, another man—apparently a fire mage—kept sending streams of fire into the open mouth of the balloon. The entire contraption looked as huge as a cottage.

"Mr. Quoken, what is that? I have never seen anything like it," said Matteo.

"My lord, Duke of Trenton, Lady Olympia, gentlemen, it is good to see you all. This—is a hot-air balloon. You will cross the lake in the basket, riding the balloon through the air," said Mr. Quoken.

"Incredible," said Olsen.

"We don't have much time. The Duke of Trenton and Lady Olympia must board the balloon. You two must come with me. The authorities are not looking for the two of you. I have tickets for Mr. Olsen and Mr. Flint on the first boat departing tomorrow for the port town of Pinella."

"How safe is that thing?" asked Olympia.

"You will be fine. It is safe. I have traveled in it several times. Trust me," said Mr. Quoken with a crooked smile.

"We can't leave Flint and Olsen," said Olympia.

"You both must go. The girls need to be protected," said Olsen.

"We'll catch up with ye when we get to Pinella," said Flint. "But for now, ye must hurry."

"I'll wait for your boat at the port in Pinella tomorrow. You two take care," said Lord Wolfson. Olympia hugged Olsen and Flint.

Olympia held her daughters firmly as she walked to the basket. The fire mage shot a long stream of flame into the mouth of the balloon. Olympia's eyes were about to jump out of their sockets. Matteo helped her climb into the balloon, then clambered in after her. Once inside the basket, she faced a young black man. He could not have been older than sixteen.

"Hello, Your Graces, my name is Elliot. I'll have you across the lake in an hour, maybe less. Here," the young pilot said, passing them some blankets, "you must wrap these blankets around yourselves. The air gets frigid as we go higher." Olympia covered herself with the blanket, ensuring her girls were protected as well.

"Go now. On the other side, my friend Pablo will be waiting for you. Safe travels, Your Graces," said Mr. Quoken. Mr. Quoken shook Matteo's hand, then shot off to unhook the anchors, tossing the ropes in the basket.

Once the beautiful contrivance was released from the ground, Elliot added a lot of fire to the balloon, and it rose quickly into the sky. It was such a marvelous contradiction.

The thing was heavy, but also light. It bounced joyously, but the fire needed for flight made it seem severe and intimidating. For Olympia, the thing was wonderfully majestic and unbelievably delicate, but the whole experience was outlandish. The basket rose from the ground; now, she was like a bird.

They were moving up and forward when all of a sudden, the basket trembled. She grabbed onto Matteo's arm and yelped. She looked up at the hole in base of the balloon, and on into the interior of the balloon, which was enormous. She could see another smaller hole at the top, covered by a flap. Elliot would pull a lever, letting some air escape from the top, and the balloon would sink slightly. By the basket trembling seemed to have abated.

As the balloon rose, they saw the whole clearing below. Olsen, Flint, and Mr. Quaken left, running into the woods on the opposite side of the clearing from where they had arrived. The things on the ground, her friends and trees, were shrinking. Moving over the lake, she could see on one side the land stretched out before her, and on the other side of the horizon the lake grew wider.

As Elliot had said, it got colder the higher they rose, but she felt warmth every time Elliot released fire inside the balloon. The breeze was light, and once they were over the lake, there was no way they could tell they were moving. The balloon's shadow over the lake below made her feel giddy.

"How are we moving?" asked Olympia.

"We are riding a current of air that moves east," said Elliot.

"What happens when there are no currents of air moving east?" asked Matteo.

"I use my telekinesis magic to move us east," said Elliot with a smile.

"How high are we?" Olympia asked.

"We are about one thousand feet up," Elliot said.

They drifted along for the next fifteen minutes, but then the girls woke, all hot and bothered. Olympia sat on the basket floor and tried to nurse the girls.

"What? You're carrying two babies under your dress? This air is too cold for those babies," said Elliot.

"I am keeping them warm by having them close to my chest," said Olympia.

"Stay seated. I'll keep the bottom of the basket warm." Elliot took off his shoes, and from his feet, heat emanated, making the basket warm. Olympia nursed the girls. Once fed, she readjusted them to fit more comfortably against her chest. She reclined against the basket's wall, falling asleep, until Matteo woke her.

"I think there is a storm approaching," said Matteo.

"What time is it?" asked Olympia. As they kept floating across the lake, the sky got cloudier and darker.

"It is a few hours till dusk. We are almost across," said Elliot.

Olympia stood up, grabbed the rim of the basket, and looked down at the world. All she saw were clouds.

Elliot moved his hands, sending exploding flames into the interior of the balloon. She felt a burst of heat warming her face, but a bitter chill returned when the flames were gone. The wind had picked up; goose bumps were extending all over her arms and body.

"How can you know where we are going? All I can see are clouds," said Olympia.

"I am using a compass that helps guide me across the lake. I have done this trip several times," said Elliot.

Matteo looked green. He had said little on this voyage. He had stayed by one corner of the basket, standing as stiff as a rod.

"We are going to descend. I am going to release a lot of air through the opening on top of the balloon. So, we will drop kind of fast. I need to fly closer to the lake," said Elliot.

Olympia held on to the rim of the basket, waiting for Elliot to release the air. The change in altitude was noticeable, causing Matteo to turn around and vomit all he had eaten that day. Olympia held a piece of cloth to wipe the babies' faces, but instead passed it to Matteo.

"I am so sorry," he said.

"It is fine. A lot people who fly with me have the same reaction." Elliot searched in his bag and found a canteen.

"Drink this. My mother makes it from the extract of ginger. It is good for an upset belly." Elliot passed the canteen to Matteo, and he took two gulps. The balloon kept getting lower until they reached an altitude where the clouds no longer obscured their path. A few minutes more and Olympia saw land on the horizon. The land came closer and closer. The mountains of Yakuta were covered in snow, giving Olympia a beautiful, tranquil feeling.

"We are almost there. It will take us another fifteen, maybe ten minutes, to reach the lake's beach." She held on to her daughters and smiled.

"I never want to return to Palermo," said Olympia.

"My Lady, it's not an option. You left the land without any traveling papers from a Trades Office or getting your passport stamped. You crossed the borders illegally. I am afraid you may never return," said Elliot.

"That is fine with me. My wife is a Yakutan citizen on account of our marriage," said Lord Wolfson.

After a further ten minutes, the balloon gently made contact with the ground. The moment the basket touched the ground, Matteo jumped out taking the ropes with the anchors, and hitched the basket. He helped Olympia climb out of the basket. When they arrived, there was a man holding open a carriage door, waiting for them.

"Where are we?" asked Matteo.

"We are about a two-hour ride to the port of Pinella. My friend will drive you to the hotel, where Pablo will ensure you meet up with your friends tomorrow," said Elliot.

Olympia turned to Elliot and took his hand into her own. "Thank You, Mr. Elliot. It was an extraordinarily amazing ride. I will never forget it."

"You are welcome, my Lady. Take care of those beautiful babies," said Elliot. Olympia turned and walked toward the carriage with Matteo following her.

Chapter 27

We Are Home

Olympia and Matteo were traveling back to Wolfson Castle in a private carriage. In the distance Olympia spied Sindu Lake, and in middle of the lake, the island with the castle perched high up on the central mountain. She couldn't contain her emotions. She hugged both girls close to her chest, and smiled as she looked out the window. Her heart filled with joy. Even the name of the lake evoked feelings of excitement and a powerful sense of pride. Her emotions made Olympia want to jump out and run to Kalbaka.

As the carriage approached the bridge that connected the mainland to the island, the lush mixture of excitement and nervousness made her take hold of Matteo's hand and squeeze it tightly. Olympia's yearning to be home filled her heart with happiness, and it showed. She didn't care that it was snowing. She wanted the carriage to move as fast as the horses could gallop. The knowledge of the wonderful life in the town made Olympia giddy.

"I want this carriage to go faster. Could you please tell the driver to move faster?" asked Olympia with a childlike excitement.

"Calm down, dear. We will be there soon enough." Matteo chuckled at his wife's elation. Olympia looked forward to seeing the people in the family. She missed the children, Lady Marina, Edith, and even Lord Findley and Lady Agatha. She even felt sorry for Katherine, but looked forward to meeting Sairah whom she'd heard so much about. The experience of returning to a place she now considered home gave her a complex tangle of thoughts and emotions. As they entered the town, it stopped snowing, and the town looked like a winter wonderland.

"Finally," thought Olympia. The carriage crossed through the gates of the castle and she could hear the children's voices shouting in a gleeful chorus.

"Father is here. Father is here," shouted Viktor.

"Is Miss Olympia with him?" asked Axel.

"I don't know," said Ivan. "Grandmother, Father is here."

The carriage reached the front door, and Lord Wolfson leaned over to whisper in Olympia's ear.

"Are you ready to greet the family as the Duchess of Trenton?"

"Matteo, step out already. We are home," said Olympia. Matteo kissed her, and the porter opened the door. He helped her step down from the carriage, and she inhaled deeply.

Lady Agatha was waiting for them by the stairs with the children and Mr. Andrews. The children ran to their father. Matteo dropped down to one knee and hugged all three of his children, who then ran to Olympia, and hugged her too.

"Miss Olympia is back," shouted Viktor. He and the other two started jumping up and down and running in circles, giggling and squealing as children do when happy.

"Father, is Miss Olympia going to be our new mother?" asked Ivan, just a tad breathless.

"Grandfather said she will be our new mother, and we needed to be extra nice to her," said Axel

"Yes, she is your new mother," said Matteo. Olympia's heart jumped at the thought of being the mother of three boys, but they had already endeared themselves to her.

"Son, it's good to have you back. Oh my stars, look at you, Miss Olympia, you look radiant," said Lady Agatha.

"No, mother, she is my duchess. We married in Palermo. I want to introduce to you the Duchess of Trenton, Lady Olympia Corona Takatsu Wolfson, and our two daughters."

"What? Daughters? I have a new daughter *and* two granddaughters. Where are the two new little ladies of Wolfson house?" asked Lady Agatha. Olympia chuckled. She opened the top buttons of her coat, showing the girls sleeping attached to her chest in a shared harness.

"They are precious. Oh, I see one is bald, just like Matteo was when he was born. The other has so much black hair. They are gorgeous. What are their names?"

"Their names are Emma Corona Katherine Agatha Wolfson and Elaria Olympia Marina Nívea Wolfson," said Lord Wolfson.

"Those are beautiful names. Oh, come and get inside. The girls need to be out of the cold," said Lady Agatha. They walked up the stairs to the main door.

Lady Agatha turned to Olympia with a smile on her usually stern face. "I love their names. Would you let me hold them?"

"They are attached to me via a harness for warmth. But once we are in our room I can release them, and I'd love for you to hold them," said Olympia.

"We must carry out their faith presentation in eight days, so I will get Matteo's sisters' dresses out of storage. I'm sure you will love those dresses, but if not, we can always have new ones made for them." Lady Agatha took Olympia's hand while she went on planning a party.

"This is overwhelming," said Olympia.

"Nonsense, you are not doing anything alone. Come, we have a nursery to decorate. My granddaughters will need many things. We only prepared for one child."

ଓଓଓ

Matteo and Olympia went to the library to greet Lord Findley. The old man was waiting for them in the grand room with Lady Marina. Olympia walked slowly. She had been feeling tired, and her feet hurt during the last few weeks of travel. She would have to nurse the girls soon.

They reached the library, followed by Lady Agatha. Matteo's father and grandmother sat facing the fireplace, their backs to the door.

"Father, Grandmother, we are here," said Lord Wolfson.

"Matteo, son, did you find Miss Olympia?" asked Lord Findley from his chair.

"Yes, Father," said Matteo. They walked into the room and stood in front of the older man.

"Oh, son, thank g-d you found her. Did you marry her as I told you to do?" asked Lord Findley.

"Yes, father, I did. She is my duchess." Lord Findley tried to stand, but Olympia hurried to his side and helped him sit back in his chair. She sat on the chair beside him.

"My dear, dear girl, I am so glad you are back home with us. Did that man di Roberti hurt you? I told Matteo to do everything in his power to make him pay if he hurt you," said Lord Findley.

"He tried, but I defended myself long enough for Matteo to get me," Olympia said, holding Lord Findley's hand.

"Good girl, I am glad. Arnold darling, could you please pass me my cup of tea," said Lady Marina, and a cup of tea levitated from the table to Lady Marina's hand. Olympia opened her eyes wide.

"My father is a telekinetic mage. I told you magic runs in my family," said Lord Wolfson. Lady Agatha walked in with baby blankets.

"Arnold, we are grandparents of twin girls. Have you shown them?" asked Lady Agatha. Olympia smiled and took off her traveling coat, revealing both girls nestled underneath.

"They are exquisitely beautiful," said Lady Marina.

Three months later, Olympia and the five children stood in front of the main door. Lady Agatha and Lady Marina each held a little girl. Matteo had to return to the battle lines. The family hated to see him go, but he was a vassal to King George, and one of the few Senior Master battlemages in the kingdom. Lady Agatha held baby Emma, and Lady Marina had baby Elaria.

He gave his mother a hug and kiss, and to his father and grandmother, and placed a kiss over each of the babies' heads. He walked down the steps to where his wife stood. Olympia hugged him, then held his hands. She placed a box in his hand.

"I have a parting gift for you," said Olympia.

"What is it?"

"Open the box and find out."

When Lord Wolfson opened the box, he found a beautiful golden pocket watch. The over the face of the watch there was a cover engraved with vines and water waves. Upon opening the lid, a small image of Olympia was engraved on the underside of the cover. The delicate arms of the watch pointed to the time: 8:30. The face was made of mother of pearl, with three dials around the center. The symbols of the four constellations used for traveling were etched around the face, and it had tiny numbers, marked in red. He closed the cover of the watch.

"Olympia, this is beautiful. How—"

"Turn it over," said Olympia. He turned the watch over and found two wolves etched on the back. One had sapphires for eyes, and the other amber."

"Wolves move in packs, and they mate for life. You will never be alone. I'll be here, waiting for you," said Olympia. Matteo embraced his wife in a tight hug.

"Thank you."

"The watch has a charm. It is a ward against demons. If a demon is around, the watch will shine blue. Carry it always with you. I love you," said Olympia.

"I loved you first." He placed the watch in his inner coat pocket, gave Olympia another kiss and hug, then went on one knee to talk to his children.

"You be good boys to your mother, grandmother, grandfather and great-grandmother. You must protect your little sisters. I love you all," and he hugged each of the boys.

"I'll protect them. I love you, father," said Ivan.

"Me too," said Axel.

"No, me also and much more," said Viktor.

"Be good boys."

He stood up, mounted his horse, and rode away with Olsen and Flint, waving goodbye. Olympia held on to Viktor's hand, knowing she would see her husband again. She considered that *she* was not the General's gift, but maybe—just maybe—her new life was the real gift bestowed by the General.

Glossary of Terms

Benanti = It is the Morai religion. Each race has their own priests who guide their spiritual needs. A religious sect derived from the Palanda religion.

Elves = Race struggling to survive with the original task of being the guardians and teachers of mages until the latter were ready to go out into the world. Elves skin is golden, and their eyes are bright. They have straight hair, often in shades of brown or red. They have pointed ears like a typical Elf, but as they grow older their ears lose their shape.

Krapens = Criminal mercenaries possessed by demons via an incantation that makes them appear larger than a normal human.

Mage = Usually an adult human or being in full control of its magical ability.

Master mage = Individual born with magical abilities who is fully trained to use his or her magic and is able to train others. This person can perform magic without the use of his or her hands and can also do so by the spoken word only.

Morai = Race, almost extinct, with an affinity to nature. Keepers of nature, mountains, forests, and water. Morai's bodies are thin and elongated, making them agile and flexible. Magical not only when born a mage. They are dark red in complexion, have four fingers, and have pale eyes.

Orc Demon = Orcs are a race of underground beings, but when enchanted they turn ugly and filthy, with prominent fangs and facial features tending toward the grotesque. Orc Demons skin is black, brown, red, or sandy tan. Violent by nature, they will fight ferociously under Jadro's orders.

Sheshlia = Main religion of the Kingdom of Alhambra. Each race has their own priests who guide their spiritual needs. The religion can be twisted if not followed with sincerity.

Slayer = A demon of a high rank. Uses its magic to enchant and place incantations to enslave those it ensnares. They are bound to any master who bests them in a fight. They are extremely dangerous.

Printed in the USA
CPSIA information can be obtained
at www.ICGtesting.com
LVHW041937151123
764048LV00003B/82

9 781959 443148